DOUBLE SHOT

BY STUART M. KAMINSKY

Lew Fonesca Mysteries

Vengeance
Retribution
Midnight Pass
Denial
Always Say Goodbye
Bright Futures

Abe Lieberman Mysteries

Lieberman's Folly
Lieberman's Choice
Lieberman's Day
Lieberman's Thief
Lieberman's Law
The Big Silence
Not Quite Kosher
The Last Dark Place
Terror Town
The Dead Don't Lie

Toby Peters Mysteries

Bullet for a Star
Murder on the Yellow Brick Road
You Bet Your Life
The Howard Hughes Affair
Never Cross a Vampire
High Midnight
Catch a Falling Clown
He Done Her Wrong
The Fala Factor
Down for the Count
The Man Who Shot Lewis Vance
Smart Moves
Think Fast, Mr. Peters
Buried Caesars
Poor Butterfly
The Melting Clock
The Devil Met a Lady
Tomorrow Is Another Day
Dancing in the Dark
A Fatal Glass of Beer
A Few Minutes Past Midnight
To Catch a Spy
Mildred Pierced
Now You See It

Porfiry Rostnikov Novels

Death of a Dissident
Black Knight in Red Square
Red Chameleon
A Cold, Red Sunrise
A Fine Red Rain
Rostnikov's Vacation
The Man Who Walked Like a Bear
Death of a Russian Priest
Hard Currency
Blood and Rubles
Tarnished Icons
The Dog Who Bit a Policeman
Fall of a Cosmonaut
Murder on the Trans-Siberian Express
People Who Walk in Darkness
Whisper to the Living

Nonseries Novels

When the Dark Man Calls
Exercise in Terror

Short Story Collections

Opening Shots
Hidden and Other Stories

Biographies

Don Siegel: Director
Clint Eastwood
John Huston: Maker of Magic
Coop: The Life and Legend of Gary Cooper

Other Nonfiction

American Film Genres
American Television Genres (with Jeffrey Mahan)
Basic Filmmaking (with Dana Hodgdon)
Writing for Television (with Mark Walker)

DOUBLE SHOT

STUART M. KAMINSKY

A TOM DOHERTY ASSOCIATES BOOK
NEW YORK

This is a work of fiction. All of the characters, organizations, and events portrayed in these novels are either products of the author's imagination or are used fictitiously.

DOUBLE SHOT

A Forge Book
Published by Tom Doherty Associates, LLC
175 Fifth Avenue
New York, NY 10010

www.tor-forge.com

ISBN 978-0-7653-1932-6

First Edition: September 2010

Printed in the United States of America

0 9 8 7 6 5 4 3 2 1

CONTENTS

NOT QUITE KOSHER

AN ABE LIEBERMAN MYSTERY

TO PETER, RIE, MOLLY,

AND NICHOLAS WITH LOVE

Terror holds me, excessive fear. Flights of wandering profit not. Father, I am spent by fear.

—Aeschylus, *The Suppliant Maidens*

1

"You sure?"

Wychovski looked at Pryor, and said, "I'm sure. One year ago. This day. That jewelry store. It's in my book."

Pryor was short, thin, nervous. Dustin Hoffman on some kind of speed produced by his own body. His face was flat, scarred from too many losses in the ring for too many years. He was stupid. Born that way. Punches to the head hadn't made his IQ rise. But Pryor did what he was told, and Wychovski liked telling Pryor what to do. Talking to Pryor was like thinking out loud.

"One year ago. In your book," Pryor said, looking at the jewelry store through the car window.

"In my book," Wychovski said, patting the right pocket of his black zipper jacket.

"And this is . . . ? I mean, where are we?"

"Northbrook. It's a suburb of Chicago," said Wychovski patiently. "North of Chicago."

Pryor nodded as if he understood. He didn't really, but if Wychovski said so, it must be so. He looked at Wychovski, who sat behind the wheel, his eyes fixed on the door of the jewelry store. Wychovski was broad-shouldered, well built from three years with the weights in Stateville and keeping it up when he was outside. He was nearing fifty, blue eyes, short, short haircut, gray-black hair. He looked like a linebacker, a short linebacker. Wychovski had never played football.

He had robbed two Cincinnati Bengals once outside a bar, but that was the closest he got to the real thing. Didn't watch sports on the tube. In prison he had read, wore glasses. Classics. For over a year. Dickens, Poe, Hemingway. Steinbeck. Shakespeare. Freud. Shaw, Irwin and George Bernard. Ibsen, Remarque. Memorized passages. Fell asleep remembering them when the lights went out. Then two years to the day he started, Wychovski stopped reading. Wychovski kept track of time.

Now, Wychovski liked to keep moving. Buy clothes, eat well, stay in classy hotels when he could. Wychovski was putting the cash away for the day he'd feel like retiring. He couldn't imagine that day.

"Tell me again why we're hitting it exactly a year after we hit it before," Pryor said.

Wychovski checked his watch. Dusk. Almost closing time. The couple who owned and ran the place were always the last ones in the mall besides the Chinese restaurant to close. On one side of the jewelry store, Gortman's Jewelry and Fine Watches, was a storefront insurance office. State Farm. Frederick White the agent. He had locked up and gone home. On the other side, Himmell's Gifts. Stuff that looked like it would break if you touched it in the window. Glassy-looking birds and horses. Glassy not classy. Wychovski liked touching real class, like really thin glass wineglasses. If he settled down, he'd buy a few, have a drink every night, run his finger around the rim and make that ringing sound. He didn't know how to do that. He'd learn.

"What?"

"Why are we here again?" Pryor asked.

"Anniversary. Our first big score. Good luck. Maybe. It just feels right."

"What did we get last time?"

The small strip mall was almost empty now. Maybe four cars if you didn't count the eight parked all the way down at the end by the Chinese restaurant. Wychovski could take or leave Chinese food, but he liked the buffet idea. Thai food. That was his choice. Tonight they'd have Thai. Tomorrow they'd take the watches, bracelets, rings to Walter on Polk Street. Walter would look everything over, make an offer. Wychovski would take it. Thai food. That was the ticket.

"We got six thousand last time," Wychovski said. "Five minutes' work. Six thousand dollars. More than a thousand a minute."

"More than a thousand a minute," Pryor echoed.

"Celebration," said Wychovski. "This is a celebration. Back where our good luck started."

"Back light went out," Pryor said, looking at the jewelry store.

"We're moving," Wychovski answered, getting quickly out of the car.

They moved right toward the door. Wychovski had a Glock. His treasure. Read about it in a spy story in a magazine. Had to have it. Pryor had a piece of crap street gun with tape on the handle. Revolver. Six or seven shots. Piece of crap, but a bullet from it would hurt going in and might never come out. People didn't care. You put a gun in their face, they didn't care if it was precision or zip. They knew it could blow out their lights.

Wychovski glanced at Pryor keeping pace at his side. Pryor had dressed up for the job. He had gone through his bag at the motel, asked Wychovski what he should wear. Always asked Wychovski. Asked him if he should brush his teeth. Well, maybe not quite, but asked him almost everything. The distance to the moon. Could eating Equal really give you cancer. Wychovski always had an answer. Quick, ready. Right or wrong. He had an answer.

Pryor was wearing blue slacks and a Tommy Hilfiger blue pullover short-sleeved shirt. He had brushed his hair, polished his shoes. He was ready. Ugly and ready.

Just as the couple inside turned off their light, Wychovski opened the door and pulled out his gun. Pryor did the same. They didn't wear masks, only hit smaller marks that lacked surveillance cameras, like this Dick and Jane little jewelry store. Artists' sketches were for shit. Ski masks itched. Sometimes Wychovski wore dark glasses. That's if they were working the day. Sometimes he had a Band-Aid on his cheek. Let them remember that or the fake mole he got from Gibson's Magic Shop in Paris, Texas. That was a bad hit. No more magic shops. He had scooped up a shopping bag of tricks and practical jokes. Fake dog shit. Fake snot you could hang from your nose. Threw it all away. Kept the mole. Didn't have it on now.

"Don't move," he said.

The couple didn't move. The man was younger than Wychovski by a decade. Average height. He had grown a beard in the last year. Looked older. Wearing a zipper jacket. Blue. Wychovski's was black. Wychovski's favorite colors were black and white.

The woman was blonde, somewhere in her thirties, sort of pretty, too thin for Wychovski's tastes. Pryor remembered the women. He never touched them, but he remembered and talked about them at night in the hotels or motels. Stealing from good-looking women was a high for Pryor. That and good kosher hot dogs. Chicago was always good for hot dogs if you knew where to go. Wychovski knew. On the way back, they'd stop at a place he knew on Dempster in Chicago. Make Pryor happy. Sit and eat a big kosher or two, lots of fries, ketchup, onions, hot peppers. Let Pryor talk about the woman.

She looked different. She was wearing a green dress. She was pregnant. That was it.

"No," she said.

"Yes," said Wychovski. "You know what to do. Stand quiet. No alarms. No crying. Nothing stupid. Boy or a girl?"

Pryor was behind the glass counters, opening them quickly, shoveling, clinking, into the Barnes & Noble bag he had taken from his back pocket. There was a picture of Sigmund Freud on the bag. Sigmund Freud was watching Wychovski. Wychovski wondered what Freud was thinking.

"Boy or girl?" Wychovski repeated. "You know if it's going to be a boy or a girl?"

"Girl," said the man.

"You got a name picked out?"

"Jessica," said the woman.

Wychovski shook his head no and said, "Too . . . I don't know . . . too what everybody else is doing. Something simple. Joan. Molly. Agnes. The simple is different. Hurry it up," he called to Pryor.

"Hurry it up, right," Pryor answered, moving faster, the B&N bag bulging. Freud looking a little plump and not so serious now.

"We'll think about it," the man said.

Wychovski didn't think so.

"Why us?" the woman said. Anger. Tears were coming. "Why do you keep coming back to us?"

"Only the second time," said Wychovski. "Anniversary. One year ago today. Did you forget?"

"I remembered," said the man, moving to his wife and putting his arm around her.

"We won't be back," Wychovski said, as Pryor moved across the carpeting to the second showcase.

"It doesn't matter," said the man. "After this we won't be able to get insurance."

"Sorry," said Wychovski. "How's business been?"

"Slow," said the man, with a shrug. The pregnant woman's eyes were closed.

Pryor scooped.

"You make any of this stuff?" Wychovski asked, looking around. "Last time there were some gold things, little animals, shapes, birds, fish, bears. Little."

"I made those," the man said.

"See any little animals, gold?" Wychovski called to Pryor.

"Don't know," said Pryor. "Just scooping. Wait. Yeah, I see some. A whole bunch."

Wychovski looked at his watch. He remembered where he got it. Right here. One year ago. He held up the watch to show the man and woman.

"Recognize it," he said.

The man nodded.

"Keeps great time," said Wychovski. "Class."

"You have good taste," the man said sarcastically.

"Thanks," said Wychovski, ignoring the sarcasm. The man had a right. He was being robbed. He was going out of business. This was a going-out-of-business nonsale. The man wasn't old. He could start again, work for someone else. He made nice little gold animals. He was going to be a father. The watch told Wychovski that they had been here four minutes.

"Let's go," he called to Pryor.

"One more minute. Two more. Should I look in the back?"

Wychovski hesitated.

"Anything back there?" Wychovski asked the man.

The man didn't answer.

"Forget it," he called to Pryor. "We've got enough."

Pryor came out from behind the case. B&N bag bulging. More than they got the last time. Then Pryor tripped. It happens. Pryor tripped. The bag fell on the floor. Gold and time went flying, a snow or rain of gold and silver, platinum and rings. Glittering, gleaming little animals, a Noah's ark of perfect beasts. And Pryor's gun went off as he fell.

The bullet hit the man in the back. The woman screamed. The man went to his knees. His teeth were clenched. Nice white teeth. Wychovski wondered if such nice white teeth could be real. The woman went down with the man, trying to hold him up.

Pryor looked at them, looked at Wychovski, and started to throw things back in the bag. Wait. That wasn't Freud. Wychovski tried to remember who it was. Not Freud. George Bernard Shaw. It was George Bernard Shaw with wrinkled brow looking at Wychovski, displeased.

"An accident," Wychovski told the woman, who was holding her husband, who now bit his lower lip hard. Blood from the bite. Wychovski didn't want to know what the man's back looked like or where the bullet had traveled inside his body. "Call an ambulance. Nine-one-one. We never shot anybody before. An accident."

Wychovski knelt and began to scoop up watches and the little gold animals from the floor. He stuffed them in his right pocket. He stuffed them in his left and in his right. A few in the pocket of his shirt.

It was more than five minutes now. Pryor was breathing hard trying to get everything. On his knees, scampering like a crazy dog.

"Put the gun away," Wychovski said. "Use both hands. Hurry up. These people need a doctor."

Pryor nodded, put the gun in his pocket and gathered glittering crops. The man had fallen, collapsed on his back. The woman looked at Wychovski, crying. Wychovski didn't want her to lose her baby.

"He have insurance?" he asked.

She looked at him bewildered.

"Life insurance?" Wychovski explained.

"Done," said Pryor with a smile. His teeth were small, yellow.

The woman didn't answer the question. Pryor ran to the door. He didn't look back at what he had done.

"Nine-one-one," Wychovski said, backing out of the store.

Pryor looked both ways and headed for the car. Wychovski was a foot out the door. He turned and went back in.

"Sorry," he said. "It was an accident."

"Get out," the woman screamed. "Go away. Go away. Go away."

She started to get up. Maybe she was crazy enough to attack him. Maybe Wychovski would have to shoot her. He didn't think he could shoot a pregnant woman.

"Joan," he said, stepping outside again. "Joan's a good name. Think about it. Consider it."

"Get out," the woman screamed.

Wychovski got out. Pryor was already in the car. Wychovski ran. Some people were coming out of the Chinese restaurant. Two guys in baseball hats. From this distance, about forty yards, they looked like truckers. There weren't any trucks in the lot. They were looking right at Wychovski. Wychovski realized he was holding his gun. Wychovski could hear the woman screaming. The truckers could probably hear her, too. He ran to the car, got behind the wheel. Pryor couldn't drive, never learned, never tried.

Wychovski shot out of the parking lot. They'd need another car. Not a problem. Night. Good neighborhood. In and gone in something not too new. Dump it. No prints. Later buy a five-year-old GEO, Honda, something like that. Legal. In Wychovski's name.

"We got a lot," Pryor said happily.

"You shot that guy," Wychovski said, staying inside the speed limit, heading for the expressway. "He might die."

"What?" asked Pryor.

"You shot that man," Wychovski repeated, passing a guy in a blue BMW. The guy was smoking a cigarette. Wychovski didn't smoke. He made Pryor stop when they'd gotten together. Inside. In Stateville, he was in a cell with two guys who smoked. Smell had been everywhere. On Wychovski's clothes. On the pages of his books.

People killed themselves. Alcohol, drugs, smoking, eating crap that told the blood going to their heart that this was their territory now and there was no way they were getting by without surgery.

"People stink," said Wychovski.

Pryor was poking through the bag. He nodded in agreement. He was smiling.

"What if he dies?" Wychovski said.

"Who?"

"The guy you shot," said Wychovski. "Shot full of holes by someone she knows."

The expressway was straight ahead. Wychovski could see the stoplight, the big green sign.

"I don't know her," Pryor said. "Never saw her before."

"One year ago," Wychovski said.

"So? We don't go back. The guy dies. Everybody dies. You said so," Pryor said, feeling proud of himself, holding G.B. Shaw to his bosom. "We stopping for hot dogs? That place you said? Kosher. Juicy."

"I don't feel like hot dogs," said Wychovski.

He turned onto the expressway, headed south toward Chicago. Jammed. Rush hour. Line from here to forever. Moving maybe five, ten miles an hour. Wychovski turned on the radio and looked in the rearview mirror. Cars were lined up behind him. A long showroom of whatever you might want. Lights on, creeping, crawling. Should have stayed off the expressway. Too late now. Listen to the news, music, voices that made sense besides his own. An insulting talk show host would be fine.

"More than we got last time," Pryor said happily.

"Yeah," said Wychovski.

"A couple of hot dogs would be good," said Pryor. "Celebrate."

"Celebrate what?"

"Anniversary. We've got a present."

Pryor held up the bag. It looked heavy. Wychovski grunted. What the hell. They had to eat.

"Hot dogs," Wychovski said.

"Yup," said Pryor.

Traffic crawled. The car in front of Wychovski had a bumper sticker:

DON'T BLAME ME. I VOTED LIBERTARIAN.

What the hell was that? Libertarian. Wychovski willed the cars to move. He couldn't do magic. A voice on the radio said something about Syria. Syria didn't exist for Wychovski. Syria, Lebanon, Israel, Bosnia. You name it. It didn't really exist. Nothing existed. No place existed until it was right there to be touched, looked at, held up with a Glock in your hand.

GLUCK, GLUCK, GLUCK, GLUCK, GLUCK.

Wychovski heard it over the sound of running engines and a horn here and there from someone in a hurry to get somewhere in a hurry. He looked up. Helicopter. Traffic watch from a radio or television station? No. It was low. Cops. The truckers from the Chinese restaurant? Still digesting their fried won ton when they went to their radios or a pay phone or a cell phone or pulled out a rocket.

Cops were looking for a certain car. Must be hundreds, thousands out here. Find Waldo only harder. Wychovski looked in his rearview mirror. No flashing lights. He looked up the embankment to his right. Access drive. The tops of cars. No lights flashing. No uniforms dashing. No dogs barking. Just GLUCK, GLUCK, GLUCK. Then a light. Pure white circle down on the cars in front. Sweeping right to left, left to right. Pryor had no clue. He was lost in Rolexes and dreams of French fries.

Did the light linger on them? Imagination? Maybe. Description from the hot-and-sour soup-belching truckers? Description from the lady with the baby she was going to name Jessica when Joan would have been better. Joan was Wychovski's mother's name. He hadn't suggested it lightly.

So they had his description. Stocky guy with short gray hair, about fifty, wearing a black zipper jacket. Skinny guy carrying a canvas bag filled with goodies. A jackpot pinata, a heist from St. Nick.

Traffic moved, not wisely or well, but it moved, inched. Music of another time. Tony Bennett? No, hell no. Johnny Mathis singing "Chances Are." Should have been Tommy Edwards.

"Let's go. Let's go," Wychovski whispered to the car ahead.

"Huh?" asked Pryor.

"There's a cop in a helicopter up there," Wychovski said, looking up, moving forward as if he were on the roller-coaster ride creeping toward the top where they would plunge straight down into despair and black air. "I think he's looking for us."

Pryor looked at him, then rolled down his window to stick his head out before Wychovski could stop him.

"Stop that shit," Wychovski shouted, pulling the skinny Pryor inside.

"I saw it," said Pryor.

"Did he see you?"

"No one waved or nothing," said Pryor. "There he goes."

The helicopter roared forward low, ahead of them. Should he take the next exit? Stay in the crowd? And then the traffic started to move a little faster. Not fast, mind you, but it was moving now. Maybe twenty miles an hour. Actually, nineteen, but close enough. Wychovski decided to grit it out. He turned off the radio.

They made it to Dempster in thirty-five minutes and headed east, toward Lake Michigan. No helicopter. It was still early. Too early for an easy car swap, but it couldn't be helped. Helicopters. He searched this way and that, let his instincts take over at a street across from a park. Three-story apartment buildings. Lots of traffic. He drove in a block. Cars on both sides, some facing the wrong way.

"What are we doing?" asked Pryor.

"*We* are doing nothing," Wychovski said, "*I* am looking for a car. I steal cars. I rob stores. I don't shoot people. I show my gun. They show respect. You show that piece of shit in your pocket, trip over thin air, and shoot a guy in the back."

"Accident," said Pryor.

"My ass," said Wychovski. And then, "That one."

He was looking at a gray Nissan a couple of years old parked under a big tree with branches sticking out over the street. No traffic. Dead-end street.

"Wipe it down," Wychovski ordered, parking the car and getting out.

Pryor started wiping the car for prints. First inside. Then outside. By the time he was done, Wychovski had the Nissan humming. Pryor got in the passenger seat, his bag on his lap, going on a vacation. All he needed was a beach and a towel.

They hit the hot dog place fifteen minutes later. They followed the smell and went in. There was a line. Soft, poppy seed buns. Kosher dogs. Big slices of new pickle. Salty brown fries. They were in line. Two women in front of them were talking. A mother and daughter. Both wearing shorts and showing stomach. Pryor looked back at the door. He could see the Nissan. The bag was in the trunk, with George Bernard Shaw standing guard.

The woman and the girl were talking about Paris. Plaster of? Texas? Europe? Somebody they knew? Nice voices. Wychovski tried to remember when he had last been with a woman. Not that long ago. Two months? Amarillo? Las Vegas? Moline, Illinois?

It was their turn. The kid in the white apron behind the counter wiped his hands, and said, "What can I do for you?"

You can bring back the dead, thought Wychovski. You can make us invisible. You can teleport us to my Aunt Elaine's in Corpus Christi.

"You can give us each a hot dog with the works," Wychovski said.

"Two for me," said Pryor. "And fries."

"Two for both of us. Lots of mustard. Grilled onions. Tomatoes. Cokes. Diet for me. Regular for him."

The mother and daughter were sitting on stools, still talking about Paris and eating.

"You got a phone?" Wychovski asked, paying for their order.

"Back there," said the kid, taking the money.

"I'm going back there to call Walter. Find us a seat where we can watch the car."

Pryor nodded and moved to the pickup order line. Wychovski went back there to make the call. The phone was next to the toilet. He used the toilet first and looked at himself in the mirror. He didn't look good. Decidedly.

He filled the sink with water, cold water, and plunged his face in. Maybe the sink was dirty? Least of his worries. He pulled his head out and looked at himself. Dripping wet reflection. The world hadn't changed. He dried his face and hands and went to the phone. He had a calling card, AT&T. He called Walter. The conversation went like this.

"Walter? I've good goods."

"Jewelry store?"

"It matters?"

"Matters. Cops moved fast. Man's in the hospital maybe dying. Church deacon or something. A saint. All over television, with descriptions of two dummies I thought I might recognize."

"Goods are goods," said Wychovski.

"These goods could make a man an accessory maybe to murder. Keep your goods. Take them who knows where. Get out of town before it's too late, my dear. You know what I'm saying?"

"Walter, be reasonable."

"My middle name is reasonable. It should be 'careful' but it's 'reasonable.' I'm hanging up. I don't know who you are. I think you got the wrong number."

He hung up. Wychovski looked at the phone and thought. St. Louis. There was a guy, Tanner, in St. Louis. No, East St. Louis. A black guy who'd treat them fair for their goods. And Wychovski had a safe-deposit box in St. Louis with a little over sixty thousand in it. They'd check out of the motel and head for St. Louis. Not enough cash with them without selling the goods or going to the bank to get a new car. They'd have to drive the Nissan, slow and easy. All night. Get to Tanner first thing in the morning when the sun was coming up through the Arch.

Wychovski went down the narrow corridor. Cardboard boxes made it narrower. When he got to the counter, the mother and daughter were still eating and talking and drinking. Lots of people were. Standing at the counters or sitting on high stools with red seats that swirled. Smelled fantastic. Things would be alright. Pryor had a place by the window, where he could watch the car. He had finished one hot dog and was working on another. Wychovski inched in next to him.

"We're going to St. Louis," he said behind a wall of other conversations.

"Okay," said Pryor, mustard on his nose. No questions. Just "okay."

Then it happened. It always happens. Shit always happens. A cop car, black-and-white, pulled into the lot outside the hot dog place. It was a narrow lot. The cops were moving slowly. Were they looking for a space and a quick burger or hot dog? Were they looking for a stolen Nissan?

The cops stopped next to the Nissan.

"No," moaned Pryor.

Wychovski grabbed the little guy's arm. The cops turned toward the hot dog shop window. Wychovski looked at the wall, ate his dog, and ate slowly, his heart going mad. Maybe he'd die now of a heart attack. Why not? His father had died on a Washington, D.C., subway just like that.

Pryor was openly watching the cops move toward them.

"Don't look at them," Wychovski whispered. "Look at me. Talk. Say something. Smile. I'll nod. Say anything."

"Are they coming for us?" asked Pryor, working on his second dog.

"You've got mustard on your nose. You want to go down with mustard on your nose? You want to be a joke on the ten o'clock news?"

Wychovski took a napkin and wiped Pryor's nose as the cops came in the door and looked around.

"Reach in your pocket," said Wychovski. "Take out your gun. I'm going to do the same. Aim it at the cops. Don't shoot. Don't speak. If they pull out their guns, just drop yours. It'll be over, and we can go pray that the guy you shot doesn't die."

"I don't pray," said Pryor, as the cops, both young and in uniform, moved through the line of customers down the middle of the shop, hands on holstered guns.

Wychovski turned, and so did Pryor. Guns out, aimed. Butch and Sundance. A John Woo movie.

"Hold it," shouted Wychovski.

Oh God, I pissed in my pants. Half an hour to the motel. Maybe twenty years to life to the motel.

The cops stopped, hands still on their holsters. The place went dead. Someone screamed. The mother or the daughter who had stopped talking about Paris.

"Let's go," said Wychovski.

Pryor reached back for the last half of his hot dog and his little greasy bag of fries.

"Is that a Glock?" asked the kid behind the counter.

"It's a Glock," said Wychovski.

"Cool gun," said the kid.

The cops didn't speak. Wychovski didn't say anything more. He and Pryor made it to the door, backed away across the parking lot, watching the cops watching them. The cops wouldn't shoot. Too many people.

"Get in," Wychovski said.

Pryor got in the car. Wychovski reached back to open the driver-side door. Hard to keep his gun level at the kid cops and open the door. He did it, got in, started the car, and looked in the rearview. The cops were coming out, guns drawn. There was a barrier in front of him, low, a couple of inches, painted red. Wychovski gunned forward over the barrier. Hell, it wasn't his car, but it was his life. He thought there was just enough room to get between a white minivan and an old convertible who-knows-what.

The cops were saying something. Wychovski wasn't listening. He had pissed in his pants, and he expected to die of a heart attack. He listened for some telltale sign. The underbody of the Nissan caught the red barrier, scraped, and roared over. Wychovski glanced toward Pryor, who had the window open and was leaning out, his piece of crap gun in his hand. Pryor fired as Wychovski made it between minivan and convertible, taking some paint off both sides of the Nissan in the process.

Pryor fired again as Wychovski hit the street. Wychovski heard the hot dog shop's window splatter. He saw one of the young cops convulsing, flapping his arms. Blood. Wychovski and Pryor wouldn't be welcome here in the near future. Then came another shot as Wychovski turned right. This one went through Pryor's face. Through his cheek and back out. He was hanging out the window making sounds like a gutted dog. Wychovski floored the Nissan. He could hear Pryor's head bouncing on the door.

The cop who had not been shot was going for his car, making calls, and Pryor's head was bouncing something out of the jungle on the door. Wychovski made a hard right down a semidark street. He pulled over to the curb. Wychovski grabbed Pryor's shirt, pulled him back through the window, and reached past him to close the door. Pryor was looking up at him with wide surprise.

Wychovski drove. There were lights behind him now, a block back. Sirens. The golden animals lay heavy in his pockets and over his heart. He turned left, wove around. No idea where he was. No one to talk to. Just me and my radio.

Who knows how many minutes later he came to a street called Oakton and headed east, for Sheridan Road, Lake Shore Drive, Lake Michigan. People passed in cars. He passed people walking. People looked at him. The bloody door. That was it. Pryor had marked him. No time to stop and clean it up. Not on the street. He hit Sheridan Road and looked for a place to turn, found it. Little dead end. Black-on-white sign: NO SWIMMING. A park.

He pulled in between a couple of cars he didn't look at, popped the trunk lock, and got out. There was nothing in the trunk but the bag of jewelry. He dumped it all into the trunk, shoved some watches in his pocket, picked up the empty canvas bag, closed the trunk, went around the side to look at Pryor, who was trying to say something but had nothing left to say it with. Wychovski pulled him from the car and went looking for water.

Families were having late picnics. Couples were walking. Wychovski looked for water, dragging, carrying Pryor, ignoring the looks of the night people. He sat Pryor on an empty bench next to a fountain. Pryor sagged and groaned. He soaked George Bernard Shaw and worked on Pryor's face with the bag. It made things worse. He worked, turned the canvas bag. Scrubbed. He went back for more water, wrung the bloody water from the bag. Worked again. Gunga Din. Fetch water. Clean up. Three trips, and it was done. George Bernard Shaw was angry. His face was red under the dim park lamp.

"Stay here," he told Pryor. "I'll be right back."

Wychovski ran to the parking lot, not caring anymore who might be watching, noticing. He opened the trunk and threw the bag in. When he turned, he saw the cop car coming down the street. Only one way in the lot. Only one way out. The same way. He grabbed six or seven more watches and another handful of little golden animals and quickly shoved them in his bulging pockets. Then he moved into the park, off the path, toward the rocks. Last stand? Glock on the rocks? Couldn't be. It couldn't end like this. He was caught between a cop and a hard place. Funny. Couldn't laugh though. He hurried on, looking back to see the cop car enter the little lot.

Wouldn't do to leave Pryor behind unless he was dead. But Pryor wasn't dead.

Wychovski helped him up with one arm and urged him toward the little slice of moon. He found the rocks. Kids were crawling over them. Big rocks. Beyond them the night and the lake like an ocean of darkness, end of the world. Nothingness. He climbed out and down.

Three teenagers or college kids, male, watched him make his way down toward the water with Pryor. Stop looking at us, he willed. Go back to playing with yourselves, telling lies, and being stupid. Just don't look at me. Wychovski crouched behind a rock, pulling the zombie Pryor with him, the water touching his shoes.

He had no plan. Water and rocks. Pockets full of not much. Crawl along the rocks. Get out. Find a car. Drive to the motel. Get to St. Louis. Tanner might give him a few hundred, maybe more for what he had. Start again. No more Pryor. He would find a new Pryor to replace the prior Pryor, a Pryor without a gun.

Wychovski knew he couldn't be alone.

"You see two men out here?" He heard a voice through the sound of the waves.

"Down there," came a slightly younger voice.

Wychovski couldn't swim. Give up or keep going. He pushed Pryor into the water and kept going. A flashlight beam from above now. Another from the direction he had come.

"Stop right there. Turn around and come back the way you came," said a voice.

"He's armed," said another voice.

"Take out your gun and hold it by the barrel. Now."

Wychovski considered. He took out the Glock. Great gun. Took it out slowly, looked up, and decided it was all a what-the-hell life anyway. He grabbed the gun by the handle, holding on to the rock with one hand. He aimed toward the flashlight above him. But the flashlight wasn't aimed at him. It was shining on the floating, flailing Pryor.

Wychovski fell backward. His head hit a jutting rock. Hurt. But the water, the cold water was worst of all.

"Can you get to him, Dave?" someone called frantically.

"I'm trying."

Pryor was floating on his back, bobbing in the black waves. I can float, he thought, looking at the flashlight. Float out to some little sailboat, climb on, get away.

He floated farther away. Pain gone cold.

"Can't reach him."

"Shit. He's floating out. Call it in."

No one was trying to reach Wychovski. There were no lights on him.

Footsteps. Wychovski looked up. On the rocks above him, Wychovski could see people in a line looking down at Pryor as he floated farther and farther from the shore into the blackness. Wychovski looked for the moon and stars. They weren't there.

Maybe the anniversary hit hadn't been such a good idea.

He closed his eyes and thought that he had never fired his Glock, never fired any gun. It was a damned good gun.

Wychovski crawled along the rocks, half in half out of the water.

He looked back. There was no sign or sound of Pryor.

2

The man sat on a polished light wood bench in the blue-tiled lobby of Temple Mir Shavot, looking at the door. A white-on-black plastic plate told him that beyond the door was the temple office and that of the rabbi. It was a little after eight on a Thursday morning, and he had been sitting for almost forty minutes.

He knew the rabbi was in. He had seen a modest green Mazda in the parking spot of the rabbi and the license plate was marked "clergy." The man had intended to stride in, find the rabbi, and beg him, if necessary, for an immediate meeting. But when he had seen the door, the man hesitated, his legs weak and heavy. He made it to the bench and sat looking first at his shaking hands, then at the door.

From beyond a door to his right, the voices of men came in a low chant. Occasionally, a voice would rise with determination and even emotion. The man, who had not been in a house of worship since he was a child, remembered the morning *minyans* his father and grandfather had taken him to even before he went to school. There was something plaintive and alien in the sound of long-forgotten Hebrew, and the man, who had regained some control of his legs, now felt as if he might begin to weep.

A few people had passed in the time he had been sitting. Most did not look at him. One woman, heavy, young, wearing thick glasses and carrying a stack of yellow flyers, gave him a smile he was unable to return.

He was, he knew, not a memorable man. Average height, not overweight, dark face now in need of a shave, very black wavy hair he had not combed but which he had brushed back and down with his fingers. He wore slacks, a sport jacket, and a tie loose at the collar. His clothes were conservative and unmemorable unless someone looked a little more carefully and noted the wrinkles and the dark irregular splash marks on his jacket and slacks and marks, which were smaller but definitely red, on his white shirt.

He sighed deeply, thinking he recognized the ending of the morning prayers by the required ten men or more who formed the prayer group. He started to rise, not sure whether he was going to leave or go to the door to the office and step in.

He was saved from the decision by the opening of the door. Two men stepped into the lobby. Their voices echoed slightly when they spoke though they were relatively quiet.

One man was large, burly, maybe about fifty and bearing the look of an ex-athlete whose pink face strongly suggested that he was not Jewish. But the man knew that Jews came in all sizes, faces, and colors. The other man was a study in contrast. He was thin, a bit less than average height, and probably nearing seventy. His hair was curly and white, and he had a little mustache equally white. The older man had one of those perpetually sad looks and resembled one of those contrite beagles the waiting man's Uncle Jack had owned.

"Rabbi," said the big man, "I'll be back here with the car in half an hour."

"Make that an hour, Father Murphy," said the smaller man.

The big man looked at his watch, nodded, and said, "That should give me enough time to check on Rabbit."

Both the rabbi and the priest wore little round black *kepuhs* as did the man who watched them. He had remembered to take one out of the box inside the entrance and cover his head in the house of the Lord.

The big priest moved past the waiting man, glanced at him, and went through the door into the morning sunlight. The rabbi turned and started down the hallway.

"Please," called the waiting man.

The rabbi stopped and looked at him.

"Yeah?"

"I . . . can we talk for a few minutes?"

The rabbi looked at his watch and said, "Me?"

"Yes, it's important."

"I know you?"

"No," said the man.

"I've got a meeting in ten minutes," the rabbi said. "What is it?"

The man rose from the bench, touched his forehead and said, "Someplace a little private?"

The rabbi shrugged and held out his hand toward white double doors across the lobby. The man followed as the rabbi opened a door and stepped into a huge carpeted room with three-story ceilings and stained-glass windows. There were wooden benches facing the platform, the *bemah*, and on the *bemah* were a podium on the left and a table on the right. Built into the wall behind podium and table was a tall curtained ark, which the man remembered contained at least one Torah, a carefully handwritten scroll containing the first five books of the Scriptures.

It all came back to him. Genesis, Exodus, Numbers, Deuteronomy, Leviticus. Hebrew words without meaning came rushing into his consciousness from the well of memory. He touched his forehead. He had not slept at all.

There were folding chairs neatly stacked against the back wall. The rabbi motioned for the man to follow him and unfolded two chairs facing each other in the back of the room. They sat. The rabbi put his hands in his lap and waited.

"I was born a Jew," the man said. "When I got married, my wife is Catholic, I converted. I don't know if I'm still a Jew."

"Tough question. As far as I'm concerned, you're born a Jew, you're a Jew forever. Maybe you can be both, like dual citizenship."

"So, I'm in the right place," the man said, whispering.

"Depends on what's on your mind."

"Confession," the man said. "Isn't a rabbi sort of like a priest?

I mean, if something is told to a rabbi in confidence, if someone confesses to something, is it protected? Is the rabbi forbidden to tell anyone?"

"Depends on the rabbi."

"What about here? This synagogue?"

"The rabbi wouldn't tell anyone."

The man sighed.

"My name is Arnold Sokol. I killed a boy last night. I think I killed a boy last night."

"Who?"

"I don't know," said Sokol touching his forehead. "Mary, my wife, and I had a fight. The minute I came home from work. I worked late last night. You know the Hollywood Linen Shop in Old Orchard?"

"No."

"That's my family's. Where was . . . Oh, yes. Mary and I we've been having a lot of them, fights. I don't go to church with her. She wants more children. We've got two. I said, 'no more.' Fight. No hitting, nothing like that. Just anger, shouting. You know, I said I gave up my religion for you, and she said she gave up friends and family and since when had I practiced any religion. The kids were in bed, but I'm sure they heard the whole thing. Mary got loud. I got loud. The baby cried. I went out."

"Out?"

"For a drive. It was about eleven. We live in the city, on Sheridan, near Loyola University. I drove to the lake, in Evanston, near Northwestern University. I sat on the rocks listening to the waves. I had a lot on my mind. Business. Mary and I haven't been getting along. It's my fault. She's educated. An MBA. Runs her own business out of the apartment. I made it through high school."

"What happened by the lake?"

"It started."

"It?"

"I guess they spotted me alone. I didn't hear them coming." Sokol went on looking toward the ark.

"How many?"

"Three. Young. White. I don't think any of them was more than eighteen, maybe a little older, maybe. I didn't know they were there till one of them behind me said, 'Hey, you.' I was startled. I turned around and saw them, standing in a line on the grass behind the rocks. They were smiling. I looked around. We were the only ones in sight. I thought about running, jumping into the water, shouting, but I knew none of them would work. And I didn't consider fighting. I exercise a little, but . . . I've never been in a real fight, even when I was a kid."

"What did they say, do?"

"One of them said, 'How'd you like to give us your watch and wallet?' Another one said, 'And your belt.' And a third one, the biggest one, a blond with short hair said, "And anything else you've got in your pockets." I stood up. The strange thing was that I wasn't afraid. I had fought with Mary. I was depressed. So many things have . . . One of them said, 'Come here.' I stayed on the rocks. Maybe deep inside I was afraid to move, but I didn't feel afraid. I didn't even consider calling for the help of God, and certainly not to Jesus. This is a confession, right?"

"Sounds like one to me," said the rabbi.

"I've been a lousy Catholic," said Arnold Sokol. "I don't believe. I did it to please my wife. Is that a sin? I mean for a Jew?"

"A mistake maybe, not a sin. Least I don't think so. That's between you and God," said the rabbi.

"But I don't believe in God either. They came toward me. I was wearing these shoes, good shoes for standing all day. Not good for running on rocks. One of them came alone. I think he was the leader. He held out his hand. He was smiling. One of the other boys was looking around to see if anyone was coming. The one in front of me said, 'Give fast, man.' I was frozen. I thought they were going to beat me, probably kill me. When he punched me in the face, I stumbled back, almost losing my balance. He came forward. One of the others, I don't know which, said, 'Hurry up, Z,' something like that. The one called Z came at me. I didn't know what was behind. Something happened inside me. I don't know what. Rage, fear. Humiliation. I grabbed his arm and pulled. He didn't expect it. I almost fell again but didn't. The one called Z went down on his face on the edge of a rock. The others stood frozen for a second. Z got to one knee and grabbed me around the waist. I don't know if he wanted my help or to kill me. His head was . . . cut, blood was flowing down his face. In the moonlight . . . I can't describe it. He sat back. The other two came forward. One of them slipped on the rocks and tumbled into the water shouting something obscene at me. The last one, a big blond with short hair, started to punch me. I doubled over and then came up. I hit the one in front of me, the big blond, in the throat. He made a gargling sound, grabbed his throat, and said, 'I'm gonna kill you, mister.'

"I thought I heard the one in the water climbing out. I tried to pull away. The big one hit me here, on the side of my head. That's when I heard the voices. I think it was a group of Northwestern students going back to campus. The one holding me hit me again, harder. I think the bone under my right eye might be broken. Maybe his knuckles are broken. The one in the water had climbed out, and he started for me, hair hanging down, hate in his eyes. 'Help Z,' the one who had hit me said. 'Let's go.' And then he looked at me, and said, 'We'll find you, mister. We'll kill you.' They went away. The one I had hit in the throat was still trying to catch his breath, the one who had said he'd kill me.

"I looked down at the one called Z. It was hard to tell in the moonlight. There was a lot of blood, and he wasn't moving. I went over the rocks back to the grass and stood shaking, my hands on my knees. The group that had saved my life passed on the pathway about thirty yards away. They were too busy talking and possibly a little too drunk to see me. I wandered, drove, and came here."

"That it?" asked the rabbi.

"No," said Sokol, looking at his hands. "I wanted to kill him. I wanted to kill them all. I want to say I'm sorry for what I did, but I'm not. I feel good. I did something. God help me, I may be a murderer, and I feel good about it and bad about it. Am I making sense? Do you understand?"

"I think I understand," said the rabbi.

"I'm not going to the police," Sokol said. "I'm not going to tell Mary. I'm going to think about this. I can kill. Somehow it's made me feel better about myself, what I think about myself. I'll keep this secret. I just had to tell someone."

"It's too late," said the rabbi.

Sokol looked up.

"Too late?"

"You've already gone to the police," the rabbi said.

"What?"

"I'm a police officer. Detective Sergeant Lieberman."

"The priest called you 'Rabbi,'" the confused Sokol said.

"He's not a priest. He's a cop, too," said Lieberman. "We call each other 'Rabbi' and 'Father Murphy.'"

"You lied," said Sokol, angrily rising from the folding chair, which clattered back behind him.

"Never told you I was the rabbi," Lieberman said, still sitting.

"You should have stopped me, told me."

"Maybe," said Lieberman. "I'm not sure what the rules are."

"I could kill you right here," said Sokol, looking around for something to attack the smaller man with. He started for the chair.

"I don't know what the punishment is for killing someone in a synagogue," said Lieberman. "I wouldn't be surprised if God struck you dead. Actually, I would be surprised. On the other hand, I don't know what he would do to me if I had to shoot you."

Sokol had his back turned to Lieberman. He had one hand on the fallen chair when he looked over his shoulder and saw the detective aiming a gun in his direction.

Sokol took his hand away from the chair, faced the detective, and began to cry.

"I'm putting the gun away," said Lieberman. "Shouldn't have brought it in here anyway. You going to give me trouble?"

Sokol shook his head no.

"You want to see Rabbi Wass?"

Again, Sokol shook his head no and tried to keep the tears back.

"Cheer up," said Lieberman, standing. "I'm not sure your confession is admissible."

Someone came through the doors, a youngish man in a suit wearing glasses.

"Lieberman . . ." he began, then saw the crying man, the overturned chair, and the detective.

"Irving," Lieberman said. "I can't make the meeting today. I'll make the one tomorrow. Today's is all yours."

The man in the glasses and designer suit and tie looked as if he were going to speak, changed his mind, and left the room. Lieberman shook his head wearily and turned toward the ark. He stood silently for about a minute.

"Are you praying?" asked Sokol.

"Something like that," said Lieberman.

"For me?"

"Not sure," said Lieberman. "Maybe. Maybe for both of us. Maybe that Irving Hamel, who just burst in here, doesn't screw up the meeting. Maybe . . . I don't use words. I don't know if God is listening. Sometimes I think God created the world and everything on it, including us, then left us on our own, went to some other world, tried again. Maybe he comes back to look in on what he left behind. Maybe he doesn't. I like to think he doesn't. If I thought he did, I'd be a little angry that he doesn't say, 'stop.' You understand?"

"I don't know," said Sokol.

"Good. Neither do I. Let's go make some phone calls."

The secretary, Mrs. Gold, had been with Temple Mir Shavot since the days when it was located in Albany Park and Old Rabbi Wass was still a young man. Now Mrs. Gold, a solid citizen of seventy who liked to reminisce with anyone who would listen about the old days on the West Side when she was a girl, considered herself the protector of the Young Rabbi Wass, who was, at forty-five, no longer quite young.

Mrs. Gold was short. Mrs. Gold was plump. Her hair was short and dyed black, and her glasses hung professionally at the end of her nose. She had perfected the art of looking over her glasses at strangers in a way that told them she had some doubts about their intentions and origin.

"Can I use the phone in Rachel's office?" asked Lieberman as Mrs. Gold behind her desk looked at the disheveled and bloodstained Arnold Sokol.

"Why not?" asked Mrs. Gold. "Aren't you supposed to be in a meeting?"

"Something came up," said Lieberman.

"You know what'll happen if you're not in that meeting?"

"Chaos," said Lieberman. " 'The sky will fall and cursed night, it will be up to me to set it right.' "

"Shakespeare?" she said, shaking her head.

"Comes from years of insomnia and reading in the bathtub," said Lieberman, motioning for Sokol to follow him into a small office next to the wooden door on which a plaque indicated the office of Rabbi Wass.

Lieberman pointed to a chair next to the desk. Sokol sat while Lieberman stood making calls and taking notes.

A resigned calm had taken over Arnold Sokol. Events would carry him. He would drift. Others would take care of him, possibly send him to prison. He had experienced his moment. It would stay inside. He was complete. He tried to remember every moment of the night before. It came in small, jerking bits in which he stood triumphant. Sokol heard almost nothing of what the detective said, and when Lieberman hung up after taking notes, Sokol had trouble concentrating on what he was being told.

"His name is Zembinsky, Melvin Zembinsky," said Lieberman. "Notice I said 'is.' You didn't kill him. At least he's not dead yet. He's in Evanston Hospital. Let's go see him."

"He's not dead?" asked Sokol. "This is a trick. I killed him. He attacked me. I killed him."

Lieberman looked at the seated man, who looked as if he were going to panic.

"And you want him dead?"

"Yes," said Sokol pounding the desk. "Yes, yes, yes. It's . . . I don't know."

The door to the office opened and a man in a white shirt and dark slacks held up by suspenders stepped in, leaving the door open behind him.

The man was thin, wore glasses and a *kepuh*. He looked at Sokol, then at Lieberman.

"Abraham, what's going on?"

"Rabbi Wass, this is Arnold Sokol. He thought I was you. He confessed to a murder, but the victim isn't dead, and Mr. Sokol is disappointed."

Rabbi Wass looked confused. He took off his glasses, which he often did to make momentary sense of the immediate world, put them on again, and looked at Sokol.

"I was working on my sermon," Rabbi Wass said.

Both Sokol and Lieberman failed to see the relevance of the statement.

"Never mind," said the rabbi. "Who did you try to kill? Why? Why are you disappointed that he isn't dead? And, forgive me, but I don't recognize you. You're not a member of this congregation."

"I'm a Catholic," said Sokol.

"He's a Jew," said Lieberman.

"I thought I killed a young man who was trying to rob me," said Sokol. "Him and his gang, three of them. I fought them off. Then I wanted to confess, to tell someone."

"You were proud of what you had done?" asked the rabbi.

"Yes."

"Why didn't you go to a priest?"

"I . . ."

"He's a Jew, a convert to Catholicism," said Lieberman. "He's as confused as Jerry Slattery."

Slattery was a convert from Catholicism to Judaism. It had come to Slattery when he was fifty. He was a postal worker, a collector of coins, a bachelor with recurrent stomach problems. Then he had become a pain in the behind. No one is more Jewish than a convert. Slattery spoke out, decried the lack of religious discipline in the congregation. He had been to Israel twice, spoke Hebrew almost fluently, and argued with Rabbi Wass on any and all subjects. And then, suddenly, Slattery had second thoughts about his conversion, went to see a priest, and dropped out of religious life of all kinds. He sat at home in his small apartment at night watching television and playing Tetris on a Game Boy.

Rabbi Wass and the priest, Father Sutton at St. Thomas's, had joined forces to save Slattery, had visited him at home, taken him to dinner, tried to argue, persuade, threaten, cajole. So far, nothing had worked, and Lieberman, to tell the truth, was happy that Slattery wasn't around to correct everyone on ritual procedure and rail against the Arab world.

Sokol wasn't a member of the congregation. Sokol was a Catholic. What was Rabbi Wass's obligation, duty? Find the name of the man's priest? Another Slattery situation?

"We're going to the hospital," said Lieberman, motioning for Sokol to rise.

"I'll go with you," said Rabbi Wass. "I'll get my jacket."

"No," said Sokol.

The rabbi paused at the door.

"I would like to go," said the rabbi.

"You can't save my soul," said Sokol. "I don't want it saved, and I don't want clichés and simpleminded advice."

"You'd be surprised at how many people find solace in simple truths," said Rabbi Wass.

"Not me," said Sokol.

"Fine, whatever conversation we have, I'll try to make it dense, metaphysical, and difficult to follow. Will that satisfy you?"

Sokol looked at the rabbi, who was serious and without expression. The rabbi left to get his jacket.

Ten minutes later, Lieberman's partner returned, was briefed, and the four men got into the car and were headed for the hospital.

"I checked with your friend Bryant in Evanston," Lieberman said in the front seat while Hanrahan drove. "Our victim is eighteen, has a long list of arrests for robbery, assault. Did six months as a juvenile offender. Father's a lawyer. Mother's a Realtor and on a state juvenile crime commission."

Hanrahan looked into the rearview mirror. Rabbi Wass was speaking softly to Sokol, who seemed galaxies away.

"What're we doing, Abe? Why not turn him over to Bryant and get to the station before Kearney puts us on report."

"I called Kearney. He was in one of his moods. Doesn't care what we do," said Lieberman.

"It would be a comfort, though a small one, if I had some idea of what we were doing," said Hanrahan, as they drove down the road between the parking structure and the rear of the hospital. Hanrahan parked near the Emergency Room and put down his visor with the Chicago police card clipped to it.

"I think we're trying to save a man's soul, whatever that is," said Lieberman.

"We'd be better off out catching a few bad guys," said Hanrahan.

"I called his wife."

"You got a lot done fast, Rabbi."

"She's coming here. Older kid's in school. She's bringing the baby."

Hanrahan looked in the mirror again.

"Looks like a true believer in nothing," said Hanrahan.

"Maybe," said Lieberman. "Let's go."

They got out of the car, two policemen ahead, the rabbi and suspect behind.

There were about a dozen people in the waiting room, none of them Sokol's wife. They had beaten her there, which was fine with Lieberman. Identification was shown, and the woman behind the counter told them how to get up to the room of Melvin Zembinsky.

At the nursing station, a thin, pretty black nurse with her hair in a bun said that Zembinsky had suffered no serious injury other than facial contusions, a concussion that knocked him out, and a cut in his head that required thirty-two stitches. He needed a few days of tests and observation, but there was no reason they couldn't see him, especially since he was a suspect in a crime.

There were two men in the other beds in the room with Zembinsky. Neither man was in any condition to notice the quartet that moved to the bedside of the bandaged young man whose eyes were closed. Hanrahan pulled the curtain around the bed to give them some sense of privacy.

"Melvin," said Lieberman.

Nothing.

"Z," Lieberman said, and the young man's eyes struggled and opened.

"I'm Detective Lieberman. This is my partner, Detective Hanrahan, and this is Rabbi Wass. I think you know this man."

Zembinsky's eyes turned to Sokol without recognition.

"He's the one who put you in here," said Lieberman. "Wanna just shake hands and be friends?"

Zembinsky's eyes now turned to the thin little detective.

"I didn't think so," said Lieberman. "You're a Jew."

"I'm nothing," Zembinsky whispered. "Religion sucks."

"Sokol," said Lieberman. "It sounds like you and your victim have a lot in common."

"Why didn't you die?" asked Sokol with resignation.

"So I could get out of this bed, find you, and punch a hole in your stomach," said Zembinsky so softly that the four men could hardly hear him. Zembinsky's eyes closed, and he seemed exhausted.

"We're gonna get you, man," Zembinsky went on, eyes still closed.

"We're gonna get you at home, or on the street when you don't know we're coming. And if you've got a family . . ."

Lieberman was at the foot of the bed facing the battered young man. Rabbi Wass stood next to the bed with Hanrahan at his side. Sokol stood next to Lieberman.

And it happened. Arnold Sokol let out an animal snort of rage, pushed Lieberman against the bed, and grabbed the detective's weapon from his holster. Lieberman's hip had caught a metal bar. Pain shot through his side.

"No," said Rabbi Wass, as Sokol aimed the weapon at the young man on the bed, who opened his eyes, looked at Arnold, and smiled.

"Put it down, Mr. Sokol," said Hanrahan, whose weapon was out and pointed at the shaking man with the gun in his hand.

"No," said Sokol. "I'm going to finish this."

"Go ahead," said the young man in the bed. "I don't give a crap. You'll make the headlines. My friends won't have any trouble finding you. Shoot. You'll probably miss and screw it up again."

"You ever fire a weapon, Arnold?" Lieberman said.

"I'm just going to pull the trigger," said Sokol. "Pull it and pull it till it's empty or the other policeman shoots me. You don't understand. It has to be, or I'm nothing."

"First the synagogue, now the hospital," said Lieberman. "And who the hell knows what you've done to my hip? And let's not forget that if you shoot him with my gun, I'm in big trouble. I've got a wife, daughter, two grandchildren, a bar mitzvah to pay for, and I'm near a retirement pension. Shoot him and who knows what I lose. All you lose is your life."

Sokol looked at the three men around the bed and hesitated.

"I have to," he said. "Don't you see?"

"Be quiet, will you," came the voice of a man in another bed beyond the curtain. "I'm supposed to, for Christ's sake, rest here."

"Sorry," said Lieberman.

Sokol aimed the gun at the young man in the bed before him. Hanrahan leveled his weapon.

Before he could move, Rabbi Wass leaned over the young man on the bed and covered him with his body, his back to Sokol.

"Get out of the way," Sokol cried.

The rabbi was eye to eye with the battered man on the bed. The pain of the rabbi's weight was offset by the rabbi's attempt at a reassuring smile.

"No," said Rabbi Wass. "Arnold, give Detective Lieberman his gun back. No lives will be lost here with the possible exception of yours and mine."

"I . . ." Sokol stammered, then screamed, "Get the hell off of him."

"I would like to get the hell of his life off of him," said the rabbi, "but at the moment, one step at a time. This is very uncomfortable, Arnold."

"You people are all crazy," said Sokol. "I'm crazy."

"And I'm calling the damn nurse," came the voice from the other bed.

Lieberman held out his hand. Sokol hesitated and handed him the weapon. Hanrahan slowly put his gun away.

"He did it," croaked Zembinsky, looking into the rabbi's eyes.

Rabbi Wass closed his eyes, let out a puff of air, and stood up on less then firm legs.

"You've got balls," said the young man in the bed struggling for air.

"I'll take that as a compliment," said the rabbi, adjusting his glasses. "Now, if you want to repay me and God for saving your life, promise that this is all ended, that you will not seek revenge. You don't deserve revenge."

The pretty black nurse came in and saw that Zembinsky was having trouble breathing.

"What happened?" she asked, looking at Lieberman and then at her patient, who was breathing loud and heavily.

"I fell upon him," said Rabbi Wass.

The nurse leaned over the heavily breathing young man and said, "You people have some damn weird rituals."

"We do," said Lieberman.

Zembinsky's eyes met those of Arnold Sokol, and he spoke as the nurse listened to his chest with the stethoscope that hung around her neck.

"Okay," the young man gasped. "I owe you one. I leave the bastard alone. He doesn't bring any charges."

"Be quiet," the nurse said.

"Sokol nodded yes and Zembinsky nodded and closed his eyes."

The nurse stood up.

"He'll be alright," she said. "I'd say this visit is over."

"Amen," said Lieberman.

"You believe the little bugger?" asked Hanrahan in the corridor outside the room.

"Yes," said Rabbi Wass.

"I think so," said Sokol.

"Yes," said Lieberman, but kept to himself the knowledge gained from more than thirty years on the street, a knowledge that one's word was only as good as the person who gave it, and rage walked the streets.

"Go downstairs, Arnold Sokol," said Rabbi Wass. "Your wife should be there. Go home. I'll call you if you wish, see how you're doing."

"I . . . I'd . . . That would be fine."

"Maybe you could come back for a service, Friday night? I think you'll be the subject of my sermon. I don't know what I'll say. Maybe

I'll surprise us both. God often gives me words I didn't expect. Sometimes they're not so bad."

"I'll think about it," said Sokol, shaking hands with the two policemen.

"I'd say you owe the rabbi," said Hanrahan.

"Yes," said Sokol, looking at his watch. "I could still take a shower, change clothes, and get to work."

"The baby's name?" asked Lieberman, as Sokol started to turn toward the elevator. "What's your baby's name?"

"Luke," said Sokol. "Did I tell you my wife's name is Mary?"

"You did," said Lieberman. "They're waiting for you downstairs."

The three men stood in the hospital corridor while Sokol got in the elevator.

"You're a hero, Rabbi," said Lieberman.

"I'm a man, that's all," said Rabbi Wass.

"So," said Lieberman. "What does it mean? What happened this morning?"

"I don't know," said the rabbi. "But it feels right."

When the three men got down to the lobby, the tattered Arnold Sokol was standing in the corner near the window arguing with a plump woman with disheveled hair and a baby over her shoulder.

"Doesn't look promising," said Hanrahan.

"They're talking," said Rabbi Wass, adjusting his glasses. "It's a start."

Sokol motioned toward them. They couldn't see a way out other than coming over to the family.

"Mary, these people helped me. I don't know their names."

"I'm Rabbi Wass. This is Detective Abraham Lieberman and Detective William Hanrahan. Chicago police."

"Thank you," the woman said, handing the baby to her husband and reaching out her hand.

They each took her hand in turn and watched while the couple moved away.

"Time for coffee?" asked Lieberman.

"Why not?" said Rabbi Wass, who walked ahead of them, lost in his thoughts.

"Abe," Hanrahan said softly. "You load your weapon yet this morning?"

"Nope," said Lieberman. "Father Murph, you know I don't load till I get to the squad room."

"Yeah," said Hanrahan, as the automatic doors opened in front of the hospital. "How about you paying for the coffee?"

"How about Rabbi Wass paying for the coffee and Danish?" Lieberman said, as the rabbi stood waiting for them.

"That'll be fine with me," said Hanrahan. "Just fine."

3

The Pinchuk sisters were seated at the Lieberman dining room table alongside each other, a thick large book that looked like a photograph album in front of them, a black briefcase next to it. At the far end of the table sat Lieberman's grandson Barry. And Lieberman's wife, Bess, standing straight, wearing a black dress and a serious look, sat across from the sisters.

Lieberman did not sigh. He wanted to. He wanted to tell them about the man who had thought he was a rabbi. He wanted to tell them about Rabbi Wass's act of courage. He wanted to tell them he was tired. He wanted to tell them he was hungry.

They were clearly waiting for him as he stepped inside the front door, looked across the darkened living room and into the dining room. Barry looked up at his grandfather, trying to show nothing but seeking a reprieve from the coming ordeal. Lieberman was in no position to grant reprieves.

He took off his shoes, dropped them in the small closet in the tiny alcove, and moved toward the table. He remembered why the Pinchuks, Rose and Esther, were here. He had it in the appointment book in his back pocket. He had chosen to put it from his mind.

"Sorry I'm late," he said, leaning over to kiss Bess on the cheek. His wife was six years younger than Lieberman. She looked at least fifteen years younger and sometimes she looked young enough to be his daughter.

The Liebermans had one daughter, Lisa, and this meeting was a direct result of that offspring.

"Hungry, Abe?" Bess asked.

He had been when he walked through the door, but he did not want to eat in front of the somber Pinchuk girls. Everyone called them "the Pinchuk girls" though Rose was seventy-six and Esther seventy-five. They were both widows. They lived together. They could have passed for twins and wore each other's clothes. The Pinchuk girls were short, looked deceptively frail, wore identical short haircuts for their identical silver hair, and bore the same face as their late mother, which meant they were unblemished and perpetually smiling as if they had a secret and knew how to tolerate even the most outrageous responses the world hurled at them. They were thin female Jewish Buddhas who were about to reveal some of their secrets in their book, briefcase, and memories to Abraham Lieberman.

"I'll eat later. Coffee?"

"I'll get it," said Barry, rising quickly. "We've got some carrot cake, too."

Barry, who was not normally so ready to serve, was almost to the kitchen door. Any respite was welcome, even serving his grandfather.

"No carrot cake for your grandfather."

The Pinchuk sisters had cups of coffee before them. Bess had brought out the good breakfast china Lieberman had gotten for her about five anniversaries ago.

Barry looked at Abe, who shrugged. Abe had a constant battle against cholesterol. God had chosen to torture him by making him love food, especially Jewish food, and then forbidding it to him. Abe had a particular sympathy for the Scriptural Jonah.

"Bring your grandfather the fat-free cookies," said Bess.

Barry went through the door. Lieberman knew his grandson would take as much time as he could get away with before returning.

Abe contemplated the coming fat-free, sugar-free, taste-free cookies that looked like real cookies just as Tarry Radlen, the drug dealer in Albany Park, looked like a real businessman. Better. Radlen's passion was expensive, tasteful clothing. He had neatly trimmed dark hair, gray sideburns, a gentle tan, and an understanding face with bright blue eyes behind stylish Italian glasses.

"Abe," said Bess.

Lieberman came out of his reverie about Tarry Radlen and pursed his lips to stifle the urge to sigh.

"The book," Rose said, putting her left hand on the large white album as if she were about to ask all at the table to swear upon it.

"I see," said Lieberman.

They were there to make arrangements for Barry's coming bar mitzvah. They had six months before that occasion when Barry was to take his place among the men of his religion, was to go through the rituals and be declared a man of Israel who, among other things, could take his place in the morning *minyan*, which required ten Jewish males who had attained manhood through their own bar mitzvahs.

Lieberman well recalled his own bar mitzvah weekend almost fifty years earlier. His own had been, because of his grandfather, an Orthodox ceremony, an ordeal that had caused him endless hours of study, nightmares for months, and, when it was finally over, the greatest sense of relief of his lifetime. Barry's bar mitzvah would be in Temple Mir Shavot with Rabbi Wass and Cantor Fried presiding. Mir Shavot was Conservative. Their joining Mir Shavot had been a compromise many years ago when the old Rabbi Wass was head of the congregation. Lieberman had held out for a Reform congregation, everything in English, a rabbi who played the guitar during services, an occasional reminder that they were Jews, a fact that required no institutional reinforcement for Abraham Lieberman.

But Bess had held out for Mir Shavot, and Lieberman had given in to her wishes as he felt he did in all matters domestic. Which was why he was sitting at the dining room table in West Rogers Park with the Pinchuk sisters who, it seemed, were particularly deferential, not because Lieberman was a policeman but because Bess was President of the Congregation.

"Invitations first," said Esther, looking at the book.

Rose opened the album. The pages faced the Liebermans.

Lieberman had a sudden flashback to his daughter Lisa's bat mitzvah. He had successfully repressed the memory the way, he thought, that women suppressed the pain of childbirth shortly after the agony.

Lisa had been a bright, no, a brilliant and defiant child of great beauty and will. She had been dragged, primarily by her mother, through the process and performed brilliantly. Lieberman remembered a sense of pride at her performance and a feeling of emotion when Rabbi Wass, Old Rabbi Wass, gave her his blessing. Above all, he remembered two other things. First, the cost. Second, the fact that when he was a boy, girls did not have bat mitzvahs. He did not object to sexual equality, only its cost.

Barry came back in, surprisingly fast, Lieberman thought, and placed coffee and a plate of six cookies next to Abe. Their eyes met. A plea.

"Where's Melisa?" asked Lieberman.

"Upstairs, homework," said Bess.

"I've got a math quiz tomorrow," said Barry, taking his seat at the far end of the not-very-long table.

"Later," said Bess firmly.

"You and Grandpa can make all the decisions," Barry said.

Barry looked remarkably like his father, Todd, who was not seated at this table taking on responsibility for a number of very good reasons. Todd, a professor of classics at Northwestern University, was not Jewish. Todd, whom Lisa had divorced three years earlier, had remarried. Todd, who loved his children and saw them often, far more often than Lisa, who had moved to California, leaving her children with her parents, wanted as little as possible to do with his former wife. Lisa had herself recently remarried, a doctor. A Jewish mother's dream. A decent, warm man. A pathologist. Tall, handsome, had studied in Israel and spoke Hebrew. But there was a catch. With Lisa there was always a catch. Her new husband was black, African-American, Negro, a *shvartze*.

Abe's and Bess's tolerance had been tested, but there had been no doubt about the outcome even before they met Lisa's husband. The Liebermans were in matters social and secular concerned only that the man was decent. He was better than that. Lieberman had grown up in a Chicago West Side ghetto on two sides of which were miles of black families. He had learned then and in later life that race was a test, absurdity, possibly a trial from God if there were a God.

"We are creatures on a small planet," he had explained to Barry and Melisa when they had been told about their mother's new husband. "Our small planet is in a small solar system around a small star. Beyond it are millions of stars, millions upon millions of solar systems. Men and women are one kind of creature on this small planet. We have small differences, different beliefs. The most truly evil man I ever met was black. But then again, the most truly good man I ever met was black. We have better things to do in our time on earth than waste it in battles over which Sneetch on the beach is better than the other."

He had practiced the speech before he had given it. Not in those words exactly, but close, and it had gone well.

He had even told them that there were others, perhaps most people, who didn't see the simple truth of man's insignificance, and that their mother and stepfather were going to have some tough times as they would probably when they were with them.

"Abe," Bess said, touching his arm as he nibbled on a tasteless cookie shaped like a leaf with little green speckles.

"I'm listening," said Lieberman, trying to appear attentive, shifting a little in his chair to ease the slight throbbing in his hip where he had bumped into the bed in Melvin Zembinsky's hospital room.

The bottom line here was that Abe and Bess were going to have to pay for the bar mitzvah. Lisa was willing to come, but she was not willing to pay. It was, she said, a matter of principle. She and God had been at war for the last two decades. The only concessions she would make were that she would attend, be pleasant, and that she and her husband would pay for the flowers on the *bemah*, the platform in the sanctuary on which the services were held. Even that had been her husband's idea.

"How many cards will you need?" Rose asked.

"We have a list," Bess answered, handing an unwrinkled sheet to the Pinchuk sisters. "One hundred and fifty. That includes everyone in Barry's bar mitzvah class, school friends, relatives from New York, California, and St. Louis."

"Most of the out-of-towners won't come," said Lieberman.

"But we're inviting them anyway," Bess said. "We agreed."

"We agreed," Lieberman agreed, picking up his coffee. Barry had prepared it just the way his grandfather liked it, hot with cream and two Equals. He had microwaved the cup so that cream and coffee were hot.

"One hundred and fifty invitations," said Rose, writing in a small black notebook that Lieberman had not noticed before. "Response cards and envelopes. You'll do the addressing?"

"Yes," said Bess.

"You've looked through the book," Esther said, hand flat on the open page. "Have you made a selection?"

"Barry?" Bess asked, looking at her grandson.

Barry shrugged, showing his complete indifference to the selection of cards.

"What's the price range?" asked Lieberman.

Bess gave him a tolerant look, the look of one who knew there were to be more of such questions to come.

"Whole package?" asked Rose.

Lieberman nodded.

"Including postage it can, for 150 invitations, range from $375 to $550 or a little more."

"For invitation cards?"

"That's a 20 percent discount figure," said Esther. "The stamps are usually thirty-seven cents to send and thirty-seven cents for the return envelope."

"I like the one on page twenty-seven," Bess said.

Esther expertly opened the album to page twenty-seven. Lieberman leaned forward to look. It was simple, ivory colored with a blue border and blue invitation lettering.

"Barry?" Lieberman asked.

"It's fine," Barry said, squirming.

"Settled," said Rose with a smile.

"Awkward as the question might be," said Lieberman, "how much will that one cost?"

"That's in category A-14," said Rose. "Three hundred and eighty, that's with the 20 percent already taken off, the response cards and thank-you notes included."

Bess gave her husband a look that told him life would be easier for him if he backed off.

"Category A-14 it shall be," said Lieberman.

But it was only beginning.

The yarmulkes with Barry's name and the date. The color and quality of the little caps that men wore to the service and were taken home as tokens of remembrance. Bess, who would have been enjoying this were it not for her husband's thoughts of their savings and her grandson's desire to escape, selected blue yarmulkes. Barry and Abe looked at each other and agreed. One hundred and eighty dollars.

Lieberman was being led into what he knew the big-ticket items were going to be.

By the time it was over, he had been cajoled, intimidated, and worked over before finally agreeing to: (a) a Kiddush, refreshments after the Friday-night service for the congregation and guests, at a cost of $900, (b) an Oneg Shabbat in the temple dining room for all following the Saturday-morning services, such lunch to include a buffet of herring in sour cream, tuna salad, egg salad, bagels, cream cheese, nova lox, a green salad, dessert table, coffee, punch, and a hot pasta dish for the kids who wouldn't eat anything else, (c) a small dinner for out-of-town guests on Friday night, (d) a small Saturday-night dinner for family and friends in the Lieberman house. All of the preceding to be kosher-catered by Carl Zimmer, a member of the congregation who owned a successful catering service.

Total cost for the preceding: $4,500, a bargain.

It could have been worse. Most of the bar and bat mitzvah kids had big Saturday-night parties at a hotel where a loud DJ kept them dancing, and adults tried to carry on conversations to no avail. There was nothing Jewish about such celebrations, and it would have doubled the cost. The house needed a new roof. Savings could go quickly for this event, and in the back of both Abe and Bess's minds was that in shortly less than four years they would be going through it again with Melisa.

Instead of the big party, however, Barry readily agreed to a trip to New York for five days. On each day, in addition to normal New York excursions to the Central Park Zoo, the Museum of Natural History, Broadway shows, and the Statue of Liberty, they would do one Jewish thing every day. The Yiddish Theater, Ellis Island, the Jewish Museum, a Shabbat with Bess's ultra-Orthodox cousin in Brooklyn. They could fly Southwest, stay with relatives. Melisa would stay with her father and stepmother, which was fine with her. She fully expected to have five days of being spoiled.

When the Pinchuk sisters had silently packed up their caravan, shook hands with Lieberman, exchanged hugs with Bess, and smiled at Barry, they were ushered to the door, where they carried on their perpetual argument about who was to drive their shared automobile back home. Rose reminded Esther that Esther had driven to the Liebermans and, therefore, it was Rose's turn.

The last thing the Liebermans heard as they closed the front door was Esther saying, "But I see better at night."

When they turned away from the closed door, Barry was gone, fled to the sanctuary of his bedroom upstairs. The house was old, small. There were two small bedrooms upstairs and Abe and Bess's bedroom downstairs.

"How was I?" asked Lieberman.

Bess touched his cheek.

"Better than I expected."

"I'm resigned," said Abe, moving back to the dining room. "I'm resigned. I'm tired. I'm hungry. I want to know what you've been doing all day, and I don't want to talk about what I've been doing."

"Kitchen," Bess said, leading the way.

Lieberman followed. There was something in the way she had said "kitchen" that made him wary. There was an I've-got-something-to-tell-you in that single word. There was further evidence at the small kitchen table with the white Formica top. A place was set for one, and Lieberman could smell forbidden food as Bess pressed the preset button on the microwave on the counter next to the sink.

"Brisket," he said.

He sat, and his wife nodded as she moved to the refrigerator to get a bottle of California wine, red wine. Normally, Lieberman drank only at the Sabbath dinner, and then only a single glass.

"You have a 'topic,'" he said, as the bell went off in the microwave.

She nodded again, removed the plate of brisket and mashed potatoes from the microwave, and poured him a glass of wine, not in the everyday tumblers they had used for more than a decade but in a wineglass. Lieberman liked the feel of a fragile wineglass as much or more than he enjoyed the wine itself.

"Eat," Bess said, sitting next to him in the small kitchen.

The brisket smelled perfect. The mound of smashed potatoes, potatoes mashed without removing the skins, looked perfect and smelled of garlic. In front of his plate was the butter dish. To actually serve him butter meant that the "topic" was serious indeed.

He ate a piece of brisket and put a small slice of butter on his potatoes before he said, "The roof."

"The roof," Bess repeated.

"You've got the estimates," he said, trying the potatoes. They were perfect. He took a sip of wine.

"All three," she said. "It's an old house. An old roof."

"The roof of this house is younger than I am," he said. "In Europe houses last for hundreds of years without needing new roofs. Why is that?"

"I don't know. What I do know is that our roof leaks, Abe. We've got to have a new roof before winter."

"We just committed our savings to a bar mitzvah," he said.

"Not everything," she said. "We can get a home improvement loan for the roof. I talked to Irv Greenblatt at the bank."

"Loans have to be paid back," Lieberman said, finding that the direction of the conversation was not curbing his appetite as he had expected. "They're funny that way."

"Monthly payments," she said.

"We haven't finished paying off the car."

"You're telling me something I don't know? Abe, the roof will cave in when we get a heavy snow."

"I'll talk to God about speeding up global warming."

"You and I will talk to Irv Greenblatt about signing for a loan for $14,000."

Lieberman stopped chewing on a particularly delicious and slightly fatty piece of meat. He met his wife's eyes.

"That's not much less than we paid for this house," he said.

"We've lived here for almost thirty-five years, Abe."

"Let's sell the house," he said. "That woman who came by last year from the real estate company. We've got her card somewhere. She said we could get at least $135,000 for the house, and we don't owe a dime on it."

"You can't sell a house with a bad roof," Bess said patiently. "And we'd have to replace the carpets before anyone would buy it. Where would we get the money for that? And where would we move? We've got the kids."

Abe ate silently for a few minutes.

"Remember Stan Taradash?" he asked.

Bess was accustomed to her husband's abrupt transitions, and tonight she was inclined to humor him.

"I remember," she said.

"High school, class clown, gangly. All arms and legs. Glasses. Dumb grin. Couldn't play basketball, baseball. Didn't even get great grades. Always had his hand up to answer questions. Shot it up in the air pumping toward the ceiling."

Lieberman demonstrated.

"He was in your class, Abe. I was six years behind."

"But you knew him."

"Everyone in Marshall High School knew him."

"Now."

"Now he's retired. Made millions in real estate. Owns a dozen office buildings in the loop. Housing developments in Northbrook, Highland Park, Park Forest. Gets his picture in the paper. Always looks serious. You have a point here, Abe?"

Lieberman looked at the food before him.

"I'm a sixty-year-old policeman, a sergeant," he said.

"Tell me something I don't know," said Bess patiently.

"You know why I've never been promoted?"

"Of course," she said. "Are we going to go over it again? If we are, I need a glass of wine."

"I'll give the short version. I have no talent for leadership. It's not in me. Wasn't in my father. Not in my brother. No talent for it. No interest in it. Consequently . . ."

Bess did pour herself a glass of wine.

"You don't make as much money as a garbageman, a teacher, as Stan Taradash."

"But I have the same expenses," he said, pointing his fork for emphasis.

"So, you'll retire in a few years, and you can be a security consultant like you've said. A Jewish detective, remember? You can line up clients, get rich in your golden years."

"When do we sign the papers? For the loan?"

"Tomorrow afternoon or morning. You stop by the bank when you can. I'll sign on my own."

"One more question," he said.

"Ask."

"What's for dessert?"

It was at that point 9:52 P.M. The phone rang. Bess got it, said hello, listened for a moment, then handed it to Abe, who had almost finished his food. The voice on the other end was Nestor Briggs, who was on the desk at the Clark Street Station. Nestor told him about the two dead men floating off the beach at Morse Avenue, told him that both corpses had been identified and that Lieberman might be particularly interested in one of them. When Nestor gave him the name of the dead man, Lieberman asked him to call Bill Hanrahan.

"Trying to find him now," said Nestor. "Not at home. His cell phone's off."

"Try the Black Moon."

"Will do," said Nestor calmly.

"How's Panther?" asked Lieberman, wiping his mouth with the napkin he had taken from his lap.

Panther was Nestor's dog, a placid, small mongrel whom Nestor occasionally brought to the station at night. Nestor lived alone with the dog. When the dog came to the station he sat quietly behind the reception desk, a bowl of water and a bowl of food in front of him. Panther simply sat, tongue out, panting, watching Nestor, who from time to time reached down to pat him gently on the head or back.

"Needs his teeth looked at," said Nestor. "But otherwise fine."

"Black Moon," Lieberman repeated, and moved to the wall to hang up the phone.

"Floaters," said Lieberman, turning to his wife.

Bess had been around policemen long enough to know what he meant and know that there was a reason he had been called. She would go to bed early, read, fall asleep after watching *Nightline*, and wake up whenever he came home. It was what she did. It was what he did.

When he did come home, he would remove his gun and holster, put them in the drawer next to his side of the bed, lock the drawer with the key he wore around his neck, kiss her gently, and tell her to go back to sleep.

Lieberman was an insomniac, which, along with heredity, accounted for his tired-hound-dog face. While he slept little, he spent a great deal of time watching very old movies on television and reading in the bathtub.

"Yes to the Pinchuk girls," he said. "Yes to the roof. Any other concessions to be made to pave the road to our eventual impoverishment?"

"Not at the moment," she said with a smile. "Be careful."

It was what she always said.

He would check the refrigerator when he got home for the dessert. He was sure it would be something special.

4

Bill Hanrahan had a favorite booth at the Black Moon Chinese Restaurant at the Lakefront Inn. The motel was located on North Lake Shore Drive a few blocks down from Devon. If you stepped out on the sidewalk during the day, you could look north and see the south end of Loyola University where Sheridan Road curved. If you looked across the street, you could see the Michigan Towers, the high-rise condo building, and you could hear the lapping of waves on the beach beyond the tall condos if the traffic was light.

Hanrahan's favorite booth was in the rear of the small restaurant near the kitchen. He sat with his back to the window. He did not like to look at the Michigan Towers. It was in the Black Moon three years earlier that he had sat at a table by the window watching the front of the condo. His job had been to watch the entrance, protect a hooker informant who lived in the building.

The hooker had been murdered while he sat in the Black Moon that night. There was a good chance she would have lived had Hanrahan been sober.

He had sat there watching the entrance across the street, a lapsed Catholic, a former football player with a pair of bad knees, a fifty-year-old cop whose wife of twenty-five years had left him and one of whose two sons wanted nothing to do with him.

On the night Estralda Valdez had been murdered, Detective William Hanrahan had hit bottom and had little interest in climbing up. But on the night Estralda Valdez had been murdered, Bill Hanrahan had begun his rebirth . . . and it was all due to the waitress who served him chicken lo mien, Iris Chen, whose father owned the Black Moon.

And now he sat across from Iris in the booth, dead sober, as he had been for almost three years, planning their wedding. Iris was clearly beautiful. Two years older than Hanrahan, who was about to celebrate his fifty-third birthday, she looked twenty years younger. Iris was svelte. Yes, it was a word Hanrahan would not have used, but Abe had described her that way once, and it fit. They looked a bit odd together, the bulky, clearly Irish cop with the ruddy face and the svelte Chinese beauty, but they also seemed somehow right together.

Iris looked nothing like his first wife Maureen, who had, with good reason, left him and moved out of the state. Maureen was tall, pale, with a sweeping head of wavy traditional red hair, a way of shaking her head no when her husband was drinking or even thinking about drinking, or when he had done something that hinted at the suicidal when he was on the job. Maureen had counted on Lieberman to keep his partner from self-destruction, but eventually Hanrahan's self-destruction was no longer the point. It was her own survival that had been at stake, and she had left him one day and Bill had understood.

"You're sure?" he asked Iris.

She nodded. The decision was much harder for her than for him. Iris's father, who was still in the kitchen, was less than enthusiastic about the marriage. Iris's family was clearly less than joyful and, perhaps most important, a certain elderly and highly respected Chinese criminal of great reputation and power in the Chinese community was particularly displeased. It had been Laio Woo's plan to marry Iris himself. It was not sex that drove him to his desire for her. He was beyond that. She was a lady, a lady in a traditional Chinese sense. She would complete his sense of worth, sitting by his side, serving tea, being respected. For respect was what this former Shanghai street gang member sought most. He prized his antiques, conducted his illegal activities at a distance, surrounded himself with able, well-dressed young men who were both educated and completely loyal sociopaths.

Iris had been promised to this man. Iris had met Bill Hanrahan. Hanrahan, with Lieberman's help, had faced the modern-day war lord. The result had been a reluctantly granted victory for Hanrahan and Iris, an agreement to wait a full year before marrying to be sure that they both wished this, to recognize what this decision would mean to her family, her honor, her future.

"I'm sure," Iris said, reaching over to touch his hand on the table.

A paper napkin with the Chinese astrological signs lay before him with his plate, a half-finished egg roll and cup of coffee resting on it.

They had decided not to wait the full year. They had decided just a few moments earlier to get married in two days.

Part of the reason was that they had remained chastely apart through their entire strange courtship with one exception.

Part of the reason was that Hanrahan felt his Irish father in him, his father who had also been a cop, his father who would have gotten the Chinese gangster alone somehow and made his head ring like a gong with his nightstick.

Hanrahan had, to some degree, returned to the church with the help of a priest, had fully returned to sobriety with the help of AA, and had certainly returned to life with the help of Iris Chen.

"Then let's do it," he said. "Two days from today. Thursday."

They couldn't get married in a Catholic church. Hanrahan was divorced. Iris was a Buddhist. It was Father Sam Parker at St. Bart's who had suggested the Unitarian minister in Evanston. The former Catholic priest at the Unitarian church had readily agreed and waited only for the date.

"Two days from today?" she asked, looking around at the only two customers in the restaurant, an older couple at a table near the window who tried not to eavesdrop on their conversation. "There is so much to prepare. I want to invite my friends, my sisters, my cousins, my family."

"Will they come?" he asked.

"I think so," she said. "Don't you want people there?"

"Abe and Bess," he said. "My son Michael. He'll come. Maybe some of the people I work with. Kearney."

"My father would like to give a wedding party."

"Your father would not like to give a wedding party. Your father would like me to disappear."

"He is learning to like you," Iris said.

"Tolerate," said Hanrahan. "I'm a white, divorced, Irish Catholic cop fighting a steep battle with the bottle. And your father's got Laio Woo on his back."

Iris's father had been opposed to the wedding, afraid of his daughter getting involved with this hulking Irish policeman, afraid of the wrath of Woo the elderly gang lord, afraid of the reaction from his own family and friends. But over the past year he had begun to adjust to his daughter's determination.

"I'll ask my father to have a party on the weekend," Iris said. "I'll invite my friends and family to that. We can keep the church wedding small."

"Sounds fine," said Hanrahan with a smile. "The party'll be here?"

"No," she said. "My father will find a place. Nothing big, but I want it to be special. I have never been married before, and I will never be married again. I may not be a young girl, but I am a woman, and I want memories. I know we won't have children. You want none, and I am beyond the age of bearing."

"We've talked about this," he said.

"William," she said. "Would you consider something for me?"

"I'll consider anything for you."

"Would you consider adopting a child, a girl?"

"A baby?"

"No, a young girl. She is six. Her mother and father are dead. She is in Taiwan. Her father was white. She is the child of an old friend."

"Adopt a child," he said to himself. "Iris, I'm a rotten father."

"You were not a good father," she said. "But you could be one *now*."

"A girl," he said. "I have two grown boys, grandchildren."

"Consider it," she said. "For me. For us."

Hanrahan was considering what to think, what to say, when he heard the phone ring on the glass counter against the back wall. Iris got up and moved to the phone.

Hanrahan looked at the red dragons and black moons that decorated the walls.

"For you," Iris called.

Hanrahan got up and went to the phone.

"Hanrahan," he said.

"Nestor. Meet Abe at the Morse Avenue Beach. Two floaters."

"Why us?" Hanrahan asked.

"There's a reason, William. You'll see. Since you're at the Black Moon, how about picking up a couple of egg rolls for Panther?"

"What . . ."

Briggs had hung up. Morse Avenue Beach was no more than ten minutes away from the Black Moon. He looked at Iris, reached over, and took her hand.

"Lot to think about," he said. "I've got to work. Can you give me a couple of egg rolls?"

Iris returned the touch and would have kissed him had the couple not been sitting at the window.

"She's a very pretty child," Iris said.

As he headed for the door after Iris had gotten the egg rolls from the kitchen and handed them to Hanrahan in a small, brown paper bag, Hanrahan found himself giving serious consideration to the completely alien idea of becoming a father again. It didn't feel nearly as strange or unpleasant as he thought it should.

Wychovski was cold. Wychovski was wet. Wychovski couldn't get the words to songs out of his head as he crossed a street heading west, away from the water. He had forty dollars in wet bills in his wallet. About eighty cents in change. There was money, not a hell of a lot, in a bank in St. Louis, if he could get to the bank in St. Louis, if the cops had not already identified him, if he could get out of town, if, if, if, if. It was all Pryor's fault. Well not all, but enough.

"'What do you do in a case like that,'" he sang softly, teeth chattering. "'What do you do but jump on your hat, and your grandmother and your toothbrush and anything that's helpless.'"

Where did those lines come from? Where had he heard that song? When he was a kid. That was it. He had a record when he was a kid. Who sang that song? Gibson something.

It was a residential street at least six blocks from the water. He wasn't sure if he was in Evanston or Chicago. Probably Evanston. He could jack a car, be gone in seconds, but someone might see him. It wasn't late enough or dark enough, and walking, at least for a while, would be safer. Maybe.

He headed south. Somehow he felt he could hide more easily in Chicago. Weighted down with golden animals and, he hoped, waterproof watches. He needed clothes or a place to dry out. He needed to find a bus or an el train. He couldn't take a chance on a cab. Cabby might remember him. Cops might ask cabbies. Cops were funny that way when a cop was killed. Not that they wouldn't care about the dead jeweler, but a dead cop was special.

He tried to walk slowly, glancing at the few cars that came up or down the street. If he spotted a cop car, he would slowly walk up the nearest driveway, take his keys out of his pocket, and pretend to be moving toward the door. If that failed to keep the cop car going, he would have run like hell, which, given his wet clothes and soggy socks and shoes, would have been difficult.

Wychovski had stayed in reasonably good condition behind the walls. He had taken up jogging and running, and lifting, more to keep away from the general prison population than for a love of the exercise; but he had gotten used to it and knew he had the endurance if not the speed for a long foot chase. He looked like a small bull. He wanted to look at least like a dapper bull and not a damp one.

No cop cars. Few people.

"There is no trick to the cancan. It is so easy to do."

Another song. He could hear a gravelly voice singing inside him. Bobby Short. That was the name. No trick to the cancan. Maybe Wychovski should cancan his way down the street. Maybe the day and night had made him a little crazy. Maybe he should come up with some plan.

Wychovski walked three blocks, passing only a couple of black kids in their teens wearing shorts. They hardly looked at him. Even if they had mugging on their minds, the wet guy walking past them looked like a compact car with a bad attitude. They were busy dribbling and singsong talking. "I could'a taken his ass to the paint any goddamn fuckin' time I wanted to. Know what I mean? But that fuckin' Stoner, man. He don't know how to set a pick or get out of the way. He just stands out there blocking the lane. Know what I mean? Wants the ball. Wants the ball."

Wants the ball, Wychovski thought. Everybody wants the ball. Now I've got the ball. Pryor is dead. Crazy Pryor. Stupid Pryor. Now I'm walking who knows where with no plan.

He came to a street, a wider street than the one he had been walking. More cars. To his left, he thought, he could see the lake, wondered if he wandered over he might see Pryor's body floating past. Maybe he would wave good-bye to him or give him the finger.

Distracted. There was an old iron fence across the street. No longer protected by the apartment buildings and houses, he felt a chill breeze off the lake and shuddered at the headstones beyond the fence. The fence extended in both directions. The iron spikes were old at the top but still pointed. He was in reasonable condition, but he was tired and wet. Chances were fair that he might slip and get skewered trying to go over it. Besides, what would he do in a cemetery? Hide? He was too cold to hide in a cemetery.

The dead didn't bother him. Almost everyone was dead, he thought as he walked to his right a little faster than he had before because there were more cars on the street. Eventually one had to be a cop.

What happened to all the dead? Thousands of years and we're not surrounded by cemeteries and up to our asses in dead bodies. Layers beneath there were probably bones from Indians a thousand, two thousand years ago. He was walking on dead dinosaurs and people. Everyone in the world was.

He passed the cemetery and in another block came to an even

bigger street. The sign said it was Chicago. Was that just the name of the street or was he in Chicago? He turned left, knowing that was where the city was. Maybe he could cross the line somewhere, be out of the jurisdiction of the Evanston cops. He didn't know how it worked.

Across the street running to and from Chicago was an embankment. At the top of it were elevated train tracks. Good. He would walk till he came to a station. He kept walking. Lots of cars coming and going now. No houses. Small businesses, closed for the night.

Think. I can't. Think. Okay. Clothes. No time. No luck. He came to another intersection with an even busier street, which the sign told him was Howard. Vaguely, he remembered or thought he remembered or just wanted to remember that Howard was the dividing line between Chicago and Evanston.

He was standing in front of a flower shop on the corner. It was closed. Across the street was an old storefront building with closed shops downstairs and a darkened beauty school upstairs, its windows shouting that haircuts were five dollars at the Hair Artists School of Beauty. "Stop in. Save." That was in one of the dark windows.

He had lost the train tracks, which had veered to the left. He moved left. Think of a reason why you're wet. Fell in the lake. Kids for no reason came out of the dark with buckets and doused him. The kids laughed and taunted. They pointed their fingers at him. Their teeth were large. They were black. They wore shorts. One of them had a basketball. They bounced the basketball off of his head. He should have gone to the police, but he didn't want trouble. He was from out of town.

Did that make sense? Maybe. It was weird enough. Weird sometimes made more sense than falling in the lake.

All the faces of the people on the street were black. He got glances but no comments, no hassles. He was tired, but he wouldn't take any hassles. He might even, in some strange way, welcome it. He was stronger than he looked.

No one better mess with him. He shouldn't have run when those kids soaked him and hit him with a basketball. Wait. That didn't happen. Hell, from now on it is what happened.

A break, or maybe. A store across the street was open, one of those stores with the big sign that says everything is a dollar but when you get in some things are two or three dollars, but what the hell.

An elevated train rattled less than half a block away. He crossed the street in the middle of the block, dodging a red car with a dented radiator.

The Big Dollar store. A black woman behind the counter. Two other black women talking to her on the other side of the counter. They weren't talking English. It sounded something like French. The woman behind the counter was young, dark, kind of pretty. The other two women were older, heavier.

They looked at him.

"Fireplug burst over on Chicago Street when I walked past it," he said. "Need some dry clothes till I get home."

The pretty woman nodded and went back to her conversation. The prices were up to five dollars, but he managed a pair of cheap blue pants made out of everything synthetic in China, a pullover blue short-sleeved polo shirt with the letter "P" in white on the pocket, three pairs of white underwear, a pair of white socks, some made-in-Indonesia cloth sneakers with plastic soles that would hold up for no more than a month, and a gray long-sleeved sweatshirt with pockets and a hood. Total bill: twenty-three dollars. Wychovski was a five-hundred-dollar suit man for chrissake. Prison gray or Big Dollar clothes. He would settle for nothing in between. But that was then. This is now.

He handed a twenty and a five to the talking woman, who looked just as pretty close up. The other two women kept talking.

"Anyplace I can change?" he said as affably as he could.

"Rest room in the back," she said. "You need a key."

She had a nice accent. The key was attached to a big round piece of orange plastic that announced in blue letters UNIVERSITY OF ILLINOIS.

Things were looking up, Wychovski decided as he changed. Not far up. Not high. Not yet. As he changed he made his decision. These were desperate times. Desperate times called for desperate measures. Who had said that? George Washington? Thomas Paine?

Wychovski had read so goddamn much in prison he couldn't remember who had written what.

Plan: Get on the train. Get off in three or four stops. Jack a car and find Walter the fence. Walter would have to buy the gold pieces in his pocket. If he didn't, Wychovski had no choice. He'd take the fence. Walter touched the Glock wedged now inside the pocket of his hooded gray sweatshirt. It was bad business robbing fences. Walter would be protected.

But desperate times. Desperate measures.

5

The bodies were lying under the white beach lights on the dark sand. The nearest light about twenty feet over their heads was sputtering, giving notice that it had had enough of graffiti-covered rocks and benches, fornicating teens, and the dumped remnants of drug users who liked to shoot, snort, and smoke to the sound of waves and the smell of dead fish.

"Looks like God and Moses," said Hanrahan, standing next to his partner.

"I think it's God and Adam," Lieberman answered, hands in his pockets, watching the uniformed cops marking off the crime scene or what regulations said was the crime scene until otherwise informed.

"The Sistine Chapel," said Hanrahan.

"I've seen pictures. Never been to Europe."

"Me either."

They both knew this about each other but it was something to say while they watched and waited. A night breeze swept in. For an instant Hanrahan thought he had something in his eye. He wiped it with his thumb. It was nothing.

It was not the first time a floater had come to a temporary stop off the beach next to the granite breaker. It was a bus stop on the way to nowhere in particular depending on the wind, the tide, and the weather. The lake pushed them against the breaker for an hour or so, then sent them on their way. The lakefront along the beach was a regular patrol stop, mostly to drive out druggies, discourage muggers, and look for the occasional body. This, however, was the first time either detective could remember two bodies turning up here at the same time.

The bodies had been pulled from the surf by the uniformed cops. Both cops had worn boots they kept in the back of their patrol car. These cops weren't kids. They knew boots were essential for surf, alleys, Dumpsters, and whatever else the human and animal world could create that smelled foul and wet and dead.

The two bodies were men. There was somewhat of a resemblance to Michelangelo's painting. The fingers of the two men, one over the other, were almost touching, but the two men looked neither biblical nor noble.

Both were dressed, one in a gray sweatshirt, the other in slacks, white shirt open at the neck, with sports jacket spread like limp wings, no tie. Both were soaked. The dead man in the sweatshirt had thin hair covering his face, pasted down. His eyes were closed. The other man's eyes and mouth were open.

One of the uniformed cops came over to the detectives, careful to avoid the marked-off area. The cop was no more than forty but carrying a beer gut and no expression.

His name was Genfredo. Bill and Abe knew him.

"ID on both," Genfredo said. "Wallets. Littler guy had eighty-seven dollars. Bigger one had seventeen."

"We know the bigger one," said Lieberman. "Who's the smaller one?"

"Name's Pryor, Matthew Alvin Pryor. Shot full of holes. Call came a few hours ago. I think he took the bullets from the Skokie police. Jewelry story robbery. Had a partner. Partner's missing. Got a description. Matthew Alvin went in the water off the rocks in Evanston after a chase. He or his partner killed a jewelry store owner in Northbrook and a cop in Skokie."

"They got around," said Hanrahan.

"They got around," Genfredo said, looking at the bodies. "The other guy hasn't been in the water as long."

"That one we know," said Hanrahan. "Name's Sokol. We saw him on a charge early in the morning. Looks like he didn't even have a chance to change clothes."

"That why they called you two?" asked Genfredo, looking back at his partner, who was going along the water's edge with a flashlight.

"I made a report," said Abe. "Copy to Kearney, copy to Evanston police. Computer did the link. Here we stand."

Alan Kearney was a lieutenant at the Clark Street Station, a handsome, tormented-looking man who had made a mistake a few years earlier that would keep him a lieutenant till he quit or retired or walked away.

"Shall we?" asked Lieberman.

Hanrahan nodded, and the three men walked over to the bodies, both of which had been laid out on their backs.

"When Davidson took the last one," Genfredo said, "he bitched because we pulled it in. I told him the lake was about to take the corpse back out. It was that or maybe lose him. Davidson didn't give a shit."

"He's got hemorrhoids," said Hanrahan.

"Shitting on me won't cure 'em," said Genfredo. "I'm glad it was your call."

"We're ecstatic," said Lieberman dryly, looking down at what remained of Arnold Sokol, which was actually quite a lot considering that the back of his head was crushed, a sharded skull open to reveal darkness and the hint of darkening brain matter. Sokol's shirt was open, and the detectives could clearly see the seven or eight dark deep bruises on his chest and stomach. One of Arnold Sokol's eyes was a dark empty hole. Fish or foul play. Too soon to tell.

Hanrahan looked back down the street at the ambulance with flashing lights but no siren heading their way. It was late. Both men in the Michelangelo pose were definitely dead. No need to give the alarm like an ice-cream truck that would bring out gawkers, beach clutterers, and the living dead.

"Poor schmuck," said Lieberman, looking down at Sokol.

"Amen," said Hanrahan.

There really wasn't more to say unless the young cop combing the beach with a flashlight came up with a weapon or something interesting that might relate to the two dead men. It wasn't likely. It didn't happen. It was up to the medical examiner.

"How do we call it?" asked Hanrahan.

It was a tricky pair of corpses. Neither had probably died in Chicago on or near the beach in East Rogers Park. But they had landed here, and the pair was theirs, though they would check in with the cops in Skokie, Evanston, and Northbrook. The Skokie cops would be interested because Pryor or his partner had killed one of theirs. The Northbrook cops would be interested because Pryor or his partner had killed a citizen. The Evanston cops would be interested because they had put the bullets in Pryor and their township had an incident report that involved Sokol.

The ambulance came to a stop as close to the beach as it could get. Two paramedics jumped out, leaving the lights on and the blue-and-white ball rotating. There was no point in telling them to slow down. The paramedics had already been informed that the men were dead, but there was procedure to follow, and who knew what might happen, so they followed the book and come running.

Both were young. Both had mustaches. Both were big.

"A pair," said the first, moving toward Pryor.

"Not a matched pair," said Lieberman. "They met by chance."

The paramedics used their eyes and stethoscopes and came to the conclusion that both men, one full of bullets, the other covered with what appeared to be knife wounds, were really most sincerely dead.

"We take 'em?" asked one of the medics, rising.

"Be our guest," said Lieberman.

There was no need to tell them to move quickly. They had other stops to make and a long night ahead. Lieberman and Hanrahan watched as the bodies were zipped into black bags and carried away. They checked the indentations in the sand where the bodies had been and saw nothing besides cigarette butts and a Zagnut candy wrapper.

The ambulance left as quietly as it had come.

"Anything?" Genfredo called to his partner, who stood in one place sçanning the shore with his flashlight.

"Nothing you'd want me to show you," the younger cop said. "Unless you're in the mood for a very large, very dead, very black Coho salmon."

The cop with the gut didn't bother to answer.

"Take down the tape," said Lieberman. "Write it up. Bring it in when you come off duty."

"You got it," said Genfredo, waving to his partner.

Hanrahan and Lieberman moved back to the street. Cars were parked illegally all along the turnaround. The neighborhood was an overnight parking nightmare. Apartment buildings four, five, seven stories high. Narrow passageways between. Not enough garages in the alleys to take in a tenth of those who lived in the neighborhood, signs all over the place telling them they couldn't park here, there, wherever. Every few weeks, cops like Genfredo and his partner would spend their shift, providing there were no floaters, muggers, or Vietnamese husbands who went berserk and hacked up their families, giving out parking tickets that helped pay their salaries.

"Station?" asked Hanrahan.

Lieberman shrugged. Not much choice. They had people to call, a suspect to find, a widow to inform, coffee to drink, another report to write while they waited for a medical examiner's report.

"How's Iris, Father Murph?" Lieberman asked.

"Holding up, Rabbi," said Hanrahan. "We're going ahead. Still up for best man?"

"I'll bring a glass for you to step on," said Lieberman.

"Would Thursday suit you?"

"This Thursday?"

"Unitarian church in Evanston. Six o'clock. You and Bess still willing to stand up for us?"

"We'll be there," said Lieberman.

"You're walking funny, Rabbi."

"Hit my hip in Zembinsky's hospital room. I'll be alright."

"Hungry?"

"When am I not?"

"Stop at Park's on Devon?"

"I'm on the way."

They stopped at a Korean shop, which called itself a deli, picked up some sandwiches, and headed for the Clark Street Station.

Nestor was on the desk. He looked up at them over the top of his glasses. He liked the effect on perps and angry victims. Nestor thought he looked a little like the actor M. Emmett Walsh. He was right. Hanrahan tossed him the brown paper bag of egg rolls.

There was no one in the small lobby. Nestor nodded thanks as they walked past and up the stairs to the squad room. That wasn't empty, but it wasn't full either. It was a Tuesday. Tuesdays were slow. No one knew why. A professor at the University of Chicago had written an article on crime patterns in the city, which days were more likely to be busy, which were more likely to be light. He had had a pair of assistants given to him on a grant doing research going back to the days of Johnny Torio.

There had been a lot of bad Tuesdays, but statistically they were definitely, over the course of eighty years or more, significantly lighter than other days. And those bad Tuesdays had been on nights when there was a full moon. Like tonight. The professor had forwarded some theories about why all this might be so. None of them had made sense to Lieberman, and none of them had made any difference. You worked your shift or were called in or stayed over if you were on a roll. No day was a vacation. One of his worst days had been a Tuesday when five uniformed cops on Montrose were gunned down by a gang of Irish kids called the Rocks. The Rocks, short for Shamrocks, were angry because their leader had been pulled in for a murder. Leaderless, they had gone to their number two, a sixteen-year-old kid named Dickey, whose answer to almost everything was "Let's kill the fuckin' bastards."

That had been a Tuesday. They had started at about six, and by midnight they had rounded up the Rocks—all except Dickey, who had seen too many IRA movies and went down in a blaze of nothing that resembled glory.

When they were seated at Lieberman's desk near the window, sandwiches and coffee in front of them, Lieberman said, "Let's see if Zembinsky is still comfortably contemplating his young life of crime in Evanston Hospital."

He was, but they both remembered that there had been a phone in the room. Lieberman made a note to check any calls Zembinsky had made.

Hanrahan went through Sokol's wet wallet, found his driver's license and his address.

"Chicago," said Hanrahan. "Sheridan Road, north of Devon. Washed up a few blocks from home. Nice address. We split up. You want the widow or the kid in the hospital?"

"Neither," said Lieberman. "Who played the lecher in *Mildred Pierce*?"

"Easy," said Hanrahan, "Zachary Scott. Unless you mean Jack Carson."

"How the hell did you know that?"

"You asked me that one before, Rabbi. You're getting old."

"I was born old. You take the widow? I'll take the hospital?"

The kid in the hospital was, at least by birth if not by choice, a Jew. The widow was Catholic. It might make no difference who took which lead, but there might be some slight touch, some contact.

The kid wasn't going to be easy, but it was a hell of a lot better than telling a woman her husband had been murdered unless she had killed him, which was always possible, almost anything was possible.

They ate slowly. Abe a tuna on white. Bill a turkey on rye with mayo and onions. Coffee. It was almost midnight.

"What about the other one?" Hanrahan asked.

"Cop killer? Let's find out who Pryor is. Maybe that leads us to the man that got away."

"It's a start. Abe?"

"I know."

"We should talk to the other widow. The one in Northbrook, the jewelry store. I'll check with the Northbrook cops, see if she can give us a description of Pryor's buddy."

"It's nights like this that make being a cop worthwhile," said Lieberman dryly.

Hanrahan looked at his partner. There was no telling if Abe was tired. He always looked the same—weary, baggy-eyed.

"How's the bar mitzvah coming?" asked Hanrahan.

"I may have to sell my boat," said Lieberman.

"You haven't got a boat."

"Then I'll sell my shares in Microsoft."

"You've got shares in Microsoft?"

"No, you?"

"No shares in anything."

Lieberman sat silently, cheeks full of sandwich. He needed a Tylenol for his hip pain.

"We're gonna keep the wedding . . ."

"Cheap?"

"Inexpensive."

"Maybe I can get Barry married instead of bar mitzvahed," said Lieberman.

"It'd be cheaper," said Hanrahan. "If you let the Unitarians handle it."

"Know any nice Jewish girls between eleven and twenty?"

"No," said Hanrahan. "Wait. Yes, your granddaughter."

"You are not being helpful, Father Murph."

Hanrahan finished the last of his sandwich.

"Sorry, Rabbi. Will you settle for a Chinese girl? Iris has a niece."

"How old?"

"Thirty-six."

"Sounds perfect," said Lieberman. "Let's discuss this further."

"Shouldn't we check with Barry?"

"I'm the patriarch," said Lieberman. "I make the decisions."

"And?"

"I'm going to empty my savings account and have a hell of a bar mitzvah, to which you are not only invited but expected to bring a substantial present I can pawn or sell to Fat Dewey to help defray the expenses."

"I'm not a wealthy man, Rabbi."

"Sell your house," said Lieberman, wiping his hands on a paper napkin. "It's for a worthy cause."

"I'm heading for the widow."

"I'm heading for the hospital. Maish's at ten in the morning?" asked Lieberman.

"Something comes up we call."

Maybe they would find time for a few hours' sleep. Maybe.

Lieberman reached down to power on his cell phone. Hanrahan did the same.

Wychovski found the car he wanted on a street called Winthrop. It was a slightly battered Honda, a 1992, maybe older. He'd pick up another one after he visited Walter. He'd pick up another one or, if he could get enough money, he would buy one, and head for St. Louis.

He wished Pryor were still alive, so he could kill him. He drove south, trying to remember where Walter's place was. Fullerton. He remembered Fullerton. When he got there, near there, he would recognize something, remember. He did not want to call Walter again. He wanted to surprise Walter. He would try to make a deal. He had pockets full of watches and little gold animals. Wychovski fingered them with his right hand while he drove with his left. Was that a horse? A zebra? A cop was dead. A jeweler was dead. A pregnant woman stood screaming in his memory.

What was the baby's name going to be? He couldn't remember. Yeah, Jessica. She would change it now. He was sure. She would name it for her dead husband. Wychovski would find a way to send a gift for the baby, he told himself. A gift from a sympathetic person who had read about the woman's tragedy. He knew he was lying to himself. He would send no gift, but he listened to his lie, and he got lost. He ran out of Sheridan Road, turned right, went by a cemetery. He tried not to look at the cemetery but he did. Graceland Cemetery. Wasn't Elvis buried in Graceland?

Wychovski remembered his grandmother in the nursing home. He had visited her just before he went back to prison the last time. She was his only living relative, and he paid her bills, at least what the government didn't cover.

His grandmother, Sophie, had been small, frail, confused, and depressed. They had tried to find something to interest her.

"You like bingo?" the young woman in large round glasses had asked patiently, kneeling next to his grandmother.

"No," she had said.

"She loves bingo," Wychovski had answered.

"Church?" the woman said. "You're a Catholic."

"I'm not."

Wychovski drove to a street he vaguely remembered, Ashland. He turned left, kept going south.

The young woman in the nursing home had come up with a list of things that might interest his grandmother. Cooking, reading, television. All "no."

"She likes game shows," Wychovski had said.

His grandmother had answered briefly in Polish. Wychovski didn't understand Polish. He understood cash, possessions, that there was only one life and nothing more and that you lived to make yourself comfortable, to satisfy your needs and wants. There was nothing more. But there was his grandmother.

"Music?" the young woman had tried.

"She likes polkas," he had said.

"No," his grandmother had answered, looking off into a corner where there was nothing to look at but a corner.

"Wait," she said, suddenly animated. "Elvis. I love Elvis."

His grandmother had decried all popular music. She had been a Lawrence Welk junkie, a Perry Como fan, and she liked Patti Page and Ginny Simms and Dinah Shore. Elvis had been an abomination to his grandmother. He had represented all that was wrong with young people. She spat three times when his name was mentioned. Chubby Checker, Fats Domino, Bill Haley, Buddy Holly were worth one spit each. The others she couldn't identify weren't worth the hint of a spit.

"I love Elvis," his grandmother declared, looking at him with a smile.

It was then he was certain of what he had only considered. His grandmother was truly out of her mind. It wasn't Alzheimer's. The doctors had assured him. It was simply dementia. She was nearing ninety years old. It happens.

"Graceland," his grandmother had said, taking the young woman's hand.

Where had his grandmother even heard of Graceland?

"I'd like to go there," she said.

"When you're better I'll take you," Wychovski had said.

Sophie had answered in Polish. The young social worker smiled. Her name was Flaherty or Flannery or something Irish. She didn't know Polish from chop suey, which his grandmother had also loved but now hated.

His grandmother had died while Wychovski was in prison. He didn't know if the nursing home had placated her with Elvis records. He had never visited her after the Elvis incident. The sight of ancient people lolling in wheelchairs in the hall outside their rooms, the one woman who kept calling "I have to be at work at nine," the old man who looked up at him, his mouth open, following Wychovski with his eyes down the long corridor, the smell of spiceless old-people food. He never went back. Not that he could have. He was arrested three weeks after that last visit with Sophie.

Past Addison, past Belmont, where he spotted a Polish restaurant. The ghost of his grandmother inside listening to polkas and Elvis and making pierogi and cabbage rolls.

Past Diversey. Dark stores, closed for the night. Past midnight. Past caring. They, the people who ran the stores, paint stores, key shops, storefront accountants, would be up in hours doing the same thing they did every day. There's safety in doing the same thing every day. No creativity. Wychovski didn't tell anyone, but he thought of himself as a master craftsman, maybe even an artist, no two days quite the same, every job a leap into a pounding blood-pressure river. Like going onstage, he was sure. Or like stepping in front of an audience to sing, or like sitting down to write a story and not knowing what would come next.

He needed a toilet.

He stopped at a twenty-four-hour Walgreen's just past Diversey near some outcropping of concrete buildings labeled Lathrope Homes. After midnight, but there were customers, mostly black. He bought a large bottle of Tylenol Plus and a generic antacid and asked for the washroom. The pharmacist on duty, old man, heavy with not much of a neck reminded him of James Earl Jones, even his voice and the way he looked at Wychovski over his glasses.

"Emergency," Wychovski said.

The pharmacist nodded, handed him a key, and pointed the way. The toilet was clean. Wychovski examined some of the animals in his pockets. He could get them melted down, but they wouldn't be worth as much as if they remained jewelry. He sat in a daze examining a cat, a pelican, a seal, a giraffe. They felt like treasure. He was a walking Noah, and the rain was falling hard.

Pryor dead. Window shattered. Cop dead.

He shoved the animals back into the den of his pocket, washed himself, and went back into the night.

If it were done, he told himself getting back into the car after downing three Tylenol and a swallow of antacid. When it is done, then better it were done quickly.

He remembered that. Wychovski was no fool. He had read in prison. Jack London, Shakespeare, anything. When he hit Fullerton it was after one in the morning. He wasn't sure whether he should turn right or left. He turned left and started to look for something that would jolt his memory.

Dark, dark, dark, but lots of traffic. Where were people going to or coming from at this hour?

Find him. Get it over with.

There was something. There on the right. A hot dog stand. Rickety, on the corner, big painting of a hot dog with mustard and onions. Wychovski had learned to like his hot dog sandwiches with mayo or ketchup. Learned it from the blacks. The place was closed, but it resonated. He was close.

Buildings that looked like dark factories. Old brick. Dirty, tired buildings. Bump over train tracks. Yes, nearby. On the left, on the corner, a bar on the first floor of a three-story building. Budweiser sign in the window. Red, glowing. Place was open. He had stopped there for a beer once, a year ago. Anniversary celebrated today in double death and overtime.

Walter was two or three doors down from the tavern. Wychovski parked, moved his gun. He hadn't noticed. It had pinched against his hip. He got out and looked across the street. Three buildings in a row. Apartments upstairs. Storefronts downstairs.

There it was. Dark. Olshan's Antiques and Used Furniture.

Wychovski waited till there was no traffic and crossed. Someone laughed in the bar on the corner. He could hear music behind the laughter. He wondered how the people who lived with the noise liked it and if they ever complained. Probably not.

He looked in the window. An old dining room set in the window with a recliner on top of the table. The recliner looked tired and heavy. There was a dim night-light at the rear of the shop. He could see furniture piled, a mess of furniture, paintings, shapes jagged and shapes round. He knocked at the door. The glass rattled. Behind the glass was a mesh of metal. It rattled, too. Nothing. He knocked again. Louder. More rattling.

"Shake, rattle, and roll," he muttered. "You never do nothing to save a doggone soul." He shifted from one leg to the other and knocked even louder, looking over his shoulder at the street, knowing that if he saw a cop car coming he would move quickly to the bar. No answer, no cop car. He moved to the bar on the corner anyway.

He pushed open the door, expecting who knew what. What he saw was a small tavern, night dark, bartender, thin, almost bald, five customers, three at the bar arguing about something on the television set, two at a table. The two at the table, a man and a woman, were old and nursing beers. They weren't even talking. They were serious drinkers. The woman was overweight. The man was fat.

Wychovski moved to the bar. One of the old men turned to look at him.

"You settle it," the man said. His face was red, and he needed a shave. His eyes were nearly closed. "The greatest Cub of all, all time, ever."

"Banks," said one of the other old men.

"Nicholson," said another.

"And I," said the man with the nearly closed eyes, "I say Sosa hands down. Funny-looking spic's going in the record books."

Wychovski shrugged and ordered a beer. The bartender nodded and brought it.

"Well?" asked the old man.

"I'm from Texas," said Wychovski.

"Rangers," sighed the old man, turning away.

Wychovski laid a couple of bucks on the bar and asked the bartender, "Walter, the furniture store. I've got to see him."

The bartender looked at Wychovski, who didn't look like a cop but wasn't a regular either. He didn't look like he was into drugs either, but there was something about him the bartender recognized and didn't want to catch.

"Closed for the night, I guess," said the bartender, with a cough, reaching for a burning cigarette in the glass ashtray.

"It's important," said Wychovski.

"I've got nothing to do with his business," said the bartender.

"Where does he live?"

"Over the store," the bartender said.

"Does . . ." Wychovski said.

"End of questions. End of answers. I'm closing up for the night. Finish your beer. Thanks for the business."

Wychovski knew when to stop. The bartender made the rounds of his remaining patrons and told them he was closing in ten minutes. He never looked back at Wychovski, who left his drink half-finished and went back into the night. There was a door next to Walter's shop, farther east than Wychovski had gone. No name. No lights. A bell button almost invisible in the dim streetlight. Wychovski pushed. Nothing. He leaned on the bell, put his life in his thumb. He would stand there pressing all night till someone answered or the bell or all his fingers gave out.

He didn't have to wait long, not if five minutes is long. A light came on beyond the wooden door. He could see it under the door, dim but there. Then steps coming down. Slow steps, someone walking down sure and heavy. Lots of steps. Then a voice.

"Who is it?"

It wasn't Walter behind the door. It sounded like a black man.

"My name's Wychovski. I've got to see Walter."

"Come back tomorrow."

"I can't . . ."

There was the sound of voices inside. Wychovski strained to hear. He thought the second voice might be Walter's.

"Don't come back tomorrow," the man with the black voice said. "Don't come back at all."

"I'm staying till you open," Wychovski said. "I've got a good deal in my pockets and nothing to lose. If the cops find me huddled here, they'll find a stolen car across the street, too, and I'll have to explain why I have what I have in my pockets and why I'm here with it."

More talking inside.

"Five minutes," came the black voice. "Then you get the hell out of here, deal or no deal. You go headfirst or feetfirst. Choice'll be yours."

"Deal," said Wychovski.

Bolts turned, and the door opened.

6

Melvin Zembinsky was in his hospital room getting dressed when Lieberman entered. Melvin had his left leg in his jeans and was trying to keep his balance while putting in his right leg. He took a little hop, made the move, got the pants on, and was pulling them up when he saw Lieberman standing at the door.

Melvin's bed was the one closest to the door. A white curtain was partially drawn between his bed and the one next to it. A television mounted on a black metal plate on the wall across from bed two was playing. It was an old game show. There was no sound. Lieberman looked up at the host of the show, Bill Cullen, who had been dead at least a decade. Shot of the audience laughing. Lieberman was not a laugher. He wasn't laughing now. He stood watching the young man.

Zembinsky's facial bruises were a darker prehealing red. A bandage was wrapped around his head, covering the stitches. He ignored the detective and reached for a shirt on the bed.

Zembinsky wasn't tall, but he was well built, flat stomach, body of an athlete. He carefully pulled the black sweatshirt over his head, keeping himself from biting his lip to keep back the pain as he eased the shirt over his bandaged head.

Lieberman folded his arms and said nothing. Zembinsky sat on the bed and began putting his shoes on. Abe had no doubt about who would speak first.

When his socks and shoes were on, the young man looked up, and said, "What?"

"You made three phone calls. Two last night. One this morning."

Zembinsky shook his head.

"One call to the home of James Franzen a little after we left you," Lieberman went on. "A second a few hours later to Franzen again and then this morning to an Edward Denenberg."

"Dean, Ed Dean," Zembinsky corrected.

"Like James Dean?" asked Lieberman.

Zembinsky laughed and shook his head again.

"James Dean? You're even fuckin' older than you look. Why didn't you ask Dean Martin? Or Dizzy Dean?"

"You know your old people history," said Lieberman.

"My grandfather's a comedian. Was a comedian. He's dead. I've got a tape of his he made at some fucking Jew resort. My grandfather wasn't funny. He spent a year dying and telling me about all the famous people he knew. Bullshit, but what the hell. Kept talking about some guy named Harry Ritz. Now you've got my life story, and I've got my pants on."

"Your father and mother, Melvin," Lieberman said.

Zembinsky looked up.

"You want my life story, you pay for it. Charge is cut-rate, rock bottom, going-out-of-business sale. You don't call me Melvin. You call me Zembinsky or Z, you get answers."

"Parents, Z," said Lieberman.

"My father was in something called SDS in college."

"Students for a Democratic Society," Lieberman said.

A shrug from Zembinsky, who stood, testing his balance.

"Except," said Zembinsky, "they weren't democratic. Most of them weren't students. And they didn't know what society was."

"And you do?" asked Lieberman.

"You a social worker or a cop? What do you want?"

"Peace of mind, but for now I'll settle for what you talked to Eddie Dean about."

"World peace," said Zembinsky. "Albanians in Macedonia. The

International Space Station. My bowel movements. Jackson Pollock's later works. None of your fuckin' business."

"It's always enlightening talking to an educated man," said Lieberman.

"Yeah, it's amazing what little pieces of useless shit you can pick up in two years in a community college. So? Sokol changed his mind? He's bringing charges?"

"Hold it down," a raspy voice called from behind the curtain. "I'm watching something here."

"Crazy fart," said Zembinsky, nodding over his shoulder. "So, am I arrested? You going to read me my rights?"

"What did you talk to Eddie about?"

"I answered that," Zembinsky said, taking a step toward Lieberman, whose back was to the door. "Now I'm checking myself out of here. It smells like iodine and old men dying."

"Eddie," Lieberman repeated.

Zembinsky shook his head and looked up at the yellow-white wall with his hands on his hips. Marlon Brando had done it better in *The Wild One*.

"You think I'm going to tell you the truth about what I talked to Eddie about?"

"I'll guess," Lieberman said, as Zembinsky took another step toward him. The young man had forty years and forty pounds on the detective. Lieberman didn't move. "You talked about getting Sokol."

Zembinsky did his best to look bored. It was caricature Marlon Brando.

"Getting Sokol," Zembinsky repeated. "Getting him what?"

"Getting him dead. Someone killed him last night, maybe a few hours after you said you or one of your friends would get him. You told James Franzen and Eddie how to find Sokol."

Zembinsky's face was inches from Lieberman's now. Zembinsky smelled surprisingly clean, and his breath smelled like mint mouthwash.

"Cop or no cop," he whispered, "there's just you and me here, and I'm going through the door. You move over, or I put you down. Your word against mine. Maybe I'll just bite your fucking nose off."

They were too close together for the young man to see the punch coming. Lieberman's right hand shot out straight, short, and hard to Zembinsky's chest. Zembinsky staggered back, mouth open, gasping for breath, holding his chest. He was about to fall to the floor when he backed against the bed and sat.

"Will you guys shut up for God's sake," the man in bed two called out. "Merv's giving money away."

"It's Bill Cullen," Lieberman called, still standing in the same spot in front of the door. "Not Merv Griffin."

"Who the hell cares?" called the curtained man.

Who the hell cares, Lieberman thought, waiting for Zembinsky to catch his breath. The young man was bruised, bandaged, and in pain from a new attack. There was no fight left in him. There might still be swagger. Zembinsky tried to talk. Nothing came out. He put his hands on the bed to steady himself, his eyes on the old cop who had done this to him.

Lieberman's hip flared up from the punch he had thrown. He was not in a good mood.

"What did you talk about?" Lieberman asked.

"You mean did I tell them to kill Sokol?" Zembinsky managed to get out.

"That's what I mean."

"And you expect me to just tell you if I did?"

"No, I expect you to lie. Tell me a lie. Then I go to Eddie and Franzen and ask them what they talked to you about and see if you were smart enough to set up a lie you all agree on. I get the phone cut off in this room and I put a cop on the door so you can't call them."

"Cops die, too," Zembinsky said, teeth gritted.

No longer Marlon Brando. Now he was Dan Duryea, straw and threat, no substance. A twig.

"Everybody dies, Z," said Lieberman. "Some people just do it later or better than others. So, you want to tell me a story?"

"No, I want a lawyer."

"I'm not arresting you. I'm just asking questions."

"I don't like the questions," said Zembinsky, breathing a little better, no longer holding his hands to his chest. "I want to call my father. He's a lawyer."

"Suit yourself," said Lieberman. "Give me your father's number. I'll place the call. You talk, then the phone comes out."

"We didn't kill him," Zembinsky said, as Lieberman moved to the phone on the night table.

There was something in the way he said it that made Lieberman pause.

"We talked, me and Eddie, about how it had all turned to shit. We puffed. You know what I mean?"

"Bragged."

"Yeah, bragged, strutted, talked like assholes about how we were walking away from this one, what we'd do next, go to San Diego or something. We didn't talk about Sokol. That's the truth. Well, I did tell him Sokol and you and the other cop had come to see me. I didn't tell it the way it happened. We didn't talk about getting back at Sokol. That was just talk for you. I'm full of shit. Okay. You happy?"

"Eddie?" Lieberman asked.

Zembinsky was trying to find another actor to imitate, but he wasn't up to it. One punch and he had caved.

"I told him I was going to be okay and to keep his mouth shut if the cops came to see him. Nothing else. Dean's not a talker."

"He say anything?"

"He said he'd take care of things."

Zembinsky looked up at the television screen. A commercial for a Jean-Claude Van Damme movie was on. Lieberman waited for the young man to try to do a Belgian accent. Zembinsky didn't say anything.

People were laughing on the television set, laughing at a joke told twenty years ago by a dead man.

Lieberman picked up the phone.

"What's your father's number?"

The way to do it was to do it calmly, gently, quickly, and that is what Hanrahan did.

It was almost two in the morning when he rang the bell to the Sokol apartment. The building was in a ten-year-old fifteen-story high-rise on Sheridan Road across from the Loyola University campus. The number on the bell next to the name was 2C, probably not high enough to get a view of Lake Michigan over the university's trees and classroom buildings.

"Yes?" came a woman's voice on the intercom.

"Mrs. Sokol?"

"Yes?"

"Police. I'm Detective Hanrahan. Can I talk to you?"

"Arnold," she said flatly.

"Yes, it's about your husband."

"Is he with you?"

"No, Mrs. Sokol. Can I come up?"

"Is he in the hospital?"

"No, if I could . . ."

A buzzer rang, and Hanrahan moved to the door to open it. It was still buzzing as he stepped inside and found the elevator in front of him. It was only one flight up, but Hanrahan's knees were bone on bone and bore the scars of three operations to keep him functioning. Football had once been his life. It was long gone, but he didn't regret the loss, not anymore.

He stood in front of the door to 2C knowing the woman was looking at him through the peephole. He stepped back, hands folded in front of him. He was wearing his sports jacket and a tie, which he had knotted on the elevator. He needed a shave, but not badly.

He was a formidable presence, broad-shouldered, holding his own in a battle of the bulge.

"Mrs. Sokol," he said softly, taking out his wallet and badge and holding it up where she might be able to see it.

Locks turned, and the door opened.

She stood there, plump, pale, maybe thirty-five, maybe older. She wore a green robe. Her hair was dark and short and as unkempt as it had been when he had seen her at the hospital when she had embraced her husband. Her eyes told Hanrahan that she knew.

He waited to be invited in but she simply stood in the doorway, one hand holding the top of her robe closed over her small breasts.

"Mrs. Sokol, I'm sorry to tell you this, but your husband is dead."

"Dead," she repeated.

"Yes, I'm sorry to tell you this. May I come in?"

"Dead," she repeated without moving.

Bill Hanrahan stepped forward, a single unthreatening step.

"May I come in?"

She looked down the carpeted hallway outside her apartment door to see if anyone else was there. Then she turned and walked back into the apartment, leaving the door open.

He followed her and found himself in a small, neat and comfortable, but not colorful, living room. There was a single light on, a table lamp next to a wooden entertainment center with a television set and CD player against one wall. In front of the windows sat a chair and desk with a computer surrounded by neat file boxes. It was still dark. He couldn't tell whether she could see the lake when dawn came. He hoped she could.

Her back was to him, and he could see that she was crossing herself. His hand started to come up, and he found himself doing the same as she turned, revealing the cross on the wall she had been facing.

"You're Catholic," she said.

"Yes."

"Was there a priest?"

Hanrahan hadn't thought about it. To him Sokol was a confused Jew, but now he remembered that he had converted to please his wife.

"No," he said.

"We need a priest," she said. "Where is he? Where is Arnold?"

"I . . . the morgue."

"Don't let them touch the body. Not till the priest gets there."

She dashed barefoot to a white portable phone on a table next to the pale blue sofa. She picked it up and handed it to Hanrahan.

"Please," she said.

Hanrahan pulled out his wallet-sized address and phone book, found the number, and called the morgue. He didn't know the attendant who answered, but he identified himself and checked to be sure Sokol's body had arrived and hadn't been touched.

"Won't get to him for hours, maybe not till tonight. Backed up. Full moon. They say it's superstition, but I'm here to tell you it's not. People go nuts with a full moon. People fall in love with their guns and knives and bottles they can break when the moon is round and white."

"I guess," said Hanrahan. "There's a priest on duty at Cook County Hospital."

"Always is," said the attendant.

"Victim named Sokol needs last rites," said Hanrahan. "Priest knows what to do."

"I'll page him," said the attendant.

"Thanks," said Hanrahan.

"Least I can do for the poor son of a bitch. Full moon. Believe in it."

"I do," said Hanrahan, and hung up. He turned to Mary Sokol, who was sitting in a blue armchair that matched the sofa. She was hugging herself, knees together.

"It's being done," he said.

"Oh my God," she said suddenly, jumping up, eyes wide. "He didn't commit suicide, did he?"

"No," said Hanrahan.

"What?" she asked, looking into his eyes for an answer.

"He was murdered, Mrs. Sokol."

"Arnold," she said. "Arnold."

She started to move back to the sofa, paused, and turned. "You want some coffee?"

He didn't, but he said that he did to keep her busy. She moved to the kitchen, and he followed her, waiting for the next question, the question that always came.

"I'll have to give you instant," she said, moving to a cupboard in the small kitchen. "Arnold grinds beans in the morning, makes it fresh. He's not really a coffee drinker. It's for me. We get it in the mail. Gevalia. You know them?"

"No, ma'am," he said.

"I can't grind. My children are sleeping. It might wake them, especially the baby, Luke. Matthew, he's six. He'd sleep through it, but . . ."

"I understand."

He sat at the round glass-topped table and waited while she microwaved water. There were file boxes on the table like the ones around the computer in the other room, but there was more than enough space to put down a few cups.

"I'm sorry about the mess," she said, looking at the file boxes. "I work at home. I do Internet research for authors, most professors at Loyola, a few at Northwestern, Roosevelt, even the University of Chicago."

She stood looking around the room as if she had never seen it before.

"You can find anything, almost anything on the Internet if you know how to . . . I'm sorry."

"No problem."

"Coffee? All I have is instant decaffeinated," she said.

"Decaffeinated is fine."

He waited. Sometimes they were numb. Sometimes they took a while, but it always came. It had to come. When she finally set the cup of coffee in front of him, she said, "He did it, didn't he?"

"He?" asked Hanrahan, putting the cup to his lips. It was bitter and not very hot.

"The man he owed the forty thousand dollars," she said.

"Forty thousand dollars?"

"Maybe more. I'm not sure. Business was bad. Arnold should have let it go, but it's been in the family for three generations. He . . . I'm sorry. I keep saying I'm sorry. I don't know what else to say."

"Who was this man your husband owed the money to?"

"He never told me. I don't know if . . . Wait."

She went through one of the doors, which led to the two

bedrooms, and returned in a few seconds with a thin, black leather briefcase. She handed it to Hanrahan.

"I never opened Arnold's briefcase. He carried it with him everywhere. Maybe the man's name is in there, in his notebook or appointment book."

"May I take this?" asked Hanrahan.

She shook her head in what Hanrahan took for a "yes."

"It's my fault," she said. "I pushed him about so many things. I did . . ."

Hanrahan finished his coffee quickly.

"Could I have some more coffee, Mrs. Sokol."

"More . . . oh, coffee? Yes."

She took his empty cup and moved into the kitchen.

"Arnold is dead," she told the sink and herself. "Arnold is dead."

Wychovski had to squeeze past the huge man at the bottom of the stairwell. The man was big, black, and in a bad mood. His breath smelled of chicken and something sweet. It would have been easier if the big man had gone first, but that wasn't the way it was done, couldn't be, wouldn't make sense.

The black man wore black. Black cotton shirt with a button-down collar, black jeans, black shoes, black mood. He patted down Wychovski professionally, even went between his legs, stuffing a thick finger into his shoes. Finding the Glock in his sweatshirt was no problem. Wychovski had carefully pulled it out and handed it to him. The black man had pocketed it and gone on searching. He took out a handful of gold animals from Wychovski's pocket and dropped them back in. He nodded when he was satisfied, and they started up.

The stairs, wood, uncarpeted, creaked as Wychovski moved upward, feeling the weight of the big man behind him. At the top was a closed door. The stairway was dimly lit. The stairs were narrow. Two doors, narrow stairway. Even a fast raid would give Walter time to hide any immediate problems. Depending on his relationship to the man behind Wychovski, Walter could simply have the black man fill the doorway, calmly demanding to see a warrant, then slowly reading it. Fences, the smart ones, were prepared for such contingencies. Walter was a smart one. Maybe too damn smart for what Wychovski needed.

When he reached the top of the stairs the black man reached past him to open the door, and Wychovski stepped inside.

The room was huge. High ceilings. It looked like something out of one of the old *Architectural Digests* Wychovski had sometimes looked at in prison. Rooms with plush, tasteful furniture and views of forests in valleys below or the Golden Gate Bridge at night. This room had no view from the windows on either side. A brick wall left. A brick wall right. Dining room left, with a table big enough for a dozen people. Table looked like it had been built for King Arthur with high-backed dark hand-carved chairs with arms. The table was bare. Sideboards flanked it. A badly faded tapestry on one wall, a knight on a horse, sword pulled back, about to slash a two-headed dragon. The tapestry on the other wall was less faded and not violent, Madonna and child surrounded by women with smiles and men with beards.

The other half of the room was a square of not matched but compatible antique furniture. Deep chairs with wooden arms. Two sofas. A big table in the middle with a bowl of flowers. The flowers were colorful, real. Against one wall was a gigantic television set in a massive carved cabinet whose doors were open but which could be closed to hide the screen that threw off the tone. This section of the room had paintings on the walls, four big ones, one of dogs on the hunt, one of a girl on a hill in a frilly dress with one hand on her hat to keep the wind from blowing it away, one of a forest with a river running through it, and one of a man with long hair and a knowing and evil smile.

"That's Count Ferdinand Devereaux," said Walter, who sat in a chair across from Wychovski, who was looking at the smiling man in the painting. Walter wore jeans that looked as if they had just come off the rack. They fit him perfectly. So did the pale blue T-shirt with the little pocket. "A real son of a bitch. A real Bugs Moran. Didn't like the way you looked at him, he ran you through or planned an elaborate torture and invited people to watch. Credited with doing in more than four hundred people, mostly innocent, but who knows. Violent man."

Walter was a lean man who kept himself in good condition. He must have been sixty, maybe more, but he didn't look it. Stuffed his face in ice water every morning. Worked out after a protein shake. Showered three times a day. He kept his head shaved and wore a full but not excessive mustache. His hero was G. Gordon Liddy.

Everyone except street trash knew about Walter. Walter told them. Walter also told them straight out with no negotiating what he would take and what he wouldn't and how much he would pay. Walter was an honest fence. Walter was a tough fence.

"I plan to be in bed in ten minutes," Walter said, looking at his watch. "Ten, no more. And I'm not in a good mood. Today's not been one of my better days."

"Yesterday," said the black man standing behind Wychovski. "It's already tomorrow."

"Right," said Walter, nodding. "Technically, it's tomorrow. No, technically it's today. I was just talking about the period of time from the moment I got up in the morning with a stiff neck."

"I'm sorry to hear it," said Wychovski, thinking that no one could have had a worse day than he was having.

"Told you not to come here," Walter said calmly, reaching for a large mug of what was probably tea. It smelled strong, but not like coffee. Wychovski could suddenly smell everything in the big room, flowers, tea, the man behind him, the old wood, the cool air.

"What I've got you can melt down," Wychovski said. "I'm gone. I never heard of you. You know my word is good."

"I know your word is supposed to be good," said Walter. "But you've had a stupid busy day. Killed a cop. Killed a jeweler. Pryor's dead. No loss. You are not a good risk, and I don't need to take chances."

Wychovski plunged his hands into his pockets, pulling out little gold animals, a zoo full. He dropped them on the table in front of Walter and went back in for more. When he had fished the last scorpion from his pocket and wiped a speck of lint away, he stood back. It hadn't been much work, but he was having difficulty breathing.

Walter looked at the glittering pile, then past Wychovski to the black man. Wychovski didn't look back to see the man's reaction.

"The table you just dumped this menagerie on is fourteenth-century Dutch. If you've put one small scratch on it, you pay."

"I pay," Wychovski agreed. He would have agreed to anything. He wanted out. In the street, in the car he had felt desperate. He would do anything. He would walk out of here with cash no matter what he had to do. But right now he would settle for just walking out of here.

Walter reached over and picked up something that looked like an anteater. He fingered it, turned it over. Put it back. Picked up a lion, turned it over in his very clean hands and held it gently in his palm.

"They're good, very good," he said. "The man was an artist, George."

Wychovski wasn't happy about hearing his first name used by the fence. It implied something. He didn't know whether it was something good, bad, or indifferent.

"They're too good," Walter said. "Too good to melt down, but too good to sell anywhere but where they don't care and won't be spotted. You know where that is, George?"

George didn't know. George didn't care. George wanted out the door and down the stairs, walking, not being thrown. George Wychovski wanted money in his wallet, two or three cups of coffee, a different car, and the road to St. Louis.

"Singapore maybe," said Walter. "Hong Kong. Maybe some sheik in Saudi Arabia. The stuff is good, George. I'll not kid you on that. But the risk. The risk. Accessory to murder. A cop. I'll have to sit on this stuff for years. And the cops are going to come see me. Now, normally the cops, especially three friends in the district, are polite and willing to accept gifts, but a dead cop . . ."

He looked at Wychovski and drank some more tea, waiting for a response.

"You'll take them?"

Walter shrugged and put his hands behind his head, supposedly to show he was relaxed, actually to show his muscles. He looked at the rampage of tiny animals and said, "Three thousand."

Wychovski said nothing. If Walter was offering three thousand knowing how hot they were, knowing that a dead cop was involved, they were worth more, much more.

"They're worth a hundred thousand," Wychovski said, more than half expecting the big man to put an arm around his neck from behind and simply strangle him. Wychovski was in good shape, but he'd be no match for the black man.

"You're right," said Walter. "But I'm offering you three thousand. Listen, George. I could simply have Mr. Dickerson remove your head and dispose of your body and not give you a nickel. Then I wouldn't have to worry about what you might tell the police if they catch you, providing they let you live long enough to tell them anything. I'd just have to ask Mr. Dickerson to clean up the mess and dispose of the remains. You know what's keeping you alive?"

"Your generous heart," said Wychovski, trying to bluff it out, hoping he wasn't sweating, unable to check.

Walter shook his head no.

"My reputation is keeping you alive," he said. "You die, and somehow word gets out, who knows how, that I might have been involved, I lose suppliers. Most suppliers, even the ones with very, very bad habits, don't want to risk their lives. So, three thousand, no, three thousand two hundred dollars and you walk out of here and start running. I was thinking of dropping the offer to two thousand and one, make it a space odyssey for you, but I'll tell you the truth George, this isn't a bad deal for me."

"I'll take it," Wychovski said.

Walter got up, went around the chair, and moved to a door. He went through the door, closing it behind him. Wychovski turned to look at the black man, Dickerson. There was no expression on the man's face when his eyes met Wychovski's.

Walter was back in a few seconds. He left the door open behind him. The light was on in what looked like a bedroom. A safe was open. Walter wasn't worried. Walter was carrying a tote bag, green with the word BELIZE in white block letters.

"Fifties, twenties, a few hundreds," Walter said, handing the bag to Wychovski. "Mr. Dickerson will show you out. We'll remove the ammunition from your gun and he'll give it back to you on the stairs. If this is the gun you used on the cop . . ."

"It isn't," said Wychovski.

"Fine. Good-bye. We don't do business again. I don't care if you walk in with the Crown Jewels, especially if you walk in with the Crown Jewels. Anything else you can think of?"

Wychovski said nothing.

"Anything you can think of, Mr. Dickerson?"

Mr. Dickerson responded by shooting Walter the fence in the face and neck. Two shots, not much noise. Walter fell face-first in the mound of golden animals.

7

"I don't know. I'd say *shpilkes*," said Morris Hurvitz, holding his toasted everything bagel above his cup of coffee and trying to decide if dunking it was a good idea. Morris was short, bespectacled, and about to celebrate his eightieth birthday. He was also a psychologist with a loyal cadre of patients who would probably visit him in the cemetery and stand over his grave with a handful of flowers asking his advice.

Morris Hurvitz, Ph.D., was not the oldest, nor the most outspoken or even the unofficial leader of the group of old men who met daily at the T&L Deli on Devon Avenue. The Alter Cockers had their own table near the window and their morning numbers varied from three or four to as many as eight or even ten.

With the exception of Howie Chen, who had owned a Chinese restaurant a block away till he retired five years ago, the Alter Cockers were all Jewish. A few spoke Hebrew. A few others spoke anything from forty words to relatively fluent Yiddish. Howie's Yiddish, after half a century of dealing with Jewish customers in the obligatory neighborhood Chinese restaurant, was more than forty words and far less than fluent but better than most at the table, including that of Morris Hurvitz. Howie had been shifting in his chair next to Morris Hurvitz, which had brought on the Hurvitz diagnosis of *shpilkes*, a less than clinical appraisal which meant that for unknown reasons the person with the affliction could not sit still.

"My grandson had a big day yesterday," explained Howie, whose fully round face showed concern.

"Congratulations," said Herschel Rosen, the table's acknowledged would-be comic, "he's finally moved his bowels. May we all join him."

"If I had my Mylanta, I'd toast to that," said Al Bloombach, who served as Herschel's second banana. Al was still called Red by his older friends though the hair that brought him the nickname was all but gone and certainly no longer red.

"Graduated, MIT," said Howie, watching Morris Hurvitz make the big decision and dunk his bagel in the cup of coffee.

"I couldn't be there," said Howie. "Doctor says I shouldn't miss a day of treatment."

Howie was being given radiation therapy for prostate cancer, a condition shared by approximately one-third of the Alter Cockers, all but one of whom admitted it. There was no question about Howie's recovery. That had been assured, but treatment had been an issue. Howie, at seventy-six, was a perfect candidate for surgery. He had opted instead for radiation after having been told privately by Lou Roth that the surgery had left him impotent. Now, having missed his grandson's graduation, he was having second thoughts.

Morris Hurvitz bit into his coffee-soaked bagel and made a face.

"Hurvitz," Herschel Rosen said, pointing a ringer at him across the table, "how many times a week are you going to do that? How many years? You dunk your bagel, make a face. You know you're not going to like it."

"It always seems like a good idea and who knows, some day, my taste will change. You gotta take a chance sometimes."

"Why?" asked Herschel. "I took enough chances in my life. Now I order the same thing every day . . ."

"Lox omelette, toasted egg bagel with a shmeer of cream cheese, and a cup of black," said Hurvitz. "Where's your sense of wonder?"

"I'm filled with wonder," said Herschel, a forkful of omelette in his hand. "I wonder about the *fercockta* Republicans, global freezing."

"Global warming," Roth corrected.

"You go away to Florida in the winter," said Hershel. "What the hell do you know?"

"You get to be our ages, and a sense of wonder comes from enjoying an omelette, not having a fight with your wife, and having a good bowel movement."

"Again with the bowel movements," said Hurvitz. "You need a few months of good analysis to deal with your infantile obsessions."

"Infantile?" asked Rosen. "*Moi.* My granddaughter says that. *Moi.* She thinks it's cute. I think she's cute, but she's spoiled rotten. Ah, here come Sergeants Friday and Gannon. They can solve the mystery."

Lieberman and Hanrahan stepped into the T&L together. It was a few minutes to ten. The morning breakfast crowd, which had dwindled since the neighborhood had become increasingly Indian, Korean, and Vietnamese, was still sufficient to make the T&L profitable in the morning, but the conversation of the past had been sustained primarily by the Alter Cockers, who had chosen not to leave the neighborhood where they had grown old.

There were two people at the counter sitting on the red leatherette swivel stools. They were a couple, young, white. They were shabbily dressed and didn't look as if they were part of the neighborhood. Wanderers passing through, whispering.

"Lieberman," said Rosen. "Is it cute to say *moi*? I'm asking because you are our resident detective. You and County Cork."

Hanrahan was tired, in no mood for games, no mood to correct the prodding old man and engage him in his favorite activity, provocation and meaningless banter. He couldn't help himself. Rosen was old. Rosen thought he was funny. Rosen, in spite of the fact that he was an old Jew, reminded Bill Hanrahan of his own long-dead father who loved nothing more than a verbal joust.

"Kildare," said Hanrahan. "My people were from Kildare. Like the street."

"*Moi*," Roth said.

The rear booth, which was Lieberman and Hanrahan's unofficial second office, was open. Maish, Abe's brother, who owned and ran the T&L, kept it open unless he had a full house. The detectives sat across from each other, Lieberman facing the window and the Alter Cockers, Hanrahan with his back to them.

"*Moi* is French," said Lieberman. "From a Frenchman in the proper context it is either a simple acceptance of responsibility or a small or large act of hubris. Coming from an American kid, it is a clichéd affectation picked up from television sitcoms reinforced by laugh tracks."

"A lecture," said Rosen, looking at the other Alter Cockers.

Maish, Nothing-Bothers-Maish, was behind the counter serving coffee to the young couple. Lieberman could see their faces now. They didn't seem to be having a good day. The young man appeared to be on the verge of tears. The woman, no, she was just a girl, with dark short hair that needed combing, was touching the back of his head, consoling him.

Their story was as clear to Lieberman as *moi*. The young man was strung out. If you had the cash, this wasn't a bad neighborhood to score drugs. There were better ones, but this one wasn't bad. You just had to have the cash, and the couple didn't look like they had it.

The girl's eyes suddenly met Lieberman's. She came up with an obviously false smile covering pain and desperation. Lieberman blinked his eyes and waited while Maish, who looked like an overweight bulldog, apron around his waist, looked their way.

"Bill?" he asked.

"Three scrambled with grilled onions and mushrooms, rye toast, coffee," Hanrahan answered.

Maish didn't bother to ask his brother what he wanted. Maish was under strict orders from Bess about what her husband could and could not eat. Maish, at five-foot-eight weighed close to 255 pounds. Abe at five-seven hit 145 on a festive day. But it was the younger brother, Abe, who had the cholesterol problem.

Abe was drawn to the T&L. He was comfortable there. He was a mile from the problems of home and almost two miles from the Clark Street Station, from which they had both just come after reporting to their boss, Lieutenant Alan Kearney. Neither Hanrahan, Lieberman, nor Kearney had slept much during the night. Hanrahan and Lieberman had been working. Each had managed a few hours' sleep. Kearney had slept fitfully in his office. He spent more and more time in his office, more and more nights. He looked haunted.

He was still a handsome man at forty-three, but his face was not as healthy and his blue eyes seldom flashed. Kearney was a good cop, one who had been pegged to move up, quite possibly to the top, chief of police. He was being groomed when disaster struck. One night his former partner had murdered two people and barricaded himself on the roof, publicly blaming Kearney for seducing his wife. It wasn't true, but it made no difference. Other things went wrong that night. Kearney relived the possible options he hadn't chosen, reviewed and imagined and went on working.

"So," said Lieberman, pulling out his notebook. "Let's do it, Father Murph."

Doing it involved a simple process in which each man reviewed and assessed what the other man had done on whatever case he was working.

Behind Hanrahan, the Alter Cockers laughed, and Hurvitz said with some annoyance, "Enough already."

"Widow knows nothing about the three who roughed up her husband," said Lieberman, "but she immediately thought it might have something to do with some money he owed. Questions you've answered. Widow says Sokol was with her from the time she picked him up at the hospital till around eight, when he said he had to take care of something. He told her that he was going to see the people he owed money to and was going to cash in his insurance policy, or tell them that he was going to do it as soon as possible. She felt he was falling apart. She says she reassured him, told him it was alright, that she had learned from what had happened to him that it was more important to have him alive and well than to have his insurance money. She said she didn't know who he had borrowed the money from but that it was forty thousand. He had used it to pay overdue business debts."

"Or so he said," Hanrahan corrected.

"Or so he said, or so she says he said," Lieberman amended. "He did mention that he had to meet the man and wouldn't be back for a few hours. She thinks he said something like, 'He's a little loco, and he likes to talk, but I'm sure he'll be reasonable. Don't worry

I'm going to give the dog his money.' And . . . 'loco,' 'likes to talk,' 'lends money.' "

"Could be plenty of people," said Hanrahan, "except here's his appointment book. His wife gave me his briefcase. I found it inside."

He handed the small black book to Lieberman, who opened it.

"There's an entry for two weeks ago at six on a Tuesday, last week on Monday, and yesterday for nine. Doesn't say A.M. or P.M."

Lieberman put on his glasses and flipped to the most recent entry.

"El Perro," said Hanrahan.

Lieberman flipped through the book, checking the other dates. Neatly inked in little block letters the words "El Perro" appeared where Hanrahan had told him to look. Abe glanced at a few other entries, all kinds of names and notations. All in the same neat block letters.

"I wouldn't want to owe your amigo money, Rabbi."

Lieberman's "amigo," Emiliano "El Perro" Del Sol, was known to have beaten Syvie Estaban nearly to death with a telephone for talking while Julio Iglesias was singing on the radio. El Perro was reported to have cut the throat of one of the Vargo brothers for accidentally stepping on his shoes. More than one person Lieberman knew had been in the Dos Hermanos bar the night El Perro beat into pleading senselessness two construction workers who dared look at him while he was painfully and slowly composing a letter to his mother. El Perro was the leader of the Tentaculos, the gang that believed it owned North Avenue and probably did.

El Perro was average only in height. He was lean, kept his hair cut short, and bore a white scar on his face from an incident Lieberman knew nothing about and did not want to know. El Perro was also clearly psychotic. He leapt from obsession to obsession and criminal enterprise to criminal enterprise. He was into selling protection, drugs, stolen goods, extortion, and occasional loan sharking. Few of those who borrowed from El Perro were the Mexicans, Central Americans, and Puerto Ricans who lived in his territory. The consequences of missing a payment were far worse than facing any creditor.

Lieberman and the Tentaculos' leader were not exactly friends though the line was thin. Lieberman had done favors for the gang leader in exchange for information and occasional assistance when Abe felt the law did not equal justice. The two men also shared a passion for the Chicago Cubs. El Perro was especially passionate about Hispanic players, and once seriously considered issuing a threat to the ball club's owners not to trade any more Hispanic players unless it was for other Hispanics. Sammy Sosa was a God. Lieberman was a tough old Jew cop who spoke pretty good Spanish and couldn't be intimidated. Most recently El Perro had taken over a bingo parlor on North Avenue, where he set up his desk on the platform and did business. On Tuesday, Thursday, and Saturday nights he usually called the numbers himself.

The relationship between the cop and the gang leader had made the news twice, once in a *Chicago Tribune* story about Chicago cops and their criminal contacts, and once in the *Tribune* and *Sun-Times* and on the six o'clock news when Lieberman testified in court giving one of the Tentaculos named Machito a solid alibi for the murder of a rival gang member. Lieberman had told the truth. He had been with El Perro getting information on another homicide when the gang member had been murdered, and Machito had been present at the meeting.

Lieberman knew Internal Affairs had a file on him with a list of questionable shootings and associations with known criminals. It was part of the reason Abe had never been promoted, but just part of the reason.

"Maybe it's something else."

"Maybe."

"But we're going to find out."

"That we are," said Hanrahan, as Maish placed a large platter with a still-simmering omelette in front of him along with toast and coffee.

In front of Lieberman he placed a coffee and a large bowl of oatmeal. Lieberman put his glasses back in his pocket and handed the appointment book back to his partner.

"One bagel, plain, toasted," said Lieberman.

"No. Take your business to Walgreen's."

"Walgreen's doesn't have bagels," said Lieberman, looking at the steaming bowl of gray cereal.

Maish shrugged, and Lieberman looked at his partner's omelette with his starving beagle eyes.

No one made a better omelette than Terrell, the short-order cook at the T&L. But it wasn't just omelettes. Terrell, whom Abe had convinced his brother to hire a dozen years earlier, had learned his skills in prison, where Abe had been largely responsible for his five-year stay. Terrell had found his true calling behind the walls. He was a cook. Jewish cooking had become his specialty, and he was brilliant at it, too brilliant at the moment for Abe, who longed for a slice of brisket or just one stuffed cabbage. There was a small blackboard on the wall near the pass-way to the kitchen. On the board were listed the daily specials. Lieberman tried not to look, but he didn't have the willpower. Cherry blintzes. It was more than a human being should be expected to endure.

Maish hovered. Abe sighed and reached for the sugar.

"I put sweetener in it already," Maish said. "Stevia."

"I appreciate your concern," said Abe, picking up his spoon. "Now if you'll let me down my medicine in peace."

"The temple caterers are going to handle the bar mitzvah dinner," said Maish.

"They're kosher," said Abe.

They had been over this a dozen times. Abe took a spoonful. It wasn't bad. It wasn't a cherry blintz, but it wasn't bad.

"Who cares?" asked Maish. "Terrell can outcook all the kosher kitchens."

Abe and Bill ate silently. Maish went on.

"You're worried about Labal and Aviva?" Maish asked.

Labal and Aviva were the Lieberman brothers' ultra-Orthodox cousins from Brooklyn. There wasn't even a certainty that they would make it, let alone their combined total of sixteen children.

"God's gonna have a conniption fit because they don't eat kosher?" Maish went on. "We tell them it's kosher. I'll tell them. They'll have committed no sin. The dinner will cost you nothing instead of two thousand dollars."

"Three thousand," Abe amended. "I'd know it wasn't kosher. Bess would know. Yetta would know. They"—he nodded at the Alter Cockers—"would know."

"They'll all shut up," said Maish.

Maish was itching for a battle with God. Ever since his son David had been murdered by robbers and his pregnant daughter-in-law shot in the robbery, Maish had entered into battle with God. It wasn't that he didn't believe. He just didn't like God and was more than willing to take him on and accept the consequences.

Maish didn't know the full truth of his son's death. Abe did. So did Bill. There was no chance either one of them would ever tell, so they ate and listened just as the congregation of Mir Shavot had to listen to Maish, who doggedly attended services and forced the patient but besieged Rabbi Wass to deal with the bulldog of a man and his challenges.

"Maish, you want to do a dinner, wonderful. Do it on the Sunday," said Abe. "I'd like that. I'd love it. I'd celebrate by eating piles of chopped liver and a half ton of brisket, but Friday and Saturday we go kosher."

"God is a pain in the ass," said Maish, turning away from the table. "And you can tell him I said so."

"You just told him," Abe said.

Maish disappeared into the kitchen.

"He's getting better," said Hanrahan.

"Yeah."

Suddenly Maish was at the table again looking not at his brother but at Bill Hanrahan.

"You going to marry Iris or you're not?" asked Maish.

"I am."

"When?"

"Thursday," said Bill.

"Good, I'll cater a dinner. Abe and Bess's house. Unless you're going to have Chinese."

"Catered Jewish will be fine with Iris," said Bill. "Thanks."

"Someone appreciates reality at this table," Maish said, heading back for the kitchen without looking at his brother.

"Iris's father's giving us a party at the Black Moon the night before," Hanrahan said softly. "Invitations will be in the mail in a few days. What about James Franzen and Edward Denenberg and our battered Melvin Zembinsky?"

"What about indeed."

"They sound as good as whoever Sokol went to see last night," said Hanrahan, continuing to eat. "Well, almost as good."

"We'll pay them each a visit. We've got a busy day."

Lieberman finished his oatmeal. Hanrahan was still eating. Maish was giving the young couple their third or fourth cup of coffee, and the Alter Cockers were debating the current state of the Israeli/Palestinian conflict.

"Be right back," said Hanrahan, rising and wiping his mouth with a napkin.

"You just inhaled a three-egg omelette," said Lieberman.

Hanrahan ignored him and headed for the men's room. There was half a bagel with cream cheese left on the side dish across the table. Lieberman was sure he could down it in no more than forty-five seconds.

"Please, sir," he said, looking toward his brother and holding up his bowl, "can I have some more?"

Maish nodded and turned to Terrell. The young girl was off the stool and moving toward Abe quickly.

"Hi," she said, standing over him and smiling.

There was a slight yellow to her teeth, but her skin was good, primarily because she was young, very young.

"Hi," he said.

"I waited till your friend was gone," she said.

Lieberman looked at the young man she had left at the counter. He was busy paying no attention. Lieberman was afraid he knew what was coming in addition to oatmeal.

"Wait," said Lieberman, reaching for his wallet.

She stood waiting and glanced back at the young man, who continued to act as if all this had nothing to do with him.

"I can do lots of things," she said softly. "You have a car?"

"Here," Lieberman said, handing her the card he had managed to pull from a small stack he kept near his cash.

She took the card and looked at it.

"I'm a cop. If a young lady were to solicit for prostitution, I'd be obligated to arrest her. I don't always meet my obligations, and I've got a busy day, so let's say you've hit a small piece of good luck. You from out of town?"

"Yeah," she said, clearly confused. "You're really a cop."

"It's my winning nature," said Lieberman. "That card is for a drug rehab center four blocks from here. Methodists run it. It's a good place. My name's on the back. Use it. They'll give you a place to spend a few days and some food and start you on a program. What've you got to lose?"

She looked at the card, reading it slowly. She'd probably give it to her boyfriend, and there was a chance they would stop in at the New Christian Center to at least pick up a meal and spend the night. It would give Dave Mahan, the minister, a shot at them. Dave was damn good. It was a shot.

"We're from New Orleans," she said. "New Orleans, Louisiana."

Lieberman nodded. Maish came over with a fresh bowl of hot oatmeal. Hanrahan returned from the men's room, and the girl went back to her boyfriend at the counter.

"That what it looked like?" asked Hanrahan.

"It was."

"She wouldn't have tried it on me."

"You look like you might be a cop. I look like a guy who might own a pawnshop or a dry-cleaning store."

"I left temptation in your path, Rabbi," Hanrahan said, nodding at the slice of bagel.

"And I resisted," said Lieberman, looking at the young man and woman, who were discussing the card she had handed to him. They looked over at the two policemen and hurried out of the T&L.

"Like a good recovering addict," said Hanrahan, picking up the slice of bagel.

Hanrahan was a recovering alcoholic. He knew what he was talking about, and Lieberman understood.

"I've joined cholesterol anonymous," said Lieberman, spooning up oatmeal. "We start each session standing up and reciting our pledge: I eat all the wrong food. I'm blocking my arteries. I'm letting my craving get in the way of my staying alive and taking care of myself and my loved ones. With your help and the help of Jesus, I will resist."

"Doesn't sound like a bad idea to me. Maybe you should start a group. You can substitute 'God' for 'Jesus' and you . . ."

The cell phone in Lieberman's pocket began to vibrate. He took it out and said: "Lieberman."

Then he listened, his eyes on his waiting partner. He took out his pen and began making notes on his pad, then he listened some more before saying, "We'll head right over."

He pressed a button, and the call ended.

"Gonna be a very long day, Father Murph," he said. "The other dead guy in the lake, Pryor. Did time in Federal and State. Strong arm. Not smart. Place he hit in Northbrook. Stole a bunch of gold animals like the one we found in his pocket. Three more were found about an hour ago in the apartment of Walter Crest."

"The fence."

"The fence," Lieberman agreed. "Walter is dead. Walter is very messy dead. Now we have a dead policeman and a dead fence and a dead ex-con tied together with a charm bracelet."

They both got up. They didn't try to pay Maish. Maish had made it clear long ago that any offer of payment from either his brother or Hanrahan would offend him.

They both waved at Terrell, who leaned out of the pass-way from the kitchen and whispered, "Maish is in the back taking in a load of smoked fish and lox."

He held out a paper bag. Lieberman hurried behind the counter to take it from him and quickly returned to his partner's side.

"You drive," Lieberman said.

They had come in an unmarked 1998 police vehicle, a tan Mustang.

Hanrahan shook his head and opened the door.

"So you're having a bar mitzvah?" Herschel Rosen called out.

"Had one about forty-seven years ago," said Lieberman. "Thought I'd try another."

"Who's catering?" asked Roth, winking at all the Alter Cockers.

"Mama Lina," said Lieberman. "Kosher pizza and calzone. You'll get your invitations."

"Tell her to make one with lox," shouted Howie Chen.

"Kosher lox pizza," said Rosen. "A new delicacy, could become a new bar mitzvah tradition. We should pass it on to the caterer."

In the car, driving toward toward Western Avenue, Abe opened the paper bag. No doubt. A cherry blintz. Two of them.

"You want one, Murph?"

"To keep you from eating it," Hanrahan said, reaching out his hand.

"You're a generous and good-hearted man," said Lieberman, wrapping a large warm blintz in one of the napkins and handing it to his partner.

"I'm up for beatification next year," said Hanrahan. "Since Mother Teresa died they've been looking for someone like me."

"You've got my vote," said Lieberman, taking his first bite from the delicacy in his hand.

"And we've got a tail," said Hanrahan. "Four cars back. Dark blue Buick with tinted windows."

"See him," said Lieberman, looking in the side-view window and chewing. "Life is interesting, Father Murphy."

"Indeed it is, Rabbi. Indeed it is."

8

Melvin Zembinsky had dressed and made it to the door of the hospital room without falling on his face. It hadn't been easy. The room and the floor did not cooperate. They fun-house wavered and wobbled. His mother and father had called. They had met the night before with the doctor, a Pakistani named Bandhari, who advised that their son remain in the hospital for another day or two of testing. They had agreed. Z had not, but he had said nothing.

He had called Eddie and asked him to come to the hospital to get him. Eddie had a part-time job as a telecom salesman. Eddie had a '93 Toyota. He agreed to be there at ten, in front of the hospital entrance.

Z checked his wristwatch. He had about eleven minutes to make it. He strongly considered going past his bed, pushing back the curtain, taking the remote away from the old fart in the next bed, and turning off the goddamn game-show channel forever. But it was easier just to get the hell out.

He moved slowly, went through the door, tried to stand up straight and look normal, which was difficult with a bandaged head, a sore back that bent him over, and a bloodshot left eye. But hell, this was a hospital. What did you expect to see in a hospital?

I expect maybe to see a cop is what I maybe expect, thought Z, keeping his eyes down as he moved past the nursing station and headed for the elevators. No one stopped him. No cop appeared.

Z was sure of lots of things. Life sucked. There was no God. His parents saw him as a disappointment and a burden, and he did not kill the guy who had put him in the hospital. Sokol, Arnold Sokol.

He pressed the button for the elevator. A woman, who looked a little like his mother only not as well dressed, joined him and waited. He watched the white lights. The elevators were on the first and fifth floors.

If he didn't kill Sokol, that made the odds pretty good that it had either been Jamie or Eddie. He had talked to both of them, told them of Sokol's attempt to kill him, told him about the two cops and the crazy rabbi. He hadn't called Jamie this morning, and when he called Eddie he did not tell him what that little Jew cop with the creepy eyes had said about Sokol being murdered. Z wanted whichever one of them who did it to tell him. He was sure they would. Maybe not directly. They were both too smart for that, but they would let something drop, strut, brag, smirk. Eddie was the most likely, the most violent. Eddie didn't think about tomorrow. Shit, he didn't even think about later today.

Z made it to the lobby and the front of the hospital with three minutes to spare. He felt as if he were going to throw up and wondered if he should do it in the flower bed a few feet away or get into Eddie's car and tell him to stop when they cleared the hospital. If he threw up here, they might drag him back in.

His goddamn head hurt. Sokol was the asshole who had done this to him and in front of Jamie and Eddie. Sokol deserved a hard one in the head from behind with a Coke bottle. Not enough to kill him but enough to make him spend the rest of his life worrying about Coke bottles from behind.

Eddie pulled up. Z managed to move forward, open the car door, and slide in. Eddie's car smelled like stale pizza.

"Get away from here and stop somewhere," said Z.

"Where?" asked Eddie.

"Just drive before I puke all over your fucking car," said Z.

Eddie stepped on the gas. He was the biggest of the three friends and, at twenty, the oldest. He lived alone in a rusting trailer behind a house in Chicago on North Rockwell. The trailer was small, but cheap. It was their unofficial party and planning space. There wasn't much to it, and it was usually filthy, but no one bothered them. They certainly bothered others, but neighbors were not inclined to complain, though once while they were drunk and blasting heavy metal at about two in the morning, two BB holes went through one of the trailer's windows. They had tried to go out in search of the shooter, but knew they were in no shape for a chase.

Eddie's phone had rung about ten minutes later. Eddie had passed out. Jamie was shaking his head to the beat. Jamie didn't like Eddie's trailer. He hated the filth and the bugs he sometimes saw, but he could get over it by downing three or four beers. When the phone had rung that night, Z answered. A frightened, angry man's voice said, "That was just the first shots in this war. I'm going to shoot your damn trailer to pieces unless you stop the noise."

"And," Z had answered, "you stupid fuck, I've got caller ID, and I know your goddamn phone number."

It was a lie, but Z could tell from the man's voice that it would make him squirm. The BB sniper had hung up. He was probably still sitting there, weeks later, waiting for a call in the middle of the night or the three friends to come out of an alley when he came home some night and beat the shit out of him. Yes, there had been good times. But this was not one of them.

"You sick?" asked Eddie, driving.

Z looked at him. Eddie was bald, skinhead shaved with a small blue tattoo of a throwing knife in the center of his head. He figured if he ever wanted to look straight, all he would have to do was let his hair grow in. He had a baby face and a decent body, and he worked out when he wasn't drunk or trying to sell people things on the phone that they didn't want or need.

Eddie wore tight T-shirts to show off his muscles, which weren't exceptional, nowhere near as impressive as Jamie's. Eddie had capped teeth and a good smile, but he smelled, and had no line to pick up or deal with women. So, except for Skank Lilly at the Woodburn Bar on Ashland, he got no sex except what he paid for.

Eddie's passion was exotic weapons. He was a survivalist. There were times when Z had to tell him to shut up about blowguns, knife fighting, and killer martial arts.

Eddie's trailer was filled with books and magazines. They piled up in and around his bed. *Zips, Pipes and Pens, Deadly Blowguns: How to Make and Use Them, The Art of Throwing Weapons, How to Make a Silencer for a .22, Thai Boxing Dynamite.* Paladin Press catalogs were piled high next to the toilet. Eddie read them all. He never used anything he read in his ragged library. Jamie, big and dumb, who read nothing but worked out constantly, could break Eddie with one hand. Even Z could take Eddie out without any sweat, but Eddie was always willing to go along with whatever Z wanted to do, and he wasn't worried about hurting people when it seemed like fun.

"Just fucking pull over," Z said.

Eddie pulled over in front of a house with a driveway. There were no cars in the driveway. Z grabbed some Wendy's yellow napkins from the dashboard and stepped out of the car on weak legs. He leaned over to vomit on the grass. No one was out on the street. Z wiped his mouth with the Wendy's napkins and threw them on the lawn. Then he got back in the car and Eddie took off.

"The Colonel can clean it up," said Eddie.

"Wendy's is Dave. The Colonel is Kentucky Fried. The Colonel is dead. Dave is dead. Know anyone else dead?"

Eddie looked puzzled and said, "No. I mean lots of people. My mother. My Aunt Joannie."

"More recent," said Z, feeling better but tasting bitter acid. "I need a drink, a Coke."

"Okay."

Z looked at Eddie, who looked back at him.

"Sure you're okay?"

"Perfect. Sokol."

"Who?"

"The guy on the rocks. The guy who put me in the hospital. The guy I talked to you about last night."

They drove south heading toward Chicago.

"Bastard," Eddie said. "We gotta find him."

Z looked at Eddie, looked hard.

"What?" asked Eddie. "What are you looking at?"

No, not Eddie. Eddie was not a total idiot, but he wasn't good enough to be pulling off this act. That left Jamie.

Z made a decision. The hell with Jamie. What the hell was Jamie to him? He would throw Jamie to the cops. He and Eddie together. Jamie was big, blond, drew the girls, but he was stupid, stupid and strong. Until a few minutes ago, Z didn't think Jamie Franzen had it in him to kill. If Jamie did it, Z was going to turn him in and save his own ass. Z had an alibi. He was in the hospital. He knew nothing about it. He could even say he called Jamie and told him to leave Sokol alone but Jamie said he wouldn't. The world was full of Jamies and Eddies and, yes, Z's, too, but *this* Z wasn't going to go down for a murder. They could have Jamie's ass and all his holes in prison in Marion.

"I'll stop at Wendy's on Western," said Eddie.

"Where's Jamie?"

"Jamie? I don't know. Maybe sleeping."

"Let's go wake him up."

Wychovski wondered why he was still alive.

"Here," said Dickerson, handing him a Big Mac from the bag in the black man's lap.

Wychovski took it. The car smelled like french fries and fat. Wychovski looked at the suitcase Dickerson's feet were resting on. It was filled with cash from Walter's safe. Who knew how many thousand. Maybe a million. All unmarked.

Staying alive was number one on Wychovski's agenda. Number two, if he made it that far, was getting that case away from the man who munched a quarter pounder with cheese next to him.

Wychovski was driving a Lexus, a black almost new Lexus. He had never driven anything this smooth before. If he ever got that cash, he could buy himself one. He wouldn't keep this one. This one, Dickerson had said, belonged to Walter. He had told Wychovski not to worry, that the car wasn't in Walter's name, but one of his nieces. Still, step by step by step.

Stay alive. Get the money. Get the hell out of town. Drive southwest or southeast. Rent a furnished room. Sit tight for four or five months. Get new ID. That was far enough ahead to think.

But to accomplish this it was pretty clear he would have to kill Dickerson, who sat within easy reach of the same shotgun, now reloaded, that he had used to tear Walter into red meat.

"I've been waiting for someone like you for almost a year," Dickerson said.

Wychovski said nothing. He followed directions. Dickerson told him where to go. He went. South and west. Past the old United Center where Michael Jordan had played, deep into a run-down black West Side.

"Racist bastard always kept the door closed when he opened the safe, always reset the alarm," Dickerson went on. "I played good nigger, tough nigger, loyal nigger. He paid well, but I wanted more. Know what I mean?"

"I know," said Wychovski.

A Lexus in Lawndale with a white guy driving. But he had Dickerson riding shotgun, and he knew Dickerson was not afraid to shoot.

"I waited. You came. Old Walter made a mistake. Last mistake. Maybe his only mistake besides his wardrobe. You've got a question."

"No," said Wychovski.

"Another burger?"

"No, thanks," said Wychovski.

"Coke?"

"Sure."

Dickerson handed him a container of Coke with a straw.

"You're thinking, 'Why didn't he kill me, too?' Right?"

"No," said Wychovski. "I was thinking why don't me and Dickerson team up. We'd make a good team."

Dickerson ate a pair of fries and shook his head.

"I don't need a partner, and with this," he said, patting the suitcase, "I won't need one for a long time. They're going to start looking for me. May take them a while, but they can probably do it, or maybe do it. No, I gotta show up and tell them what happened."

"What happened?" asked Wychovski.

"You came in, killed Walter," said Dickerson. "Sure you don't want another burger? Got a double cheese left."

"No, thanks. I lulled Walter, took his money, and ran?"

"Back a step," said Dickerson. "Mind if I listen to the radio?"

"No," said Wychovski.

Dickerson reached over and pushed some buttons. Sixties rock came on. Dickerson turned down the volume, and said, "You killed a cop last night, killed a jewelry store guy, came with your pockets full of little gold wolves and such, and tried to make a deal. You had the shotgun. I was surprised. You blasted poor old Walter, took the money in his pocket, and took me hostage."

Wychovski had watched Dickerson fill the suitcase with cash and lock the safe. The money was free and clear.

"So," Dickerson went on, "if I blasted you back in Walter's now redecorated apartment, I'd have to hide all this money."

"Why am I taking you hostage?" Wychovski asked. "Why didn't I just kill you, too?"

"I'm working that out," said Dickerson with a smile. "I'll tell you when I do. I'm not sure whether you're gonna kill yourself or get jacked on the street. But you'll have the shotgun."

"And you?"

"I escaped. Jumped out of the car when you came to a stop. Ran to the phone and hit nine-one-one. Good citizen. Mayor'll give me an award maybe. Nah, but I've got my reward. Any more questions?"

"No," said Wychovski.

He was wearing a seat belt. His door was locked. He was sweating. Smell of fried meat and fat stronger. Smell of himself in fear. Shotgun out of reach. Dickerson's hands full. Fries in one. Burger in the other.

Woman walking a buggy with two little ones on one side of the street, Roosevelt Road. A cluster of winos outside a storefront bar named Willie's. The "W" in Willie was faint against the dark glass. The "illie" still stark and white.

Wychovski went through it in his mind. It was just past dawn. It was just about too late. He went over it in his mind like a bowler imagining his moves, a great free throw shooter seeing what he was going to do. There was a light. He stopped. Now. Who knew where Dickerson was taking him, how soon he would die if he just kept driving. Now.

He took his left hand off the wheel, and said, "Supposing we . . ."

He pushed the button on the door with his left hand, hit the seat-belt buckle button with his right, pushed the door open, and took his foot off the brake as he rolled into the street.

Dickerson and the Lexus shot forward. Bruises, not bad, knee was going to hurt, but Wychovski rolled and got to his knees as the Lexus sailed into the front of a condemned building with a closed store on the corner. The Lexus, driver's side door open, hit at about twenty miles an hour.

Nothing exploded. Nothing burned. Nothing but the car was damaged. If you don't count Dickerson, who came out of the car limping, shotgun in one hand, suitcase in the other, tan slacks stained with spilled Coke.

Wychovski stood up and ran. He didn't know where he was running. He ran down the street. It looked as if it should be a busy street, but it was still early.

Dickerson fired. A storefront window, hardware store, shattered, spraying glass. Wychovski ran, covered his head to ward off the sharp rain that cut into the backs of his hands and his scalp.

He hadn't been hit. He was still running, not fast, but running. He was in reasonably good shape. He had the feeling from Dickerson's body that the man behind him was in even better shape even though he might be limping. Better shape, determined, and closing in on him.

A pair of well-dressed black children, a boy and a girl no more than six, holding hands watched the bleeding white man run by. Wychovski saw no fear in their faces. Maybe cars crashed here every day. Maybe people were gunned down on the street here every morning. Maybe they talked about it in school. The little boy would raise his hand, and say, "Ms. Holmes, we seen a white man get blown up on the way to school this morning." And Ms. Holmes would answer,

"That's interesting, Ronnie. Why don't you draw us a picture for the bulletin board."

A space between two buildings on his right. Another shotgun blast. Had the kids stepped back into a doorway? Were they cut into pieces? Would Ms. Holmes not get her report?

Wychovski was safe for the second inside the passageway. He ran. It was narrow. He had to run sideways over broken bottles, garbage, more smells, shit smells. Dying in this alley, having to fall into this. No. He moved as fast as he could. All Dickerson would have to do was turn the corner and fire. Couldn't miss. A door on the left. Wychovski put his back against the right wall and kicked at the door, kicked hard, kicked for his life. The door creaked. The hinges gave way. He jumped into darkness hearing Dickerson's footsteps hurrying down the narrow passageway.

Wychovski groped, saw light under a door, tripped over a box, got up fast, kicked the box back toward the door he had come through. He was in a storefront room. Counters, shelves with nothing much on them. Cots. People in them. All black faces looking at him in fear. A family? Mother, father, three kids in cots lined up next to each other.

Wychovski ran to the front door, threw the bolts, and opened it, jumping into the street. The same street where the Lexus sat snub-nosed. People were opening its doors and taking whatever they could carry. Radio, seats.

He turned right and ran. Getting tired now. Followed by the Terminator. The Black Terminator. He ran. Came to a corner. Turned right, glancing over his shoulder. No sign of Dickerson.

Side street. A few people passing him going to work or to nowhere. A running white man. White man with bloody scratches on his hands. The play of the day. Eighty yards to the next corner.

He made it. Touchdown. Six points and still alive. What was that football movie with Al Pacino where the guy's eye popped out during the game and they put it in a plastic bag? *Any Given Sunday.* But was this Sunday? No. Maybe. It was Wednesday. Maybe Tuesday. He wasn't sure.

This street was even smaller. A few people were coming and looked at him. Would they give him away? He ran up a concrete stairway, holding the rusting iron railing of a three-story brick house. An old woman with a big white purse in her hand looked at him. She wore thick glasses and a white dress with big blue flowers on it.

"Hide me," he panted.

"Police after you?"

"Crazy man with a shotgun," he managed to get out.

The woman stepped back to let him enter and closed the door after him. He put his back to the hallway wall and pushed closed the curtains on the window next to the door. Then he pushed them back just a bit. Pushed them back far enough to see Dickerson turn the corner and look both ways, shotgun in his right hand.

The old woman's face was next to his, peering through enormous lenses.

"That's him," Wychovski said. "He stole my money and my car and he wants to kill me. I ran away."

He looked out the window again. Dickerson couldn't decide which way to go. He looked right and then left. As his eyes turned toward the house where Wychovski was, Wychovski pulled the woman away from the curtain. He stood breathing hard for five or six seconds, then looked again. Dickerson was gone.

"We'd best call the police," said the old woman. "Come with me."

Wychovski followed her, amazed to be alive, wondering how he would keep her from calling 911.

The universe is very large, he said to himself. And life is very hard.

9

The two detectives who caught the case were happy to cooperate with Lieberman and Hanrahan. Hell, they were happy to turn the whole damn thing over to them.

On the green board in their captain's office was a list of open homicide cases. It was a long list. The only things that made it shorter from time to time was the apprehension and arrest of a suspect or the fact that more space was needed on the board so that the oldest cases went from the board but stayed on the computer.

Williams and Bustero had their names next to the most open cases on the board. Had they any hope of catching the killer that day, they would have entered into some kind of give-and-take, but they weren't working with much confidence lately. Williams was young, lean, black, and good-looking enough to be a news anchor. He was even dressed like one, in a well-pressed navy blue suit and a red tie. Bustero was short, homely, and a few years older than Bill Hanrahan. Bustero had no place up the ladder to go, and his rumpled jacket and slacks, cop belly, and open collar made it clear he had no illusions.

Chicago was averaging about two murders a day this year. The number had been going down slowly but steadily for years if the police department wasn't playing too loose with the figures.

That was the good news. The bad news was that over the past decade, the police were able to solve just over 40 percent of those murders. When the number of murders was high back in the eighties, the clearance rate had hit 76 percent. If you added in the old murder cases, some dating back a dozen years, that were cleared, you started approaching a 50 percent clearance rate.

Which meant, simply, that half the murderers in Chicago got away with it. Detroit and Los Angeles were just as bad.

The department said the problem lay with overworked detectives, undertrained detectives, too many new detectives coming in to replace veterans who walked out the door the minute they hit pension age. More and more were taking early retirement.

And so, Bustero and Williams knew their captain would be only too happy to turn the case over to someone else.

Only one thing stopped them from just walking away.

They stood in the big room where Walter the Fence lay dead. Actually, he was reclining on a bloodstained sofa. The wall and the paintings behind him were Jackson Pollack sprayed with the blood and brain matter from the dead fence.

Williams held the palm of his right hand up and open in front of Lieberman and Hanrahan. Resting in it were two small gold figures, one a snake, the other a possum.

"Hansel," said Hanrahan. "Leaves a trail for us. Think he wants to be caught?"

"I think he killed a cop," said Bustero. "I think the case is yours, but unofficially we stay on it and it stays off our board. Suit you?"

"Suits us," said Lieberman. Someday he and Hanrahan might need a similar favor.

"Tell us what you need," said Bustero.

Lieberman watched as the crime scene people puttered, printed, sampled, and scraped with gloved hands and plastic zipper bags.

Lieberman told them about Pryor.

"He did time in Stateville. Armed robbery. We'd like names and photographs of people he knew there who are on the street, people he knew well. Might be something. Might not. Then you take a trip out to Northbrook with whatever you get and show the pictures to the widow. See if she can identify any of them. The widow's description and the one from the dead cop's partner say Hansel is white, maybe mid- to late forties, a little chunky, graying hair."

Williams and Bustero nodded.

"We'll dig," said Bustero. "Give me your number."

Hanrahan gave him a number. Bustero wrote it in pencil on a napkin he pulled from his pocket.

"One thing is screwy here," Bustero said as Abe and Bill started to leave. "Walter had a wallet full of cash, more than two thousand dollars. Our guy comes here to sell his animals, blows Walter away, doesn't take his ready cash, leaves a trail."

"Who's Walter's hooligan?" asked Lieberman.

"Black guy named Dickerson," said Williams before his partner could be politically correct and label Dickerson "African-American." Williams didn't see himself as African-American. He was American. He was black. Well, actually he was a light chocolate brown, but he was more black than his partner was white. Bustero was a pale pink. No one identified perps as Italian-Americans, Jewish-Americans, Russian-Americans, Venezuelan-Americans.

"Dickerson have a record?" asked Lieberman.

"Odds are good," said Bustero. "We'll find him."

"Well, Rabbi," Hanrahan said when they were back on the street.

They both knew what their next stop was. They moved toward their car parked in front of a fire hydrant. A handful of people were standing in the street watching nothing but knowing something was going on.

"What's goin' on?" asked an old woman, her coat pulled tight around her.

The two policemen didn't answer.

"I got a right," said the old woman. "Someone get killed or robbed or what? I got a right. I live right over there."

"You see anything last night, anyone going in that door?" asked Lieberman.

"No, besides, it's none of my business," she said defensively.

"I rest my case," said Lieberman, getting into the driver's seat while his partner rounded the car and got in.

They pulled into light traffic, past the car Wychovski had stolen the night before, went to the next corner, and turned right. The car with tinted windows that had been following them pulled out behind them and followed a half block behind.

When they got to North Avenue they turned right, went a few blocks, and parked. They locked up and walked half a block to the bingo parlor. The windows of the parlor were plastered with signs in Spanish, and a young man who stood near the door stepped in front of them. Lieberman didn't recognize him.

"¿Donde esta El Chuculo?" asked Lieberman.

"¿Que quieres?" asked the young man, looking from man to man, one hand in his pocket.

"Queremos hablar con Emiliano," said Lieberman.

"No es posible. El esta ocupado."

"Es necesario," said Lieberman.

"No puedo hacerlo," said the determined young man.

Hanrahan suddenly reached out and grabbed the hand the young man had in his pocket. The young man struggled, but Hanrahan held him tightly.

"Rabbi, tell him if he shoots, he'll blow his balls off," said Hanrahan.

"He knows," said Lieberman. "He may be more afraid of El Perro than becoming a eunuch."

"Soy El Viejo. Emiliano es mi amigo," said Lieberman.

"¿Es verdad?" asked the young man, his eyes fixed on Hanrahan's with hate.

"Si. ¿Que es su nombre?"

"Esteban."

"Abre la puerta, Esteban. *Tengo que hablar con Emiliano cerca de Sammy Sosa."*

Esteban really had no choice. Lieberman was giving the new man in the Tentaculos a little wiggle room.

"Okay," Esteban said. "Let me go in and have someone tell him you're here."

There was only the slightest touch of an accent to his English.

"We don't know what's in your pocket, Esteban, and right now we don't want to find out," said Lieberman. "I just want to talk baseball with an old friend."

Esteban nodded and gave Hanrahan a cold you-haven't-seen-the-last-of-me look. Then he went inside and called someone's name.

"You've made a friend for life, Father Murphy."

"I try to spread goodwill wherever I tread, Rabbi."

Esteban was back almost instantly. He said nothing. Lieberman began counting to himself. When he got to ten, he was going in with or without the permission of Genghis Del Sol. When he reached eight, the door opened and the two cops saw a face and body they recognized.

His name was Piedras, Stone. He was a block of brown granite with a flat face. Piedras was even bigger than Hanrahan. He was also extremely stupid and loyal to El Perro. He knew nothing, derived no meaning in life but through that loyalty and a passion for amazing quantities of food.

"Buenos dias, Piedras," said Lieberman.

"Dias," answered Piedras.

"¿Esta Emiliano dentro del edificio?"

"Venga," said Piedras, turning and entering the building.

The policemen followed him.

They moved through the inside doors and into the bingo parlor. Folding chairs and tables were missing, stored away. It looked like a dance floor.

"Viejo," called El Perro from the platform where he stood behind the table on which rested the steel-barred bingo machine.

El Perro was lean and smiling, apparently genuinely glad to see the older policeman. He ran one finger over the white scar on his face and opened his palm to look at a white bingo ball.

"Come on up," he said. "You too, Irish. Cubs are gonna be rained out today. They said. We can't go. And tonight . . ." He motioned around the empty room. "Tonight there's gonna be a dance here, for the church. We're gonna raise money to fix the walls."

"You're a saint," said Hanrahan.

"Fuckin' A right," said El Perro.

He wore black chinos and a white T-shirt.

"You see this ball?" he asked, holding up the ball in his hand. "I've been thinking. It's the only ball that's also a name, B4. That makes it special. Before. You know what I mean, *Viejo?*"

"B9," said Hanrahan.

"Huh?"

"Benign," Hanrahan repeated.

"What are you talkin' about? That's no fuckin' word."

"We've got a few questions, Emiliano."

Piedras stood behind the two policeman along with another member of the Tentaculos whom Lieberman recognized but whose name escaped him.

"B9," said El Perro. "You're a little loco like me, Irish."

"Arnold Sokol," said Lieberman.

"Are no so gal?" asked El Perro. "What the hell kind of question is that? Are no so gal? *¿Diga en Espanol?*"

"It's the same in Spanish," said Lieberman. "A name. Arnold Sokol." He said the name slowly.

"You want us to do something to this guy? Write his name. Tell me what you want. It's done. For you, *Viejo*, anything. You got *cojones.* That night you put the gun down Crazy Juan's pants in the Border Bar. Man, you were crazy. Place full of his friends. You all alone. Walked him right out. Didn't give a shit. He tried to run, and you shot in him the foot. Took two toes. I like you, *Viejo*, like a second father."

"I couldn't be more pleased," said Lieberman. "Arnold Sokol. He borrowed money from you, lots of money."

"I don't know this guy, Sokol," said El Perro. "You got me mixed up with some other Del Sol."

"He wrote your name in his appointment book," said Hanrahan. "El Perro."

"He wrote 'the dog' in his appointment book, and it's me? Bullshit, Irish."

El Perro laughed. Piedras stood stone-faced. The other Tentaculo smiled, afraid to laugh, afraid not to.

"You wouldn't lie to me would you, Emiliano?" asked Lieberman.

"Fuckin' A. Sure I'd lie to you. I lied to you a thousand times, but I got no reason to lie. I don' know this guy. I never loaned him no money."

"And you didn't kill him," Lieberman said.

"No. Not me. No Tentaculos. I never heard of this guy. Listen, *Viejo*, I'm having a very bad day. No baseball. No bingo. I think I'm coming down with something you know? Like a bug? Something. So don't hack me no Chinese."

Lieberman laughed.

"What's so funny?" Hanrahan.

"You mean don't '*hock me a chinek*,' " said Lieberman.

El Perro shrugged. He had picked up the Yiddish phrase from Lieberman, asked him what it meant, stored it away. Lieberman imagined him saying it to Piedras and wondered what other Yiddishisms the mad gang leader had picked up from him.

"Whatever," said El Perro. "I don't know this guy Sokol. *Cree o no?*"

"*Creo*, I believe you," said Lieberman. "You might want to check around and see if someone is using your name and reputation to loan shark."

"I'll check," said El Perro. "But they would have to be crazy to do it. Almost as crazy as I am."

Lieberman and Hanrahan turned and started to leave.

"What about next Saturday?" called El Perro. "Pittsburgh Pirates. Day game."

"I'll let you know," said Lieberman. "If I'm there, I'm there."

"Okay. *Adios*, B9," El Perro called.

On the street they moved past Esteban, who gave Hanrahan his best frightening look. Hanrahan paid no attention.

"You believe him, Rabbi?"

"Yeah, you?"

"I think so. So, someone's using his name and reputation," said Hanrahan.

"Someone's doing something."

"Like killing Arnold Sokol maybe?"

"Like killing Arnold Sokol maybe, Father Murphy. Let's check out our other suspects."

"Other business first," said Hanrahan. "What do you say you drive over to the guy who's been on our tail."

Lieberman saw the car. He knew what to do. He got in their car and started the engine while Hanrahan moved slowly around as if he were about to get in the passenger seat. Before Hanrahan reached the door, Lieberman hit the pedal, burned tire, and cut in front of a slow-moving battered pickup truck. He pulled alongside the car with tinted windows, blocking it in the space between the car ahead and the one behind.

The pickup truck driver cursed and slowed down as Hanrahan ran, pain surging through his knees, weapon in hand, to the sidewalk beyond the trapped car. Lieberman was out on the street now, his gun out and leveled in both hands at the driver's door.

"Open it up," Lieberman commanded.

There was a pause, and the window on the driver's side slid down slowly. Hanrahan moved to the front of the car, weapon pointed, then to the driver's side.

The man behind the wheel was familiar. Hanrahan had seen him four times before, and Lieberman had seen him twice. He was calm, wore sunglasses, and was definitely Chinese.

He was one of Laio Woo's personal bodyguards.

"Out of the car," Hanrahan commanded, coming to the open window and aiming his weapon.

The man behind the wheel sat calmly, his hands on the steering wheel. He reached up slowly to adjust his sunglasses and opened the door.

Hanrahan was on one side of him, Lieberman on the other.

The man who emerged from the car was slim and wore a navy blue Armani suit and red tie. He stood next to the open door, hands at his sides. Hanrahan reached over and patted him down. He was unarmed.

"You may not search my automobile," he said in clear, precise English. "I've committed no crime. My vehicle is properly registered, and my driver's license and license plates are current. You have no cause for invading my property."

"You were driving recklessly," said Lieberman. "Weaving in and out of traffic."

The man, who could not have been more than thirty, nodded in understanding and stepped toward Lieberman.

"There is a gun in my glove compartment," he said calmly. "Along with a license to carry it. My employer deals in very rare antiques and jewelry."

"Driver's license," said Lieberman.

The man slowly reached into his inner jacket pocket, produced a black leather wallet, and handed it to Lieberman.

Hanrahan slid past the man into the driver's seat. It was a tough squeeze but he managed to reach across and open the glove compartment.

"A Luger," he called back. "And registration with a permit to carry."

"There is nothing else of possible interest to you in my car," the young man said, "but if you wish to waste your time . . ."

Hanrahan came out of the car and slammed the door, almost catching the young man's right arm.

"What the hell are you doing? Why are you following me?" Hanrahan said evenly.

"I am your conscience," the young man said without a smile. "You promised Mr. Woo that you would not marry Miss Chen for one year, that you would consider the reasons why this might not be a good or proper union. There are still eight months to go on your promise."

"I promised nothing," said Hanrahan.

"That is not Mr. Woo's interpretation of the situation," the young man said. "Nor that of Miss Chen's father. And it is Mr. Woo's understanding that you intend to marry precipitously."

A small crowd had gathered on the sidewalk and in the street where Lieberman had parked. All of the faces were Hispanic. Behind him Lieberman heard the voice of El Perro.

"What's goin' on?" he said. "What's this Korean gook doin'?"

Lieberman's cell phone began to buzz.

"He's Chinese," said Lieberman.

"Same difference," said El Perro, looking at Mr. Woo's man, who turned his tinted glasses toward the gang leader with a look of complete disinterest. "What's he doin' here?"

"He's a bad driver," said Lieberman. "*No puede manajar un automóvil muy bien.*"

The phone kept buzzing.

"*No lo creo. ¿Digame, Viejo, que pasa?*"

"This gentleman," Lieberman said, looking at the driver's license in the wallet, "Mr. Ye, is being given a warning for reckless driving. Mr. Ye is now being told that if we see him driving recklessly, which means if we see him driving, we will be forced to arrest him for a variety of infractions. Which means we don't want to see Mr. Ye anymore."

He handed the wallet back to Ye, who returned it to his pocket. Lieberman answered the phone.

"Lieberman."

"Abe, you know what time it is?" came Bess's voice.

He looked at his watch. It was a few minutes past noon.

"You're supposed to be at the temple for the fund-raiser lunch meeting," Bess said wearily. "Did you eat this morning? Did you get any sleep?"

"You're up to something, *Viejo*," said El Perro. "Pull away and don't look back. You know, I think our Chink here is going to have an accident. I think our Chink here is maybe not gonna live, and if he does, he's gonna know what part of the city to stay out of."

"I ate oatmeal at Maish's," Lieberman told Bess. "I caught a few hours in the car. I shaved at the station, put on fresh underwear and a shirt from my locker. Bess, I'm kind of busy right now."

"Filth," said Ye, looking at El Perro, then away.

"What?" shouted El Perro. "What'd he call me?"

"I didn't hear," said Lieberman. "Mr. Ye, I suggest you get back in your car. I'll back up and let you out, and we'll watch you drive away."

"What's going on, Abe?" Bess asked.

"I'm busy. I can't make the luncheon. Go in my place."

"Where do you think I am? I'm at the luncheon."

"Then tell everyone I'm sorry. There's been a death in the family. The family of man. Ask Rabbi Wass if he's seen the news about Arnold Sokol. He'll understand."

"Abe, you told them you would be there," Bess said firmly.

"Okay, I'll get there as soon as I can. Half an hour."

Lieberman hung up and pocketed the phone.

"Tell Woo if he wants to see me," Hanrahan was saying to Ye, "he knows where I live, and he has my number. I don't like mind games."

Ye got in his car and turned to look at El Perro.

"What is the word your people are called? Spics?"

"You are dead sushi," screamed El Perro, now being held back by Hanrahan and Lieberman.

"The Japanese eat sushi not the Chinese, you racist spic."

"I've got your fuckin' license number," El Perro screamed. "You disrespect me in front of my people." He spread his arms, indicating the crowd. "I'm gonna find you and cut your *pequeño* yellow dick off."

Ye shook his head.

"I'm gonna kill him, *Viejo*. You didn' hear me say it, remember, but I'm gonna kill him."

"You'll have to go to Chinatown to do it, Emiliano," said Lieberman. "He works for Woo."

"I give no shit about that Chinese gang, tong shit," said El Perro, the white scar on his face pulsing. "I'll go in there alone."

"Cubs. Saturday," Lieberman said.

"He's dead, *Viejo*."

"Lieber's pitching, I think," said Lieberman. "I'll see you at Wrigley."

Hanrahan held El Perro back while Lieberman went back to the car and backed up so Ye could get out. Ye seemed to be in no hurry.

The street was full of people now, all looking at El Perro, knowing who he was. Tentaculos surrounded their leader. Someone was going to suffer and soon. If it wasn't going to be the Chinese guy, it might be someone on the street who made the mistake of looking at El Perro too long or the wrong way. The crowd began to disperse.

When Ye was out of sight heading toward Michigan Avenue,

Hanrahan got in the car and Lieberman drove away looking into his rearview mirror. He could see El Perro looking around, fists clenched in rage. He didn't want to see more.

"Congratulations, Father Murphy. It looks like you've started an unusual if not unique gang war. Latinos and Chinese. They don't even have a border or business dispute. Just reputation."

"Reputation means everything," Hanrahan said, looking straight forward.

Lieberman wasn't sure if his partner was talking about the Chinese, the Tentaculos, both, or himself.

10

Z and Eddie got to Jamie's one-room basement apartment in a wooden frame house on Kimball at around eleven. Z wasn't feeling too well. Actually, he felt like shit. His head hurt, hurt like hell. Little shocks on top of a constant pressure and ache in his head. The rest of him didn't feel that great either.

Sokol was dead. Good. Jamie killed him. Let's give him a medal, Z thought as he led the way down the five steps to Jamie's apartment. No, let the cops give him the prize.

"Good job," Z would say. "Thanks for doing the bastard. You should have driven a truck over him. Sorry Eddie and I had to give you up, but hey, what can you do? Cops are after us, and we're clean. Cops are going to come after you soon, and you are stupid.

Z knocked at the door.

"Who's it?" called Jamie.

"Z and Eddie."

The door opened. Jamie stood there in his jeans. No shirt, no socks or shoes. He was the biggest of the trio, the strongest, the dumbest. His hair was blond, cut short, and an island of fine yellow hair nested on his chest. His mouth was open, and he looked at Z.

"You okay?" he asked, stepping out of the way.

"Do I look okay?" asked Z, stepping in with Eddie behind him.

"You look . . . I don' know. Not so good I guess."

The room was neat. Jamie hated dirt and was afraid of roaches, rats, spiders, anything that crawled. He had nightmares about a roach crawling on his chest. Jamie kept cans of bug spray and scrubbed the room almost every day. He kept the sheets, blanket, and pillowcases on his bed in the middle of the room clean. He didn't want to sleep against a wall. Something might crawl up or down the wall, and if there were rats, and there almost certainly were in the old building, he would hear them.

Whenever he spent time at Eddie's trailer, the first thing he did when he got back to the apartment was throw all his clothes in the washing machine, including his sneakers, then take a long hot shower.

"I was doing laundry," he said, as Z moved to the park bench against the wall. The bench had been stolen from a park in Des Plaines. Jamie used it as a couch. Two pillows, plain brown, which he had dry-cleaned every month. There was a small wooden table with three chairs, an ancient electric range against one wall, with a noisy refrigerator next to it, and a dresser in a corner of the room with a big-screen color television sitting on it.

There was a soccer game going on on TV. The sound was off.

"It's in Italian or something," said Jamie nervously, moving to turn off the television. "I can't understand Italian."

"I know," said Z.

Eddie moved to the refrigerator and opened it. He knew he wouldn't find anything he wanted to eat, but there might be a Coke or something. There wasn't.

Z sat on the sofa bench and looked at Jamie, who stood in front of him. Eddie went to sit on one of the wooden chairs by the table.

"So," Jamie said. "You're okay."

"I told you."

"Yeah, that's right. You did. You're not okay."

Jamie rubbed his pants nervously against his sides.

"So he's dead. That guy who . . . the other night," Jamie went on.

"He's dead."

"It was on television," Jamie said. "Guy's name. Stuff."

"Yeah, thanks," said Z. "You got any aspirin, anything?"

"Motrin?"

"Yeah."

"Why did you say 'thanks'?" Jamie said, moving to the cabinet next to the refrigerator. He opened the door. Everything was laid out neatly. Every box that had been opened was in a sealed see-through bag.

"For doing Sokol," said Z. "For getting back for me."

"And me, too," Eddie added.

Jamie had the Motrin now. He brought the bottle to Z, who opened it, poured about five of them into his hand, and threw them into his mouth. For years he had been able to take only one pill at a time and with lots of water. A year or so ago he found that he could suddenly swallow pills without water, just gulp them down. He couldn't figure, but who cared. Right now he didn't care about anything but a confession from Jamie.

"So, thanks," Z said.

"You're welcome," said Jamie.

"Yeah, thanks," Eddie added again.

Jamie turned his head to look at him and nodded with a smile.

"Where'd you find him?" Z asked.

"Find him?"

"The guy. You killed him for all of us," said Z. "Right?"

"The dead guy?"

Jamie was looking at Z and trying to think. Z smiled, a smile that looked like gratitude and respect.

"So," said Z. "How'd you find him? I mean before you killed him?"

"Over by the rocks," said Jamie slowly. "He went back there. I went back there."

"Why?" asked Eddie.

"Why?" Jamie repeated. "To look for something I dropped."

"What?" asked Z.

"My watch. He was there. I beat the shit out of him and pushed him in the water. He hit his face on the rocks."

"You didn't mean to kill him?" asked Z.

"Just rough him, hurt him, for you," Jamie said.

"Cops are gonna come," said Z. "You better make up a story."

Jamie stood running his tongue back and forth over his lower lip.

"I was with you, you and Eddie at the hospital. You'll back me. Same story. With you all night."

"Should work," said Z, standing up, feeling no better. "I'm going over to Eddie's for the night."

"Okay," said Jamie. "We getting together later?"

"Depends on how I feel," said Z. "We'll call. Let's go, Eddie."

"See you, Jamie," said Eddie, following Z to the door. "Thanks again."

"See you," said Jamie.

Out on the sidewalk heading toward the car Z said, "Cops want us all."

"Yeah," said Eddie.

"You and I didn't do anything."

"No."

"So, we give them Jamie," said Z.

Eddie went to the driver's side and got in. When they were both inside, doors closed, Eddie said, "We give 'em Jamie."

"Can't wait for police," Wychovski said, grabbing the woman's arm.

She turned to face him. She knew. He could see she knew. Not the details. Not even a general idea of what was inside the circle he was trapped in. But she knew the outline. She had seen people there, maybe been there herself.

"Man trying to kill you, man with a shotgun. There's no place you can walk or run around here. You're a white man. Try looking in the mirror sometime."

Wychovski didn't want to look in a mirror. He didn't want to run.

"Somebody you can call?" she asked.

"No. I can boost a car."

"Nothing you find on the streets around here," she said. "People lock their cars up in garages if they got 'em, or keep an eye on 'em. You see a lot of cars parked out there?"

Wychovski remembered seeing cars. Not a lot but some.

"Go try and steal a car. You'll have a whole gang of black faces coming for you. You kill someone? Wait. Don't answer that. There's a door back down this hall, leads to the basement. There's a table and a chair near the furnace. Just sit there till it gets dark. I've got my son's sweatshirt with a hood in the dryer, along with his other stuff. Yours has blood on it. My sons'll fit you. Put it on and wait. I'm gonna be late for work."

"Here," said Wychovski, reaching into his pocket and taking out a golden turtle. "It's real."

She took it, turned it over, and put it in her pocket.

"Be gone from here when it turns first dark. Hear what I'm sayin'."

"I hear," he said.

The woman nodded and went back out the front door without looking back. He moved to the window, parted the curtain, and watched her walk down the stairs and across the street.

She was going to sell him out. He was sure. Why shouldn't she? Dickerson was roaming. She might find him if she were dishonest enough. Or she could find a phone and call the cops. Either way he wasn't going down into the cellar. He would take his chances in the street. This was a big goddamn city, the toddling town. Big, bad, millions of people. Head east down the alleys. Head toward downtown, toward State Street. That great street. Find a car. Take a chance. Get the hell out of the city.

He still had some of the watches. He still had golden animals left. How many people were dead? He fingered something hard in his pocket, wondering what it was. A tiger? How many were dead? Pryor. The cop. Walter. Three.

The street looked clear. Near the corner three girls, teens, maybe a little older, were standing. They looked as if they were waiting for a ride.

He could feel the pulse in his forehead. He could feel, really feel, his heart beating. He stepped through the door and heard the voices of the girls on the corner though he couldn't make out what they were saying.

Dickerson had gone west. Wychovski went down the steps and

moved east, toward downtown. Don't run. Don't hurry. No, he had to hurry. And what was the difference if he ran. Dickerson would recognize him two blocks away.

He jogged, looking down each street as he came to a corner. Avoiding the eyes of the few people he passed. He wanted rain. It looked as if it were going to rain. Rain would bring daylight darkness. Rain would discourage Dickerson. Well, it might. Dickerson had the money, but he wasn't safe. He needed Wychovski, and he needed him dead.

As he moved faster, he considered things he could have been and done. He could have been a good salesman. He could have been a dealer in Atlantic City or on some Indian reservation. He looked as if he might have some Indian blood in him. He could make it up. He would be a good dealer. Used cars. New cars. He could sell them. He could fix them. He could drive them.

He had been in Daytona once. The noise from the track was deafening. If the noise were here and it had been blackness instead of thick sound, he could hide.

Hungry. He hadn't considered it. He was hungry. He was probably also tired, but he didn't feel tired.

Bring it together. Boost a car. Get to another car outside the city. Boost it. Make his way to St. Louis, where he had money.

Now he had a plan. It was good to have a plan, to work out the details as he moved. He had been walking about ten minutes when he heard the siren. He couldn't tell where the sound was coming from. He moved down the street to his left. A big street. Dickerson might think twice with cops around. Might think twice about walking around with a shotgun and a suitcase full of money.

Wychovski found himself on Van Buren Street. The cop car was coming down the street toward him. He pulled the hood over his face, put his hands in his pockets, moved to the nearest store, and went in. Through the window of the neighborhood grocery no more than the size of a two-car garage, he watched the cops.

"Car crashed down the street," a man's voice called out. "Big new car. Brother came out with a gun shooting at a white ma . . ."

The man had been in the back of the store putting something on a shelf. Now he spotted Wychovski and knew from his eyes who he was looking at.

Wychovski held up both hands, palms out to show they were empty. He put his right hand back in his pocket and came up with a woman's watch with a gold-and-diamond band. He also came up with a golden parrot.

He put them both on the small cluttered counter, looked into the eyes of the old man and shook his head no. The old man shook his head no in return, and Wychovski went out the door and back to the street.

Thunder now. It was definitely going to rain. He walked quickly for half a block, and the rain began. People were running for cover. He ran too, ran east, ran fast. His pockets jingled with what remained of the disaster he and Pryor had created.

What was there in man that sought out punishment for imagined misdeeds? Lieberman wondered. Well, actually, Lieberman had to admit that some of his own misdeeds were not imagined.

He sat in Rabbi Wass's study pretending to listen to Irving Trammel. Irving was a lawyer, not yet forty, well dressed, fully suited, even had a pocket watch. His dark hair was brushed straight back and he was lecturing.

It was a dour group. Rabbi Wass, seated behind his desk, didn't seem to be listening, though his unfocused eyes were aimed at the man Lieberman unaffectionately called Erwin Rommel. Lieberman was sure the Rabbi's mind was on the death of Arnold Sokol. Ida Katzman, who was moving in fast on her eighty-eighth birthday, sat in the chair next to Lieberman, leaning on her cane. Ida Katzman could not shrink much more and still exist. She did not bother to look at Irving Trammel. Her eyes were on Lieberman. Ida Katzman didn't have to pretend to look at Irving. She was ancient and rich, both of which gave her the advantage of not having to pretend to deal with people she didn't like. She didn't like Trammel, Abe knew, but Irving knew what he was doing. The ancient woman was the financial core of the congregation. The lawyer was the corporate center, and the rabbi the reminder that the temple existed for spiritual reasons.

Syd Levan was the only one paying attention to Irving. Syd was Lieberman's age, owner of two children's furniture stores in the suburbs. He wasn't rich. He wasn't poor. He kept in reasonable shape, had great false teeth and a winning smile. His hair was a well-dyed black, and he felt truly honored to be in the inner circle.

Lieberman had dropped Bill Hanrahan at the station, and they agreed Bill would pick up his partner at Lieberman's house at two-fifteen. That gave Lieberman time to make an appearance at the meeting and an excuse to leave it within an hour. Bill said he had some things to take care of, too. Abe hadn't asked what they were.

"So," the Desert Fox continued, or, Lieberman hoped, concluded, "if we can get a really big-name speaker, we can charge one-fifty a plate and make a profit of $15,000 if we sell all the tickets."

"Providing we don't have to pay the speaker," said Lieberman.

"We can pay four thousand and still make fifteen," said Trammel with a knowing smile. "I've worked the numbers. If we get a big enough name, we can get the bigger dining room at the Hyatt. We pay three thousand more and it is not beyond the realm of real possibility that we could make $30,000 or more."

He had someone in mind. They all knew it, but only Syd seemed the least curious.

"Who?" he asked.

"Lieberman," said the Desert Fox.

Everyone looked at Abe.

"No," Trammel corrected, "Joseph Lieberman. We give him an award, let him name the date."

"We just call his office and ask him?" asked Syd.

"Abe calls his office and asks him," said Trammel. "One Lieberman to another. Maybe you're distant cousins."

"I see a family resemblance," said Syd, studying Abe.

"I defer to the orator," Abe said, looking at Trammel.

Trammel wouldn't take up the ball. He would just pass it. He would not want to come up with the idea and then fail to have it succeed. Far better to come up with the idea and let Abe fail.

"I respectfully decline," said the Fox. "Syd and I are already talking on the dinner. I checked with the temple president about this before I proposed it."

The temple president was Abe's wife, Bess.

"When?"

"An hour ago," Irving said, now a step ahead in the chess game of responsibility.

Abe looked to the rabbi for help. There was none there. He looked at Ida Katzman. She could reach into her little beaded purse, pull out her checkbook, and write a check for $30,000. She had done it many times before, but there was a limit to the number of times the committee could go to Ida. The library was named for her long-deceased husband. The building carried a bronze plaque thanking her for making the move to the new temple a reality. From Bess, Abe knew that the old woman had donated more than two million dollars to the temple over the ten years since her husband's death.

"Because I have the same name as the senator? That's a reason?"

"Why not?" asked Syd.

"And you're a police officer," Irving added. "You're more likely to get through to him."

Abe looked at Ida, who shrugged. He couldn't tell what the shrug meant. He hoped it meant that she would not cast the vote her money gave her to make him do it. It might also mean she sided with Syd's "why not." And then again she might simply have felt a chill.

Everyone was looking at Abe, who reached up to run a finger along his gray mustache, a sign Bess would recognize. Abe Lieberman was trapped.

"I didn't even vote for him," Abe confessed.

"You voted for Bush?" Rabbi Wass said, jolted to life.

"I voted Libertarian," said Lieberman. "Now you know my politics. An open book."

"And Bess . . . ?" Ida Katzman said, now paying attention.

"She voted Democratic," said Abe. "It's in her genes. You don't want me to make this call."

"We do," Ida Katzman said.

That ended the conversation.

"I'll call," Abe said with unconcealed resignation. "No promises. I'll call his office."

"I have his office number," said Trammel, reaching into his pocket and pulling out his wallet.

"Why does that not surprise me?" Lieberman asked, as the lawyer handed him a card. It was Irving's business card. On the back was the name: Senator Joseph Lieberman. There was a telephone number, an e-mail address, and a fax number.

"You can call today," said Irving.

Lieberman pocketed the card.

"I've got a couple of murderers to find today. I'll call in the morning," said Abe.

"Then," said Trammel with a small but triumphant smile, "I have no other items on the agenda."

"Then we're finished," said Rabbi Wass.

Lieberman knew that he was. He was suddenly very, very hungry. If he were lucky, Bess would be home. If he were lucky, there would still be some of last night's dessert in the refrigerator. If he were lucky, he could get her to call Joe Lieberman's office. It would cost him something. Bess would have a price, but Abe would probably be willing to pay it.

"You play golf, Abe?" Syd Levan asked, as Trammel moved quickly to talk to Ida Katzman and help her up.

"No, Syd. How long have you known me?"

"Thirty, forty years," said Levan, showing his expensive teeth.

"Have I ever played golf with you?"

"No, but it doesn't hurt to ask."

"I don't play golf, Syd. I do drink coffee, and on rare occasions I eat. You want to get together for lunch at the T&L sometime and kibbitz, I'm open."

Syd had lost his wife to cancer about a year ago. It had been sudden, unexpected. Syd had seemed to recover quickly, to handle it well. He threw himself into his work along with his two daughters and sons-in-law. He joined temple committees, and he developed a passion for golf, which, Lieberman had heard, he played well.

"Lunch sounds good," said Syd. "You really have two killers to find today?"

"If possible," said Abe, looking at the forlorn rabbi, who was moving around the desk slowly to say his good-byes.

"Gotta talk to Irving," Syd said, touching Lieberman's arm and moving to flank Ida Katzman and help her out the door.

"Abraham," Rabbi Wass called, as Lieberman moved toward the door behind the slowly departing trio, "you have a minute?"

Lieberman turned, and Rabbi Wass moved forward, hesitating till the other three committee members were gone. Rabbi Wass looked about five years older and ten pounds heavier than he had the day before. He was wearing a clean white shirt and dark trousers and the usual black yarmulke on his head. He also wore the look of a troubled man.

"Arnold Sokol, the man in the hospital, was murdered?" asked the rabbi softly.

"Yes," said Lieberman.

"Did the young man at the hospital, Zembinsky, is there a chance he killed Mr. Sokol?"

Lieberman thought he knew where this was going.

"It's a possibility," said Lieberman. "We're working on it."

"So," said the rabbi, adjusting his glasses, "I may have kept Arnold Sokol from killing Melvin Zembinsky in the hospital, but Melvin Zembinsky may then have murdered Arnold Sokol?"

Lieberman stood waiting till the rabbi went on.

"It's a difficult question. Was I destined by God to be a part of this human . . ."

"Joke?" Lieberman supplied.

"No, 'puzzle' perhaps. Is one life worth more than another? And why was I the instrument of this . . . I'm sorry, just thinking aloud. I've learned to accept the will of the Almighty even when I don't understand it."

"And my brother has learned to reject the will of the Almighty when he doesn't understand it," Lieberman said.

"God has a sardonic sense of irony," said the rabbi with a shake of his head. "There's a sermon in all of this somewhere, but I don't know where. I'll work on it. Please let me know if Melvin Zembinsky was in any way responsible for the murder of Mr. Sokol."

"I'll let you know," said Lieberman, who had no intention of thinking about divine nonintervention in the affairs of man.

Things simply were, Lieberman had long ago concluded. Read the Torah, and that's the lesson you get. At least that was the lesson Lieberman got. Don't look for reasons, for why bad things happen to good people or good things to bad people. The first five books of the Scriptures are filled with God's playing favorites, playing tricks, playing games, manipulating for no other reason than that's the way he feels like doing it. Therein, Lieberman had decided, lay the lesson. Learn to accept whatever happens, to be ready for anything if you can, and to blame not God but man or chance or God's whim. Sometimes Lieberman felt that there was no such thing as a simple God, but there were very wise people who wrote the Torah and put in the simple message: Don't try to understand or explain. Simply accept that anything can happen.

Lieberman's thinking, however, had gone a step further. If God wasn't going to do anything when bad things happened to good people, and if the law didn't take care of the problem, Abraham Lieberman was willing to take on the responsibility. He would discuss his actions with God if and when that opportunity arose.

There were only a few cars parked on Lieberman's street. One of the cars was Bill Hanrahan's. Abe parked in front of his partner's car, moved across the lawn and up the three concrete steps to his front door. He could hear his wife talking when he opened the door.

He stepped in and saw her sitting next to Hanrahan.

"Joseph Lieberman," Abe said when he had closed the door.

"Will it hurt you to call?" said Bess.

She was wearing her red suit. She had somewhere to go or had just come back. Abe liked her in red. He was in a red mood.

"You call. I'll clean the garage. Fair exchange."

He walked into the dining room and sat across the table from his wife and partner.

"Abe," she said with a sigh. "What's the worst that could happen? He could say 'no.' "

Abe was about to further his protest, but he looked at his partner. Hanrahan clearly had something on his mind. His big fingers were playing with his coffee cup. A small pool of coffee sat in the saucer.

"What?" Lieberman asked.

"Bill and Iris want to get married."

"I know."

"Tomorrow," said Bess. "They've got the license. That Unitarian minister will marry them. They want us to be there."

"Tomorrow," Lieberman repeated.

Hanrahan nodded.

"Iris agreed. Later we'll have a celebration or something for our relatives, friends. Woo isn't going to give up. When it's done, over, he'll have to accept that what's done is done."

"And if he doesn't?" asked Lieberman.

"What's he going to do? Kill the bridegroom? Iris isn't going to marry him, and he's too smart to try to kill me."

"I'm not sure 'smart' would have much to do with it," said Abe. "Maybe 'smart' is killing you and letting his people know that he's as dangerous to cross as they already know he is."

"Iris says she doesn't think so," said Hanrahan. "Rabbi, we're gonna do it. Bess says she's in."

"Then I'm in," said Lieberman. "Tomorrow I call Joe Lieberman and witness a wedding. On the side we can try to find a couple of killers. Congratulations and good luck."

"We might need it," said Hanrahan, taking his partner's hand.

"Now," said Lieberman. "What do we say to a small repast?"

"I called Kearney. They picked up Zembinsky and his two friends. They weren't hiding. Got 'em waiting for us at the station."

"Then we'll eat fast, and they can have a little time to contemplate their sinful ways."

"Amen," said Hanrahan.

"Lox omelettes," said Bess. "With or without onions?"

"With," said Lieberman.

"Definitely 'with,'" echoed Hanrahan.

"And cream cheese," said Lieberman as Bess rose.

She gave him a reproachful look and a shaking of her head.

"Just a little," Lieberman said. "It won't kill me. And whatever that secret dessert from last night was if there's any left."

Bess went into the kitchen. He had no idea if she would return with cream cheese in the omelettes and a dessert.

11

The thin black woman in her fifties sat back straight, both feet firmly on the worn wooden floor of the Clark Street Station squad room. She wore a brown dress and carried a tan cloth bag, which she clutched to her almost nonexistent breasts.

The flabby white man who was probably less than forty sat rocking forward and back, both legs vibrating from side to side. The flabby man who was either trying to grow a beard or simply hadn't shaved in a few days was making a hissing sound through his teeth as he rocked.

Wedged between the thin woman and the flabby man on the narrow wooden bench was Eddie Denenberg, who wanted to move away from both of them but had no place to go. When he tried to get up, the detective at the desk about a dozen feet in front of him motioned for him to sit back down.

The detective's name was Rodriguez. It said so in white on the black plaque on his desk. He looked like a Rodriguez to Eddie, dark, tough, and not in a good mood.

Rodriguez was talking to a girl no more than sixteen, who sat in the chair next to his desk. She talked quietly and earnestly, using her hands a lot. The girl wore a short skirt and a halter top and kept brushing back her long, straight hair. Rodriguez listened to her and kept an eye on Eddie as Lieberman had asked him.

Eddie pointed to his crotch and squirmed, doing his mime of a man in urgent need of a toilet. Rodriguez didn't care. Eddie sat. The thin black woman kept looking straight ahead. The flabby man kept rocking.

The squad room was busy, very busy. Every desk had a detective behind it. Noise, voices, someone belched, someone cried, more than one voice was raised in indignation and anger. All the cops seemed to wear the same look, weary, resigned. Not angry, not unsympathetic, just resigned.

They had all been picked up together, Eddie, Z, and Jamie at Eddie's trailer. The cops who came just asked them to show ID, told them not to talk, and took them away in a patrol car.

When they got to the station, they sat Eddie on the bench and took Z and Jamie away. Z had gone over it with him before Jamie had come to the trailer.

"Tell 'em nothing," Z had said. "They ask. You say nothing. They tell you me or Jamie talked, you make a deal, you hold out, and when they threaten you with all kinds of bullshit, tell them you'll give 'em what they want if they let you walk. Then you tell them what Jamie said about killing Sokol."

"The truth?"

"The truth," Z had said.

Now Eddie sat. The squad room door opened. A big cop came in, looked toward Eddie, and motioned for him to follow. Eddie got up. The flabby man spread out to fill the void. The black woman inched farther toward the end of the bench.

The cop led him into the corridor where cops, perps, victims, and witnesses were being ushered in and out and up and down.

A short fat woman with her straight gray hair held back tight with a rubber band was being supported by a black policewoman.

The fat woman was saying, "I kin make it. I kin make it."

The big cop opened a door right across from the squad room. The fat woman pointed at Eddie, the flab under her upper arms shook.

"That him? That the bastard who cut up my Bonny?"

"No," said the policewoman. "Just come with me."

Eddie went into the room in front of the detective. The large room was almost empty. There were two unmatched folding chairs in the middle of the room. The floors had a fresh coat of something green that looked like concrete. One wall was painted green, and someone had stopped halfway through painting another wall. There were cans of paint on the floor and a large rolled-up drop cloth.

"Gonna be the new lockup," said the big cop. "Have a seat."

Eddie moved to one of the folding chairs and sat. The big cop sat in the other chair and said, "My name's Detective Hanrahan. I'm in a pretty good mood, but I'm Irish, and I'm not a patient man. You've got a little room to wiggle but not much. Now, let's talk."

In the interrogation room at the rear of the squad room, Lieberman sat on one side of the scarred, scratched, and stained wooden table. Melvin Zembinsky sat on the other side. There was a cup of Dunkin' Donuts coffee on the table in front of Zembinsky. Lieberman was drinking from a similar cup.

"I drink it with cream and sugar," said Zembinsky, leaning back and folding his arms.

"I've got some Equal."

"Forget it," said Zembinsky, reaching for the coffee and glancing at the mirror that covered most of the wall to his right. There were no windows in the room, but it was bright. A bank of eight fluorescents tinkled overhead.

Zembinsky knew that he was being watched by someone behind the mirror, maybe another cop or two, someone who could ID him for something, a prosecutor. He had an audience. Good. He'd play to them, have some fun before he turned Jamie over.

He was wrong. There was no one behind the mirror in the little observation room.

"You like oranges?" Lieberman asked.

"Sometimes. You offering me an orange?"

"No, just curious. You like baseball?"

"Sometimes."

"Cubs or Sox fan?"

"I don' know. You want to ask me something that makes fuckin' sense, then ask."

"You kill Arnold Sokol?"

"No," Z said, reaching for the coffee.

"You know who did?"

"No."

"I think you killed him. The man in the bed next to yours in the hospital said you got up during the night and were gone for a couple of hours."

"I was in the John reading *People* magazine," said Z. "Cover to cover. I like to keep up. I was in there half an hour, maybe less."

"You like Johnny Depp?"

"He's alright. What the hell has this . . . ?"

"I still think you killed him."

"You arresting me? Read me my rights and get me a lawyer."

"Your father? He's a lawyer, isn't he?"

Z put down the coffee carefully and very slowly said, "I don't want my father. It's a mutual kind of thing. I don't want him. He doesn't want me."

"It's good when a father and son don't want the same thing," said Lieberman. "I've got a daughter. We never want the same thing."

"She got a nice ass?" asked Z, with a glance at the mirror.

Lieberman shrugged.

"My daughter is too old and too tough for you," said Lieberman. "She'd have you pleading to murders you didn't commit just to get someplace safe. Might be a good idea. Turn my daughter loose on you for four hours. Just the two of you locked in a room talking."

"I didn't kill anyone. I don't think I'm gonna need a lawyer. I need some aspirin, maybe codeine."

Z let his right hand move to the bandage covering the section of shaved scalp in which he had a dozen stitches.

"Want me to take a look at your head?" Lieberman said with a smile.

This wasn't going the way Z expected. The little Jew cop was nuts.

"No. I didn't kill Sokol."

"Coincidence," said Lieberman. "One night you try to mug him, and he sends you to the hospital. A day later he's murdered, and you don't know anything about it. I think we've got you for all kinds of things if not murder. Attempted murder is a good one. Or we drop down to assault and attempted robbery. That's not really up to me."

"What happens if, and this is just an 'if,' if I know who killed Sokol?"

"We charge you with withholding evidence and maybe being an accomplice," said Lieberman. "Or maybe if you tell me everything and fast, you walk away, a good citizen. Maybe I recommend you for a medal. You go to City Hall, shake the mayor's hand, and he hangs a medal on a ribbon around your neck."

Lieberman sat back, drinking his coffee. He looked toward the mirror and nodded, though he knew no one was in the observation room.

Melvin Zembinsky had something to say. Lieberman knew it the second he had sat the young man in the chair. The game was to get Lieberman to push him into talking. At least that's what Zembinsky's game was. Lieberman's was to make Zembinsky squirm and talk.

"Let's talk a deal," said Zembinsky, leaning forward across the table.

"Let's talk Polish," said Lieberman. "Listen, I think you need a lawyer. I've got another case to work on. Just ask me for a lawyer. I'll put you in holding. Your lawyer will come and . . ."

"Jamie did it," Z said.

"James Franzen? Your coffee's getting cold."

Z drank some more coffee.

"I can stick it in the microwave for a minute," said Lieberman, reaching for the cup.

"Forget the fuckin' coffee. Jamie did it. He told me and Eddie this morning. We went to his place from the hospital. Ask Eddie."

"You told him to kill Sokol."

"Hell no."

"You willing to write out what Jamie told you and sign it?"

"Yeah."

"I'll get you a pen and paper. When you're done, you can read it into a tape recorder."

"Fine."

Lieberman looked at the mirror. So did Z. Z saw faint outlines of moving bodies where Lieberman knew there were none. Lieberman left the room to let Zembinsky work out his act.

The squad room did smell. No doubt. Only Cooper denied it. Cooper had no sense of smell. He thought all the other cops made up the business about the smell to fool around with him. Cooper didn't care. He had five years to go until retirement. Compared to what they pulled on Connie Faldo, squad room smell gags were a walk on the yellow brick road.

Hanrahan wasn't at his desk. A new detective, young, caved-in chest and bad skin, sat in Hanrahan's chair playing with his suspenders and shaking his head while two old men sat across from him imploring. Lieberman moved around desks and bodies, went into the corridor, where he saw Hanrahan standing at the window near the stairs, looking out at the rain.

"Yours?" asked Lieberman.

"Turned over his friend Franzen. Took all of ten minutes. Yours?"

"Beat you by three minutes."

"Get 'em on the jury. They'll vote to get the death penalty moving again. It's good to have friends, Rabbi."

"Good indeed," Lieberman agreed. "Time for Jamie."

"Time."

Melvin Zembinsky was moved to a desk in the squad room, where he could write his statement and be watched by Rodriguez. He could see Eddie five desks over doing the same thing. Their eyes met. Z nodded. Eddie nodded back. Jamie was history.

Jamie Franzen, golden-haired and in a clean blue T-shirt and jeans, stood in front of the same table in the interrogation room where Z had sat minutes before.

This time when Lieberman entered the room there was someone behind the mirror, Bill Hanrahan and Alan Kearney.

"Sit down," Lieberman said.

"I like standing," said Jamie.

"I'm already having a long day," said Lieberman wearily. "Make both of our lives easier."

"This place isn't clean," said Jamie. "I heard something in the trash basket."

He looked at the wastebasket in the corner. The basket was full, topped by two Dunkin' Donuts coffee containers.

"You going to run if you see a roach come out of the can?" asked Lieberman.

"Maybe. What do you want?"

"Your best buddies, Melvin and Edward, say you told them this morning that you killed Arnold Sokol last night," said Lieberman.

Jamie stood blinking for a few seconds. He didn't glance at the mirror. All he saw was the little cop sitting across the table.

"What did you do to them?"

"Talked to them for about a minute or two," said Lieberman. "They couldn't wait to turn you in."

"You're lying."

"Got you nailed, James," said Lieberman with a shake of his head.

"Is prison dirty?" asked Jamie.

"No," said Lieberman. "It's pretty clean. They keep it that way. Plenty of time and Lysol and not enough to do. Now I can't vouch for the jail."

"Jail?"

"Cook County Jail till your trial," said Lieberman. "We'll see what we can do about getting you a place without roaches."

"Or ants, or spiders, rats, mice, beedes. They're so goddamn dirty," said Jamie. "You gotta work all the time to keep them out of everything."

"I know," said Lieberman. "You know you are now under arrest for the murder of Arnold Sokol. You have . . ."

"I know," Jamie said. "I don't want a lawyer. I want to tell you what happened. If Eddie and Z don't want to stand up for me, I'll show 'em I'll stand up for them."

"Because they're your buddies?" asked Lieberman.

"Because you stand up for your friends even if they don't stand up for you."

"Then tell me," said Lieberman.

Jamie Franzen pulled out the folding chair, examined it, then picked it up and turned it over to inspect the underside of the seat. Satisfied, he put the chair down and sat.

Franzen: Last night I went to his house.

Lieberman: Whose house?

Franzen: Sokol.

Lieberman: To kill him?

Franzen: Beat him to shit. Yeah, maybe kill him for what he did to me and Z.

Lieberman: How did you know where he lived?

Franzen: Phone book.

Lieberman: Were there any other Arthur Sokols in the phone book?

Franzen: No, I don't think so. I went there and called him from a pay phone, told him I had something of his, that all he had to do was come downstairs and get it.

Lieberman: And he came?

Franzen: No. He said he was going to call the police. So, I asked if he was Joe Jones. He said "no," and I said I had the wrong number.

Lieberman: And . . .

Franzen: I just waited, figuring maybe he'd come out for a walk or something.

Lieberman: And he did?

Franzen: After an hour maybe.

Lieberman: Can you describe the house?

Franzen: It was a house. That's all.

Lieberman: Go on.

Franzen: He walked down Sheridan Road to Morse and then toward the lake. I followed him. He just went to the beach and stood there looking at the water. It was getting dark. There were some people around, but they left.

Lieberman: Go on.

Franzen: I killed him.

Lieberman: How?

Franzen: Sidewalk near Morse is cracking. Chunks of concrete all over. I picked one up, a big one, came behind him, and hit him in the head.

Lieberman: He went down.

Franzen: Yeah, I hit him again, but I think I killed him with the first hit. It worked out fine. He started it by the lake. I finished it by the lake.

Lieberman: What did you do with the piece of concrete?

Franzen: Heaved it in the water. Then I heaved the body in the water.

Lieberman: You didn't get your chance to beat him then?

Franzen: Didn't have to. He was dead.

Lieberman: Then?

Franzen: I went home. I walked.

Lieberman: You want to write all this out for me and sign it?

Franzen: Yes.

Lieberman: You think of anything else, you just put it in. Anything I can get you?

Franzen: Get that garbage in the corner out of here or put me in a clean room.

Lieberman: I'll see what I can do. I'll go get you some paper.

Franzen: I'm not a good speller.

Lieberman: I'll get you a dictionary.

Franzen: It won't help.

Lieberman: Just write it like it sounds. I'll be right back with paper and a pen.

Franzen: Don't forget the garbage.

Lieberman went to the corner of the room, picked up the almost overflowing trash can, and went through the door into the squad room. He put the can down, took a few steps to the left, and went into the soundproof observation room.

The lights were off, but there was enough light from the interrogation room for the three detectives to see each other.

"He's either one hell of a smart con artist or he didn't kill Sokol," said Kearney.

"I don't think he's a con artist," said Hanrahan, looking at Franzen through the mirror.

Franzen was still seated, but he was looking back at the corner where Lieberman had picked up the garbage.

"I don't think so either," said Lieberman.

"Okay," said Kearney with a sigh. "His confession is full of shit. Wrong name for the victim, saying Sokol lived in a house. We could get around that, but that crap about a piece of concrete . . . Sokol's head was bashed in with something smooth and definitely wooden. Pieces were in his scalp. Whoever killed him also hit him in the face and kicked him or punched him hard on his chest and stomach. There was no piece of concrete in the water with blood on it. No bat or piece of wood either. So . . ."

"He didn't do it," said Lieberman.

"But he confessed to his friends," said Kearney, leaning back against the wall and folding his arms. "And to you."

"Wanted to take credit for it," said Hanrahan.

"Stand-up guy," said Kearney with a sigh.

"Martyr," said Lieberman.

"Friends turn him in, and he still wants them to think he did it," said Hanrahan. "What kid of a kid thinks like that for Christ's sake?"

"Nobody thinks like that for Christ's sake," said Kearney. "It's for his own sake. So, what do we have?"

"A very sloppy liar," said Lieberman.

"What does that leave us?" asked Kearney.

"The other two," said Lieberman.

"And El Perro," said Hanrahan.

Lieberman didn't answer. Something struck him, not hard but a small slap of memory.

"Hell of a coincidence," he finally said. "Sokol gets killed, and one of the hundreds of bad guys is someone we deal with."

"It happens," said Kearney.

"I think we need some search warrants," said Lieberman. "Judge Roscoe reachable?"

Kearney nodded yes. Albert Samuel Roscoe was one of the people who had stood by Kearney when the Shepard disaster had taken place. Albert Samuel Roscoe had great sympathy for the working police. Albert Samuel Roscoe gave out search warrants the way child molesters gave out candy. Albert Samuel Roscoe, who was dangerously close to retirement, was the policeman's friend, always willing to overlook the narrow niceties of the law.

"I'll give him a call," said Kearney. "Where you want to look?"

Lieberman told him. Kearney and Hanrahan exchanged glances.

"That's a stretch, Rabbi, even for Roscoe," Hanrahan said.

"You sure about this, Abe?" asked Kearney.

"No," said Lieberman.

When Kearney headed back to his office, Lieberman told a uniformed cop talking to another cop to bring a pad and pen into Jamie Franzen, then stay with him while he wrote his confession.

"When he's done, don't put him in the lockup. Just have him sit on the bench. I'll ask Rodriguez to keep an eye on him."

The cop nodded and went in search of pen and pad.

"I think you're wrong on this one, Rabbi," said Hanrahan, as they waited for Kearney to arrange for the search warrants.

"You mean you hope I'm wrong, Father Murph."

"Yeah."

Hanrahan shrugged.

Kearney opened his office door. He motioned for Lieberman and Hanrahan, who sidestepped a cop in a hurry carrying a handful of papers.

"I'll have the search warrants first thing in the morning. Right now, get over to Van Buren and Aberdeen," he said. "Someone plowed a Lexus into a store. Car's been stripped, but uniforms on the scene found some little gold animals on the floor under the mat."

"We're on the way," said Lieberman. "The warrants?"

"I'm working on them," Kearney said, glancing around his squad room. He looked as if he were going to say something, but changed his mind and went back into his office.

"Your turn to drive," said Lieberman.

12

No farther. That was it. It was raining now. Raining hard. Pouring. Bullets of water that stung when they hit your open skin.

Wychovski sat on the cracked concrete stoop of a boarded-up three-story redbrick factory. He huddled, knees up, clutching them, shivering, trying to keep them from knocking together.

The rain came after him. He pulled back against the boarded-up door. It didn't help much. He watched the cars go by slowly, splashing, spraying in the daylight-clouded darkness. Thunder, wind, waves in the water of the rivulets that had formed on both sides of the street and ran into the drains.

To his right about a block down was the Chicago River. He could see the bridge.

He was not simply soaked. He was a sponge; his weight felt as if it had doubled. His legs wouldn't listen to his commands or pleas. He had a cold, the flu, pneumonia.

No people were on the street now. They had all found shelter somewhere, somehow. Rain jabbed at his legs. He tried to pull himself into a tighter ball.

Across the street a solitary old man, small, black with a white beard, walked slowly, his hands plunged into the pockets of his green Army surplus raincoat.

Crazy son of a bitch, walking wounded, Wychovski thought.

The man stopped as if he had been called by a voice Wychovski couldn't hear over the pounding, drumming of the rain on the sidewalk and street and the whooshing and spray of the passing cars.

The old man turned and began crossing the street. He was heading toward Wychovski. For a few seconds after he had crossed the street the old man stood in front of the figure huddled in the doorway. The old man seemed oblivious to the rain.

Wychovski mustered a look that he was sure said, Keep walking you crazy son of a bitch. I'm in no mood for company.

The old man either took the look as an invitation or ignored it. He sat next to Wychovski, his legs straight out onto the sidewalk, ran thumping against his already soaked pants.

"Troubles?" asked the old man.

Wychovski said nothing.

Troubles? Hell no. The cops were after him for killing a cop. A guy with a shotgun was after him to blow him away. He was cold, coming down with something, too wet, weak, and tired to move, and not knowing where to go. He was definitely beginning to lose his sense of humor.

"Like to be someplace else?" the old man said gently.

Someplace else? St. Louis, Kansas City, Moscow, Shanghai, the fucking North Pole, a hospital in Oslo, Wychovski thought, but he said nothing.

"Wouldn't do much good," said the old man, reaching into his pocket.

Wychovski released his grip on his legs, ready. His arms were deadweights, but he could handle this skinny old man if he came up with a knife or a gun. They were only inches apart, bodies almost touching.

The old man pulled out a Magic Marker, a red Magic Marker, and half turned toward the damp boards nailed against the door behind them. He also pulled out a pair of glasses and propped them on his nose.

The little alcove was covered with graffiti—boards, door, walls in marker, some of it color. "Lawndale Raiders Eat Shit," "Phanesha Simms Sucks. Call Her. 343-3494," "Burn A Pig," "K.J. and Emma Two Gether," "I Clean Up My Own Shit." Not very creative, though some of it had been written with some skill, especially a few gang names: Devil Rats, Lost Boys, Men With Guns.

The old man found a space and wrote carefully, slowly as the rain beat down and cars sprayed and splashed and thunder boomed. People hit their horns. In the daytime darkness, car lights skimmed the alcove. A light show. Wychovski was sure he had a temperature.

The old man leaned back to inspect what he had written and with slow dignity put the top back on his marker and returned it to his pocket.

Wychovski looked at what the old man had written: "Embrace Infinity."

"Sometimes I write, 'Accept Infinity,'" the old man explained, putting his glasses back in his pocket. "Depends on the weather, how I'm feeling, and who I'm writing for."

Maybe Wychovski could crawl to another doorway. He considered it, but the rain, anticipating his possible move, beat down even harder.

"When I was a boy," the old man said, looking at the traffic as it passed, "I was afraid of the infinite. I was supposed to be in awe, but I was just flat-out scared. I liked the sky, the stars, but one of my worst experiences when I was about ten was going to the Adler Planetarium on a school field trip. In that dark room, looking up at the ceiling, moving deep into space, hearing that voice, deep, you know, saying it went on forever. You understand?"

Wychovski didn't understand. He didn't want to understand. He considered singing a song inside his head to block out the man whose voice was raised so his alcove partner could hear him over the onslaught of nature.

"Grew up afraid to fall asleep in big rooms. Had this dream where the room kept getting bigger, I kept getting smaller. Youngest of seven children. Slept in a bed with three brothers. They all dreamed of someday living alone. I felt comfortable when I was in that small bed in that small room with a body on both sides."

The man let out a sigh. From the corner of his eye Wychovski could see that the man was shaking his head and smiling.

"Grew up," the old man said. "Read a lot. Went to school. Right through. University of Illinois. English literature. Taught at Marshall High School. You go to college?"

"No," said Wychovski.

"Well, one day I read this book. Picked it up at a used book store for a quarter. Ragged trade paperback with the cover coming off. Something about the title. *One*. That was what it was called. Turned out to be about Hindu and Buddhist myths and such. One story hit me. Right away. Right through my eyes, deep into my head. I was brought up storefront Baptist. Never believed it. Didn't like dressing up. But that book. That story. Man, a king, was afraid of the same thing I was, that he was a piece of nothing on a piece of nothing, that both he and the piece he was on would be around for no time at all. You with me?"

"Where the hell would I go?" asked Wychovski.

"You look sick. Want me to help you get to a hospital?"

"No."

"Where was I? Oh, this king started to reincarnate. Always something smaller. First a dog. Then a cat. Then a rat. Then a cockroach. Then a flea. He never made it to virus, or maybe he did. But each time he got smaller, he felt more like he belonged, like not being the king or a mouse or anything wasn't all that important. Hell, wasn't important at all. Well, eventually he became a simple cell, though that's not what the book called it. He just became part of everything. The whole universe. He was content. Buddhists call it Nirvana."

"I know," said Wychovski.

"Well, I read that story, and I wasn't scared of the universe anymore. I could sleep outside. Strange thing is that after I read that story I slept better, no bad dream, never. Don't know the connection, but I know there's one. We're all scared of something. Dying mostly. Being nothing. Or, put it another way, not being something."

Enough. Wychovski wanted the old man to get the hell out of his corner of hell.

"I figure I know what you're scared of," said the old man.

"What's that?" asked Wychovski, his teeth chattering.

"A man in a leather coat carrying a suitcase in one hand and a shotgun under that coat."

Wychovski look at the old man, who tilted his head down and looked at him as if he were looking over the glasses he was no longer wearing.

"Heard it in the neighborhood," said the old man. "Big news of the day. White man crashes his big new car into a store three, four blocks that way, gets out. Black man gets out after him, shoots at him, and the white man goes running."

"And you figure the white man is me?"

"And the black man is the one who's coming down the street over there with the suitcase and the shotgun under his leather jacket."

Wychovski jerked his head around and looked into the downpour. Dickerson was about a block away, dim, coming through the darkness and thunder, moving steady, a slight limp.

"Here," said Wychovski, forcing himself to his feet and reaching into his pocket.

The old man got up and helped Wychovski to his feet. From deep in his pocket Wychovski pulled out a small golden lizard. He handed it to the old man.

"Salamander," said the old man, examining the golden lizard. "Good luck sign."

The rain was stopping, definitely stopping. The thunder was far away. It was still raining but not as hard. If he hadn't seen him before, Dickerson definitely saw him now. He stopped for an instant, his head aimed directly at Wychovski.

"Want me to stay and die with you?" the old man said.

"You're fuckin' nuts."

"I'm old, dying of cancer, a bad heart, and who knows what else. Might not be a bad way to go, and you'd have someone next to you so you wouldn't be so scared."

Agony weighed him down, but there was something left. Not much, but something. Wychovski began to stagger toward the bridge.

The old man put the salamander in his green raincoat pocket and started back across the street.

There was no one Wychovski could ask for help. He knew cops. They had decided by now that he had killed one of them. They would probably shoot him just as surely as Dickerson would.

He slogged his way so slowly, so heavy, so tired. The rain had stopped now. The rivers in the gutters on both sides of the street ran swiftly. He stepped in sidewalk pools, socks heavy, water sloshing in his shoes.

He didn't look back. The bridge. If he could make it to the bridge, he could jump in. Dickerson would take a shot at him, but he would have a chance. He still clung to that, a chance. He tried to move faster.

The cop in the doorway held out his hand. Nestled in his palm were a small golden porcupine and another animal Lieberman couldn't identify.

"I think it's a mongoose," said Hanrahan.

Lieberman looked at the Lexus, or what was left of it.

"They got out," said the young uniformed cop with a mustache that made him look a few weeks older than his twenty-four years. "Black guy shot and took off after the white guy. Lots of witnesses. About an hour ago. Woman who lives two blocks that way and one block over gave me this one."

He pulled another little golden animal from his pocket. Lieberman took the tiny bird.

"One more," said the young cop, a magician in blue, going back into his pocket, this time pulling out a golden rabbit. "Got it from a guy who has a little store right down the street."

"Honest citizens," said Hanrahan.

"Who knows how many our Hansel has given out?" asked Lieberman.

The rain had stopped. People were coming back on the street to watch the show. A passing car almost hit a woman carrying a baby, honked his horn, and kept on going.

"Pardon me," a voice came from Lieberman's side.

He turned to see a little black man in a green raincoat. The man had a white beard and steady brown eyes.

"Mine is a salamander."

He held his palm open, revealing the treasure to the police.

"I believe the man who gave it to me is about to be shot," the old man said. "That way. By the bridge."

The uniformed cop motioned at his partner, who was trying to keep the small crowd back. They ran for their patrol car. Lieberman and Hanrahan moved to their unmarked car. Both cars sped off in the direction the old man had pointed to, leaving him alone, hand out, palm up, salamander resting on it. The old man pocketed the golden animal and moved on.

Wychovski was almost at the bridge. A few more feet. He didn't want to look back. Dickerson couldn't be far behind. He expected the sting of the pellets into his back and head, penetrating his skull, lungs, liver, every organ. He couldn't go over the side yet. Below him was the embankment and pieces of concrete, wood, broken bottles. A few more feet.

Cars passed. Their lights were still on, though the sun had suddenly come through the clouds. Bright day.

His sense of horror was worse than in the rainy darkness.

He had one leg over the railing when he looked back and saw Dickerson about twenty feet away.

"There are witnesses all around," said Wychovski.

"Chance I'll have to take," said Dickerson.

"My prints aren't on that gun. Yours are. The gun that killed Walter." Dickerson shook his head and laughed.

Poe, Wychovski remembered. He remembered the lines he had memorized in his cell. Poe always sounded good. Sometimes he gave a chill.

"'And as the Demon made an end of his story, he fell back within the cavity of the tomb and laughed,'" Wychovski said to himself. "'And I could not laugh with the Demon, and he cursed me because I could not laugh.'"

Dickerson took a step closer.

"I took it from you when you crashed the car after taking me hostage. I came looking for you. You killed my boss. You're a cop killer. You've got a gun. I'll catch a little shit, but I'll be a hero."

"I don't have a gun," said Wychovski.

"You will after I blow your ass away," he said. "I've got one for you, your Glock."

"You'll lose everything," said Wychovski.

"Didn't have to be this way," Dickerson said. "But I'll take what I can get. I'll take over Walter's business and turn in what you stole. Wouldn't be surprised if I did get a medal. You got a name?"

"Wychovski, George Wychovski. You?"

"Dickerson, Robert."

Dickerson raised his shotgun. Cars zipped past. Wychovski could see eyes turn toward the scene, then turn away as the cars moved even faster. Wychovski heard them first and saw them first. The patrol car and the unmarked car heading toward them. The patrol car. Both cars were flashing their red lights. The patrol car turned on its siren.

Wychovski leaned over the railing. He knew he didn't have the strength to climb over. As he started to go over, Dickerson fired. A pepper of pellets drilled into the falling man's legs. Hot pain like the long deep scratches of a dozen cats.

He fell. But it didn't feel as if he were falling. He could see the sky. He had the sensation of rising. Embracing the infinite. Accepting the infinite. The sensation lasted about a second. He hit the dirty water hard. His breath escaped, and he began to sink. His clothes weighed him down, and he couldn't move his legs. They had no feeling. He flayed with his arms but kept going down.

The two cars stopped at the end of the bridge. The uniformed cops got out of their vehicle and leveled their weapons from behind their open doors. Lieberman and Hanrahan did the same.

"Put it down slowly," called Lieberman.

Dickerson put down the suitcase and the shotgun.

"Now, clasp your hands behind your head and look right at me."

Dickerson obeyed, and Hanrahan dashed toward the low fence at the end of the bridge. He scrambled over it and slid down the embankment, tearing his pants, scratching his palms. He almost slid into the rushing river but stopped at the wooden pilings.

Hanrahan caught his breath and looked toward the water.

Wychovski had been carried more than thirty feet away. Hanrahan searched for some sign as he took off his jacket and holster and kicked off his shoes. He searched. Nothing.

Wychovski was still struggling. He frantically pulled watches out of his pocket, jettisoned whatever he had in his pockets, tried to hold his breath. He couldn't, however, fish out the last of the golden animals. He gave up trying for them. He gave up trying for anything, closed his eyes, and let the filthy water into his mouth.

Noah's ark was sinking. The end of the world had come. The animals went down not two by two but one by one. He embraced the infinite. What choice did he have?

13

When Lieberman got home just before seven, he took off his shoes, put them in the front closet, and looked over at his granddaughter. Before coming home he had stopped at the drugstore on Touhy and California to make a phone call. He didn't want to use his cell phone, and he didn't want to make the call from home. He had reached Emiliano "El Perro" Del Sol and explained what he wanted.

"*Por supuesto, Viejo.* Now you owe me another one."

"No," Lieberman had said. "I think you still owe me about five or six, but I'm not keeping count."

El Perro had laughed and said, "*Tan loco, mi amigo.*" Then he hung up, and Lieberman had gone home.

Melisa was sitting in the living room reading a book and watching television at the same time. Well, she wasn't actually sitting. She was sprawled on her back with one leg on the seat of his leather armchair and the other on the floor. She was watching something with a laugh track. From her position, she was watching it upside down.

"Grandpa," she said, scrambling to a sitting position. "They're coming."

"Who?"

"The Pink Cheek sisters," Melisa said, holding the book open on her lap.

"Pinchuk," Lieberman corrected, walking into the room.

"I know," Melisa said. "I'm being funny."

"They do have pink cheeks," Lieberman conceded, moving toward her with his arms open.

The girl placed the book facedown on the floor and moved into her grandfather's arms.

With Lisa, his daughter, it had never really been like this. Lisa had read. Lisa had seldom watched television. Lisa was not a hugger. Lisa had called him "Abe," not "Pop" or "Dad" or "Father" or "Abba."

His granddaughter's face was pressed against his chest, her arms tight around his waist.

"What are you reading?" he asked.

"One of your books," she said.

"Which one?" Abe asked, looking into the brightly lit dining room, which was set up for four people, which meant Rose and Esther were not joining them for dinner, just for dessert and harassment. No, that wasn't fair. They were there to help, and Lieberman was ultimately grateful for their assistance. He had simply had a long tough day, and, if he were right, tomorrow would be even harder.

They had taken Dickerson in, booked him on everything from murder, grand theft auto, grand theft, carrying a loaded shotgun, firing said shotgun on a city street, and leaving the scene of an accident, to obstructing traffic. There would be no chance of bail on this one.

Wychovski's body had been recovered more than a mile from where he had gone into the river. Kearney had called the widow of the dead jeweler and the widow of the dead cop. Alan Kearney had been taking on such calls for more than a year. Hanrahan and Lieberman agreed that he was doing some kind of psychological penance or maybe finding some solace in comforting people who had even sadder stories than he did. Though he wasn't responsible, Kearney carried the guilt of his own partner's death, a death that ended Kearney's promising future.

"I'm reading *War and Peace*," she said, stepping back to look up at him with a pleased grin.

"You understand it?"

"Not really," she said. "Too many people with Russian names. Too many big words. It's a challenge. It was the fattest book you had.

I wanted to read the fattest. That one or the unabridged copy of Stephen King's *The Stand*."

"Unabridged," said Lieberman. "I suggest you put off the challenge of both books for a few years."

"Good. I'll read one of the Harry Potters again."

"Better," said Abe. "Where's your grandmother?"

"In your room."

"Barry?"

"In his room, working on his Torah portion," she said, moving into his chair. Her feet dangled. She bounced.

"You have no homework?"

"Did it. Easy," she said. "I told you, my school underestimates us."

"That's bad," he said.

"No, I like it that way."

"I see your point."

Lieberman walked through the living room to the bedroom door and stepped in. He closed the door behind him. Bess was wearing a blue robe and drying her hair with a bath towel.

"The sisters are coming," she said, as he removed his jacket, took off his holster and gun, and locked them in the drawer next to the bed with the key he wore around his neck.

Only then was she ready to meet him for a kiss. Bess was a good kisser. She felt after-shower warm and smelled like some flower he couldn't place.

"News of the day," she said. "Lisa and Howard will pay for the flowers at the bar mitzvah, the flowers on the *bemah*, and the ones for the Oneg on Friday and the Kiddush on Saturday afternoon."

"Good news," said Lieberman.

"Todd and his wife are definitely not coming," she said, rubbing her hair, which was still quite naturally dark and shiny.

"Barry know?"

"Yes. He's relieved."

"More good news," Lieberman said, sitting on the bed and removing his wet socks.

"Something's on your mind," Bess said.

"The Pinchuks are coming."

"That's not it," she said, still drying her hair but keeping her eyes on him.

"We found the man who killed the policeman in Skokie," he said.

Dead policemen were not one of Bess's favorite subjects.

"He drowned in the Chicago River," he said. "It'll be on the news. We can watch at ten."

"There's something else, Abe. I've got dinner on. I've got to get us fed before Rose and Esther get here. Tell me, or you know I'll keep after you till you do."

"Something I have to do tomorrow, maybe," he said. "Something I hope I'm wrong about. I'll tell you when I know."

"For now, I'll accept that if you don't brood," she said, moving toward the closet and dropping the towel onto the chair in the corner.

"Brooding is over."

"Dinner is in twenty minutes."

"And?"

"Baked chicken with sweet potatoes."

"Skinless?" he asked, wiggling his toes.

"Skinless," she called from the closet where she was pulling out a solid blue dress. "Thai peanut sauce. Low cholesterol sugar-free chocolate pudding for dessert. I plan to keep you alive, Avrum, in spite of yourself. Give me a hand."

"With the dress or my diet?" he asked.

"Both," she said.

A minute or so later Lieberman climbed the narrow stairway. He could hear his grandson's voice in his room. Barry's voice hadn't changed yet.

Lieberman could not understand Hebrew, but he knew Barry was working on his portions for the bar mitzvah. Barry would have to read a section of the Torah in Hebrew, the section for that Sabbath weekend. He would not only have to read it but to chant it with the proper traditional trope. The Torah is the first five books of the Holy Scriptures. Each year Jews read the Torah through at services from start to finish, and when they get to the end they have a celebration holiday, Simchas Torah, and immediately begin again.

In addition to chanting from the Torah, Barry would have a designated chanted reading from the Haftorah, that part of the Scriptures that comes after the Torah. Barry's reading was from Ecclesiastes.

"Come in," Barry called, when Lieberman knocked.

Lieberman found his grandson seated in front of his computer. On the screen was whatever he had been working on in Hebrew letters.

Melisa looked like her mother. Barry looked like his father, which meant he looked nothing like Lieberman. Barry was as tall as his grandfather and broader. He had escaped the Lieberman downcast face and not been blessed with Bess's beauty, but he was a good-looking boy who could have passed for a Swede or a Norwegian.

Lieberman smiled. It wasn't much of a smile, but it wasn't sardonic, resigned, or cynical. It reflected his sincere joy in his grandson.

"Dinner ready?" Barry asked.

"No," said Lieberman, moving to the wooden chair next to Barry. "We've got twenty minutes. Can you check some things for me on the Internet?"

"Police business?" Barry asked seriously.

"Some of it," Lieberman conceded. "Some of it temple business."

Barry pushed some buttons and moved the computer mouse.

"What do you need?"

"Can you get old newspaper articles on the Internet?"

"A lot."

"See what you can find on me," said Lieberman. "Then see if you can get me some office phone numbers for Joseph Lieberman. The one I've got is wrong."

"The senator?"

"Yes."

Barry had already been told that Joe Lieberman wasn't a relative, but he liked the idea that the senator and almost vice president had made the family name well known and acceptable and even a little famous.

It didn't take Barry twenty minutes to find both of the things that his grandfather had asked for. He printed out a few of the documents, finishing just as Melisa came through the door after knocking but not waiting to be invited in.

"Dinner," she said.

She left the room, door open, and went down the stairs. Lieberman took the sheets of paper. He had hoped he had been wrong, but the sheets in his hand, while they did not prove him right, certainly made his theory a real possibility.

When Hanrahan got to his house, the dog was sitting on the porch, waiting.

Hanrahan grinned. He was an ugly mutt, a mongrel, big, white, and gray, shaggy. He was not Hanrahan's dog. He didn't even have a name. Lieberman and Hanrahan had saved him from the Humane Society. The dog was not young. He had been particularly wary of people, but Lieberman and his partner had treated him with dignity in the alley where a man had been murdered, and Hanrahan had reluctantly taken him home.

The dog now had a collar on which was written simply "Dog" and Hanrahan's address. The dog was free to roam outside or come in the house and be fed or sleep. Sometimes Hanrahan didn't see him for days. Sometimes he would come every day for a week or more.

"Well," Hanrahan said, opening the door. "You don't seem to have any new wounds or scars. I've got a few."

The dog listened intently as they went through the door.

"Tore my legs some and cut my hands," Hanrahan said, holding his hands out.

The dog sniffed at his palms.

"It's a long story," Hanrahan said, taking off his shoes and putting them on the mat near the door. "Maybe I'll tell you later if I don't start thinking I'm going a little nuts talking to a canine."

The furnishings in the small two-story house were old but clean. The house was immaculate. Bill Hanrahan kept it that way. At first he had done it in the hope that his wife, Maureen, would return someday and find that he had kept it as clean as she had and as ready for her return as he was. He had driven her away with his drinking. She hadn't had much choice other than risk the wrath of God or be a good Catholic wife and stand by him, watching her life pass and having no effect on her husband. While they had made peace with each other, Hanrahan was sure his former wife would never fully forgive him for making her go against the Church.

Hanrahan had joined AA, even returned to the Church himself, but it had been too late. Both of their grown sons had sided with their mother. They had witnessed the truth. Maureen had divorced him even though the Church had made it clear that there would be no annulment granted. Even then Hanrahan had hoped she would change her mind.

He had given up hoping three years ago and been drinking again when he met Iris at the Black Moon while he was watching an apartment building. He had been drunk on duty. Should have lost his badge, but Lieberman had covered for him and, for reasons he still didn't understand, the beautiful Chinese woman who waited on him sensed something in him that he didn't sense himself.

Now he was straight and sober, back in the Church, and about to be married. He would have said all this to the dog as he filled the big yellow bowl in the kitchen with Dog Chow, but the dog had already heard it more than once. The plan for the evening was simple. Call Iris. See if there were any last-minute changes or needs for the wedding, eat a cold leftover meat loaf sandwich with a Coke, take off his clothes, have a bath, clean his wounds, and go to bed early.

The doorbell rang when he opened the refrigerator.

Hanrahan had no children in his house, and there was no danger of the dog getting his paws on his guns and firing one of them. Hanrahan kept several weapons nearby. He had reasons. He had killed one intruder to the house a few years ago, a lunatic he had lured there for the express purpose of ridding the world of him and saving the madman's wife and small son from being his next victims. Twice, Laio Woo had come to the house to try to persuade him to give up his relationship with Iris. One of those times Woo had been in the house with two of his men in the kitchen when

Hanrahan got home. One time Woo had come to the door with his men to warn him about his relationship with Iris. The next time Woo or a dozen of his men came to the door, he might not be coming to do any talking.

Hanrahan had his weapon in his right hand behind his back when he stood to the side of the door and asked, "Who is it?"

"Morales," the voice came. "El Perro sent me."

Hanrahan opened the door and backed away. In front of him stood a young man in a blue blazer, navy slacks, white shirt, and red tie. He was tall, reasonably good-looking, and holding his hands together in front of him waist high.

Behind him Hanrahan could hear the dog growling softly.

"Mother and father's anniversary," the young man explained, seeing Hanrahan examine his clothes. Then his eyes turned to the dog. "Thirty-eight years."

"Congratulations," Hanrahan said. "To what do I owe the pleasure."

"Can I come in?" the young man asked.

"It's a warm enough night," said Hanrahan. "We can talk here. Besides, the dog doesn't like visitors."

"Okay. Let's keep the dog happy."

"You alone?"

"Car down the street," the young man said, looking over his shoulder.

The young man had no accent at all. Hanrahan had never met a Tentaculo who didn't have an accent either brought with him from Puerto Rico, Mexico, Cuba, or someplace else or acquired in the ghettos of Chicago where Spanish was the first language. It wasn't unusual to come across a young boy or girl who spoke no English even though they had been born in the city.

"And what can I do for you, Morales?"

"For me? Nothing. It's what El Perro is doing for you."

Hanrahan waited.

"That Chinese guy this morning. El Perro did some checking. He works for Woo the Chink. Woo the Chink doesn't like you."

"I'm aware of that fact," said Hanrahan.

"You're marrying a chink woman," Morales said.

"A Chinese woman," Hanrahan corrected.

"Right. Sorry. Looks like Woo doesn't want you marrying her."

"So?"

"So, we're going to have some guys sort of watching out for you. They'll be cruising tonight or parked or strolling. They'll be there till you get married. El Perro figures after you're married, Woo will realize he's lost and back off."

"That's the way El Perro figures?"

Morales shrugged. The dog was growling louder now.

"He just wanted me to tell you so you don't spot our guys and shoot them or arrest them or something."

"El Perro doesn't like me," said Hanrahan.

"He doesn't like you a lot," said Morales with a smile. "But *El Viejo* is his friend. You're *El Viejo*'s partner."

"What if I tell you I don't want any protection?"

"I'm supposed to tell you you're getting it anyway and it won't cost you a dollar. You got a gun behind your back and a mean dog behind you, but they don't stop maybe three or four chinks with automatic weapons."

"And what does El Perro want in exchange?"

"Nothing," said Morales, looking at his watch. "They offended him by coming into his territory. Hey, look. I've got to go. You do what you want. I delivered my message."

"Anything else?" asked Hanrahan.

"Yeah, you look like shit. Dog go after you?"

"Long story," Hanrahan said, "and I already told it to the dog."

Morales sauntered down the steps, and Hanrahan closed the door.

He locked the door and moved back to the kitchen. The dog remained at the front door in a crouch, growling softly.

"He's gone," said Hanrahan. "How'd you like to try some meat loaf?"

The dog followed him into the kitchen. Hanrahan took out the plate, removed the layer of Saran Wrap, cut off a chunk of meat loaf for himself and one for the dog. He threw the dog's into the air. The dog's piece was devoured before it hit the floor.

Z and Eddie celebrated by having two Big Macs each and two bottles of beer in Eddie's trailer. Z's father had come to the police station with a briefcase full of papers he had placed on the desk of Alan Kearney. Neither Z nor Eddie had been present.

There wasn't enough to hold either of them, and Kearney knew that there would be a pretty good case for false arrest if he didn't let them go. It wasn't worth the effort. He knew where to find them.

"They're material witnesses," Kearney had said, knowing he would fall back but wanting some promise or commitment on the record and in his notes.

"They will both be available to a grand jury and for trial," Andrew Zembinsky had said. "And I understand that the young man who committed the murder has confessed, confirming what my clients have told you."

"He confessed," said Kearney, sitting back while the lawyer stood.

What Kearney failed to say was that the confession was useless. He could hold Franzen, but even a shiny new public defender could get him off on minimum or low bail. Why not let these two walk thinking they were clear? They would have no reason to run, and Lieberman and Hanrahan could keep digging, harassing.

"I'll release them," Kearney said, patting the stack of papers Andrew Zembinsky had placed on his desk. "You have them ready to testify."

"I will," said Zembinsky, snapping his briefcase shut.

Kearney looked at the man standing on the other side of his desk. Zembinsky was a solid man in a dark suit that showed wrinkled signs of his having been through a long day. His dark hair could have used a comb, and his face was at four o'clock on the shave scale. He wore a tie but it was knotted loosely. The man looked bone tired.

"Can I tell you something?" Zembinsky said. "Off the record?"

"Yes as long as it's nothing that could incriminate any of them," Kearney answered, folding his hands on his desk, reminding himself of Father Gellen when Alan Kearney had come to him after Kearney's world had fallen apart.

"I don't like my son," the man said, shaking his head and smiling painfully. "Haven't liked him for the past four or five years. My wife and I haven't raised him badly. Or maybe we have. I don't think so. He wasn't particularly spoiled or punished. Somehow he gradually became the kind of kid parents want their kids to stay away from. You have any kids?"

"No," said Kearney.

"I'll give him one thing," Zembinsky said. "Through all the crap he has been into, he's never asked for my help. I wouldn't be here now if it wasn't for my wife. I don't think she has any more love for Melvin than I do, but she feels a lot more guilt. She's not sure why. My son is going to walk out of here, not come home, not call his mother, and not thank me."

"Some kids are just born that way," said Kearney. "Nothing much you can do to stop it. My sister was like that. But my father spoiled her. He was a cop."

Kearney didn't know what his father having been a cop had to do with his sister's history of defiance, but Kearney somehow felt the connection.

Zembinsky reached out his hand and Kearney stood to shake it. The lawyer's grip was firm but not trying to prove anything.

"Thanks for listening," said Zembinsky.

"My job," answered Kearney.

And the lawyer left quickly.

Z and Eddie were unaware of the conversation. All Z knew was that his father had gotten him out without being asked. He owed neither of his parents thanks.

"No one asked to be born," he said, holding his beer bottle up for a toast.

Eddie clinked his bottle up to meet Z's.

"Nobody asked," he said.

There was a knock at the door.

"Gina," Eddie guessed. "You feel like Gina tonight?"

"No," said Z. "If she brought her black friend, what's her name?"

"Matty," said Eddie, moving toward the door, bottle in one hand, leering back at Z.

"Then it's different," said Z. "If not, tell her you just got tested for HIV and you're waiting for the results."

"I'll tell her you got tested, and you're the one waiting for the results."

Z's head hurt like a son of a bitch. Even if Matty did come through the door, he doubted that he could do anything about it. The beer wasn't helping. Pain suddenly shot through the side of his head away from the stitched wound.

As Eddie opened the door, Z felt like saying he thought he should go back to the hospital.

The door blocked Z's view. Eddie said nothing. There was no greeting from Gina or whoever was there.

"Who is it?" Z called, putting down the beer bottle, feeling definitely sick to his stomach.

The door pushed open all the way, revealing Jamie Franzen. Jamie stood with his feet apart, a baseball bat in his right hand.

"Join the party," Eddie said carefully. "We're celebrating. They let us all out. We're clear."

Z didn't like this, didn't like the dull, distant look on Jamie's face. What the hell was Jamie doing out? He had confessed. Eddie and Z were going to testify. And what the hell was he doing with that bat?

"They didn't believe me," Jamie said, still standing in the door.

"Didn't believe what?" asked Eddie nervously.

"Didn't believe I killed Sokol. You both turned me in, but they didn't believe me. I told them I did it. They didn't believe me. I stood up for you."

"We knew they'd let you out," said Z, closing his eyes. He thought he tasted blood in his mouth. "We were celebrating, waiting for you. Have a beer."

Eddie backed away, eyes on the bat.

"Wanna know what I see?" asked Jamie. "I see two beers and two empty Big Mac boxes. You didn't know they were letting me out."

"We thought they were letting you out in the morning," Eddie tried.

"You killed that Sokol," Jamie said. "You killed him, and when I told you I did it to show off to you, make you think I had balls, you turned me in."

"We didn't kill him," Z said, sitting back on the couch. "We thought you did. We believed you."

"And you turned me in. I don't believe your lying mouth," Jamie said calmly. "I don't want you anymore."

"Sorry you feel that way," Eddie said, looking to Z for help. Z was the talker. He needed Z's mouth, but Z looked like shit. His eyes were dancing.

Jamie stepped in and swung the bat at Eddie. The blow cracked Eddie's arm. Z could hear it, could hear Eddie scream in pain as Jamie moved across the room. Z could see Eddie running out the door.

He tried to get up.

"Stop a second," Z tried, shaking his head. "We can talk. I can explain."

Jamie brought the bat down with all his might on Z's head as the seated young man tried to stand up. The bat against Z's skull made the sound of a hammer hitting a coconut. That's what Z thought. That was the last thing he thought. The coconut. The hammer. He must have been seven or eight. His father and he had drained the coconut of cloudy milk and they had taken turns smashing at it as it skittered across the concrete floor of the garage. They had chased it like a trapped animal, taking turns, laughing, having a good time.

If he lived, he'd describe it that way to his father.

But he didn't live.

14

The Hollywood Linen Shop was in the Old Orchard Shopping Center in Skokie off of Skokie Boulevard. It was a sprawling mall of midscale and upscale stores and a few restaurants. It had been one of the first malls in the area and had undergone frequent changes. Shops came and went. New ideas were tried. One place tried to specialize in chocolate-covered pretzels and twenty flavors of popcorn. It lasted almost a year.

But the Hollywood Linen Shop had been in the same location on the south end of the mall for almost thirty years.

Lieberman had the warrant in his pocket. He preferred not to use it and probably wouldn't have to, but it didn't hurt to have it.

Lieberman and Hanrahan had met at the T&L just before eight in the morning before going into the Clark Street Station to pick up the warrants.

"Abe tells me it's the big day," Maish had said, serving them coffee at their regular booth.

"The big day," Hanrahan had agreed.

"I'll have the food at Abe's house all set up after the wedding. Your favorites."

"Won't be many people," said Hanrahan. "We're keeping it small."

"Make it bigger," said Maish, hovering over the table. "Terrell's got a special today. Fried kosher salami and grilled onion on a toasted bagel."

"I'll take it," said Hanrahan.

"Should I even bother to second the motion," asked Abe, "or am I going to be consigned a bowl of oatmeal?"

"Exception today," said Maish. "Special occasion. In honor of your partner's wedding. But no butter. If I catch you putting butter or jelly on the sandwich, I break your arm."

"I can live with a broken arm," said Lieberman. "Can you take my order, Maish?" a voice called behind them.

The T&L breakfast crowd was rolling in. Maish waited the tables himself and handled the cash register. He was dumpy, overweight, and, like his brother, looked a decade older than he was, but when he moved inside the T&L he had the full-court-press speed and efficiency he had displayed for three undefeated seasons back at Marshall High.

Maish turned to the Alter Cocker table, where Al Bloombach, Sy Weintraub, and Howie Chen sat waiting. It had been Bloombach who had called out to Maish.

"The usual?" asked Maish over the talking of the nine other customers on the counter stools, in the booths, and at the tables.

"I'm living dangerously," called Bloombach. "I'll have the special. Extra salami."

Howie and Sy said nothing. Sy was still in his sweatsuit. He was somewhere in his eighties, but he ran every day, rain or shine. In the winter he ran laps around the gym at the Bernard Horwich Jewish Community Center. He didn't jog. He ran, not fast, but there was no doubt it was running. His "usual" was decaf coffee, two eggs scrambled, orange juice, and a toasted bialy. He would have no part of bagels. He was a loyal bialy man. Howie's usual was a lox omelette.

"See the paper?" Bloombach said, holding the *Sun Times* up and open to an inner page. "You're famous again."

Lieberman had seen the paper at home. He had been up at five to take it from the front steps and retire with it to the kitchen, where he heated coffee and had time to read before he woke Bess and the kids.

It had been a good night for Lieberman. Four hours sleep, maybe a little more. He had soaked in the tub till his thin body gave up and wrinkled. He had added hot water four or five times while he read a book about Bruno Bettelheim. He didn't even bother to go to bed till a little after midnight. When he awoke a few minutes before five, he got up as quietly as he could. Sometimes he simply lay there next to Bess, waiting for first light. He had no illusions about getting back to sleep.

He had dreamt, but he didn't remember his dream or dreams, only that they had been there. All in all it had been a better than average night.

The article was small, five paragraphs buried on page eight. It told about the incident on the bridge, the bizarre death of the cop killer, and it speculated on the connection to the death of the jeweler and the antiques dealer. Lieberman's name and Hanrahan's were in the article.

"Fame is fleeting," said Sy Weintraub.

Howie and Al looked at the old man. Sy Weintraub seldom spoke at the Cockers' table and when he did people listened.

"Fame is fleeting?" said Bloombach. "I'll write that one down so I don't forget to tell Rosen when he gets here. You get that from one of Howie's fortune cookies?"

"Everything is fleeting," Weintraub said seriously, ignoring Bloombach's attempt at wit.

"I'll drink to that," said Howie.

The three Alter Cockers raised their coffee mugs. So did Lieberman, Hanrahan, and some of the patrons who had heard the words of wisdom.

"*La Chaim*," said Sarah Bass, who more than filled the stool on which she sat at the counter. Sarah was seventy-three, an honorary Alter Cocker who was allowed minimal participation in the group of old men, who had an unalterable and unofficial rule that only men could sit at the table and that during the morning hours wives were not permitted in the T&L. This was fine with the wives. There had been one exception. Sol Mandelbaum's wife Rose had come one morning five years earlier and sat at the counter drinking tea and tearing with her teeth at an egg bagel with cream cheese.

Rose was angry with Sol. No one knew why. Neither Sol nor

Rose talked about it. She simply sat there, ate, drank, and glared. There had been no conversation at the Alter Cocker table that morning. Sol Mandelbaum had left after a quick cup of coffee. He left his bagel with cream cheese untouched.

Rose never returned to the counter but Sol, a retired insurance salesman, had suffered the slings and arrows of the table for more than two years, acquiring the nickname "the Henpeck Man."

Abe and Bill ate in silence. Bustling from customer to customer, Maish kept an eye on his brother to be sure he wasn't shmeering cream cheese or grape jelly.

"The Tentaculos can't watch me forever, Rabbi," Hanrahan had said.

"Woo is a realist," said Lieberman.

"Woo is one angry, tough old bastard is what he is," said Hanrahan.

"You're not changing your mind again?" asked Lieberman, savoring his treat with small bites that he chewed slowly.

"Nope. It's on. I'm just saying . . ."

Hanrahan had hesitated.

"Maybe I should take early retirement and Iris and I should pack up and move away."

"It's an option," said Lieberman. "But that's not what you have in mind."

"After the wedding, I'm going to talk to Woo again," said Hanrahan.

"About what?"

"Survival and revenge," said Hanrahan. "He understands them."

"He specializes in them," said Lieberman. "But it's worth a try."

"No more Tentaculos," said Hanrahan. "We're not going to live under siege."

"I'll tell El Perro," said Lieberman. "Anything else for the wedding planner?"

"No."

"Then let's go."

Ten minutes later they had picked up their warrants from Kearney, who, again, looked as if he had spent the night in his office. His face was shaved. He wore a clean shirt, but he still had on the same slacks and jacket as the day before.

"Melvin Zembinsky is dead," Kearney had greeted them soberly. "Franzen beat his head in and broke Denenberg's arm. A reporter from WBBM picked it up, did some checking, talked to Denenberg, called me asking why a confessed murderer had been let loose to kill again. I told him I'd check with the chief and get back to him. Had five calls since from the newspapers and television. You don't talk to reporters on this one."

Lieberman and Hanrahan agreed.

"Franzen is in holding," Kearney said, going to his desk and picking up a coffee mug. He looked at the liquid, changed his mind, and put the cup back down. "He wants to talk, to confess. We've got a legal in there with him."

Kearney didn't have to say that the situation looked bad. These were white kids from good families. Zembinsky's father might sue the city, but Kearney had the feeling that he wouldn't. If they had been black kids, there wouldn't have been a story here. The papers would have made a little check mark next to the police report and assumed a dumb-ass fight over drugs, an affront, too much to drink. But white kids from decent families in a story like this were news.

Alan Kearney was once again going to take some heat. He had spoken to Terry Banovich downtown and the chiefs assistant had cautiously suggested that the now-dead Melvin Zembinsky, with or without Denenberg, had killed Sokol and tried to frame Franzen, who in a state of rage had effectively closed the case.

Kearney could probably get Denenberg to agree to dump the murder on his dead friend. The public defender could possibly be maneuvered to help Jamie Franzen remember Z's confessing the murder in exchange for a manslaughter plea. The state attorney might offer Franzen a deal he couldn't refuse in exchange for a lie. Or maybe it was true. Kearney didn't know. Lieberman was given the two warrants. They might turn up an even more sensational answer, might save Kearney's ass to fry another day.

And so Abe Lieberman and Bill Hanrahan, on a slightly overcast and cool May morning, entered the Hollywood Linen Shop and introduced themselves, showing their badges to a well-groomed woman in her thirties with short blonde hair, a clean, clear face, and thin lips she kept together to keep them from trembling.

"We'd like to see Mr. Sokol's books," said Lieberman.

"Why?" the woman asked.

"Well Miss . . ." Lieberman began.

"Mrs., Mrs. Althea Glide."

"It's routine," said Hanrahan.

Althea Glick looked confused. There were no customers in the store, which had opened only minutes before.

"I thought about closing today," she said, looking around at the tables and shelves of merchandise. "But . . . I wasn't sure what would be right."

"Opening is right," Lieberman said.

The shop smelled good, faintly flowery, completely clean.

"Life goes on," Althea Glick said. "Is that it?"

"Something like that," said Lieberman. "How's business been?"

"Business? The shop? We had a slight downturn last quarter, but we're back up. The other two Hollywood shops are about the same. I don't . . ."

"The company is losing money," Hanrahan said.

"The company is not losing money," Althea Glick said with a flash of pride. "We had a very good last year and overall a good one this year. Hollywood Linen is very healthy financially. Arnold, Mr. Sokol, has been talking about opening another store in Wheeling."

Lieberman and Hanrahan glanced at each other.

"The books . . ." Lieberman began.

". . . will confirm what I've just told you. Please follow me. There really are no books. Everything is on the computer, but I'll access whatever you need."

Althea Glick was going to protect her dead boss's reputation. No warrant was needed.

Twenty minutes later the detectives left the shop with thirty printed sheets inside a manila folder. There were seven customers, all women, in the shop when they left.

The baby, about three months old, was on his back in one of those bouncing seats. He was reaching for a dangling plastic ball in front of him. Once in a while he managed to make contact. The rattle of the ball seemed to startle him.

Lieberman and Hanrahan sat drinking their third cups of coffee of the morning. They sat across from Mary Sokol.

"Matthew is in school," she said, reaching over to touch the corner of the baby's mouth with a clean tissue.

They had needed no warrant here either. Mary Sokol had allowed them to look in the desk drawer in the bedroom. Hanrahan had found some documents written by Sokol and brought them out to the living room.

He handed it to Lieberman along with some other papers. There was a computer on the desk with a speaker on each side. Cards with writing on them were stacked on the desk.

"I use the desk more than Arnold," she said. "My work. Arnold worked at the shop."

"Yes, ma'am," said Hanrahan. "We know."

"Would you like some coffee? I should stay with the baby."

"Coffee would be fine. These were written by your husband?"

He showed her the items, and she looked puzzled.

"Yes," she said. "Why?"

"Let's talk over coffee," Lieberman said.

The two policemen sat in the living room while the widow, dressed in a black dress, got the coffee. Hanrahan smiled at the baby, who took a beat to decide, then smiled back.

"Got a way with babies," he said.

"I scare them," said Lieberman.

"Well," said Mary Sokol, sitting back in the chair next to the baby, "I got a call early this morning. If I have it right, one of the men who beat him the other night stalked Arnold and killed him.

And then you let him go, and he killed one of the other men who had beaten Arnold."

"It's not really clear yet," said Hanrahan.

"No," she said, looking at the baby. "Nothing is clear."

"Can we ask you some questions?" Lieberman said.

"Questions? Yes."

"One important one," said Lieberman. "I want you to think about it, then I want to say something to you before you answer it."

"Yes," she said, brushing back her hair.

"Why did you kill your husband?"

Hanrahan was watching her closely. They both were. The widow seemed to have no reaction. She touched the cloth to the gurgling baby's mouth again and sat back.

Lieberman read her her rights and asked her if she understood. She said she did.

"You want a lawyer before you answer the question?" asked Hanrahan.

"No," she said.

Lieberman handed her the file from the Hollywood Linen Shop.

"Your husband's business isn't in trouble," he said. "It's doing very well. He didn't have to borrow money from anyone."

"I don't understand," she said.

"I've checked his appointment book," said Lieberman. "The one in his desk. The book is filled with entries. I've got these copies of your husband's handwriting. The entries in the appointment book were not written by your husband. They are close, but not close enough. We'll show them to an expert, but it doesn't take an expert to tell. I'm going to guess that you filled this appointment book."

Mary Sokol looked at Hanrahan.

"You sure you don't want a lawyer?" he asked.

"No lawyer," she said with a shake of her head, looking toward the window.

"You do research on the computer for a living," said Lieberman. "After you met me and my partner at the hospital, you had our names. You checked and found stories linking me with El Perro. My grandson did the same thing last night. You filled in that appointment book and gave it to my partner so we would go after El Perro."

"I went to confession this morning, early," she said, her face blank. "I took the baby after I took Matthew to school. One of the cleaning ladies who works at the church watched the baby. I confessed. The priest told me I should tell you what I did, but he absolved me. I couldn't just come and confess. I have two babies."

"How did you kill him?" asked Hanrahan.

"The children were asleep," she said. "Arnold was so depressed. He said he had to take a walk. I went with him. We weren't going to leave the children alone for more than ten or fifteen minutes. We talked about his medication, that he wasn't taking it. We walked down to the lake. I listened to him. I always listened to him. We were sitting on a bench just looking at the stars and the water and he told me he had to go away, had to start again. He said he was sorry. He cried. I consoled him. I was frightened. And then, suddenly, I was angry. He was going to walk away from me and our children. I got up and found the block of wood."

"And you hit him," Hanrahan said.

The baby hit the dangling plastic ball with a random swipe, and it rattled gently. Mary Sokol smiled at the infant.

"I hit him," she said, turning back to the policemen. "I hit him. I hit him again and he fell to the ground and I kept hitting him and hitting him."

"You hit him till he was dead," said Lieberman.

"I hit him till he was dead. Then I dragged him across the beach and pushed him into the water."

"You had it all planned?" Hanrahan asked.

"No," she said. "It just happened. He was crying, saying he was going to leave me and the children. I told him that it was a sin in the eyes of our Savior. He said he didn't believe in Jesus."

"And that's why you killed him?"

"I don't know. I don't think so. My sin in killing him was greater. I didn't plan to do it. I didn't do any planning till I got home and saw the children sleeping. Then I checked your name on the Internet and filled in the appointment book."

"Would you like more coffee?" she asked.

"No," said Lieberman.

"They're going to ask me more about why I did it, aren't they?" she asked.

"Yes," said Hanrahan.

"I don't have the answers," she said. "Don't you have people who do things, terrible things, and don't know why? Sometimes regular people like me?"

"Yes," said Lieberman.

"And they say we're crazy," she said with a sigh. "I'm a Catholic, but I don't believe in possession by demons or traps of the devil. And I'm not crazy. Maybe I was for a few seconds or minutes or hours, but I'm not crazy. Confession didn't help. A priest can't absolve me. I killed my husband. My children are going to be taken from me. If God forgives me, he can forgive anyone, and there are people, people even worse than I am, who should never be forgiven."

"You have someone who can watch the baby, pick up your son after school?" asked Lieberman.

She rose, moved to a corkboard in the kitchen, and removed a sheet of paper held by a pushpin. She brought the sheet into the living room and handed it to Hanrahan.

"It's a list of everything you'll need," she said, standing over them. "My sister's name, address, and phone number. A backup friend if you can't reach her. I've written a note for my sister. I'll get that. You can give it to her. There's nothing in it about what I did, just how to take care of the children and what to do with the apartment."

"You had this ready?" Hanrahan said heavily.

"I prepared it months ago," she said. "I expected her to use it when I died. I've been expecting death for a long time. I didn't expect this, didn't think about Arnold when I wrote it. As God is my judge. God punished me. He . . . I . . . I think I should call my lawyer now. His name is Charles Angotti. His number is on that sheet. I called him yesterday and told him I might be needing him sometime soon or in a little while."

There was something more than chilling in the woman's careful preparation, her resignation.

"You see," she went on, "I wouldn't have been able to let an innocent person go to prison for killing Arnold. I know that now. I knew it yesterday."

"Call your sister and your lawyer," Lieberman said. "We'll wait."

Mary Sokol nodded and moved to the telephone on the table against the wall. She picked up the phone and began punching the buttons. And then she stopped. She stood there with the phone in her hand and turned to the policemen.

"Could you? Please?"

She held the humming phone out to them. Hanrahan moved quickly to take it from her and lead her back to the chair next to the baby.

15

Lieberman did not believe in miracles. He did believe in coincidences. He had seen too many to deny their existence. Once he had gone out at two in the morning unable to sleep, unable to read, nothing on television to watch. He had gone out intending to go to Dunkin' Donuts, have a decaffeinated coffee and a plain donut, and talk to the night man or read an article or two in the *Smithsonian Magazine* he had rolled up in his coat pocket.

He didn't know what changed his mind, but instead of going to Dunkin' Donuts he stopped at a Denny's. When he walked through the door he saw that there was only one other customer in the place, William James Sinett.

Now that was where the coincidence came in. Lieberman had spent the day looking for William James Sinett in connection with a series of armed robberies. Sinett did not live in this neighborhood or anywhere near Rogers Park, nor had he committed any crimes that Lieberman knew of in the area. But there he was, sitting, having a cup of coffee, eating a large piece of some kind of cream pie.

After he had arrested Sinett, Lieberman had asked him why he had gone to this Denny's.

"I don't know," Sinett had answered. "I was just driving, and I felt like having a piece of pie."

Coincidence. But such things happened more than once in a person's lifetime.

After booking Mary Sokol, Kearney heard their story and wasn't sure whether to be happy that he was off the hook for letting Franzen and the others go the day before or he was sad because of what Mary Sokol had done.

"And that's her best reason?" he had asked, standing at the window of his office.

"That's all she gave us," said Lieberman.

"It's better than no reason," said Kearney. He had seen dozens, maybe a few hundred or more cases in which someone who seemed completely sane attacked or murdered someone else and could give no good reason for the crime. Kearney believed there was always a reason, but sometimes the criminal had no conscious idea of what it was.

That was the job of the shrinks. They would work on Mary Sokol. The prosecutor's psychiatrist. The defendant's psychiatrist. They'd both find reasons. Maybe the right one. Probably not.

"You're still getting married tonight?" Kearney asked.

"Tonight," said Hanrahan.

"I'll be there," said Kearney.

Hanrahan had expected Kearney to give an excuse.

"What are you two working?"

"Definite multiple arson," said Lieberman. "Last night. Two homeless people were killed. Hit-and-run on Lunt near Western. Victim's an old woman. She's in Ravenswood Hospital. Critical but alive."

Kearney nodded.

"Take the afternoon off," he said. "Both of you."

They thanked him and went into the squad room, which was a little less busy than the day before. The smell was no better, but the bodies were fewer.

"A superstitious man might say what we saw today was a bad omen," said Hanrahan, as they walked toward the door.

"What we saw today?"

"Mary Sokol. I'm getting married today, and I meet a woman who seemed to have a decent marriage, a Catholic woman, and she murders her husband. That strikes me like it might be an omen."

"You look for omens, you find them," said Lieberman. "Good and bad."

"So our coming down on Mary Sokol is just a coincidence?" Hanrahan asked, as they moved down the narrow stairs and into the lobby, where Nestor Briggs behind the desk nodded at them as he talked to two old men with beards who might have been twins.

"You made the connection, Father Murph. You remember me finding William Sinett? That was a coincidence. This is not, not a coincidence, not an omen. Maybe it's an excuse, but if it is, and I say this as your best man before I go home and put on my best suit, then don't use it. Don't blame it on God, magic, or chance. Do what you have to do and take responsibility. You want to get married?"

"I do."

"Then get married."

They moved into the parking lot. The sky was overcast, but it definitely didn't look or feel like rain. Lieberman and Hanrahan had both driven in to the station.

"Six o'clock," said Lieberman. "Unitarian church."

"I'll be there," said Hanrahan, pulling out a smile.

"Don't bring the dog."

"I won't bring the dog," Hanrahan said, moving to his car.

"Bring the ring," Lieberman said, calling across from his car.

"I'll bring the ring."

"Wear pants."

"I'll think about it," said Hanrahan.

"Good," said Lieberman.

Hanrahan drove away first. Lieberman, windows open, took out his notebook and removed his cell phone from his pocket. This was as good a time and place to do it as any. He dialed the number his grandson had found on the Internet.

"Senator Lieberman's office," came a woman's voice.

"My name is Abraham Lieberman. I'm a detective in the Chicago Police Department. How do I get to talk to the senator?"

"One moment please," she said.

Two minutes later a man's voice said, "Who are you and what is it you wish to speak to Senator Lieberman about?"

Lieberman repeated what he had said to the woman and added that he wanted to talk to the senator about a possible speaking engagement.

"Are you related to the senator?"

"I doubt it."

Lieberman explained to the man that the temple wanted him as a featured speaker at a luncheon, a dinner, a breakfast, anything and almost anytime the next month or the month after.

"Do you have a number where we can verify your identity?"

Lieberman gave him the station number.

"Ask for Lieutenant Kearney," he said.

"And is that the number where we can reach you?"

Lieberman gave the man his home phone number and cell phone number.

"And you said you're a Democrat?" the man asked.

"As a matter of fact," Lieberman said with a deep sigh, "I'm a registered Libertarian. If you want to know if I voted for Senator Lieberman, the answer is no. I voted for Harry Browne."

"Someone will get back to you, Detective," the man said abruptly.

"Thank you."

The man hung up. Lieberman had done his duty. He started to head home but checked his watch. There was a day game at Wrigley. He had forty-five minutes to make it. He could watch at least five innings before he had to go home and change. He turned out of the parking lot and headed south.

Hanrahan pulled over on his way home and called the Black Moon. There was no answer. He called Iris's home number. She answered.

"Haven't changed your mind?" he asked.

"No. Have you?"

"No. You sure you want to take a cab with your father?"

"I'll go with him and leave with you," she said.

"Sounds good to me. How's your father doing?"

"Resigned," she said. "He's afraid I'll try to have a baby. He thinks I'm too old. He thinks the baby might come out not looking the least bit Chinese. He wants his grandchild, should there be one, to be Chinese."

"We're not even married yet," he said. "And you're talking babies again."

"And that upsets you?"

"It used to," he said. "I'm not sure anymore. Can we put that one off for a little while?"

"Not long," she said. "If we decide to adopt a baby, it must be soon. My father is right. I'm too old."

"You are young and beautiful," he said. "You are perfect."

"I don't want to be perfect," she said. "It's too much work."

He laughed.

"See you at five at the church."

That was it. No turning back now. He didn't want to turn back. He didn't want a drink. He didn't want to think about Mary Sokol and her children. He wanted a long, very hot shower.

There were twelve people at the wedding, including the bride and groom. They gathered in the chapel, which was capable of comfortably holding 150 people though there had never been a service there approaching that number.

The minister was no more than forty, clean-shaven, a former Catholic priest. He had straight dark hair that dangled in a lock over his forehead. The minister's wife, who was also a minister, was there to greet people. She looked enough like the minister to be his sister.

Gathered were Abe, Bess, Maish, Yetta, Kearney, Iris's father and sister.

The minister's voice echoed in the emptiness of the hall. The lights had been left bright at Iris's request. She was dressed in white, not a wedding dress, but something that they all knew she had made with her sister's help. Hanrahan wore his best suit. His cheeks were pink from shaving closely. Lieberman thought his partner's knees looked a little uncertain, but Hanrahan had two bad knees that often failed to cooperate.

The service had been short, with a very brief few words of congratulations from the minister. Everyone shook hands, and the small motorcade headed back to the Lieberman house, where Terrell had laid out the food on the dining room table with the help of Barry and Melisa.

That was the part Hanrahan had expected.

What he didn't expect was that the small house would be full. Five of the Alter Cockers were there. Nestor Briggs was there. But most important, Hanrahan found himself facing his son Michael and not only his son but his daughter-in-law and his two grandchildren.

"Congratulations," Michael said, giving his father a hug, then doing the same to Iris.

"Congratulations, Bill," his daughter-in-law said, giving him a sincere smile and a hug and moving to Iris.

Hanrahan knelt to hug his two grandsons, who had been prepared for such an event, had been told about the grandfather who had not seen them since they were babies.

"Food's hot," said Herschel Rosen.

They were serving themselves from the buffet, talking in small and somewhat odd groups: Kearney and Sy Weintraub, Iris's father and Terrell, Maish and Yetta and Hanrahan's daughter-in-law. Howie Chen was lost in a serious conversation with the five- and six-year-old Hanrahan boys, and Barry and Melisa were talking to Iris.

Then the doorbell rang.

"Party crashers," said Bess, moving to the door.

When she opened it, there stood a young Chinese man, Ye, the young man who had confronted Lieberman and Hanrahan in the street in front of El Perro's bingo parlor.

The young man seemed to be dressed exactly and as neatly as he had the day before except today he wore no sunglasses.

Everyone went silent. Hanrahan stepped in front of Iris and Lieberman moved to his side. Neither of the policemen were armed.

The young man looked around the room from face to face, then stepped into the house and out of the way as a huge Chinese man entered hugging a massive, shiny black vase that must have been five feet tall. The vase was decorated with golden dragons and flowers.

"A wedding gift from Mr. Woo," the young man said. "He regrets that he is unable to deliver it himself."

The young man stepped forward and handed an envelope to Hanrahan, then backed away. He looked at Lieberman, who said, "You want a slice of brisket for the road?"

"I think not."

"Want us to make up a plate for Mr. Woo?" Lieberman asked amiably.

"Abe," Bess whispered at his side.

"Thank you, no," said the man, nodding to the huge man, who went back through the door. The young Chinese man nodded and left the house, closing the door behind him.

Hanrahan opened the envelope and read. He handed it to Iris and turned to Lieberman.

"It's over, Rabbi. He wishes us a long and happy life and marriage."

"You trust him?"

"He wouldn't do this if it weren't true," said Iris. "Mr. Woo is a criminal, but his word is better than a written contract."

People were gathering around the huge vase. Iris's father moved toward it, touched, and turned to his two daughters, saying something in Chinese.

"My father says this is a very valuable gift," Iris said.

"So far so good," said Hanrahan.

There was another knock at the door.

Abe opened the door. Emiliano "El Perro" Del Sol stood there, white box in hand. He was dressed in a suit.

"You cool with the chinks?" he asked Lieberman. "We were watching them to see if they started trouble."

"We are cool with Mr. Woo and his friends," said Lieberman.

El Perro looked around and saw Kearney.

"I can't stay," said El Perro. "Got places to go. Here Irish," he added, handing Hanrahan the box. "*Su esposa es tan bonita.*"

"He says Iris is beautiful," Lieberman translated.

"Thanks," said Hanrahan. "I can't take this."

"You took that big ugly piece of glass from the chink," El Perro said. "You can take this from me. Open it. Take a look."

Hanrahan opened the box and started to laugh.

"You don't want it, give it to someone. See you around sometime, *Viejo. Usted, tambien Irish.*"

And El Perro was gone.

"What is it?" asked Bess.

Hanrahan pulled a football from the box and turned it over.

"It's got Dick Butkus's and Mike Ditka's signatures on it," he said.

Hanrahan looked at Kearney, who shrugged.

"Keep it," said Kearney. "And the vase. I don't see a football and a big vase turning you into a rogue cop."

Everyone applauded.

This time the phone rang. Melisa ran to get it. People were talking, milling around, eating and drinking. The men were handing around the football.

There were about ten presents of various sizes on the coffee table in the living room. Iris was moving to open them when Melisa came out of the kitchen with the phone.

"Grandpa, it's for you," she said. "It's your cousin or something."

Lieberman took the phone, covering his open ear with his right hand and moving toward the bedroom.

"Lieberman," he said.

"Lieberman here, too."

There was no mistaking the voice.

"Senator."

"Detective. Am I calling at a bad time?"

"No, we're having a wedding party for my partner."

"He a Libertarian, too?"

"No, he's a Democrat."

"Maybe I should talk to him. Can you give me some more information on this fund-raiser?"

Abe gave him the information. The senator listened, spoke, asked a few more questions, and ended the conversation saying, "Maybe we are related."

"I've just concluded that anything is possible."

Lieberman stood for a few seconds, moved into the kitchen, and hung up the phone. Then he went back into the noisy living room.

"Was that Ernie in Cleveland?" Maish asked. "If it was our cousin Ernie, I wanted to talk to him."

Lieberman moved over to Bess, who took his arm.

"Who was it?" she asked.

"Senator Joseph Lieberman," said Abe. "He's going to be in Chicago for three days in July. If we're flexible, he'll come to a breakfast fund-raiser."

"This is one of your jokes, Avrum," Bess said. "It's not getting you out of cleaning the garage."

"I've got a number and the name of a woman to call in his office to set it up," said Abe, showing her his open notebook.

"They'll throw a dinner in your honor at the temple," Bess said.

"I'll settle for being retired from the fund-raising committee."

"Retired? They'll probably want you to be permanent chairman."

She kissed him on the cheek.

"So, do I get a reward?"

"What do you have in mind?"

"A moderate to large slice of the wedding cake Terrell is about to bring out of the kitchen. A moderate to large slice without looks of recrimination and arrows of guilt and betrayal."

"Granted," said Bess.

"Ladies and gentlemen," Lieberman said aloud, "I have a greeting for Bill and Iris. That was Senator Joe Lieberman on the phone."

Everyone laughed.

"It's true," said Bess.

Everyone stopped laughing, and Lieberman reached for a glass of wine set up with others on the sideboard. He lifted his glass and said, "From the groom's partner and the senator from Connecticut, *mazel tov.*"

BRIGHT FUTURES

A LEW FONESCA MYSTERY

TO NATASHA MELISA “THE PERLL” KAMINSKY,

FROM DAD WITH LOVE.

AND THANKS FOR THE IDEA.

PROLOGUE

Twelve hundred years before I drove my dying car into the parking lot of the Dairy Queen on 301 in Sarasota, saber-tooth tigers, mastodons, giant armadillos, and camels roamed what are now the high-end malls that house Saks, Nieman-Marcus, Lord & Taylor, and twenty-screen movie theaters.

The land that is now the Florida Keys was part of a single landmass double the size of the present state.

People who inhabited Florida twelve hundred centuries ago were hunters and gatherers who lived on nuts, plants, small animals, and shellfish. There was a steady clean water supply, good stones on the ground for toolmaking, and more firewood than they needed. Complex cultures developed with temple mounds and villages. These villages traded with one another and developed cultivated agriculture.

As ocean waters wore away land, the peninsula shrank.

Juan Ponce de León landed in 1513 in what became St. Augustine. He called the area "La Florida," in honor of Pascua florida—the feast of flowers. In 1539 Hernando de Soto arrived, and a short time later, in quick succession, came settlers, slaves, and hurricanes. The natives were gone, though remnants of natives and runaway slaves created the Seminole tribes. By this time the peninsula had already long since shrunk to its present size.

Soon came the railroads, the airplanes, and the almost endless stream of cars on I-75 and I-95 carrying snowbird Canadians and retirees from Illinois, Minnesota, New York, Michigan, and even California. The few remaining Seminoles were herded into casinos, which they fought over and operated at a profit.

Towering buildings rose, blocking out view and sun. The more that were built, the more they cost and the greater the crowds.

Then my wife was killed by a hit-and-run driver on the Outer Drive in Chicago. With a Chicago Cubs cap on my head and in need of a shave, I came 1,044 miles looking for the end of the world and settled in an office at the rear of the Dairy Queen parking lot in Sarasota when my car broke down forever.

Now the DQ is gone, replaced by a bank. The less-than-shabby, concrete block two-story office building I live and work in will be torn down in a few days.

There are twenty-nine banks and numerous branches in Sarasota County, and only one DQ remains.

There are more than 360,000 people in the county. Florida progress.

My name is Lewis Fonesca. I find people.

I

PLAYING WITH CHILDREN

1

"There's a man sleeping in the corner of your office," the boy said.

"I know."

"He's Chinese," the kid said. "You want to know how I know?"

"He looks Chinese," I said.

"But he could be Japanese or Korean," the kid said, looking at Victor Woo, who was lying faceup on his bedroll with his eyes closed.

"He's not."

"Pale skin, small eyes, and his . . ."

The boy was seventeen, a student at Pine View School for the Gifted. His name was Greg Legerman. He was short, nervous, and unable to sit still or be quiet. Next to him sat a tall, thin boy with tousled white hair and rimless glasses. Winston Churchill Graeme, also seventeen, was tall, calm, and sat still, looking at whomever was talking.

"Am I right? Winn, am I right?" Greg said to his friend with a laugh as he punched the other boy in the arm, punched him hard.

Winn Graeme didn't answer. Greg didn't care.

"You're moving," Greg said.

"How could you tell?" I asked.

"The six cardboard boxes over there near the Chinese man."

"I'm moving," I said.

It had taken me less than an hour to pack. I lived in the adjacent room, a small office space, and I owned almost nothing. We were sitting in the reception room, which had a desk, three chairs, and four small paintings on the wall. That was it. My friend Ames McKinney would be by later to pick up the desk, the boxes, the TV with the built-in video player, and the knee-high bookcase.

"They're tearing this building down," said Greg. He grinned.

He was easily amused. He punched Winn Graeme in the arm again.

"Why do you keep punching him?" I asked.

"We're kidding. He punches me sometimes."

Winn gave a halfhearted tap to the arm of Greg Legerman.

"Am I right? They're tearing the building down?"

"Yes."

"You have another place for your office?" asked Greg.

"Yes."

"The Dairy Queen used to be right out there," said Greg.

"Yes," I said.

"They should tear down banks and put up DQs," Greg said.

I agreed but didn't say so. He didn't seem to need anyone agreeing with him about anything.

Victor Woo stirred in the corner and rolled toward the wall.

"Mind my asking who that is?" asked Greg.

"Victor Woo."

"And what's he doing sleeping on the floor of your office?"

"He walked in one afternoon," I said.

"Why?"

"He killed my wife in Chicago. He feels guilty and depressed."

"You're kidding, right?" asked Greg.

"No," I said.

"Wow," said Greg.

I called out, "Don't punch him."

Greg hesitated, shrugged, and let his hands fall into his lap for a few seconds before they started to roam again.

"Let's go," Winn said, starting to rise.

Winston Graeme had the remnants of a Russell Crowe accent.

"No wait," said Greg. "I like this guy. I like you, Mr. Fonesca. You come highly recommended."

"By who and for what?"

"By a Pine View student."

"Who is nameless?"

"No, the student has a name," he said with a laugh.

I couldn't open my mouth fast enough to stop him from punching his friend.

"I'm a process server," I said.

"You find people. You help people."

I didn't respond. He hadn't really asked a question. I make enough money to live by serving papers for lawyers. I didn't want more work. I didn't want money in the bank. I wanted to be able to pick up my duffel bag, which was always partially packed, add a few things, and walk out the door.

"We can pay," said Greg. "What's your fee?"

Victor got up on his elbows and looked over at us. He was wearing a red sweatshirt that had a Chicago Bulls logo and the word "Bulls" on the front. The sleeves on the sweatshirt had been roughly cut off.

Something in my face told the two boys that I wasn't interested.

"You can listen," said Greg, starting to rise, changing his mind and sitting again. "Ten minutes."

"Five minutes. What's your problem?" I asked.

"Ronnie Gerall is in jail, juvenile. He's seventeen. They say he murdered a crazy old man. He didn't. The police aren't even looking for anyone else."

Winn Graeme adjusted his glasses again and glanced at Victor.

"Okay," said Greg. "We want you to find someone—the person who killed Philip Horvecki."

I had read about the murder of Philip Horvecki in the *Herald-Tribune* a few days before. He had been beaten to death in his home. Horvecki was one of the Sarasota superrich. Semiretired, he had earned his money in land development when the market was hot. He was involved in local politics and had run without success for everything from property appraiser and tax collector to city council, and his causes were many.

His latest cause was something called Bright Futures, a program to provide financial aid to high school students going to a Florida college or university. Horvecki wanted the program abolished. He didn't want to pay for people's college education. The argument that the program was paid for by the Florida lottery made no difference to Horvecki.

His second most recent and continuing cause involved Pine View School for the Gifted, a public school for high-IQ and high-achievement students who could test their way in. Pine View was consistently ranked in the top ten high schools in the United States. That didn't matter to Horvecki, who thought taxpayers shouldn't have to pay for elitist education. He wanted to turn Pine View into an open-admissions high school like the others in the county. For this position he had a lot of support.

All of this was in the article I had read. I remembered having the feeling that more was going on.

"Ronnie didn't do it," said Greg, looking around the room as if he had lost something or someone.

"He was found over the body covered in blood," I said.

"Circumstantial," said Greg.

"He was there to fight with Horvecki about his Pine View and Bright Futures positions," I said.

"Ronnie's got a temper I admit," said Greg. "But he's not a killer."

I looked at Winn whose accent was more pronounced now as he said, "Ronnie's not a killer."

"Winn's from Australia," Greg said with something that sounded like pride at having an exotic trophy at his side.

"He was Australian thirteen-and-under golf champ before he moved here with his mom two years ago. Winn's a state runner-up in golf. Winn's also on the soccer and basketball teams at Sarasota High. Pine View doesn't have sports teams. Tell him."

I wasn't sure how Winn Graeme's athletic achievements qualified him to determine that Ronnie Gerall was not a killer.

"We have a rowing team," Winn said. "And cross-country."

Greg started to laugh again. He held up his fist and was stopped by the hoarse morning voice of Victor Woo saying, "Do not punch him again."

"Victor doesn't like violence," I said.

"How did he kill your wife?" asked Greg.

"Hit-and-run," I said.

"Tapping each other's just a joke with my friend," said Greg to Victor. "It's a joke. Don't be lame."

Victor was on his knees now, palms on his thighs. He was wearing purple Northwestern University sweatpants. They didn't come close to being compatible with his Bulls shirt.

"Nonviolent hit-and-run Buddhist, right?" asked Greg. "Do you know there are an estimated seven million Buddhists in China?"

Victor was on his bare feet now, touching his face to find out if he could go another day without shaving. He didn't answer Greg Legerman, who turned to me and said, "Well, will you take the job?"

"You haven't told me who you want to find."

"Horvecki's daughter," said Winn. "She was a witness. Ronnie says she was there when he died. Now she's missing. Or find who killed Horvecki, or both. Charge double."

"No," I said.

"You haven't heard what happened," said Greg.

"I don't care. I'm sorry."

Greg looked at me, stood up, went behind his chair, and rocked it slightly. He was a short, reasonably solid kid.

"You don't look sorry," Greg said.

"I don't need the work," I said.

"We need the help," Greg said.

Nothing he said had turned it for me, but something happened that made me open the door at least a little.

"Let's go, Greg," said Winn. "The man has integrity. I like him."

Greg was shaking his head "no." Victor walked behind the two boys and headed out the front door. He was almost certainly headed to the washroom at the end of the outdoor second-floor concrete landing. Either that or he was headed back to Chicago barefoot. It would not have surprised me.

"Wait," Greg said, shrugging off the hand that his friend had put around his bicep.

In style and size, the two boys were a study in contrast. Greg was short, compact, and slightly plump; Winn tall, lean, and muscular.

Earlier that morning, I had bicycled over, shaved, and washed at the Downtown YMCA on Main Street. I had brushed my teeth, too, and looked at my sad, clearly Italian face.

"How old is Horvecki's daughter?" I asked.

"I don't know," Greg said, looking at his friend for the answer, but Winn didn't know either.

"What's her name?"

"Rachel," said Winn.

"You have a car?" I asked.

"Yeah," said Greg.

"You know where Sarasota News and Books is?"

"Yes."

"We drive over there, you get me two coffees and two biscotti to go, and I listen to your story."

"Fair enough," said Greg. "What about Victor?"

"He knows I'll be back. I need to know who told you about me. I don't have a private investigator's license."

"Viviase," said Winn.

"Ettiene Viviase, the policeman?"

"No," said Greg. "Elisabeth Viviase, the freshman daughter of the policeman."

Sarasota News and Books wasn't crowded, but there were people dawdling over coffee at four of the six tables on the coffeehouse side of the shop. A few others roamed the shelves of firmly packed rows of books and circled around the tables piled with new arrivals.

We sat at a table near the window facing Main Street. The television mounted in the corner silently played one of the business channels. I wasn't tempted to watch.

"I've got to tell you," said Greg. "I am not filled with confidence about you."

"Why?" I asked.

"Well, no offense, but you're a little bald guy in jeans and a frayed short-sleeved yellow shirt. You've got a baseball cap on your head and you look like someone just shot your faithful dog."

"I'm not offended. What do you have to tell me?"

"What? Oh."

Greg grinned and punched his friend's arm again.

"You really are funny."

"I wasn't trying to be," I said.

"I think that woman on television is talking about aliens," said Greg.

"No," said his friend.

"I don't mean illegal aliens. I mean the kind from outer space. Wishu-Wishuu-ooooo."

"That sounds like an Ivy League football cheer," said Winn.

"Get out," said Greg.

"Hit him and I walk," I said.

Greg, fist cocked, looked hurt, but he didn't deliver the punch. Instead, he said, "I did one of my blogs about so-called alien visitors. There aren't any. Aliens with two eyes and two legs aren't coming millions of miles to pluck people out of their beds to probe their rectums with metal rods."

A woman who had been talking to a younger woman at the table next to us looked over at the last comment.

"No aliens," I said.

"No, they're humanoids from the future, maybe hundreds of thousands of years in the future. They're archaeologists or anthropologists or whatever those sciences will be like. They appear and disappear so fast because they zip in and out of time. The shapes of the craft differ because they come from different times in the future."

"Why didn't the ones from farther in the future go back and visit the ones from more recently and coordinate?" I said.

Greg had finished something filled with caffeine over ice and topped with whipped cream. Just what he needed to calm him down. Winn had an iced tea. I played with my coffee and looked at the two extra cups of Colombia Supremo Deep Jungle Roast and the two biscotti to go.

I learned that Ronnie Gerall had come to Sarasota in his junior year, that he was a natural leader, passionate about protecting the school from politicians and social gadflies, particularly Philip Horvecki.

"Everyone likes Ronnie," said Greg. "Particularly the girls."

Greg considered a punch, but his eyes met mine and he dropped his hand to his lap.

"What about his parents?" I asked.

Greg and Winn looked at each other before Greg said, "His mother's dead. His father travels. We've never met Ronnie's father."

"I don't think his father makes much money," said Winn. "He drives a twenty-year-old Toyota."

The ride over and the two biscotti and coffee was the price I had to pay for the information. I listened.

"Did you know that, in their duel, Alexander Hamilton fired at Aaron Burr first, and that Hamilton had been undermining Burr, who at the time was Vice President of the United States?"

"What has this to do with the murdered man and your friend in jail?"

"Nothing," said Winn, adjusting his glasses. "Greg is a master of non sequiturs."

"A connection will occur," said Greg with enthusiasm. "String theory."

"Any other connections between Ronnie Gerall and Philip Horvecki?"

"No," said Greg, squirming in his seat.

The woman at the next table was trying not to listen for more talk about rods being applied to orifices. She was failing.

"Who else would want Horvecki dead?"

"Everybody," said Greg.

"I didn't want Horvecki dead," I said.

"You didn't know him," said Greg.

"Lots of people are happy that Horvecki is dead," said Winn.

"Can we narrow that down a little?"

"Horvecki had legal trouble with people," said Winn.

"Like?"

"We don't know for sure," said Greg. "It was all kept quiet, but everybody knew. Okay, okay, you didn't know."

"Just talk to Ronnie, please," said Winn. "Start there. What do you charge?"

"Eleven thousand dollars a week, but in your case I'll give you a discount because I was recommended by Ettiene Viviase's daughter."

"Eleven thou . . . ," Greg began.

"He's joking," said Winn.

"I'm not good at jokes. I'm making a point. What would you pay for your friend to be found innocent?"

"Five hundred dollars a week plus expenses," said Greg. "We can get lots of people to contribute. My grandfather could write a check for four thousand and not miss it."

"That's comforting," I said.

"It is to Ronnie," said Greg. "I've got cash."

I let the bills he took out of his pocket rest on the edge of the desk.

"It goes back to you after I talk to your friend," I said, "if I'm not happy with his answers to my questions."

"Then you'll find the killer?"

"Then I'll try to find Rachel Horvecki."

"And the killer," said Greg.

"And the killer," I agreed.

I got a paper brown paper bag from the counter and carefully placed coffees and biscotti inside and then neatly folded the top over before cradling it against my chest. The heat was lulling. I had told the two boys that I wanted to be alone to think and that I'd make it back to my place on my own. Greg wanted to say a lot more. Winn guided him out of the News and Books.

Normally, I would have turned the possible job down with thanks for the refreshments, but I could use the money. I was moving. It didn't cost much but there were things I needed and my bike wanted repair. The number of court papers to serve for my lawyer clients was down for the summer. The snowbirds who came down to their condos, homes, and rentals wouldn't be back to engage in and be the victims of crime for at least three months. There were fewer criminals being brought to justice or just being hauled before a judge for not paying child support. I didn't need much, didn't want much, but now I had Victor Woo to feed and a weekly dinner out with Sally Porovsky and her two kids at Honey Crust Pizza, which would eventually present a challenge even if Sally and I split the bill. And though I was a project for my therapist, Ann Hurwitz, I still had to pay something each time I saw her, even if it was only ten dollars.

When this meeting of the minds was over, I walked down the block to Gulf Stream Boulevard, across from the Bay, to get to my appointment with Ann.

I stepped through the inner door of Ann's office and held out my ritual offering of coffee and biscotti. She looked up from her blue armchair, and I sat in its duplicate across from her as she removed the lid from the cup and dipped an almond biscotti into it. I took off my Cubs cap and placed it on my lap.

"Make me smile," she said.

Ann is over eighty years old. I'm not sure how much over. I do know she doesn't like it when people say she is "eighty years young."

"I am by no stretch of the imagination young unless I have morphed into a tortoise. I've earned my years. It is the end of them I regret and not their number which I savor."

She had said that to me once when I told her I wasn't interested in growing old. Now she wanted a joke. For almost a year now, I had not only been responsible for refreshments but also for telling a joke. I do not smile. I do not laugh. When my wife, Catherine, was hit and killed by Victor Woo's car, I had lost my ability to consider happiness. Ann worked to have me lose my hard-earned depression, and I struggled to hold on to it. A joke delivered was a concession. It took research on my part.

" 'I have of late, but wherefore know I not, lost all my mirth,' " I said. " 'This goodly frame seems to me a sterile promontory.' "

"Shakespeare," she said.

"Yes, and *Hair*. Catherine liked *Hair*. We saw it four times."

"You liked it?"

"No."

"But you remember it."

"Yes."

"A joke, Fonesca. It is time to pay the toll."

Ann was well groomed, wore colorful tailored dresses, and had her white hair neatly trimmed short. She always wore a necklace and a wide bracelet. She had dozens of baubles of jewelry either made by her husband, a long-retired investment broker, or chosen by them during one of their frequent travels all over the world.

She skillfully managed to get the soaked end of her biscotti from cup to mouth without dripping—a skill I admired.

"A psychologist's receptionist says, 'Doctor, I have a man out here who thinks he's invisible.' And the psychologist answers, 'Tell him I can't see him now.' "

"I'm sufficiently amused," Ann said. "You think this joke is funny?"

"No."

"But you understand why others might?"

"Yes."

"Progress. Tell me about your houseguest," she said finishing the last moist bite of biscotti.

"Tell you what?"

"Whatever you wish to tell me. Does he like biscotti?"

She took a sip of coffee, looking at me over the top of her cup.

"I don't know. He killed my wife."

"Catherine."

"Catherine."

"And now he lives on the floor of your office and is going to live with you in your new office?"

"I think so."

"Why?"

"Why do I think so?"

"No, why is he going to live with you?"

"He doesn't say."

"No, I meant, why are you letting him live with you?"

This struck me as a good question.

"I don't know."

"Think about it and give me the best answer you can in your next office visit."

"No joke?"

"When you laugh and mean it, you can stop bringing me jokes."

"I'll bring you a joke."

She finished her coffee, examined the bottom of the cup, daintily reached in with her little finger to retrieve a biscotti crumb, and deposited it on her tongue.

"Some boys want me to help their friend get out of jail."

She looked up, definitely interested.

"What did this boy do?"

"They say he did nothing. He's accused of killing a man named Philip Horvecki."

She shook her head and said, "So I have read. He has a daughter?"

"She's missing," I said. "She may have witnessed the murder."

"From what I have heard and read about him, Horvecki was an angry man, a very angry man, and proud of it. He could have used intensive therapy."

"He was angry about Pine View School."

She smiled. "And many other things," she said. "Taxes, landfill, religion, the price of gasoline."

"But mostly Pine View and Bright Futures."

"So I understand."

"You know something more about him, don't you?" I asked.

"Nothing I can talk to you about."

"He's dead."

"And you wouldn't mind my talking about our sessions if you were to die?"

That gave me pause.

"I wouldn't like it."

"He was a patient of yours?"

"No," she said.

"His daughter?"

I was about to push the issue when Ann rose from her chair with a bounce. I got up. "There's someone in the waiting room who is here to see me. Do you mind going out the other way."

"The other way" was through a door that opened into the offices of a Hispanic real estate and law office. I went through the door. A young woman, pretty and dark, was at one of the two desks in the outer office. She was on the phone and speaking in Spanish. I nodded as I went out onto Main Street, turned left, and then left again down Gulf Stream. My plan had been to walk back to my office.

But before I had gone five steps, someone offered me a ride.

2

He was smiling. He was one of those people who wore a perpetual smile. It didn't mean he was happy or amused. He walked at my side, a few inches taller than me, a few pounds heavier, a few years older, and much better dressed. His dark hair was brushed back. His dark eyes were moist.

"You want a ride," he said, his voice almost Robert Preston musical.

"No, thanks," I said.

"It wasn't a question," he said, keeping pace with me. "I was letting you know that your fondest wish at the moment was a ride in an almost-new red Buick LeSabre. The car was washed this morning and sprayed inside with the scent of a forest. You're not allergic to scented sprays, are you?"

"No," I said, continuing to walk.

"Good, very good. I'm new to Sarasota," he said. "Been here a few weeks. I like what I've seen so far. Air smells good, fresh. Know what I mean?"

"Yes."

He looked to our right, beyond the manicured bushes and well spaced trees, toward the bay.

"And the birds, magnificent," he said. "I'm from L.A. . . ."

We were just passing a high-rise apartment building on our left.

"We have to turn around," he said. "I'm parked back there."

"I'd rather walk," I said.

He reached over and flicked the brim of my Cubs cap.

His smile remained, but his voice changed. We weren't just chatting anymore.

"Too hot to walk."

"No."

"It's not open for discussion."

I recognized him now, but I couldn't place him. He had the tough look of a television heavy. He caught me looking. His smile got a little broader. He put his left hand on my shoulder to stop me and turn me toward him.

An old woman with a small, fuzzy white dog leading the way on a leash came out of the apartment building. She glanced at us, moved past, and started across the street.

"She wasn't carrying a plastic bag," he said, watching the woman and the eager dog pulling at the leash. "She doesn't plan to clean up after the dog."

"She's old," I said.

"Then she shouldn't have a dog."

"Maybe that's all she's got," I said. "Jeff Augustine."

"Son of a gun. You not only recognize me, you know my name. I'm impressed, flattered."

"I used to watch a lot of old television shows. Rockford, Harry O."

"I want you to meet a guy," he said seriously.

"Mike Mazurki as Moose Malloy in *Farewell My Lovely*," I said.

"Right, but it's also Jeff Augustine on a street in Sarasota. I really have someone who wants to meet you."

"And if I don't want to be met?"

He shrugged and said, "Suit yourself, but I think it would be a good idea if you met this fella. Besides, he'd be very disappointed in me if I didn't deliver you."

"What happened to your career?" I asked.

He shook his head and watched the old lady and the little dog, which was now making a deposit under a small palm tree.

"Twenty-five years waiting for checks so I could pay my phone bills and my rent and eat reasonably. Toward the end I was singing second banana in dinner theaters. My biggest role was Judd Frye in *Oklahoma*, in Knoxville. When Judd Frye died that last time, I said good-bye to my career."

"Now you . . . ?"

"Yes, I work out, wear nice clothes, and persuade people to do things. It pays well and some people like the idea of having a guy with a familiar face getting things done for them."

"Is Steven Seagal really tough?" I asked.

"You remember."

"He threw you through a factory window and you fell four floors to your doom."

"Doom?"

"It's been nice talking to you," I said. "Now I'm walking home. I've got packing to do."

"You haven't been listening closely . . . Look at that. She's just leaving it there."

This was all said calmly, more with regret than anger.

"You want an appointment," I said, "give me a call or just drop by my new office. I'll give you the address."

"No, now," he said, his smile even more friendly.

"I don't think so," I said.

He opened his jacket to show a holstered gun.

"You're going to shoot me on the street because I don't want to get in your car?"

"The car smells like a forest, and I've got a small cooler with bottles of water," he said. "And yes, I could shoot you a little bit."

"No," I said, turning to walk away.

"You're a real phenomenon. You're not afraid, are you?"

"Worst you could do is kill me. This isn't a bad place, and it's a nice day for dying."

"You're a little crazy," he said.

"You caught up with me just when I ended a session with my shrink. You know any good jokes?"

"Jokes?" He looked puzzled now.

"Jokes," I repeated.

"Yes, lots. I did stand-up for a while. The good jokes weren't in my act, but I remember them from Larry the Cable Guy and Diane Ford."

"I'll go with you if you tell me five good jokes," I said.

The old woman with the dog was no longer in sight, but a shirtless black man with sagging slacks, unlaced shoes, and no socks was advancing on us, scratching his belly. I recognized him, had given him coffee and an occasional biscotti. He said his name was Clark, or maybe Cleric, and he claimed that he wasn't homeless. His home, he said, was under the second bench in Bayfront Park, not far from where the dog had just relieved himself or herself.

"Five good jokes?"

"Five."

"Deal."

"This way."

Clark was headed right for us.

"A friend of yours?"

"I don't know," I said as Clark lifted his chin, reached into his pants to adjust his testicles, and said, "Too many midgets. Too many."

"It's a problem," I agreed.

Clark looked at Augustine and pointed a finger.

"You shot ol' Kurt Russell. Some soldier movie."

I gave Clark two quarters and said to Augustine, "The scent of the forest in a Buick LeSabre?"

"That's right," said Augustine. "Let's go."

"The Cubs," said Clark, looking at my cap as if he had suddenly realized it was there. "Andy Pafko."

"Who?" asked Augustine.

"Never mind," I said. "Tell me jokes on the way."

The LeSabre did smell like a pine forest. I turned down the offer of Evian water. Augustine drank one as he drove.

"Five jokes," I said, index cards and pen in hand.

"Okay," he said.

He told the jokes. I wrote them down. I didn't laugh or smile.

"You don't think they're funny?" he asked as we headed north on Tamiami Trail.

"They're funny," I said, tucking the cards into my appointment book.

"I like you," he said. "Do people generally like you?"

"Yes."

"Why? I mean, I like you, but I'm not sure why."

"It's my curse," I said.

"That people like you?"

"They expect to be liked back."

"And you can't?"

"I don't want to," I said. "The cost is too high, and people die."

He looked at me, one hand on the wheel, one grasping a bottle of water, which he squeezed, making a cracking sound.

"So you have no friends?"

"Too many," I said.

The big two-story gray stone house was right on a cul-de-sac on the water a few blocks south of the Ringling Museum. The house had a front lawn that looked as if it had been manicured with a pair of very small scissors. At the top of the house was a turret which probably had a great view across the water to Longboat Key. A blue Porsche was parked in the driveway in front of a three-car garage. The street had no curb. There was no sidewalk.

Augustine led the way. I followed up the redbrick path to the front door. Gulls were complaining out over the water, and waves flopped against the shore.

Augustine pushed a white button in the wooden paneling next to the door. I heard chimes inside, deep and calm. He rang only once, stood back, clasped his hands in front of him, and rocked on his heels waiting.

"The hat," he said.

I took off my Cubs cap folded it over and shoved it in my back pocket. The door opened. The woman who strode out was in a hurry. She was dark and beautiful and maybe in her forties. She wore a gray business suit over a black blouse and the necklace she wore was a string of large, colorful stones. She walked past us as if we didn't exist, her heels clacking on the red bricks. Augustine and I watched her get into the blue Porsche and pull smoothly away.

I didn't know who she was. I didn't know who I was about to see. Augustine was no help. We went through the open door that the woman had not closed behind her.

We were in a white-tiled entryway with an open glass elevator, which was on its way down. A large man in it was wearing a pair of tan shorts, a matching polo shirt, and sandals over bare feet. He had a full head of brown and white hair and a white-toothed smile of what looked like real teeth that were carefully tended. He was a well-kept sixty-five or seventy years old. I knew his name before the elevator door opened and he stepped out.

"Mr. Fonesca," he said, extending his hand. "Thanks for coming."

I took it. His grip was firm, but he wasn't trying to win any macho hand-squeezing contest.

"You're welcome," I said as he held out a hand, palm up, in invitation for us to follow him.

He ushered us off to the right. He smelled like something slightly sweet and musky and displayed the redness of someone fresh out of the shower.

We went through a large kitchen that opened into a family room and library.

"Please sit," he said, sitting on a yellow leather chair.

Augustine and I sat on a matching yellow leather sofa.

He poured three glasses of something dark brown from a pitcher full of ice on a low, ornately carved table with inlays of white stones. It could have been from India or Serbia. It could have been Wal-Mart.

The drink was strong iced tea. The three of us drank.

"You know who I am," he said.

"Yes, D. Elliot Corkle."

"And?"

"You sell gadgets on television."

The tea was good and strong. I could have used a biscotti.

"Used to. Household aids," he corrected, chewing on an ice

cube. "For nineteen-ninety-nine, your kitchen fantasies can come true. Our products are all made of the finest durable Oriental plastics and South American metals."

"My favorite's the steamer chopper," I said.

"You have one?"

"No, I watch infomercials. Insomnia. I don't get cable."

"Want to know why I asked Mr. Augustine to invite you here?"

"No. I just want a ride back to my place. I've got packing to do."

"It's taken care of. Right, Jeffrey?"

"It's taken care of," said Augustine. "Mr. Fonesca is fully moved."

"There," said Corkle. "Now we can have a brief but leisurely few minutes."

"That should be pleasant."

"D. Elliot Corkle will see that it is," said Corkle. "I would appreciate your doing something for me."

I nodded and drank some more tea.

"After your hospitality, how could I refuse?"

"D. Elliot Corkle would like you to politely return whatever money may have been advanced to you this morning by Gregory Legerman. I will give you a check for double the amount plus a ten-percent bonus if you decide right away. I'm a gambler."

"If I act right away, you pay shipping costs," I said.

"And I throw in a set of four eternally sharp cutting knives with handles made from the hulls of salvaged ships—a forty-nine-dollar value."

He laughed. He was having fun. I didn't laugh.

"Why?"

"Why do I want you to return the money and go about your business?" he asked, looking at Augustine, who smiled attentively. "Greg is my grandson. He is smart, full of energy and vigor, and inclined to do things without thinking that might get him in trouble."

"Like hire me?"

"Like trying to prove his friend didn't murder Phil Horvecki. I think it's possible, even likely, that there are people who are not unhappy that Horvecki is dead, people who might have killed him, people who do not have the conscience of an orange beetle or a lovebug. Horvecki was not a nice human being."

He leaned toward me and lowered his voice.

"And if such a person or persons were responsible for the demise of Philip Horvecki they would not be happy to know that you are trying to help that young man in jail, a young man who, I might add, is not the most socially acceptable of characters. They would prefer that young Mr. Gerall go to a juvenile facility for the crime."

"Got it," I said.

"Do you? Good. Take it from me. D. Elliot Corkle loves his grandson. Word has already gone out that D. Elliot Corkle will be seeing to it that his grandson is no longer pursuing this inquiry."

"No," I said.

"No?" said Corkle.

"I took your grandson's money and told him I would at least talk to Ronnie Gerall and look around, and that I fully intend to do."

"Randolph Scott in *Comanche Station*," said Augustine.

Corkle looked at the ex-actor with something less than approval. Augustine shrugged.

"My grandson could be hurt," Corkle said, smiling no more.

"Your grandson could hire someone else if I walked away."

"Perhaps someone not quite so stubborn."

"This could wind up costing a lot," I said.

"I can afford it. You know how many Power Pocket Entertainment Centers I sold last year?"

"No."

"Three million."

"I'm impressed."

"You're damn right you are," he said, plunking his almost empty glass on the table. The remaining ice cubes clinked musically.

"I'd like to go now," I said.

"Who is stopping you?" asked Corkle.

I put down my glass, which didn't clink as musically as Corkle's, and stood. So did Augustine and Corkle, who wiped his hands on his shorts.

Corkle silently led the way back through the kitchen and to the front door, where we paused while he made a stop at a closet and came up with a white box about the size of a large book. He placed the box in my hand.

"Forty-two songs on three CDs," he said. "Best of the original jazz crooners. Bing Crosby, Dick Powell, Russ Columbo."

"I don't have a CD player," I said.

"Not in your car?"

"I don't own a car."

He shook his head and said, "Wait."

I looked at Augustine as Corkle disappeared back in the closet and came up with a white box even smaller than the one with the CDs. He placed it in my free hand.

"Big seller in its day," he said. "Nine ninety-five. Thirty-dollar value. Great little CD player."

"Thanks," I said.

"Think about my offer," said Corkle. "D. Elliot Corkle is as good as his word. You a poker player, Fonesca?"

"Used to be."

When Catherine and I were first married, I played poker twice a month with two cops, an assistant district attorney and another investigator who, like me, worked for the state attorney's office. Well, he wasn't quite like me. He was in prison now, for murder.

"I host a weekly Wednesday game in my card room. If you like, I can let you know when we have an open seat. You can join us, see how you like it, how we like you."

"Game?"

"Five-card stud. That's it."

"Stakes?"

"Ten, twenty-five, fifty for the first hour," said Corkle. "Last hour, one to two in the morning, we go up to twenty-five, fifty, and a hundred. We start at nine at night. I know where you can get the money to play. Think about it."

He started to close the door as Augustine and I stepped out and said, "If I can't get you to say 'no' to Greg, can I hire you?"

"To do what?"

"Exactly what my grandson hired you to do, with one exception."

"Yes?"

"I don't care if you find evidence to clear Ronnie Gerall or get him locked up till he is ready for Social Security."

"I'll think about it," I said.

"D. Elliot Corkle doesn't work that way. The offer is going fast. Just fifteen seconds to decide. I'll make it a cash offer, payable right here on my doorstep. Two thousand dollars."

"Your grandson is still my client."

"Now you've got two clients. You just have to report to me and keep a protective eye on Greg."

I looked at Augustine, who gave me no help, and then back at Corkle.

"Why not?" I said.

Corkle reached into his pocket and came out with an envelope and folded sheet of paper.

"Two thousand in hundreds and fifties in the envelope. Just sign the receipt. It's made out 'for consulting fees.' "

"You were sure I'd agree."

"Reasonably," he said. "D. Elliot Corkle could always put the cash away and tear up the unsigned receipt. One should always be prepared for contingencies."

I took the envelope without checking the contents and said, "I can't sign this receipt."

Corkle smiled in understanding.

"I'm a process server, not a consultant."

"Then," said Corkle, "we'll just have to trust each other. Call when you have information."

He closed the door behind us as Augustine and I walked down the path.

"I think he likes you," said Augustine. "He's never invited me in on that poker game, not that I could afford it."

"I'm glad," I said, putting the envelope in my pocket.

"He's a good guy. You don't know him."

"And you do?" I asked.

"He sells gadgets, has millions of dollars, and refers to himself in the third person," said Augustine. "Also, he loves his grandson and he never leaves the house."

"Never?"

"For the last four years at least, I've been told. I don't know what his reasons are."

I shifted my gifts and got in the car.

"Corkle produced the only movie I ever starred in."

"*Shoot-out On a Silent Street*," I said, closing the car door. "You and Tim Holt."

He started the car. I put on my Cubs cap.

"Who was the woman who ran out of the house?" I asked.

"Alana Legerman."

"Greg's . . . ?"

"Mother. D. Elliot's daughter. If you ask me . . ."

I never found out what he wanted me to ask him. The front window exploded. Glass shot toward my face. I covered up. Augustine lost control. We spun around three times, skidded onto the freshly cut lawn of a large ranch-style house and came to a stop against a row of trimmed bushes.

I looked at Augustine. He was silent. Blood dripped like a red tear from the corner of his right eye and made its way down his nose. I was fascinated. Then I passed out.

Ames McKinney looked down at me. He was tall, lean, a little over seventy years old with tousled gray hair and an accent that came from the West. He always wore jeans with a big buckled belt and a flannel shirt, even when the temperature hit a humid one hundred. He never sweated. Ames was the closest thing I had to a best friend.

"You're lookin' tempered," he said.

My face was scratched in four or five places, and my shirt was torn. Nothing was broken.

"I feel fine," I said trying to stand. "Augustine?"

"Other fella in the car? He's a bit chiseled down but he'll survive."

"Envelope? Money?"

"Right here," said Ames, holding up the bulging envelope.

I tried to stand.

My legs didn't cooperate. I started to sink back on the bed. I had been taken to Sarasota Memorial Hospital by ambulance, treated and asked if there was anyone I wanted the people in the ER to call. I came up with Ames, who I knew would be at the Texas Bar, where he worked as a handyman, cleanup man, occasional short-order cook, and bartender. Big Ed, who owned the place, had been taking more time off to visit his children and grandchildren back in New Jersey. The only person Ed trusted was Ames.

Ames and I had met four years ago when I tried to stop him from having a shoot-out on Lido Beach with his ex-partner, who had gathered every dime in their company and run off to Sarasota to change his name and spend his way into what passed for society on the Gulf Coast. Ames had done some jail time, but not much, since I had testified that the partner had shot first.

"Steady, partner," Ames said, grabbing my arm and easing me back when I tried to rise again.

"What happened?" I said.

"Don't know."

"How long was I out?"

"Four hours," Ames said. "Besides those cuts on your face, you have yourself a concussion."

The room tilted at a slight angle and then tilted back the other way. I closed my eyes.

"Augustine?" I said.

I passed out again.

When I next opened my eyes, Detective Ettiene Viviase of the Sarasota Police Department was standing next to Ames.

"You all right?" he asked.

He was a burly man of about fifty who pretended to be world-weary. We had experienced a number of close encounters of the third kind.

"Fine and dandy," I said.

Augustine would have known I was quoting Earl Holliman in *The Rainmaker.*

"You were serving papers?" he asked.

I didn't answer.

"Lewis is confused," said Ames. "Trauma."

Viviase nodded and said, "What's it all about?"

"How is Augustine?" I asked.

"He'll live," said Viviase. "Maybe they can save his sight. He had a .177-caliber pellet lodged in his right eye."

"A pellet? Someone shot Augustine with Ralphie's Red Ryder you'll-shoot-your-eye-out BB gun?" I asked.

"And came close to shooting his eye out. Something like that," said Viviase. "Any idea who shot at you?"

"Me? What makes you think they were shooting at me?" I said. "They could have been shooting at Augustine, or maybe it was just kids shooting at a car."

"Ronnie Gerall," Viviase said.

I closed my eyes and started to lean back, and then I remembered. I touched the top of my head. The hair was definitely thinner with each passing crime. Ames reached back into his pocket and came up with my Cubs cap. He handed it to me. I clutched it like a teddy bear.

"You had Gerall's name and the words Greg and Winn in your notebook."

He held up my notebook and handed it to Ames.

"Think it might have something to do with your getting shot at?"

"No."

"Doc says you can go when you're up to it," said Ames.

"In a minute," said Viviase, eyes fixed on me. "Are you getting involved with the Philip Horvecki murder?"

"I promised a friend I'd drop in and see Gerall, talk to him."

"Need I remind you that you don't have a private investigator's license?"

"I tell people that all the time. I'm just doing a friend a favor," I said.

"The Gerall kid did it," said Viviase. "Caught inside the victim's house kneeling by the corpse. Kid had motive. Kid's a hothead. Only thing the kid said when he was arrested was, and I quote, 'I'm glad the son-of-a-bitch is dead.' Who's the friend who asked you to stop in and see Gerall?"

I hesitated. Viviase's daughter Elisabeth had told Greg and Winn about me. A few more questions and I'd have to lie or tell her father that she was the one who got me involved.

"I'd like to talk to Augustine," I said.

"Jeff Augustine, onetime actor, minor arrests in California, looks tough, maybe. I know he's working for D. Elliot Corkle. It's not clear in what capacity, and he is too narcotized to explain or talk to you. You happen to know what he does for Corkle?"

"I think he's a kind of companion," I said.

"We talked to Corkle," Viviase said.

"What did Corkle tell you?" I asked Viviase, making another effort to get up. Ames reached for my arm.

"Lie down, partner," he said.

I did. The thin pillow felt just right behind my head, and I wanted to go to sleep. I was sure I had been given something to ease the pain.

"Corkle had nothing much to say," said Viviase. "He did refer to himself in the third person and compared life to a game of poker twice. He tried to give me a box with a Wonder Chopper inside. I told him I couldn't take it. Your mini CD player and the CDs are being held as possible evidence."

"Of what?" Ames asked.

"I don't know," said Viviase. "I have a headache and I don't know. Just answer the questions, Fonesca, and don't ask any. I have places to go and things to do, and my wife promised me that she would have chicken in duck sauce for dinner tonight. I plan to be there for it."

I nodded. Ames stood straight and silent.

"You moved to a new place," Viviase said.

"Yes. Had to. DQ is gone. My office building goes down tomorrow. I'm right around the corner, off of Laurel."

"Life goes on," Viviase said.

"Even when we don't care."

"The Chinese guy?" said Viviase.

"He's moving with me, I think."

"You're nuts," said Viviase.

"No . . . Maybe. It doesn't matter."

"Get better. Come and see me," he said taking a deep breath. Then he turned his head toward Ames and added, "Take care of him."

"I aim to," said Ames.

When Viviase was gone, I stood again, this time without Ames's help.

"We going to look for whoever took the shot?" he asked.

"We are," I said. "Either that or I buy a car and head out of town forever."

"That won't work."

"I guess."

"Where do we start?"

"In juvenile detention," I said, adjusting my Cubs cap and noticing that it had a slight but real tear on the right side. "First we talk to Augustine."

I didn't fall on my face as we moved to the elevator to go up to the private fourth-floor room where Jeff Augustine was lying on his back. He wore a white hospital gown with a thin white blanket pulled up to his chest. An IV was going. His left eye was closed. His right eye was covered by a taped-down gauze pad. His hands were folded in front of him. He looked like a one-eyed saint.

"Jeff?" I tried.

Augustine made a sound but didn't open his eye. I tried again.

"Augustine."

This time his left eye popped open and he let out a pained groan as he reached up with his right hand to touch the injured eye.

"Hurts," he said.

"I know," I said.

"How would you know?"

"I have a natural empathy. Besides I got caught by flying glass."

"We get a medal or something?" Augustine asked, closing his eye again and explaining, "Hurts less when both eyes are closed. I may lose the eye."

"Maybe so," said Ames.

"Who is he?" Augustine said, being careful not to turn his head.

"My friend," I said. "Ames McKinney."

"Weren't we both in an episode of *The Yellow Rose*?"

"Not an actor," said Ames.

"I could have sworn, but . . . Damn, what if this killed me? My obit would make a single line in *Variety*, 'Bit Player Killed by BB Gun.' Bitter irony."

Alana Legerman walked in. She wafted perfume and looked sleek, dark, and beautiful.

"What happened?" she asked, moving to the side of the bed next to Augustine.

She was as tranquil as her offspring Greg was wired.

"Someone shot BBs at us," said Augustine. "Hit me in the eye."

"Who did it?" she asked.

No one had an answer, but Alana Legerman had a question. She looked at Augustine and said, "Are you all right? Are you going to lose your eye?"

She tried to say it nice, but it was as if she were asking if the dime dropped on the floor was his. I couldn't be sure if she was just saying the right thing or if she had shown concern to her father's employee beyond that of an heiress.

"I'm all right," Augustine said. "I've still got one twenty-twenty eye."

"I'm all right too," I said.

There was no way even a casual glance would have failed to reveal the scratches on my face and neck.

"I'm sorry," said Alana Legerman. "How are you, Mr. . . ."

"Fonesca," Ames supplied. "Mr. Lewis Fonesca. And my name's Ames McKinney."

"And what have you got to do with my father and Jeff?"

"Your father has asked me to look into the murder of Philip Horvecki."

"You're a private investigator?"

"No, a process server."

She was unimpressed.

"You think my son's friend killed Horvecki?"

"The police think so. The television stations, the newspaper, and most of the people in Sarasota probably think so."

"Why don't you just ask Ronnie Gerall what happened?" she asked.

Jeff Augustine's left eye was open wide and looking at Alana Legerman. I moved toward the door, Ames at my side.

"I think we'll do that," I said.

3

The problem was immediately clear after we talked to Ronnie Gerall across a table in the visitors' room in the county jail. I got the impression that he worked at being independent, superior, and unlikable, but I could have been wrong. He could simply and naturally be what my uncle called a *Merdu*, which roughly translated from the Italian means "dickhead."

Ronnie was about six feet tall and had the build of an athlete, the drawn-back, almost blond hair of a teen movie idol, blue eyes, and a look of total boredom. He could easily have passed for twenty-one, which I was sure he did when it suited him.

It had started badly. Gerall had been ushered in. He wore a loose-fitting orange jail suit and a look that said, "Look at what those jerks sent me." He didn't offer his hand to Ames and me or ask or say anything at first; he just sat in the wooden chair with his right leg extended and half turned as if he planned to escape at the first sign of ennui.

Ames and I took seats. The full-bellied, uniformed guard, who looked almost as bored as Ronnie Gerall, stood with his back to the door, arms folded. The room was large enough that the guard wouldn't hear us if we whispered. Ronnie had no intention of whispering.

"Greg Legerman told me you were coming," he said.

That required no answer so I just kept sitting and watching him.

"Please do me a favor before we have anything that resembles conversation," he said.

"Yes."

"Would you mind taking off that dopey baseball cap."

"Yes, I would."

"I watched you and an old man drive up on a motor scooter," he said, ignoring my answer.

"And . . . ?"

"You can't afford a car?"

"Don't want the responsibility," I said.

"How did Greg Legerman find you?" he asked shaking his head and looking first at Ames and then at me.

"Luck," I said.

We sat in silence for about a minute, during which he found his fingernails fascinating and the palms of his hands, particularly the right one, profound.

"I did not kill Philip Horvecki," he said, looking up.

"Tell us what happened."

"Why not? I've got time. It was Thursday night. He called, said he would meet with me. Horvecki said he wanted to talk."

"You sure it was Horvecki?" I asked.

"Old men all sound alike, either like sick hummingbirds or gravel pits. This was gravel pits. Pure Horvecki."

He looked at Ames, who could have been number five on Mount Rushmore.

"Go on," I prompted.

"I went to his house."

"Right away?"

"Yes."

"You told someone you were going?"

"No. Can I go on?"

"Yes."

"I rang the bell. No answer. I tried the door. Open. I went in. The place is a nightmare. Black wood, black tile floors, white walls. Even the paintings are almost all black and white. No wonder someone killed him."

"I don't think you should say that," I said.

"You don't think so?" Ronnie said with a smile.

"He doesn't think so," said Ames. "And you'd best heed what Mr. Fonesca tells you."

"Or what, old man?"

"Or I reach across this table and slap you three or four times. And you won't stop me, because even though I just warned you, you won't be able to," said Ames, eyes fixed on Ronnie Gerall's face.

"He'll do it, too," I said.

"Then he'll be in here with me," said Ronnie.

"Is that where you want him? Respect means a great deal to Mr. McKinney."

The uniformed guard slouched a little more. He wasn't interested in what we had to say.

"You found Horvecki," I said.

"On the floor in the hallway. Definitely dead. Lots of blood on his face and shirt. Mouth open. I thought I saw someone in an open doorway on the right. Then I saw someone go out the window."

"And you followed him," said Ames.

"No. I mean yes. I went out the front door looking for him. Whoever it was was gone."

"You saw nobody?" I asked.

"No . . . wait. There was a man in a pickup truck, but it wasn't the one who was in the house. The guy in the pickup was there when I got to Horvecki's. I thought he was waiting for somebody."

"Could he have seen the man who jumped out of the window?" I asked.

"Could have? He would have had to," said Ronnie.

"Can you describe the man or the truck?" I asked.

"It was a small pickup, not old, not new. Guy in the truck had on a baseball cap. Couldn't see his face. I think he was black. Maybe. Couldn't tell you how . . . Wait, I had the feeling he wasn't an old guy like Stokes over here."

Ames did not take kindly to the remark, but he held his tongue.

"And I don't know how tall he was," Ronnie went on. "He never got out of the truck. I only saw him for a few seconds."

"Did he look at you?" I asked.

"Yes."

"We'll find him," I said.

I must not have filled the room with my infectious optimism, because Ronnie said, "You don't believe me."

"No matter if we believe you," said Ames. "It matters if we find him."

"What did you do after you went outside and didn't see him?" I asked.

"I went back in the house to be sure Horvecki was dead. Before I could call 911, I heard the door to the house open. Then a voice saying, 'Throw your gun toward the door and stand up slowly with your hands high and your palms showing.'

"I did. I was read my rights and arrested."

"Did you tell them about the person in the doorway and the man in the truck?" I asked.

"I did. They didn't believe me, either. I'm glad Horvecki's dead, but I didn't kill him."

"You have a lawyer?" I asked.

"You're not a lawyer?"

"No," I said.

"Goddamn it!" he shouted loud enough to make the guard almost slump to the floor. "I'll kill Greg when I get my hands on him."

"You really know the right things to say," I said.

"What the hell are you then?"

"A process server," I said. "And someone who finds missing people."

"Who the fuck is missing here?"

"The person who shot Philip Horvecki," said Ames, "provided that person is not you."

"And," I added, "whoever might have been standing in the open doorway when you went into Horvecki's house."

"Guard, get these two out of here," said Ronnie. Then he turned to me and said, "I'll get my own lawyer."

"Suits me," said Ames rising.

I got up, too. The guard was alert now.

We got to the door. Then Ronnie Gerall said, "Wait."

I turned as the guard moved toward the prisoner.

"I think the person in the doorway was a woman."

"Horvecki's daughter?" I asked.

He shrugged. "I don't know."

"Whoever it was might have seen the person who went through the window kill Horvecki," I said.

"Or might have been the person who killed Horvecki," said Ames.

"I've got no money, but I don't want a public defender," Ronnie said. It sounded like a challenge.

"I'll see what I can do," I said.

Ames and I went past the guard and into the corridor.

"He's scared," Ames said.

"He's scared," I agreed as we walked toward the thick metal door.

"Full of hate," Ames said.

"Full of hate," I agreed.

"You gonna help him?" Ames asked as we got to the door.

"It's why I get the big bucks," I said.

"Philip Horvecki," I said.

There were twenty-two wooden steps leading up to the three rooms under a pitched roof into which I had moved. This was on Laurel, around the corner and about half a block from the departed Dairy Queen. The steps had once been white. The railing, which shook if you put a hand on it, had once been green. I couldn't call it an apartment. You had to move carefully under the ceiling or you would bump your head. The first room was a big, blank square with a bathroom across from the front door. The second room, about the size of a prison cell, looked as if it had originally been installed by indifferent Seminoles and recently painted white by someone who wanted to set the record for speed painting. There was a third room, a little bigger than one of Superman's phone booths. With luck you might be able to get a rocking chair into it.

The walls of the big room were white-painted plasterboard under which the smell of sad and ancient wood managed to persist. The big and little rooms were connected by a varnished wooden door. There were no overhead lights, but Flo Zink, who had found the place, had not only painted it but put two bright floor lamps in each room. I had met Flo shortly after I came to Sarasota. I had found her husband, Gus, who was dying from too many diseases to count. Gus had been kidnapped to keep him from voting on a land issue in the City Council. Ames and I had gotten him to the meeting, where his last act on earth was to cast the deciding vote. He left Flo with enough money to sustain five widows comfortably for a lifetime. Flo felt responsible for me. Finding my new home was just one of the ways she had shown it over the last four years.

There were three small windows in the big room and one in each of the other two rooms. Ames had already moved the air conditioner from my last place overlooking the defunct DQ to a window in the big room. It was already clear that the air conditioner wouldn't be able to adequately cool one room let alone two or three. There was more space than I needed.

As Augustine had said, my boxes and furniture had been moved. My meager furniture looked sad and frightened in these rooms.

The first thing Victor Woo had done was put up my Stig Dalstrom prints, including a recent painting Flo had given to me as a housewarming present. Victor had pinned the Dalstroms to the wall in about the same places they had been in my former space.

"Philip Horvecki," I repeated into the cell phone which I now reluctantly owned.

The phone was another housewarming present. It was from Adele, who was just about to become a freshman at New College in Sarasota. She could have gotten into dozens of colleges, but she wanted to continue to live with her baby, Catherine, in Flo's house. No dorm experience for Adele, but she wouldn't regret it. Adele's father had sold her to a pimp when she was fourteen. Getting her away from Dad and pimp had had its complications, but when Flo took her in, Adele blossomed, turned her life around, became an A student in high school, and was now going to college. There had been one major speed bump in the path. Adele had gotten pregnant by an older man who was now doing time in prison for murder. Adele had named the baby Catherine in honor of my dead wife.

"Horvecki. Did he have a criminal record?" I asked.

"I'll check," said Viviase. "The county might have something. If that doesn't work, I've got another place you can look."

I had walked back out to get better reception.

Victor Woo had followed me out and sat next to me on the top step. The Serita sisters, friends of Flo, lived in the bottom two floors of the brightly painted white and green wooden house. They owned the building, so I'd be paying rent to them, the same rent I had been paying behind the DQ.

From my seat on the top step, I could look past the freshly painted house across the street and into a yard where the edge of a screen-enclosed pool was visible. I stared at the water of the pool flecked with light from the setting sun and decided that I needed a shower.

"Check with Sergeant Yoder in the sheriff's office," added Viviase.

"Thanks," I said.

The sun seemed to be dropping quickly now. I heard something below.

"Fonesca, you are one hard dog to find."

It was Darrell Caton, which usually meant it must be Saturday, but I knew it wasn't Saturday. Darrell was the fourteen-year-old that Sally Porovsky had conned me into being a big brother for. She was a county Children and Family Services social worker I had been seeing socially and seeking in ways I didn't understand.

Darrell was lean and black, wearing baggy jeans and a T-shirt that had something printed on the front. I couldn't make out the word from twenty-two steps up.

"It's not Saturday," I called.

"I know that," said Viviase on the phone. "You losing it, Fonesca?"

"Darrell just showed up," I said.

"It's not Saturday," said Viviase, who knew of my weekly commitment to Darrell.

"I know," I said.

Darrell had grown in the time he had been trailing me once a week. He looked forward to being with me because, as he said, "Man, something's always happening with you. Guns, dead people, and shit. You are an education, Fonesca."

I did not want to be an education, but I had grown used to seeing Darrell.

Darrell started up the steps. Victor started to move over so Darrell could sit.

"One more question," I said into the phone.

"Yeah."

"Why are you helping me?"

The pause was long. He was considering telling me something.

"He may not be guilty, and it's not really my case, but if you're looking into it . . ."

Darrell was almost in front of me now. He had bounded up the steps. He wasn't panting. I remember once, when I was fourteen, lying in my bed and praying to God to let me live through Saturday because I had a soccer game on Saturday. We lost the game to Lane Tech, and I missed an easy goal. God did let me live, but it didn't look as if he were about to do the same for Darrell.

I could now clearly see what was printed on the front of Darrell's T-shirt. It read, in black block letters, "Pope John Paul II Girl's Volleyball Team Kicks Ass."

There was a crack in the air, a sudden sharp pinging sound from somewhere on the side of the house with the pool. Darrell lifted his head toward the sky as if he were startled by the sudden appearance of a UFO. Then he arched his back, groped over his left shoulder blade as if he had a sudden itch.

He was about to tumble backward down the stairs.

I dropped the phone and reached for him. His right hand almost touched mine and he bent over backward. Victor Woo was up, behind Darrell now, stopping his fall, setting him gently on the small landing in front of my door. Victor was holding the rickety handrail and taking the steps two at a time.

I knelt next to Darrell and groped for the phone.

"Fonesca, what the hell is going on?" asked Viviase.

"Someone shot Darrell. Send an ambulance."

Victor hit the ground running like a sprinter. If he was lucky, he would catch up with the shooter. If he wasn't lucky, he would catch up with the shooter. Victor was armed with nothing.

"I'm on the way," Viviase said and ended the connection.

Darrell was groaning. A good sign.

"What the fuck, Fonesca? Oh. I like the action, but I don't want to be the victim. You know what I'm saying?"

I rolled him gently onto his side.

"This isn't for real," he whimpered. "Why'd anyone want to shoot me?"

"I think they were trying to shoot me," I said. "You got in the way."

"I took a bullet for you?"

"Yes, but I'm guessing it was a pellet, not a bullet."

"Hurts like a bullet."

"You've been shot before?"

"Hell no," he said and then gasped. "Life's funnier than shit. You know what I'm saying? My mother's going to be all over your ass, Fonesca. Jesus, it hurts. Am I going to die?"

"Yes, but so am I. You're not going to die for a while."

"You know how to make Christmas come early, don't you, Fonesca?"

"Ambulance is on the way," I said.

"You ever been shot at, Fonesca?"

"Yes."

"When?"

"A few times."

"Last time?"

"This morning." An actor took that pellet in the eye.

There was no doubt where the pellet had entered Darrell, just below the left shoulder blade. The hole was small, the T-shirt was definitely ruined. There was blood dripping from the wound, but it didn't look as if anything vital had been hit.

Police headquarters was, at maximum, a five-minute drive from where Darrell lay bleeding. Viviase made it in three, and somewhere in the distance an ambulance siren cut through the twilight.

4

The emergency room triage nurse, a wiry thin woman with wiry thin straw-colored hair, looked up at me and said, "You're back, Mr. . . ."

"Fonesca."

"Are you . . . ?"

"I'm fine. I'm here about Darrell Caton. He was brought in here by ambulance a few minutes ago."

"What's your relationship to him?"

"I'm his big brother," I said. "It's complicated."

She looked from me to Ames to Victor and said, "He's being taken care of by a doctor. His mother is on the way. Just have a seat."

We had a seat.

That was when Victor told his story.

"I took your bicycle from under the stairs," he said.

"Okay."

"I went after the shooter, who I saw running from behind the house across the street. He was carrying a rifle."

"What were you planning to do?" asked Ames.

"I don't know."

In a seat across from us, a drunk cradled a limp arm with his good arm like a baby. He snorted in half sleep.

"You chased him," I said, getting Victor back on track.

"He ran down Laurel. When I turned the corner onto the street . . ."

"Laurel," I said.

Victor knew almost nothing about Sarasota geography. He had spent most of his time in town squatting in my two former rooms.

"What'd he look like?" Ames asked.

"I don't know, it was starting to get dark. He was a block away. He opened a car door, threw the rifle inside, climbed in, and started to drive away when I was about forty yards from him."

"He got away," said Ames with a touch of disapproval.

"He drove west. I followed him. I don't know where we went. North, I think, then west again. He ran a light on Oxbay . . ."

"Osprey," said Ames.

Victor nodded.

"Ran a light and then went way over the speed limit. I would have caught him on Fruit Street."

"Fruitville," I said.

"He went right through without stopping, almost hit a couple," said Victor. "I stopped."

"Why?" asked Ames.

I knew. Victor had killed my wife in a hit-and-run accident. He didn't want to be the cause of another hit-and-run.

"You get a license plate number?" I asked.

The drunk across from us snorted louder than he had the first time. He was definitely asleep when he grunted, "Can there be any doubt in the mind of the jurors?"

Then he slumped over on his left side.

"No," said Victor. "I think it was a dark-colored Nissan. Late model. As he crossed Fruitville, he went under a streetlight. I'm sure he gave me the finger."

"When we find him," said Ames evenly, "I shoot him."

"Ames . . ." I began.

"He shot the boy," said Ames. "Could have killed him if Victor here didn't keep him from tumbling down the stairs."

"He was aiming for me."

"More's the reason," said Ames.

"No," said Victor. "No killing."

"I'll not kill him," said Ames. "I'll just give him some sense of what it feels like to get shot in the eye or the back."

"No," said Victor.

The drunk roused himself, blinked his eyes, rubbed his chin, and tried unsuccessfully to flatten his bushy hair. Then he looked at us and said with a cough, "You're just puttin' on an act for me, right? I like the story, but it lacks romance. You know what I'm talkin' about?"

That was when Darrell's mother came through the emergency room doors, looked around, saw us, and moved in front of me. She was a dry, tired brown stick of a woman who had touches of good looks left over from only a few years earlier.

"You were supposed to look after him," she said.

"Yes," I agreed.

"You got him shot."

"Yes. I'm sorry."

She stood, looked around the waiting room, and saw the drunk, who either bowed in his seat or was about to fall over again.

"I want to be angry at you, but I can't do it. You're a crazy man, but a good one," she said. "Darrell thinks you . . . I've got to go see him."

She turned and hurried to the desk where the wiry triage nurse came around and led her through the double doors to the treatment area.

"I'm sorry I didn't catch the shooter," said Victor.

"You probably saved Darrell's life," I said. "A fall down those stairs might have killed him. I'll settle for that."

"I am the click-clack man who never made it to Oz. I am the bold deceiver who winks to those who understand, who winks only to himself in the mirror, a store window, the dark screen of a computer. I am the truth, which is a lie. I'm looking down at everyone from a spot reserved for me in the asshole of a serial killer with the blood of children in the webbing between his fingers."

He had called about ten minutes after Victor, Ames, and I got back to my new rooms, which would always smell like decaying wood. He didn't announce himself, just began talking with a muffled, high-pitched Latino accent that was more Billy Crystal than Ricardo Montalban.

"You're the click-clack man," I said. "You almost killed a fourteen-year-old. I've got that much."

"Stop looking. Visualize yourself in dark glasses looking only straight ahead," he said.

"I'd fall."

Ames was reaching for the phone in my hand. He was not to be denied. Victor sat against the wall on his open bedroll.

"Someone here wants to say hello," I managed as Ames took the phone from my hand and put it to his ear.

Ames looked very calm. I'd learned that Ames always looked calm when he was angry—dangerous and determined. I knew, given enough time, that Ames would find the shooter as Ames had found his former partner when he came to Sarasota. He had found him on the Lido Key Beach. There had been a shoot-out. The partner, a plaster pillar of the community who had cheated Ames out of a small fortune, had not survived the volley.

"Where did you get blunt-force .22 bullets?" asked Ames.

"What?" the caller said.

"The ones you used to shoot out that man's eye, and to shoot the boy. We can trace them."

"No, you can't," said the caller.

"Here," said Ames handing me back the phone and moving back to lean against the wall with his arms folded.

"My friend is angry," I told the caller.

His voice betrayed a quiver and went a little higher when he said, "I didn't intend to kill him or even shoot him."

"You wanted to shoot me?"

"Yes. And I will if you don't stop."

"Stop what?"

"You know."

Ann Hurwitz would say I should stop fighting my emergence

from depression over my wife's bloody death against the grille of the car Victor Woo had driven down Lake Shore Drive. It had happened as Catherine was crossing at the light. I think we were going to have steak for dinner. Or was it chili?

"Fonesca?" said the caller. "You listening?"

"Not really. Why are you calling?"

"Stop looking," he repeated with some frustration.

"Or you'll try to shoot me again with a pellet gun?"

"I have a real rifle," he said.

"Having it and using it are different things," I said, looking at Victor, who was gently bouncing his head against the wall as he sat.

"I don't want to kill you," he said.

"Then don't."

"But you might make me."

"Then do. You want to tell me now what I'm supposed to stop doing?"

"Whatever you're doing," he said.

"I'm talking to a frightened person on the telephone," I said.

"Looking for the person who killed Horvecki," he said.

Ames was looking at me. I met his eyes.

"You killed him?"

"Yes, I did. The police have the wrong person in jail. Ronnie didn't do it. They have to let him out. You've got to stop looking."

"This doesn't make much sense," I tried. "Ronnie didn't do it, but you don't want me to look for who did."

The pause was long. I could hear breathing.

"What can I do to convince you?"

"Stop shooting at me, that would make a nice start," I said.

"Lewis," Ames said firmly.

"What's your favorite movie?" I asked.

"What?"

"Your favorite movie. Mine's *The Third Man*, or *Mildred Pierce*, or *The List of Adrian Messenger*, or *On the Waterfront*, or *The Seven Samurai*, or *Once Upon a Time in America*, or *Comanche Station* . . ."

"You're crazy," he said.

"Deeply neurotic," I corrected. "You have a favorite movie?"

"*Gone with the Wind.*"

"And?"

"*Wuthering Heights. From Here to Eternity.*"

"You didn't kill Horvecki," I interrupted.

"I did."

"Let's meet for coffee."

"I don't drink coffee," he said. "I hate the stuff."

"Tea?"

"Tastes like water someone pissed in."

"A cheeseburger."

"You'll arrest me. That other guy, the old one. He'll shoot me or break my face."

"I'll persuade him not to. And I'm not a cop, I can't arrest you," I said.

"Citizen's arrest."

"You have something to tell me, don't you?"

"I'll think about it."

"You almost killed that boy on the steps."

"I'm sorry. I'll let you know about meeting you."

He hung up.

"He didn't do it," said Ames.

The phone rang again. I pushed the button and put it to my ear. The phone was a gift to keep me in touch with the world. I did not wish to keep in touch with the world.

"Philip Horvecki was a murderer," came the voice of the person who had just hung up. "He deserved to die."

The connection clicked, and the line went dead. I pushed the button and handed the phone to Ames, who wanted no more to do with it than I did. Ames handed it to Victor, who put it in his pocket.

"The shots at you were pellets and that business about blunt-force .22 bullets was a small pile of cow chips," said Ames.

"I know," I said.

The next call came that night, from Sally Porovsky.

"Lewis," she said wearily.

"Sally," I said.

"Darrell's mother doesn't want him to see you again," she said.

"He's all right?"

"Whatever it was he was shot with didn't go very deep," she said.

I had been going with Sally for about two years. We didn't see each other much because she was a child services worker who regularly put in ten-hour days and spent whatever hours she had left with her two children. I was at the fringe of her schedule, which I understood. It was fine with me.

We had never slept together, though we had come close a few times. I had to admit that it was less and less out of a commitment to the memory of Catherine and more an unwillingness on my part to take the symbolic and real action.

I wanted to hold on to the belief that at any moment I could simply fill my duffel bag, get on a Greyhound bus, and head somewhere, anywhere, where no one expected anything of me and I could nurture my depression. I was increasingly aware that my belief that I could do that was becoming an illusion. Ames, Flo, Adele, Darrell, and Sally—I knew I could not easily ride away from them. I'd need a major blow to let me escape.

"Darrell's fine," she said. "He's weirdly proud that he took a bullet—"

"Pellet," I corrected.

". . . that he took a pellet meant for you," she said.

"I don't like Ronnie Gerall," I said.

"He takes some getting used to."

"You know him?" I asked.

"I handled his transition when he came from San Antonio to Sarasota."

There was something in her voice, an unfamiliar impatience or something I couldn't quite grasp.

"His friends are paying me to prove he didn't kill Philip Horvecki," I said.

"I've got to go."

"Meet me tomorrow?"

"We'll see. Call me in the morning," she said. "We can set a time when I can come and see your new . . ."

"Lodgings," I said.

"I'll talk to Darrell's mother," she said. "I'll make her love you again."

"You can do that?"

"No," she said. "I can't."

"Thanks."

"Take care of yourself, Lewis Fonesca."

"Yes," I said. "And you too, Sally Porovsky."

I had not been doing a good job of taking care of myself since Catherine had been struck and killed by the man sitting on the floor, against the wall. Ann Hurwitz said progress was being made.

The last time she had told me that, I suggested that maybe we needed either another hundred thousand troops in Iraq or a small team of psychologists to speed my progress.

"We'll talk in the morning," Sally said.

She didn't seem to want to end the call.

"Something wrong?" I asked.

"Nothing."

"Okay," I said.

What I really wanted to say was, "I'll see you if I'm alive. I'll see you if I don't run away. I'll see you if I don't curl into a ball on the floor next to Victor, hugging my knees."

I turned off the phone and looked at Victor.

Ames walked in from the other room and said, "Beer, Dunkin' Donuts, or ice cream?"

Victor shrugged. He didn't care.

"Make it doughnuts," I said.

Ames left, and I picked up the phone.

I called the number Greg Legerman had given me. A woman answered after three rings. I said I wanted to talk to Greg. She politely said she would get him. About thirty seconds later he came on the phone with a wary, "Yes?"

"Do your Cheech Marin for me again," I said. "It's bad, but probably a little funny for anyone who has a sense of humor."

"What are you talking about?"

"You called me," I said. "Told me to stop looking for whoever killed Horvecki. Meet me at the Waffle Shop at eight tomorrow morning."

Silence.

"You're at a loss for words?" I said.

"I didn't call you," he finally said.

"I think I'll just give your money back and continue to try to locate a reasonably sane world."

"Tomorrow at eight. Waffle Shop on 301," he said. "I'll be there."

I made one more call, to Dixie Cruise, and told her what I needed and what I would pay.

"I'll work on it tonight," she said. "Call me after ten tomorrow."

"Tomorrow," I repeated and turned off the phone.

Dixie was a waitress. She had just moved to the Appleby's on Fruitville near I-75. Dixie was pert, energetic, in her thirties, and working online toward a business degree from the University of South Florida. Dixie was also a first-rate computer hacker with a small apartment in a 1920s apartment building on Ringling Boulevard.

When Ames returned, Victor took one plain, Ames had a double chocolate, and I had a strawberry iced. We ate, drank decaf coffee, and said nothing for the rest of the evening.

There was nothing to say.

5

The Waffle Shop is on Washington, also known as State Road 301 or just 301 to the locals. The shop is just before the point where 301 meets Tamiami Trail, known as 41 to the locals. It's across from a car dealership, half a block from a McDonald's, and another block from Sarasota High School. It was also a five-minute walk from where I now resided. It didn't feel right yet for me to say I "lived" there. It probably never would.

The Waffle Shop is semi-famous. Elvis once stopped there. The sign outside says so. There's a big poster of The King on the wall inside. He was a frequent topic of conversation.

There were regulars at the shop, which looked like it belonged in the 1950s without trying to create the illusion. There was a wrap-around counter with red leatherette-covered stools. There were tables against the walls by the windows where morning cops, hearse drivers, car salesmen, high school teachers, truckers and deliverymen, and all kinds of people just hung out.

I sat on a stool and got a coffee from one of Gwen's daughters, who served as hostesses, waitresses, and owners of the landmark.

For an instant, as I looked at Elvis, I felt like a regular. I did not want to be a regular anywhere, but such things happen.

"Carrots are bullshit," said the old man who climbed up on the stool next to me.

I knew him. He was a regular. His name was Tim—Tim from

Steubenville. Tim said he was sixty, but he was closer to eighty and looked it. He lived in an assisted living home a short walk away at the end of Brother Geenen Way. He spent as much time as he could at Gwen's, reading the newspaper, shaking his head, and trying to lure people into conversations about eliminating the income tax. Almost everything he said about income tax, abolishing drug laws, and eliminating gun laws ended with the punctuation, "damn government."

He always had a newspaper and commented on stories ranging from war and devastation around the world to cats and dogs waiting, hoping to be adopted before they had to be urged to pass away, making room for others to wait their turn.

"Do animals have souls?" Tim asked, the blue veins undulating over his thin bones.

"I don't know."

"What about carrots?"

"Carrots don't have souls," I said.

"What's the matter with your Cubs?" Tim asked in one of his familiar dancing changes of subject.

"They're cursed," I said as he was served his coffee and a slice of pineapple upside-down cake.

"I'll drink to that," he said, lifting his coffee mug and bringing it to his lips.

"No," I said.

"I won't drink to that?"

"No," I said. "Animals don't have souls."

The coffee was hot. I could see the steam rising, feel the heat with my fingers through the porcelain mug. I hadn't drunk any yet, even after adding milk from the miniature aluminum pitcher. My grizzled counter partner took no such precautions. He sipped, made an "uhh" sound to indicate he had made a mistake, and put the coffee down.

"You do that all the time," I said.

"I do what?"

"Add the milk and then remember that you don't like it with milk."

"My problem," he said. "Just like Jesse always said when she was living—that I don't learn from my mistakes. I'm just doomed to keep repeating them. What about people? They have souls?"

"I don't think so," I said.

"Cubs, here's to you."

He raised his mug and drank more cautiously this time after having cooled down his coffee with the milk I had passed to him. He called me "Cubs" because of the Chicago Cubs cap I wore. I wore the cap for several reasons. First, it was a memento of my affection for the Cubs. Catherine had bought it at Wrigley Field one afternoon when she and I had taken the day off to catch a game with the Pirates. The Cubs had won 4-1. Catherine had bought it for me. I had put it on her head. She looked cute in it. It made her smile. Now she was dead and I wore the cap. Second, it covered my increasing baldness. It was not a receding hairline. It was a steady retreat. Vanity? Maybe. I didn't take time to analyze it. Old bald men look younger in hats. They don't necessarily look better. Men my age who wear baseball caps either look tough or would like to be thought of as athletic.

Greg Legerman showed up. He was alone. I couldn't tell if he was any more nervous than he always was, but he was sufficiently nervous to make the patrons uncomfortable. He wore jeans and a short-sleeved buttoned shirt with a collar. The shirt was green with yellow lines. He sat on the open stool to my right.

The old man leaned forward to get a better look at Greg and said, "Young man, you think people have souls?"

"Good question," said Greg, avoiding my eyes.

I thought serving this permanently wired kid coffee would not improve the coming conversation, but I was too late. Gwen's daughter, the one with two kids, including a teenage boy who sometimes worked in the shop after school, put a mug of hot liquid in front of Greg and said, "Decaf. Breakfast?"

"Waffles," Greg said.

She nodded and moved off. You ordered waffles here. You got waffles, butter, maple syrup. You didn't get built-in blueberries or bananas or bacon bits. You didn't get wheat or bran waffles. You got the old-fashioned kind. Just the way Elvis had eaten them half a century ago.

"I can explain," Greg said.

"I'm sure you can," I said.

"I was just joking," he said. "I do things like that for no reason. I get excited . . ."

"Carrots are bullshit and so are you," I said. "How did you know someone had shot at me?"

"Everybody knew," he said.

"Everybody? The King of Jordan knew? Brad Pitt knew?"

"Oh come on," he said. "I mean . . ."

"First you hire me to help Ronnie Gerall. Then you call me to warn me off. You think he did it."

"No, it's just that I . . . it's too dangerous."

"For who?"

"I gave you five hundred dollars to find the real killer. I'll give you five hundred dollars to stop looking."

He reached into his pocket and came up with a roll of bills wrapped in a thick rubber band, which he placed in front of me. I pushed it back and added to it the money he had given me the day before.

"My teeth need fixing," the old man said. "If neither one of you want that money . . ."

Greg Legerman and I ignored him and looked at the money.

"Leave it there," said Gwen's daughter as she placed the plate of waffles in front of Greg, "and it'll be the biggest tip anyone ever left here."

"What about Elvis?" I asked.

"His tip is legendary," she said moving on.

"Someone shot at me in a car and probably blinded the man with me," I said. "Then someone shot a pellet into the back of a fourteen-year-old I'm responsible for. He could have died if he tumbled down my steps. It seems pretty likely that someone was trying to shoot me. I'm getting interested in finding out who killed Philip Horvecki."

"Why'd they shoot at you?" asked the old man.

"To scare me off."

"Please stop," Greg said. "You could get killed."

"My therapist says I'm suicidal, only I'd never kill myself. I wouldn't, however, object to someone else doing it for me."

"Why are you suicidal?" asked the old man with interest.

"Because my wife was murdered and the killer was never arrested."

"Then go look for him, Cubs," said Tim.

"I know where he is."

"Where?"

"Sleeping on the floor of the place I'm living in."

"You are a strange duck, Cubs. Kid, you think people have souls?" he asked again.

This ignited Greg. "No definitive evidence," he said. "Though research at universities in France, Germany, England, and the United States, including Princeton, is inconclusive, there seems to be evidence that electrical impulses . . ."

"Greg," I interrupted.

"He's just getting started," said the old man.

"I know. Who are you trying to protect?"

Greg shook his head no.

"Winn doesn't know what you did, does he?"

Greg shook his head again.

"No. You're not going to tell me, are you?"

"You don't even like Ronnie," he said. "No one does."

"He hasn't been arrested because people don't like him. He has been arrested for killing Philip Horvecki."

"Lots of people wanted to kill Horvecki," Greg said, looking at his waffle.

"Put the butter and syrup on 'em kid," said the old man, "and whale away while they're still hot."

There was an early-morning breakfast hubbub in the Waffle Shop. All the stools and all the tables were full. Men in suits laughed at each other's jokes. Men in work clothes talked softly and tended to concentrate on eating. The smell of waffles wafted, and Gwen's daughters bustled. I put enough on the counter to cover my coffee and a tip and said, "I have work to do."

"Please," said Greg. "Take the money. Stop looking."

He looked as if he were about to cry.

"Don't be a dumb shit, Fonesca. Take the money."

Greg nodded. I moved toward the door as the old man sidled over to sit next to Greg.

I didn't listen to find out if they were talking about the existence of the human soul, teeth in need of repair, or Elvis. I did have work to do.

No one shot at me as I stepped out of the Waffle Shop. So far, it was a good day.

I had the papers in the back pocket of my jeans. They stood up, scratched my lower back, and reminded me it was time for them to be served.

My bicycle, which Ames had named "Steadfast," was locked in a storage bin under my twenty-two stairs. I had a key. That made two keys in my pocket. One for my front door and one for the locker. Two keys too many.

I rolled Steadfast into the street, adjusted my Cubs cap, pedaled to Laurel, and then made a right toward Pineapple. On Pineapple I turned left, went through downtown, and walked Steadfast across Fruitville Avenue when the light turned green. From there it was three minutes to the house I was looking for.

It was, as all the houses in the neighborhood were, a small one-story cement-block building with long-dead orange siding. The slightly slanted roof was almost completely covered with leaves and pinecones from a big tree which looked as if its roots went right under the house. Grass, or what passes for it in Southern Florida, still fought a losing battle to live in the stony rubble of the front yard. A severely rusted pickup truck of unknown vintage stood next to the house.

I walked up the narrow and cracked concrete path to the door. The day was already hot. I didn't mind. The heat didn't bother me.

I didn't sweat. Even the coldest mornings of winter in Chicago hadn't affected me very much. When I was fifteen I had a mild case of frostbite from being out too long in subzero weather. I hadn't felt cold, but even now I get occasional tingling at the top of my ears.

I looked for a bell button. There was one. There was a badly rusted small door knocker. I decided against using it lest it fall off. I knocked.

"Coming," the high, almost child's voice inside called.

The door opened.

Below me, head only about thigh high, stood a small black man of no clear age in jeans, a blue T-shirt, and a Cubs cap, though a more expensive one than mine.

"Zo Hirsch?"

"That's right."

I handed him the folded order for him to appear at a divorce settlement hearing in the office of my lawyer client. I never deliver court orders or summonses in an envelope. I was supposed to deliver papers, and that I did.

"Shit. Shit. Shit."

He muttered, looked at the papers I had just handed him, and shook his head.

"Do I look like I can pay six hundred dollars a month?"

"No," I said.

"Want a beer?" he asked.

"No, thanks."

"Dr Pepper, Mountain Dew, Diet Pepsi?"

"Diet Pepsi."

"Come in."

He stepped back. Had I reached down, I could have rested the palm of my hand on his head. I resisted the urge to do so.

"This way," he said.

A few things struck me as we moved past the living room on the left and another room on the right, which must have been a dining room at one point, but was now a library filled with shelves and books. A desk stood near the front window which, if he had been sitting there, meant he would have seen me coming. Another thing that struck me was that everything looked immaculately clean. The furniture looked Arts & Crafts and the many framed photos on the walls were crisp, clear, and signed by Major League Baseball players. The other thing that struck me was that not one piece of furniture was a concession to Zo Hirsch's size.

"Sit or look around," he said pointing to the living room.

I examined some of the photographs while Zo Hirsch moved down the short corridor.

There were photographs of Bobby Bonds, Deon Sanders, Andre Dawson, and even Sammy Sosa. All of the players on Zo Hirsch's walls were black. He returned quickly with a can of Diet Pepsi in one hand and an Amstel Light in the other. He handed me the Pepsi. We sat.

"You meet my wife?" he asked, after taking a long drink.

"No."

He reached into his pocket awkwardly, took out his wallet, flipped it open, and handed it to me. The woman in the photograph looked of normal size, darkly Hispanic, and quite pretty. She was smiling. Her left arm was draped over the shoulder of Zo Hirsch, who was also smiling.

"Pretty," I said, handing back the wallet.

"Fucking beautiful," he said, accepting the wallet and stuffing it back in his pocket.

"Cubs fan?" I said.

He seemed puzzled and then got it. He touched the brim of his cap and pointed to mine.

"Not especially," he said. "Billy Williams gave me this one."

"Vintage," I said.

He shrugged and drank some more.

"What happened to your face?" he asked.

"Flying glass. Someone shot at me."

"Why?"

"I'll ask when I find him. Nice collection," I said looking around.

"I make my living writing about baseball," he said. "Mostly for Spanish language newspapers, magazines, and websites. My mother is Haitian. My father was a Jew from Cuba, a fisherman. He's gone. They were both normal-sized, if you were wondering."

I had been wondering, but I said, "No."

He looked at the photos on the wall and said, "I'd rather be playing right field anywhere for half of what Emilio Vezquez is getting."

"Emilio Vezquez?"

"The Double-D level pitcher my wife walked off with who will never, never make it to the majors. You want to know why?"

He finished his beer and looked at the empty bottle as if it had betrayed him.

"His fastball never hits ninety and he is scared shitless of line drives."

He sat back and took off his cap, a look of satisfaction on his face. He looked around the room at the photos of the men whose photographs surrounded him as if they had just applauded his observation.

"I've got to go," I said, rising and placing my empty can on a coaster on the table between us. The coaster had a Cincinnati Reds logo on it.

"Think you might forget I was home?" he said, holding up the papers I had served him. "I'll have a check from a Dominican newspaper coming in a few days and I'll be able to hire a lawyer."

"I don't—" I began, but was cut off by the ringing of Zo Hirsch's phone.

"Hold on," he said and moved to the library, where I heard him pick up the phone and say, "Yeah. Okay. Hold on."

He came back into the living room carrying a black phone, which he handed to me.

"It's for you," he said.

I took the phone and moved to the window, being careful that someone parked and watching wouldn't be able to see me. No one knew I was at Zo Hirsch's, not even the lawyer I was serving papers for. Conclusion: I had been followed here.

"Fonesca," I said.

"You're supposed to be working on the Horvecki murder."

The car parked across the street was familiar—a red Buick

LeSabre. The window blown out by the BB had been replaced, but the left fender definitely needed work and the left front headlight was missing. Jeff Augustine's right eye wasn't missing but it sported a black eye patch. He held a cell phone to his ear.

"You should be in bed," I said.

Zo Hirsch held up his empty beer bottle, inviting me to join him in a morning brew. I shook my head no. He shrugged and got another beer. Maybe a steady diet of bottled beer had contributed to the departure of Zo's wife.

"I can't afford to be in bed," Augustine said in that musical Robert Preston voice.

"You ever play the Music Man?" I asked.

"Yes, dinner theater. You want me to sing 'Seventy-Six Trombones'?"

"Maybe later."

"How's the investigation going? Corkle wants to know."

"I'm working on it."

"I know. You're in the home of one of Philip Horvecki's few friends."

I looked at Zo who, with pursed lips, appeared to be deciding if a burp were in order.

"My eye aches," said Augustine.

"I'm sorry. You should take something for it."

"I am. I've got a container of painkillers that begin with the letter B. Make my life easier. Tell Corkle you can't find anything so I can go back to simply taking care of his nuttiness. I'm in pain and may never have three-dimensional vision again. I'm in desperate need of a Corkle Pocket Fishing Machine."

"You are?"

"No, but I still seem to have something resembling a sense of humor."

"I don't have a sense of humor," I said.

"It's my turn to be sorry. Do we understand each other? Do we share the common language of English? Corkle wants to protect his grandson from anyone who might be unhappy about his paying you to look for an alternative to jolly Ronnie Gerall. We've been over this."

"We have. Can I buy you a cup of coffee or a sandwich?" I asked. "The Hob Nob is five minutes away. Great sandwiches."

"I'm supposed to be threatening you," Augustine said. "I can't do it if you feel sorry for me and offer me coffee and sandwiches. Tell the little man I'm sorry."

"For what?" I asked.

"Playing the role," he said.

Augustine turned off his phone before I could ask him what he meant. I turned back to Zo Hirsch. It couldn't have been more than ten seconds later that a rock came through the window, showering the room with glass. I turned to the window again and watched Augustine drive out of sight to the metallic clank of a piece of dragging undercarriage.

I handed the phone back to the stunned Zo Hirsch who seemed to be baffled by the gift. Then he hung it up.

"What did he do that for?" Zo asked.

"His job," I said. "Sorry."

"His job is to throw . . . forget it. It's just another piece of crap thrown at me."

"Want another soda?" Hirsch asked, looking at the rock near his feet.

"No thanks, but I do have a question."

"Ask."

"You were a friend of Philip Horvecki?" I said.

"Phil the Pill, Phil the Eel," he said, sitting down in what appeared to be his favorite chair. "Much beloved by all who knew him. He was almost a saint."

He looked at me and waited.

"I'm lying," he said.

"I know," I said.

"Phil Horvecki was an asshole."

"You weren't friends?"

"He was on the bowling team I manage," said Zo. "Zo's Foes.

Phil Horvecki was a man of many alibis, always ready to criticize the play of others. He will be easily replaced. I wish he had had a funeral so I could stand up and say it. Rest in peace you A-number-one asshole. I did have an occasional beer with him and some of the other bowlers. Small group got together at Bennigan's on Monday nights after our league games."

"Was he friendly with any of the bowlers?"

Zo was smiling now.

"The cost of further information is your forgetting to deliver your papers till the end of the week."

"What papers?" I said.

"Just me," said Zo. "But I wouldn't call the relationship friendly. We shmoozled."

"Shmoozled?"

"Talked."

"About?"

"Who knows? We have a deal?"

"Not yet," I said.

"He told me about people he had cheated out of property. He didn't think it was cheating. He went after old people, mostly."

"Old people who might want to kill him?"

"Old people who have sons or daughters who might be mad enough to do some killing. Phil the Pill had a restraining order against two such offspring who threatened to kill him."

"You know their names?"

"No," he said. "I've been dreaming about my wife. Bad dreams."

I moved toward the door.

"Ever meet Horvecki's daughter?" I asked.

"Once," he said. "She stopped by the bowling alley and just sat there watching. Skinny thing. Big scared eyes. I didn't talk to her. Horvecki didn't even introduce her, just said, 'My daughter,' once when he saw me looking."

"How did he say it?"

"Say what? 'My daughter'? I don't know. Almost as if he were apologizing or something."

I had no response, so he continued as I opened the door.

"I've been thinking about killing Vezquez, but there are too many damned Vesquezes out there and too much killing."

"The phone book probably has a couple of columns of Vezquezes," I said.

"I don't mean people named . . . forget it. Leave me with my thoughts of Roberto Clemente."

I offered to help him clean up the mess, but Zo just looked at it and said, "I'll take care of it."

"Can I . . . ?"

"No one can," he said.

I left him. I had another appointment, maybe another client.

I sat on my bike and called Dixie Cruise at the coffee bar on Main Street where she served espresso and kept the Internet-connected patrons happy and their electronics running. Dixie was slim and trim, with very black hair in a short style. Dixie lived in a two-room apartment in a slightly run-down twelve-flat apartment building on Ringling Boulevard, a block from the main post office. The apartment was almost laboratory clean, neat, and filled with computers and electronic gear.

"Working on it, Mr. L.F.," Dixie said in her down-home Florida accent. "Lady knows her stuff. Horvecki's daughter Rachel seems to have migrated to an alternate universe. Since her father's murder, she hasn't used a credit card, written a check, flown on an airplane, booked a room at a motel or hotel, or rented a car, at least not in her own name. She's running on cash and another name. Every Sarasota business, from dry cleaners to Red Lobster, has no record of her having been there."

"Keep looking," I said.

"You keep paying in cash, I keep looking. I've got bills to pay and things to buy for my wedding."

"You're getting married?"

"Didn't I tell you?"

"No."

"Wedding'll be in June. First Baptist. Reception after at Cafe Bacci. You and the cowboy are invited. You'll get an invitation."

"New address," I said, and gave her the address.

"My beau's name is Dan Rosenfeld. He's an airplane mechanic at Dolphin."

"Congratulations," I said.

"Thanks. I'll keep looking for her. Today, I check on unidentified bodies found from North Carolina to Key West."

6

I would have forgotten about the appointment if I hadn't written it on one of the three-by-five index cards I carried in my back pocket. The call had come in early the day before. With everything going on, I had almost forgotten about it. The index cards got dog-eared quickly from my sitting on them, but I wrote my notes to myself in clear block letters and had no trouble reading them.

At the age of forty-three, I was having trouble remembering simple things like why I was going to the refrigerator or what I was planning to do when I opened the medicine cabinet in my bathroom.

The card read:

Bee Ridge Park softball field. 11 a.m.
Monday. Ferris Berrigan

The bike ride to Bee Ridge Park was long. It was made longer by my expecting that someone might pull alongside me, roll down a window, and take a few shots, or that someone would run me into oncoming traffic on Beneva Road. It would be fitting, to die the same way Catherine had, but I wasn't really ready for that. Progress, Ann would say. I no longer welcomed accidental death.

Traffic wasn't too heavy, but a pickup truck did pass by when I crossed Bee Ridge, and the passenger did throw something out the window in my general direction. The sight of a somewhat lean man in a Chicago Cubs cap riding a bicycle seemed to bring out the redneck in some people. Actually, this was better than the panic that the sight of me brought to ancient drivers who often came near losing control and running me down.

I made it to Bee Ridge Park just before 11 a.m. I was familiar with the place. There were two softball fields. No one was playing on or standing by the nearest field, the one next to Wilkinson Road. But on the more distant field, a group of men were playing ball. As I rode across the parking lot and down the narrow road that marked the west side of the park, I heard the cool aluminum-on-ball clack followed by the shouting of men.

"Take two, Hugo!"

"Take three! What do you mean, two?"

"Dick is coaching at first."

"He took second easy, you dumb cluck."

"Grow up, John."

I parked my bike in a bike rack next to the field. I could see now that the players were all wearing uniforms, white ones with the words "Roberts Realty" on one and "Dunkin' Donuts" on the other. All the players were men who looked like they were in their sixties or seventies or eighties.

A few of the players glanced in my direction. There was a lone spectator, a man in a black cloth on a dark wood folding director's chair. Next to him there was an identical chair. I moved toward the man in the chair. He was sitting forward with his elbows on his knees and his chin in his hands. The pose of a bad boy who has been caught.

The man in the chair was even leaner than I am and a little older, maybe fifty. He wore brown slacks and a matching short-sleeve pullover shirt with what looked like a guitar etched on the lone pocket over his heart.

He sat back, waiting, and removed his glasses. He was clean shaven and nervous.

The empty chair next to him had "*Blue*" written on it in fading white paint.

I sat and looked at the game. Hugo scored.

"What's the score?" I asked.

"The score?"

"What inning is it?"

"I don't know. I don't really understand baseball."

"This is softball," I said.

"That ball doesn't look soft."

"It isn't," I said.

Another ball was hit with that pleasant bat-kissing-ball sound.

"You know who I am, don't you?"

"Ferris Berrigan?"

"Yes, but who else?" he asked.

"Who else are you?"

"Do you have any children?"

"No."

"Still," he said. "You should know who I am."

"You're the man who wants me to find out who is blackmailing him," I said.

"Something like that. You know what he said he would do?"

"No," I said.

"He'd go to the newspapers and television with a lie. You sure you don't know who I am?"

"No. Did you lose your memory?"

He looked puzzled and reassessed whatever positive feelings he had drawn from a first impression of me.

"No, I did not lose my memory. Someone wants to take it from me."

My fond wish at that moment was that whoever the good guys were out on the field full of battling voices and hoarse calls would win and go home.

"Okay, who are you and who is trying to take your memory?"

"Actually, it's all my memories they wish to take. You are positive you don't know who I am?"

"You're King Solomon, Master of all the Aegeans."

"If you can't take this seriously . . ."

"I'll take it seriously," I promised.

"I'm Blue."

"I'm sorry. I know how it feels."

"No, I'm Blue Berrigan, Blue the Man for You, Blue with Songs Ever New. Blue. The one on television. Fourteen years on television. I'm syndicated all over the world. Two generations of children have grown up singing my songs. Go to YouTube. One-year-olds dancing to Mitchell and Snitchel, The Great Big Blue Starfish, Empty Bottles of Juice."

"I've heard of—"

A clack, a shout of "Look Out!", and a yellow softball whizzed past Blue's head.

"You aren't in a safe place," the first baseman said as he ran after the ball.

"You're telling me," Blue said. "What was I saying?"

"Television."

"Television," he repeated, sitting back. "You want some walnuts?"

"No, thanks."

"Suit yourself. I'm semiretired. I don't need the money anymore, but it's my money and I'm not giving it away to fake blackmailers."

"They aren't really blackmailers?"

"Extortionists. They have photographs of me in bed."

"Yes."

"With two naked people."

"It happens," I said.

"One of the naked people is a man; the other is a woman, a very young woman who could pass for sixteen or even fifteen, but she's twenty-four and reasonably well known. Since you didn't recognize me, you probably wouldn't recognize her."

"Show business," I said.

"I work with kids. TV, tabloids, newspapers, magazines, blogs, they'll all show it and say I'd been in bed with a minor. I'll have to say it's a lie and no one will believe me. Even the suggestion will end my career. I don't want to end my career, but I can live with it. What I can't live with is what it will do to my reputation, my reruns, as unsuccessful as they've been everywhere but Guam and Uganda. You know why I asked you to meet me here with the softball players rather than the playground where kids are playing? A man in his forties, alone. Pedophile. You get it?"

"We could have met someplace else."

"I live right over there, across the street, on Wilkinson. This is convenient and, dammit, I don't want to hide."

Long pause. A skinny guy who couldn't have weighed more than Ames's broom hit a line drive out to shortstop.

"Come on," said Berrigan.

The teams changed positions while we folded up the director's chairs.

"I'll take those," he said.

I followed him to the road and a parked Mazda SUV. He opened it to put the chairs inside.

"What do you want me to do?" I asked.

"Find the blackmailers, expose them, tell me who they are, kill them, break their legs, feed them to the stingrays at Mote Marine Park. Find a way to blackmail them back."

He reached into his pocket and with difficulty came up with a CD. He handed it to me. "Take the job. Don't take the job. The CD is still yours."

"Thanks," I said, putting the CD into my back pocket.

"I signed it with a Magic Marker."

"One more perk and you'll have me."

He slammed down the door.

"Do you have a note? A recorded message? How did they contact you?"

"A young woman came to the door of my house and told me they, whoever they were, had the photographs. She gave me some of the pictures, said there were more. She was perky, bright, pretty, dark, possibly Hispanic. She said they would call and would expect me to have an initial payment of fifteen thousand dollars ready when they did. She wished me a nice day and bounced away like a teen in a toilet bowl commercial.

"Did you do those things, the things in the photographs?"

"Does it make a difference? Consenting adults."

"I think you should go to the police."

"I think I should not. I live there."

He pointed across the field and to the street a good hundred yards away.

"The yellow house. They put those photographs on the Internet and I won't work again, and then I'll find pickets outside my house demanding that I move away from the playground."

"None of the photographs were of you with underage children?"

"Not one," he said. "Two generations. Two generations of people who grew up and are growing up with my music will have a childhood dream broken, a friend lost, a trust betrayed."

"We don't want to do that," I said.

"We do not. So?"

"I'll look into it. I'll take the photographs and talk to some people. If you're contacted, call me."

"What will it cost?" he asked.

"Two hundred dollars flat fee for two days of work to see what I can find."

He took out his wallet and paid the money in twenty-dollar bills.

"Want a receipt?"

"No," he said.

I wrote my number on an index card and handed it to him.

"Call me when they get in touch with you again."

"I will," he said. "Want to put your bike in back and I'll drive you home?"

"No, thanks," I said.

"Looks like rain."

"Let's hope," I said.

"Let's hope," he said.

He had lied. Not everything, but a lot of it. He was a nervous look-away liar, his act semirehearsed, his voice low. Lying didn't mean he was guilty of what the blackmailer claimed. People lie for many reasons—because they are ashamed, because they like to seem to be more or less than they are, because they want to protect themselves or others, or because lying was automatic. I didn't know what kind of liar Blue Berrigan was.

Throughout the ride home I was sitting on the CD in my back pocket and hearing its plastic cover crack. I took it out and drove with it in my hand. The photographs were tucked inside my shirt. It did rain, not hard at first but coming down in a heated, pelting shower by the time I hit Tamiami Trail and Webber.

No one tried to kill me, either intentionally or inadvertently.

When I hit Laurel, I did not look at the building that had replaced the Dairy Queen where, had it still been there, I would have stopped for a chocolate-cherry Blizzard and a few minutes of conversation with Dave, who had owned the place, about the call of the Gulf as we sat under a red and white umbrella. No more. Dave had been forced out by what passed for progress. Dave had also made over a million on the DQ's death.

I felt wet and was not filled with a sense of merriment as I went up the steps to my new rooms. My pants clung heavily to my legs and, not for the first time, I considered buying a cheap car, leaving a cheap note, and going to Key West to sit for a decade and look toward Cuba as I cheaply lived out my life.

When I opened the door, Flo and Adele were there with Catherine in Adele's arms. Ames was there, too, and by the sound of the toilet flushing I figured Victor would soon make an appearance. The people in front of me were all reasons why I wanted to leave. They were also reasons I wanted to stay.

"Nice place you have here, Lewis," said Flo, her silver earrings tinkling if you listened quietly.

"We've got a ride to take, Lewis," Ames said.

Adele put Catherine down so I could see that she could now stand on her own with arms outstretched. I looked at Ames.

"Darrell," he said. "Doing poorly. You'd best put on something dry."

Catherine took a lone baby step toward me.

"Ain't that something?" asked Flo in her best Western drawl, which decades ago had replaced the twang of Brooklyn.

Victor appeared and looked at Catherine, who looked up at him and smiled. Victor knew the baby was named for my dead wife, the woman he had run down while he was drunk. Victor tried to smile back.

"Lewis," Ames said, "we'd best go."

Darrell's mother, dark and angry, came out of the intensive care unit at Sarasota Memorial Hospital. She said nothing to me or Ames. She didn't have to.

"I'm sorry," I said.

For an instant, her anger seemed about to turn to fury. I waited for the outburst. I would welcome it. But just before the anticipated attack, something changed. The tightness in the lean woman let go and her shoulders dropped. The anger turned to pure sorrow.

"You didn't do it," she said. "I know that. Fault's mine for letting Ms. Porovsky talk me into letting Darrell spend time with you. I should have known what kind of business you were into. I should have asked. And then Darrell started liking you, talking 'bout you, changing, gettin' better in school and such. You find the man who shot my only boy. You find him and shoot him back before you give him up to the police. You hear?"

"I hear," I said, acknowledging that there was nothing wrong with my hearing but not that I was agreeing with her order for me to commit murder. I owned no gun and wanted none. As long as Ames was nearby, I wouldn't need one.

"How is he?" asked Ames.

"Poorly," she said. "Poorly. That BB or whatever it was infected him. Poorly."

Victor had driven Ames and me to the hospital. It was not the car he had driven when he had killed my wife, but he was the driver. Once again I searched for anger. Ann Hurwitz had urged me to find the anger, to purge it, to deal with it. Though she couldn't tell me, I had the distinct impression that she would have considered it a step forward if I suddenly attacked Victor in a bitter rage. It wasn't in me. The hate button in my psyche didn't seem to exist. I had witnessed much in my life that would put others into squinting anger. I should probably have felt that way about whoever had shot Darrell. Nothing came except a sad determination to confront the person who had put Darrell in that hospital bed.

It was still raining. Flo, Adele, and Catherine went home, and I promised to stop by the house and report.

Darrell's mother went back into the intensive care unit with us. Darrell lay on his side, knees up near his chest, hands under his face on the pillow, eyes closed. Curled up, he looked like a dark, peaceful baby. The usual machines were blinking and beeping in the darkened room.

"She's right," Ames whispered. "We should shoot him when we catch up with him."

Darrell's mother couldn't hear the whisper, and I chose not to respond.

The rain was down to a steady shower with a full bright sun shining round, red-orange, and happy when we got back to the place I was now expected to call home. Victor parked on the gravel path next to the stairs.

All three of us got out slowly, ignoring the rain. A clump of small white and yellow flowers yielded to rain drops and then popped up again for another gentle assault. Before I hit the first step, I heard her.

Parked on the street was a familiar car. When the window rolled down I saw Sally Porovsky looking at me. She didn't call out or wave. She just looked at me.

"You've got work to do," Ames said.

"I know."

Victor stood silently, a thin trail of rain wending its way down his nose. Ames nodded at me and said no more. My door was open. Ames knew it. He led Victor upward, their shoes clapping on each wooden step.

I went to the street and moved around Sally's car to the passenger door. It was open. I got in and sat.

"You're wet," she said.

I nodded.

"There's a beach towel in the trunk. You want to get it?"

"No."

Her hands were tight on the steering wheel as if she were about to peel into a drag race. She looked forward. The shadow of rain rolling down the front window danced against her face. She looked pretty. She was pretty. Her skin was clear and pale, her hair dark and cut short. She was slightly plump and normally totally in control of herself, but not at this moment.

"I was going to call you," I said.

"I remember," she said. "I decided not to wait. How is Darrell?"

"I don't really know."

"His mother won't answer my calls."

I didn't know what to say.

She went on. "I think she blames me for getting Darrell involved with you."

"She does."

"She told you that?"

"Yes."

We went silent for about half a minute and then she said, "Let's go someplace where we can talk."

I could have said, "What's wrong with right here," but I sensed that she wanted to talk about something other than Darrell.

"FourGees?"

FourGees is a coffee shop, a decent place for lunch and late-night live music, at Beneva and Webber. It was dark in the daytime, with amber shadows and places to talk quietly.

"I can't stay long," she said as she drove. "I have to go back to the office."

The office was children's services, about ten minutes from FourGees.

I nodded. She drove. I like company when I drive alone. I'll listen to conservative talk shows, ball games, religious evangelists, but not music. I want no music. I want company. When I'm with other people in a car, I like to listen to them talk, which they seem to do whether or not I'm doing the driving.

Look at your watch or the time on your cell phone and count off a minute, then two, then three. Minutes become interminable when you count them. Silences become an anticipation of bad news.

We said not a word as Sally drove to FourGees and found a space directly in front of the shop.

The rain had stopped.

Silently, we got out of the car and went inside. Only two of the tables in the front room were occupied, one by a man and a small boy, and the other by three older women. The boy was playing with the straw in his drink. The women were eating slices of cake and drinking coffee. They seemed happy with one another's company.

Sally and I marched solemnly past the counter near the rear, where a tattooed girl in her twenties said, "I'll be right with you."

The second room was empty. Sally hesitated as if this wasn't what she had had in mind, and then she decided to sit on a wooden chair as far from the window as she could get. I sat too. I sat, and I waited.

"I have to tell you something, Lewis."

She leaned over and put a hand on mine.

"Your husband isn't dead," I guessed.

"He's still dead," she said.

"You have cancer."

"No. I think you should stop guessing."

The girl with the tattoos appeared and asked if we had made up our minds. I ordered a plain black coffee and a slice of the same kind of cake the women in the other room were having.

"Nothing for me," Sally said. "No, wait. Tea. Hot. Mint if you have it."

"We have it," the girl said. "Two forks for the cake? It's big."

"Sure," Sally said.

When she was gone, Sally looked down and said, "Lewis, I'm moving."

"I'll help."

"No, I'm moving to Montpelier."

"France?"

"Vermont."

This time, the silence almost insisted that no one break it.

"For good?" I asked.

"For good."

"People move here from Montpelier. They don't move from Florida to Vermont. Why?"

"My family, cousins, brother, people I've known all my life, people I went to school with. Besides, I have a good job offer at a hospital as social services director. Double my present salary."

"And?"

"And," she said, "I've been doing what I do for more than twenty years. I'm burned out, Lewis. I can't stand getting up in the morning and facing children who keep getting sent back to drug-addicted parents, kids who are hurt, abused, ignored, and dumped on the system, on me, with no resources other than whatever we can get by with off the books and paperwork. I don't want to think about the pile of cases on my desk that keeps growing. I want to be with my kids more, come home without feeling the footsteps of those kids behind me, silently calling for attention."

"I understand."

All the things she said were true, but I felt that something was missing, another reason that haunted her, a reason she didn't want to share.

"Do you? Do you understand without just feeling sorry for yourself because you're going to have to deal with another loss?"

"I don't know," I said.

Music started. It came down from a speaker mounted high on the wall. Lilly Allen was singing one of those songs that sways gently but carries lyrics as sharp as the edge of a sheet of newspaper.

"Lewis, how many times in the more than two years we've known each other have we made love or even had sex?"

"None," I said.

"I've respected your memory of Catherine with you, but we both have to move on. How many times have we kissed, really kissed?"

"Seventeen."

"I make it twenty, but you're almost certainly right. You never forget anything."

"My curse," I said.

"It's the way you want it," she said.

"When are you leaving?"

"As soon as the school year ends, so the kids won't be too disrupted."

"Seven weeks," I said.

"Seven weeks," she repeated.

The girl with the tattoos came back and placed the drinks in front of us and the cake between.

"Two forks. Enjoy."

I would not cry, but not because of pride. It just wasn't in me, but I would feel it. I would feel it, alone, sitting on the toilet, lying on my bed, listening to someone speak or Rush Limbaugh rant. I would feel it.

"I'm sorry," Sally said.

I handed her a fork and answered without saying that I was sorry, too.

"It's banana-chocolate," I said.

7

"Seven weeks," Ann Hurwitz said, dunking one of the two biscotti I had brought her into the cappuccino I had also brought to her office. A bribe.

"Seven weeks," I said.

"How do you feel about it?"

"Helpless. Relieved. I'm thinking of buying a cheap car and leaving."

"Again."

"Again," I said. "This time maybe I'll go west till I hit the Pacific Coast somewhere."

"And you'll look out toward Japan but see nothing but water."

"Maybe it will be clean."

"Pollution is everywhere."

"Sally's leaving me. Someone is trying to kill me or at least frighten me. I have a new client I don't like and another client who lied to me and may be a child molester."

"Lied about what?"

"I don't know, but I know he lied. Lies are heavy, dark, deep behind too much sincerity. And there are people depending on me, Ames, Flo, Adele. And Victor."

"Your houseguest from Chicago."

"Yes. And I don't like my new rooms. Too big. I like things, and places, small."

"Cubicles," she said, leaning forward to ensnare the moist end of a biscotti with her teeth. "What else are small places?"

"Boxes, caskets, car trunks, jail cells, monks' cells, closets."

"You can hide in all of them," she said. "You can even die in them. All both protect and threaten."

"I guess. You're supposed to tell me that people can't run from their problems, that nothing is solved by running away."

"No," said Ann. "You got these biscotti at News and Books?"

"Yes. I always do."

"They taste different. Very good. Sometimes things are solved by running away."

"I should run away?"

"If you feel that you must," Ann said, wiping her chocolate-tipped fingers with a napkin and then discarding it in her almost empty wastebasket. "I would miss you. You would miss Ames, Flo, Adele, and the baby."

"Her name is Catherine," I said.

"I know. I wanted you to say it."

"Because she was named for my wife, and it ties me to Sarasota."

"It ties you to people," she said. "You're not going to run away."

"I suppose not."

I leaned forward, my head between my legs.

"Are you all right? Are you going to be sick?"

"No," I said. "I'm trying to find a box to hide in."

"Have you been having nightmares again?" she asked.

"Yes."

"Tell me."

My head still down, I said, "I'm in New York City, at a hotel. I look out the window, across the street, at another hotel. On the seventh floor of that hotel, there's an open window. A child, about two, is about to climb out the window. It's New York during the day. The distance and the city noise let me know it would do no good to yell."

"So what do you do?"

"Nothing. I stand there, looking, hoping, praying. I can't move away. I can't close my eyes. I'm crying, muttering."

"Muttering what?"

"Oh, no. God, no. Jesus, no."

"Does the child fall?"

"The child looks over at me and smiles over the chasm, the canyon of buildings and streets. I try to wave her back, but she just smiles and waves back at me. I push my hands forward. I'm afraid to scream or make a frightened and frightening face for fear she will fall."

"She?"

"Did I say she?"

"Yes."

"So what do you think?"

"The child is Catherine or the baby we never had. She is about to die and there's nothing I can do about it."

"What does the child look like?"

"Dark curly hair. Wide eyes, brown eyes. Even at this distance I know they are brown."

"And," said Ann, "Catherine's hair was curly?"

"No."

"Not even as a child?"

"No," I said.

"And her eyes were wide and brown?"

"No, her eyes were blue."

"Who is the baby?"

"Me," I said. "She looks just like my baby pictures."

"Breakthrough," Ann said, sitting up in her well-padded swivel chair.

"But why is it a girl?" I asked.

"We save that for another time, to give you something to think about between now and then. Time for one more quick dream."

Knowing I would stare into the eyes of that baby who was me, looking for answers, I said, "Thalidomide man."

"Thalidomide man?"

"You know. About fifty years ago in Chicago a lot of women who were given thalidomide and had deformed babies, withered arms or legs or both. In my dream I see a man with a deformed right hand advancing toward me in slow motion. He's smiling and holding out his hand to shake my hand. I don't want to shake his three-fingered stump of a hand, but I extend mine to him. I always wake up then, and almost always it's 4:13 in the morning."

"How did you know about thalidomide?" Ann asked.

"I'm not sure. I think my mother and father talked about it, or I ran across it in a newspaper or magazine."

Ann looked puzzled, as if there were something she was trying to recall.

"Lewis, think."

I thought. Nothing came.

"The man with the withered right arm?" she prompted.

Nothing.

"The boy whose parents abandoned him."

I remembered. "I forgot."

"You never forget anything," said Ann.

"That's what Sally said."

"The boy?"

"His name was David Bryce O'Brien. I met him when I was investigating a homicide for the Cook County State Attorney's Office. You know this."

"Tell me again," she said. "I'm ancient and often forget what I move from one room to the next for."

"His father was a suspect."

"And?"

"His father was the murderer. He killed his dry cleaner. Then he killed his wife and son."

"David Bryce O'Brien."

"Then he killed himself."

"And what did he do to the body of his son?"

"No," I said.

Ann went silent. So did I. A waiting game. I could get up and leave, but I didn't. Then I said, "He cut off his son's withered arm and left a note saying, 'I'm sorry.' It's the most common suicide note in the world."

"Biblical," she said.

"Biblical?"

"If my right hand offends . . . ," she said.

"It wasn't his right hand."

"How old was David Bryce O'Brien?"

"Almost two years old."

"About the same age as the child in the window in New York?"

"Yes."

"That feels true?"

"Yes. You want me to think about it?"

"Yes, but not consciously. Let it go. When the time comes to talk about it, you will. You forgot to bring me something, Lewis."

I looked at the empty white bag that had held coffee and biscotti. The pungent smell of coffee and pastry hung lazily. She shook her head.

"I have a joke."

"Good, but you were supposed to bring something else. You were supposed to bring me the first line of a book. Do you have one?"

" 'And he shall turn the heart of the fathers to the children, and the heart of the children to their fathers, lest I come and smite the earth with a curse.' "

"And that is the first line of what?" Ann asked.

"It's the last line of the Old Testament. The only line I remember."

"Come back next time with first lines," she said. "Who told you the joke?"

"A man with one eye I met outside your office the last time I was here."

"The joke," she said.

"Actually, he gave me five of them."

I took out my index cards.

"One will be enough."

"Treat each day as if it's your last. One day you'll be right."

"That's a joke?"

"Yes."

"You think it's funny?"

"No."

"Next time, first lines," she said.

Augustine was waiting for me outside of Ann's office again, but this was a very different Augustine from the one who was there the last time I emerged into sun and heavy, moist air.

"Need a ride?"

"Yes," I said.

"I put your bike in my trunk. I'll buy you a new lock."

"Thanks," I said.

He walked us slowly to the corner and made a right turn onto Main. He was silent. So was I. I was trying not to think about what Ann and I had talked about, but I was doing a bad job.

"How is your eye?" I asked.

His hand reached up to be sure the patch was still there.

"Hurts," he said.

"I'm sorry," I said, and I was.

"Corkle fired me."

"What for?"

"Failure to get rid of you."

We hit the first corner and I was tempted to invite him across the street to News and Books, but I had had enough darkness for one day.

"Get rid of me? He just hired me."

"He wants to scare you away from the job. He's nuts. I'm glad I'm no longer in his employ. He gave me a check for five thousand dollars and an instant electric machine that both cores and peels apples, pears, and even peaches and plums."

"How will you get it on a plane?"

"I don't know."

"Why does he want to scare me away?"

"Don't know. Ask him."

"And you're telling me this because . . . ?" I asked.

"I like you," he said. "And I don't like loose ends."

His car, a gray two-door Mazda rental, was parked halfway up the block. Parking space downtown was always at a premium. I didn't consider telling him he was lucky. He had almost lost an eye. It could have been much worse.

"I think the kid shot at us," he said when we were driving.

He was one of those people who instantly turns on music when you get into their car. It made intimate conversation difficult. The music was '40s and '50s pop. Rosemary Clooney was singing "Come On to My House." She bounced.

"The kid?"

"Corkle's grandson, Gregory Legerman."

"Why?"

"Because Corkle thinks the kid killed Philip Horvecki."

"And then hired me to find himself?"

"Go figure," he said, making a turn on Orange and heading south. "We're talking about crazy people here."

"Corkle's daughter, too?"

"Why not?"

We drove silently for a few minutes, and then he said, "I'm not supposed to drive till I get another driving test. Hell, I can drive better with one eye than all these old farts with two."

"Someday you may be an old fart," I said.

"Great, an old fart with one eye."

He went to Laurel and turned left. A minute later he parked in front of my new home, the one with rooms too big and visitors too many.

"I'm cashing Corkle's check and heading for the Tampa airport," he said. "I'll work in commercials if I'm lucky, dinner theater, wherever a one-eyed character actor is wanted. Who knows? This . . . ," he said, pointing to his patched eye, "may be the opening of new career opportunities."

"Who knows?"

"We both do," he said with a smile as bitter as orange peel.

I got out of the car.

"Watch yourself, Cub fan," he said.

I touched the brim of my cap in a gesture of good-bye. He tore down the street with a drag racer's abandon. The tires weren't his. The car wasn't his. It was too bad the Dairy Queen two blocks down was closed and torn down. He could have had a Blizzard to ease the rush-hour trip to Tampa.

"Let's go," Ames said when I went through the door.

He was standing to my left, near the wall. Victor, in his Chicago Bulls sweatshirt with the sleeves cut off, was seated on the floor, his bedroll wrapped neatly in the corner. Ames was wearing black corduroy pants, a red-dominated plaid shirt, and boots.

"Where this time?" I asked.

"To see a man," said Ames. "Brought you this."

He held up a wooden plank about the size of a rolled up newspaper. Burned into its dark, grainy surface were the words *LEWIS FONESCA*.

"So people will know you're here," said Ames. "I can mount it outside somewhere."

"I don't want any more people to know I'm here," I said.

"Suit yourself," he said, placing the plank faceup on my desk. "Let's go. Victor'll drive us."

In response, Victor Woo got up from the floor.

"Where are we going and why?" I asked.

"I found a man who knows all about Philip Horvecki."

Victor chauffeured. Ames and I sat in back. Ames gave Victor directions. They weren't easy. We drove up I-75 to the University Parkway exit and headed east. Ames gave clipped driving directions like, "Next right," and Victor drove without speaking.

"Fella came into the Texas a few hours ago," said Ames. "Heard him talking. Sheriff's deputy. Talking about the murder. Told another fella that the detectives should ask Pertwee about it. I asked him who this Pertwee was. He told me."

Ames went silent. Long speeches were not his medium.

After telling Victor to go down a narrow dirt road, Ames went on.

"Seems Pertwee knows a lot about old crimes in the county," said Ames.

Silence again, except for the bumping tires and the *rat-tat* of pebbles against the undercarriage of the car.

"How do you know where to—" I started.

"Came out here on my scooter when the deputy gave me directions," Ames interrupted.

We had gone almost twenty miles from my apartment. On a scooter, going over this road, one would have to be very determined.

"Look out on the right over ahead. Hardly see it, but there's a low wooden fence and an open gate."

Victor turned into a rutted path even narrower than the dirt road. Ahead of us about fifty yards was a mobile home with a small addition. It was a house of aluminum waiting for a hurricane to wash it away.

The closer we got the better it looked. The place was recently painted white. A small, umbrella-covered metal table with three wrought-iron chairs sat in front of the mobile home's door.

Victor parked. We got out as a man lumbered through the door and held the sides of the doorway to keep from slipping on the two steps to the ground. He was short, with a sagging belly. He wore jeans with suspenders over a blue-striped polo shirt that was sucked into the folds of his neck. He was about sixty years old.

He looked at the three of us with amusement.

"A visit from a formidable trio," he said. "A cowboy, a chink, and a gingerbread man. What brings you, and would you like a beer?"

We all said no. Pertwee shrugged and said, "So be it. What brings you here?"

"Deputy I met said you know a lot about Philip Horvecki," said Ames.

"That I do," said Pertwee. "And who did you say you were?"

"My name is Lewis Fonesca and I—"

"Lewis Fonesca," he said. "Formerly an investigator in the state attorney's office in Cook County, Illinois. You came here four years back after your wife was killed in a hit-and-run on Lake Shore Drive in Chicago. The driver of the red convertible that killed her was an Asian man who has yet to be found by the police."

"This is the man," I said, nodding toward Victor.

Pertwee bent forward and looked up at Victor. Not much could happen that would surprise him.

"And this is Ames McKinney," I went on.

"Four years ago, beach at Lido," said Pertwee. "You shot your ex-partner. Fonesca was there. You did a little time. I sit out here, keep track. Retired detective, Cincinnati police. Come on in."

We followed the wobbling Pertwee into his house. The living room was larger than I had expected. It had the musty but not unpleasant odor of dried leaves. Family portraits hung on the walls, and the sofa and matching chair were each covered with a bright blue knitted blanket. Beyond the living room and down a step into the one-room addition to the home was an office lined with file drawers. A computer with a large screen sat next to a printer and a fax machine. There was a duplicate of the sofa in the other room complete with knitted blanket, only this blanket was brown.

"Wife's in town at a photography class at Selby Gardens," Pertwee said. "Won't be back for a long while. She'll have a portfolio full of photographs of flowers and trees when she walks through the door."

He nodded toward the wall over the sofa. Color photographs were mounted one after another, all around the room. All the photographs were of flowers or bright fish in a pond.

Pertwee sat in front of the computer and pressed the power button. While the machine was firing up, he rose and waddled to a file cabinet, opened it, rummaged in a lower drawer, and came up with a manila file folder.

"Cold cases," he explained as the image of a red flower appeared on his computer screen. "Sheriff's office lets me see what I can find. Won't find stuff like this on the Internet."

"Horvecki was involved in a cold case?" I asked.

Victor had sat on the sofa. Ames stood at my side looking at the screen. Pertwee's face was red with the reflected color of the flower before him.

"Two cold cases," said Pertwee, opening the file folder and placing it on the table next to him. "First case was back in 1968. Young Horvecki was but a stripling. Two fourteen- and sixteen-year-old black girls were raped and beaten. They were found wandering the byways. Both girls identified Horvecki as the attacker. Both later changed their minds. Case still open. Both girls are grandmas now. One's a great grandma. One has a son who is not fond of Mr. Horvecki and has been known to speak ill of the now deceased. Son's name is Williams, Essau Williams. Detective in the Venice Police Department. Detective Williams has been given disciplinary warnings because Horvecki claimed Williams has been stalking him for years."

"And the other case?" I asked.

Pertwee said, "Ah" and flipped pages until he found what he was looking for.

"Here 'tis, 1988, same year Cynthia and I arrived in the State of Florida and purchased this little bit of heaven. Costs almost as much to get an Internet hookup and dish TV as it cost to buy Buddenbrooks."

"Buddenbrooks?" I asked.

"The abode in which we sit, away from civilization in a field of rattlesnakes, raccoons, and seldom-seen rodents of unusual size and appetite. I can shoot them at my ease from one of those chairs under the umbrella. My principal physical exercise."

"Sounds like fun," Ames said.

"Yes, 'tis. However, all in all, I'd rather be back in Cincinnati. Cynthia, however, longed for Paradise, and we wound up here. I'm not complaining."

"The second case in your files," I reminded him.

He turned the page of the stapled sheets in the folder and said, "One Jack Pepper, sophomore at Riverview High School. Attacked from behind while crossing an orange grove on his way home from school. Assailant told him to pull down his pants or die. Assailant proceeded to attempt anal intercourse. Failed. Boy stepped out of his pants and drawers and ran. Pepper turned and saw the attacker coming after him. Pepper ran faster, covered himself with a damp, dirty newspaper and entered a gas station. Pepper identified Horvecki but Horvecki had the best lawyers money can buy and some friends in the right places. That was nineteen years ago. Jack Pepper is now thirty-six years old and living in relative tranquillity in Cortez Village. Thrice Jack Pepper confronted our Mr. Horvecki in public places, broke his nose and cheekbone with a well-placed and probably knuckle-hurting punch, and kicked him into unconsciousness. Attempted murder, but . . ."

"Horvecki did not press charges," I said.

"He did not. No other incident involving the two of them in the last nineteen years."

"You have Pepper's address?" I asked.

"That I have. I'll give you both his and Essau Williams's address," said Pertwee. "And I shall print some possibly pertinent information for you."

"Cost?" asked Ames.

"Close those two cold cases and find out who killed Horvecki," said Pertwee. "These cases of open files challenge and mock me. The fewer there are, the lighter my burden, even though I know others will come to fill the drawers."

We started back to the car, and Pertwee called out, "A sweet fella like Horvecki probably had lots of people who didn't much care for him besides Williams and Pepper."

We kept walking. One of the people who didn't like Horvecki was Ronnie Gerall, sitting in juvenile lockup for killing a man everyone seemed to hate.

Cell phones are wondrous things. They keep people connected regardless of where they are. Going to be late for an appointment? Call. Have an accident on the road and need AAA? Call. Lapse into drunkenness at the side of the road and need AA? Call. Supposed to meet someone and they don't show up? Call. Cell phones are wondrous things. They take photographs and videos, tell you the temperature and baseball scores, let you order pickup at Appleby's, tell you what time it is and where you are if you get lost, and play music you like.

People can find you no matter where you are.

The problem is that I don't want to be connected, don't want to order braised chicken to be picked up at Appleby's, don't want to take photographs or videos, and am in no hurry to get baseball scores.

But the machines give us no choice.

The young don't have wristwatches.

Phone booths are dying out.

Good-bye to all that.

Still, I had a cell phone in my pocket, a birthday present from Flo Zink. Adele had programmed in a ringtone version of "Help!" that was now playing.

"L.F., unless her body is enriching a wood or bog, Rachel Horvecki is not dead. And she is still not leaving her footprint on the sands of time. I can tell you stuff about her. Got time to hear?"

"Yes."

"She is twenty-seven years old, went to Sarasota Christian High School where she was on the yearbook committee, Spanish Club, Poetry Club, Chess Club, Drama Club, cross-country team; did three years at Manatee Community College, where she was on no club, went to a small school called Plain River College in a small town in West Texas. Her major was English Lit. No extracurricular interests or clubs. Plain River College registrar records show she dropped out. Reason stated: Getting Married. Sarasota Memorial Hospital records show she had an appendectomy when she was seventeen and came into the ER once, when she was fourteen, for a broken arm and bruised ribs. Hospital reported possible abuse, but Rachel insisted she had fallen down some stairs. Want me to keep looking?"

"Yes. See if you can find out who, if anyone, she married."

"Will do."

We hung up. I called Winn Graeme's cell phone and told him I wanted to talk to him without Greg at his side pummeling him. He had something to do at school but would call me when he could get away.

I called the home of D. Elliot Corkle and left a message when he didn't pick up. Since he said he never left the house, I wondered where he was. Maybe he was taking a shower or a swim or just didn't feel like being connected to someone beyond his front door. I gave my number to the machine and said, "Please call me soon. What's the 'D' in your name for?"

I called Sally. She answered. I said nothing.

"Lew?"

Cell phone. Caller ID. She knew who was calling.

"Yes."

"What is it?"

"Nothing," I said. "I hoped that words would come when I heard your voice, but they're not coming."

"We can talk later," she said. "I'm with a client now."

"How is Darrell?"

"Better, much better. I'll call you later. Promise."

She ended the call, and I tried to think of other people to call. I wanted to wear out the charge in my phone so it would go silent, but I couldn't bring myself to do it.

I was tempted to launch into baseball metaphors.

Victor drove me to the Fruitville Library, where I got my bike out of his trunk.

"I can come back for you," said Victor.

"No, thanks," I said.

Ames said nothing, just looked at me and nodded. I nodded back. They drove off. The sun was high, the air filled with moist heaviness and the smell of watermelons from a truck vending them on Fruitville, just beyond the parking lot.

I chained my bike to a lamppost and went inside.

The cool air struck and chilled for an instant.

Two minutes later I had an oversize book of World War II airplanes open on my lap. I didn't want to look at it. I wasn't interested. It was a prop to keep a vigilant librarian from making a citizen's arrest for vagrancy.

No more than five maybe six, minutes later, Blue Berrigan sat down across from me.

8

"You just happened to see me hiding here behind the fiction," I whispered.

He was wearing a pair of dark corduroy slacks and a short-sleeved green-and-white-striped polo shirt.

"I . . . I followed you."

"From where?"

"You're going to get angry," he said. "It can't be helped. We're talking about my life here."

He looked over his shoulder and out the window and gently bit his lower lip.

"You're talking," I said. "I'm listening."

"I put an electronic tracer under the rear fender of your bicycle," he said. "I removed it before I came in. They're really cheap now. You can get them online."

He held up both hands in a gesture designed to stop me from rising in indignation. I didn't rise. I wasn't indignant.

"I was afraid you didn't believe me when we talked in the park."

"I didn't," I said.

"I do lie a lot. People always say you should tell kids the truth; you shouldn't lie to them. But there are truths you want to keep from children. There are truths they are better off without. What are you reading?"

A thin woman with wild hair came down the aisle perpendicular to us carrying a load of books she wouldn't be able to read in a generation. The books at the top and in the middle of the pile threatened to fall. Blue Berrigan was silent until the woman rounded the corner, went up the next aisle, pulled out two more books, and balanced them on top of her heap. Then she went out of sight.

"I'm looking at pictures of old airplanes," I said.

"Good."

I wasn't sure why he might think that was good.

"You're not being blackmailed," I said.

"No."

"Then . . ."

"I'm being paid to distract you," he said with a great sigh.

"From what?"

"Whatever you're working on."

"Who's paying you?"

"A man who called me, said he knew my work, knew I was down on my luck. I'm supposed to keep bothering you, sending you on wild-grouse hunts, tell you someone tried to kill me. Improvise."

"How much is he paying you?"

"Five thousand dollars in advance. I've got it back in my room."

"But you've decided . . ."

"The guy sounds nuts, is what I'm saying. I'm keeping the money, packing up, and moving west. I'm only renting a room here. He's got someone keeping an eye on me. I'll have to lose whoever it is."

I was tempted to say I'd join him in his getaway, but it wasn't temptation enough.

"Don't go yet," I said.

"Don't go?"

"He calls you?"

"Yes."

"Tell him you have me looking for grouse."

"Ah, I see," he said.

"What's a grouse?" I asked.

Neither of us knew for certain.

"Let's leave separately," I said. "He might have followed you. I'll get back to you."

He got up without certainty and said, "I'm really very good with kids. I just, you know, got lost."

"I know," I said.

"You don't live near here."

"No. I come here when I want to be alone, where no one can find me unless they plant tracking devices on my bicycle. You want to give me a ride home?"

"No, can't," he said standing quickly. "I've got to go."

He strode away quickly. I waited about ten seconds and then followed him to the glass doors at the entrance to the library. I stayed against a wall inside, watching him find his car in the lot and leave. It was a well-used jeep of uncertain vintage. I got the first three letters of his tag before he turned left. That's when whoever was in the backseat sat up. I couldn't see who it was.

"Embarrassing, demeaning, humiliating, abasing," Darrell said. "It brings me down. Know what I mean?"

He was out of intensive care and propped up on a couple of pillows. There was an IV in his right arm and a look of exasperation on his face. He was out of danger, but not out of flaunt.

"Almost killed by a BB in my back," he said with a single shake of his head. "How do I explain that? How do I strut that? 'Hey man, I got shot.' 'Yeah, with what?' 'A BB gun.' "

"It almost killed you," I said.

"That makes no difference on my street. Take that back. Shot with a BB gun? That's below a misdemeanor on my street."

"Sorry. Maybe you'll be lucky next time and get shot with a machine gun."

"Not funny. I was lucky. Bad lucky," said Darrell. "Hey, do me a favor and get the shooter. Then let old Ames shotgun blast him a second asshole."

I nodded. He was still hooked up to the machine with the green screen that painted white mountains and valleys to the sound of a low *beep-beep-beep.*

"I'll find him," I said. "You want my hat?"

"Your Cubs hat? I'm touched, Fonesca. I know what that hat means to you but a, it's your sweat in there, and b, I'm not a Cubs fan."

I nodded again.

"My mom still mad at you?"

"Sort of."

"Ms. Porovsky?"

Sally was more than Darrell's caseworker. She was someone who cared. Sally knew she couldn't save the children of the world one abuse at a time, but she couldn't help trying.

"She's fine," I said.

"You?"

"I'm fine."

"Why don't you look fine? I don't look fine," said Darrell.

"Nurse says you can go home in a few days," I said.

"From almost dead to back to school in three or four days," he said.

"It happens."

"But not much," he said. "Old Chinese Victor saved my butt from going down the stairs."

He made a tumbling motion with his free hand.

"I decided something," he said, licking his lips.

I poured him water from a pitcher into a plastic cup on a table near his bed. He took it and, with my help, drank.

"Don't laugh. Don't even smile, and don't tell anyone, not even my mom."

"I won't."

"I know," said Darrell. "I'm going to try out for the play at Booker."

Booker High, I knew, had a big annual musical production. I'd been told by Sally and Flo that they were very nearly professional.

"You sing?" I asked.

"That's what I like about you, Fonesca. You are dribbling down with emotion. I can sing. I can act."

"What have you done?"

"Nothing yet," he said. "I just know I'm good. I'll tell them on the street that I'm going to be the next Will Smith or Denzel or Cuba. Maybe they'll buy it, you know?"

We went silent and I listened to and watched the green mountain-and-valley machine.

"Get the guy who shot me, Fonesca."

"I'll get him," I said. "Darrell, he was trying to shoot me."

"I know that. It didn't hurt less because of that. I'm tired."

"I'll be back," I said.

"I might be out of here first," he said so softly I could barely hear him.

Darrell's eyes were closed. He was asleep.

I had people to see and a bicycle parked outside. I made a decision.

There were only two cars parked in the small driveway of the EZ Economy Car Rental. The EZ was a converted gas station, a half-block north of the now-demolished DQ on 301. It wouldn't last much longer. The banks were moving like relentless giant Japanese movie monsters gobbling up small businesses and looking for more along the strip of 301 from Tamiami Trail to Main Street.

This didn't matter to Alan, the formerly jovial partner of Fred, who was now dead with one heart attack too many. Alan had been the more likely candidate for heart trouble. In his late forties, Alan was twenty years younger than Fred but fifty pounds heavier. Alan was addicted to strong coffee. Alan had lost the sense of sardonic humor he and Fred had shared. It had kept them both sane between infrequent customers.

"Fonesca, the man from whom there are no secrets," Alan said when I walked through the door.

He was seated at his wooden swivel chair behind the counter with a cup of coffee in his hand, a cluttered desk drawer lying in front of him. The coffee was in a black thermos. The suit and tie he usually wore had been replaced with slacks and a wrinkled white dress shirt with an open collar.

"You came at the right moment," he said. "Today is the third and final day of liquidation. No more rentals. Two cars out there to sell. Take your pick."

"I don't want to own a car," I said. "I want to rent one."

"You don't want to own anything," he said. "And until Fred went to automobile nirvana, I wanted to own everything. The price is right. Both cars will be gone by tonight even if I have to give them to Goodwill."

"How much for the Saturn?" I asked.

I had rented the gray 1996 Saturn before. There had been a little over 110,000 miles on the odometer when last we met. In its favor, it had behaved, though hollow clanks echoed under the glove box. The last car I had owned was the one I escaped from Chicago in and managed to get as far as the DQ parking lot. Cars and I are not friends. One of them had killed my wife. One of my many fears was that I might one day accidentally hit someone and spend the rest of my life like Victor Woo. Perpetual apology. Perpetual shock.

"What do you have in your wallet?" Alan asked after another sip of coffee followed by a face that suggested the coffee or life or both were bitter.

"I'm flush. Two clients."

"Okay, how does sixty-six dollars sound to you?" he asked.

"For the Saturn? Reasonable."

"You just bought a car. Congratulations. Enjoy. No, wait. You don't enjoy anything."

He picked up a pair of keys on a small metal hoop and threw them in my direction. They arced through the air, tinkling as they flew. I caught them.

"I've got the papers right here," he said, shifting his considerable bulk so that he could dig into the exposed desk drawer.

I took out my wallet, extracted the sixty-six dollars and placed it on the counter. Alan shifted out of the chair, which let out a weary squeak. He placed the papers on the counter, signed them, asked me to sign, and said, "You want another car?"

"No."

"Gift for a friend?"

"No."

"We're having a two-for-one sale."

"No."

"You are a tough customer."

He held out his hand. We shook.

"Are you all right?" I asked.

"Decidedly not," he said, "but I am solvent. Fred and I owned this business and the land on which it sits. I have a generous offer, which I have accepted. Fred's widow and I will share right down the middle. Want to know how much we're getting?"

"No."

"A million six. I'm heading back to Grosse Pointe as soon as the papers are signed and the check is in my hand."

"Good luck," I said. "All right if I leave the car here for an hour?"

He shrugged, a good shrug that shook his expansive body, and said, "Till the wrecking ball descends."

Outside, I used the cell phone, called Ames, and asked if he could meet me. I told him where. He said he could and would be right over. I walked across the street and into the Crisp Dollar Bill, where Sammy Davis, Jr., was singing "There's a Slow Boat Sailing for New York." The familiar smell of beer reminded me of Mac's bar, back in Chicago, when I was a kid.

I made out the shape of four people at the bar to my left. No one was in any of the booths across from the bar. I sat in a booth where I could watch the door, looked over at Billy the bartender and owner, and nodded. He knew what I wanted.

Some say that good things come to those who wait. Bad things come, too.

The comedian Steven Wright says, "When worse comes to worse, we're screwed."

Blue Berrigan came through the door and sat across from me.

"I followed you again," he said.

"I figured that out."

Billy placed an Amstel and a mug in front of me.

"You want a beer?" I asked Blue.

"A beer?" He didn't seem to understand.

"A beer, to drink."

"Blue doesn't drink alcohol. Dr Pepper."

Billy nodded and moved off. Sammy Davis, Jr., had moved on to "What Kind of Fool Am I."

"You ready to tell me who hired you?"

"No. Well, maybe."

Blue was fidgeting, whispering, casting glances at the people at the bar who were not looking in his direction. Billy turned on the television set mounted up near the ceiling. He changed channels until he found what looked like a rerun of a high school football game. He turned off the sound. Blue had watched Billy.

"I think I know who it was," I said. "I think it was a man who hides in the backseats of jeeps."

He started to slide out of the booth, but before he could, Ames sat next to him, blocking his exit.

"Blue Berrigan, this is Ames McKinney. Ames has done time for killing his former partner. Ames is a man of honor who has a fondness for weapons, usually of an older vintage."

Ames was wearing his very old, very well cared-for tan leather Western jacket. He held it open so Blue could see something against Ames's waist. I couldn't see it from where I sat. I didn't have to.

Berrigan looked frightened, very frightened, and said, "Wait, I have evidence that Ronnie Gerall didn't kill Horvecki."

"What evidence?" I asked.

"I've got it at my place."

"Let's get it," Ames said.

Billy appeared with a bottle of beer for Ames and said, "Burger'll be up in a few minutes. One for you?"

"No thanks. Ate at the Texas."

"Blue Berrigan," Ames went on when Billy left. "Kids' singer?"

"Yes," Blue said, moving farther into the corner.

"'How Many Bunnies in the Hole'?"

"Yes."

"You believe in coincidence?" Ames asked.

"Yes," Blue said, growing smaller.

"I just bought a CD of yours for Catherine and Adele."

"Coincidence," Blue said. "This whole thing has gone too far."

"It went too far when someone murdered Philip Horvecki," I said.

The burger came. It was big. I knew it had grilled onions and tomato on a soft bun.

"I told you the truth. About distracting you, I mean. Listen, Blue needs the bathroom. He needs it bad, real bad," Blue said.

"'*The Potty Is Your Friend*,'" Ames said, looking at me.

"Let him out," I said.

Ames sidled out of the booth, letting Blue get out and hurry toward the bathrooms at the rear. Ames got up and followed him. Then I heard Ames say, "He locked it."

Two of the bar patrons looked toward the bathrooms. One was a shaky woman who kept blinking, the other a skinny man who tried to keep his elbows from slipping off the bar.

There was a window in the men's room. It was high on the wall and narrow, but it was definitely possible for a man to squeeze through. I left my burger and called out for Billy to open the men's room with a key. He got the urgency in the situation and moved quickly. So did I, but not toward the bathroom. I went past the bar and onto the street.

The red jeep was parked half a block down, to my left. Blue Berrigan was racing for it and moving fast, fast enough to get into the car, make a U-turn, and be on his way before I got twenty steps, but not fast enough to keep me from seeing something move in the backseat of the jeep.

Ames appeared at my side.

"Gone?" he asked.

"Gone," I said.

"Know where?" asked Ames.

"I think so."

We went back inside. I paid Billy, who said, "Always a pleasure having you. You bring a touch of chaos into an otherwise tranquil bar."

I had the feeling he meant it.

I took my burger and led the way out the door and to my Saturn.

"Nice car," he said.

"I bought it."

"Needs help."

"We all do."

We got in, and I ate while I drove.

I came to three conclusions:

The Saturn would definitely not qualify for the Indy 500.

There was no radio in the car.

I still didn't like driving.

Ames sat silently, jostled by what might be a weeping loose axle.

This was my kind of car.

Traffic wasn't bad. It wasn't snowbird weather, but as I tried to pick up speed I did pass three kids in a pickup truck wearing baseball caps. The kid in the middle had his cap turned around.

"Why do they wear their caps backward?" I asked Ames, who wasn't likely to know but was the only other person in the car.

"Insecurity," said Ames. "Want to look like millions of other kids."

"Insecurity," I said as I considered trying my Cubs cap backward. I decided not to. I already knew what a fool looked like.

"Only catchers behind the plate should wear their caps backward, to accommodate their masks," I said.

I was in the right lane, going south on Beneva. The pickup pulled next to me. The kid in the window gave me a one-finger salute. Ames leaned over me and showed his long-barreled gun. The kids pulled away fast.

I tried for fast, too, and failed as the Saturn let me know that quick turns to the right were subject to grinding. We were on Wilkinson now. When we got in sight of the park I looked down the block at the parked red jeep. I pulled in behind it and got out quickly, Ames right behind me as I hurried toward the yellow house after checking to be sure there was no one hunched down in the back of the jeep.

I knocked at the front door of the yellow house. Ames was still behind me, his hand under his jacket. I knocked. There was a wheezing sound behind the door, which then opened.

The old woman who opened the door in an orange robe and slippers carried a yellow cup of steaming something.

"Blue Berrigan," I said.

"Are you those paparazzi people?"

"No," I said. "We're fans."

Ames gently pushed the door open and stepped in. I followed and closed the door.

"Don't, for Jesus' sake, sing me one of his songs, especially that one about the rabbits."

"We won't," I said. "We just . . ."

"Mr. Nelson Berrigan isn't here and he doesn't give autographs or signed photographs to fans who seek him out. You'll have to wait till his next public appearance. Besides, he's not home."

"His car is parked outside," I said.

She looked at Ames with suspicion, took a sip of her brew, and leaned between us to look at the jeep at the curb.

"He's still not here. No way he could get to his room without getting past me, no fucking way. Pardon my French."

"Could he have gone around the back?" I tried.

"Yes, but there's no way to get upstairs back there. Doesn't the old guy talk?"

She wheezed mightily and fished an inhaler out of the pocket of her robe. A wad of tissues came with it and drifted to the floor. She caught them deftly without losing a drop of whatever she was drinking.

"Used to be a juggler," she said, putting the tissue wad back in her pocket and taking a deep puff of the inhaler. "Long time ago. I suppose that's how Nelson got the show business bug. His father was a tombstone carver."

"He's your son?" I asked.

"He is definitely not my son. He lived next door to us when he was a kid. Now I definitely want you the hell out of here. Good-bye."

She closed the door. We turned and walked to the curb. I looked through the window of the jeep. Nelson Blue Berrigan was slumped over on the floor, legs beneath the steering wheel, head and torso on the floor near the passenger door. He was not taking a nap. The deep reddish black oozing wound on the back of his head felt like death, but I made sure by opening the door and reaching over to see if there was a pulse. There wasn't.

We had been inside the house for no more than two minutes.

Maybe we should have gone back and told the old woman he was dead.

Maybe we should have called 911.

Maybe we should have looked for clues.

Maybe we should have looked for the killer. He couldn't have been more than a few minutes away, but a minute or two was enough if he had a car parked very close by.

I slid into the backseat and looked at the floor. There were splatters of blood. On top of one of the splatters were two little pieces of plastic, one white, one red. I knew what they were, but I needed to get the answer to a question before I could decide what to do.

"We've got to go back inside the house," I said. "Keep her busy."

Ames and I went back to the door. The old woman in the orange robe opened it a crack and said, "What the hell you want now?"

"I've got to call 911," I said. "Berrigan is in his car. I think he's dead."

"Dead?"

"Where were you the last half hour?" Ames asked as I slipped by her and went to Berrigan's room.

"Me? I didn't kill him."

I didn't call 911 right away. First, I looked around. I didn't see what I was looking for. I tried the closet. It wasn't there. When I was satisfied, I called 911 and then went to get Ames.

The old woman was saying, ". . . a quiet man."

"Sorry ma'am," Ames said. "Can we get you anything?"

"You call the police?" she asked seeing me.

"Yes. I have one more question."

"Question?"

I asked her. The answer confirmed what I found, or failed to find, in Berrigan's room.

Ames and I moved to the door.

"You're not staying till the police get here?" the old woman asked.

"Can't," Ames said gently. "Police will be here in a minute."

She seemed bewildered as we opened the door. She looked out at

Berrigan's jeep, pulled a pair of glasses from her pocket and put them on, saying, "You sure he's in there? I don't see him."

"He's there," I said.

We got in the Saturn and drove away, not quietly, but definitely away.

9

Half an hour later I was seated behind my desk, looking across the room at the Stig Dalstrom paintings on the wall. They were the only art I owned—four small paintings given to me by Flo Zink. They were of dark jungles and mountains at night with just a small touch of color, a single bird or flower, the distant moon.

Outside, Ames was working on the Saturn. He knew guns, machines, trucks, and automobiles, but it would take a lot of knowing to make the Saturn live again.

I half hoped he would fail. I felt uncomfortable owning anything larger than a DVD player.

My cell phone was on the otherwise empty desktop in front of me. I was waiting. On the way home I had told Ames that it would probably take an hour or less for the police to arrive, so he had better do as much as he could on the car before men in blue appeared bearing guns in the usually quiet street.

The old woman former juggler in an orange robe would describe us to the police. That would be enough.

"A tall old man wearing a coat in the heat and a not-too-tall, sad-looking fella wearing a Cubs baseball cap," Ames had said as we drove.

"Driving in a noisy old car," I added.

"Won't be hard," he said.

It was at that point that I called Detective Ettiene Viviase to tell him about the body in the jeep across from Bee Ridge Park. It was better to have a cop I knew around.

Viviase arrived thirty-five minutes into my longing for the comfort of dark jungles. It was just enough time for him to take a look at Berrigan's body, leave someone to take over the crime scene and get back to Ames and me.

I heard the footsteps on the wooden stairs and watched the door open. Ames was at Viviase's side.

Once, I had heard Viviase referred to as "Big Ed." He wasn't particularly big, maybe a little under six feet tall and weighing in at a little over two hundred and twenty pounds. He was wearing his usual uniform, a rumpled sports jacket, dark slacks, a tie with no personality, and a weary look on his face.

"Got a little more to do on the car," said Ames. "Need a few parts. Should get it working within reason."

"I'm glad to hear it," said Viviase, stepping into the room and closing the door behind him. "Now tell me a story. Nonfiction preferred."

"Mind if I wash up my hands?" asked Ames.

"Please do," said Viviase moving to the desk and facing me across it.

Ames walked slowly through the bathroom door and closed it behind him. Then I heard the water start to flow.

"We didn't kill him," I said.

"I know that," said Viviase. "If you had, you probably wouldn't have walked up to his door asking for him after you crushed his skull."

"I definitely wouldn't have," I said.

"Talk," he said.

"Berrigan found me at the Crisp Dollar Bill," I said. "He said he wanted my help. He was nervous. When Ames showed up, Berrigan went to the bathroom and out the window. You can check with Billy the bartender and the customers who were there. When Berrigan went through the bathroom window, we followed him. He was frightened. I thought maybe we could help. I ran outside and saw him pull away in the jeep. There was someone in the car with him. I couldn't make out who. My car—"

"Your car?"

"I bought it this morning."

"The Saturn McKinney was working on?"

"Yes."

"It's a gem."

"Thanks. It moves at its own pace."

"Two questions," said Viviase. "First, what did Berrigan say he wanted?"

"He didn't have time to tell me."

"Thin, Fonesca. Very thin. Third question: Why did you leave the scene of a murder?"

"Because we didn't want to get involved."

"Then why did you call me?"

"I changed my mind."

"Civic duty, right?"

"I knew you'd find us."

Ames emerged from the bathroom and joined us.

"I'll talk to McKinney now," said Viviase. "Let's see if he remembers it the way you do."

Ames did. We had gone over the story as we clunked our way home. Ames got it down perfectly. He told it tersely.

"This have anything to do with the Horvecki murder you've been asking about?"

"Don't know," I said, and I didn't, though it was more than likely that the two were related.

"Since I'm here, would you like to tell me how you got involved in the Horvecki business?"

I didn't want to tell him for many reasons, not the least of which was that I had been recommended for the job by Viviase's own daughter, Elisabeth, but I had to tell him something.

"Two kids just came to me. Friends of Gerall."

"Why you?"

I shrugged and said, "Ask them."

"I will," he said. "Fix your car. Stop trying to get the Gerall kid off. Lighten up this room. I'll get back to you. You listening?"

"Yes," I said.

"But you won't back off, will you?"

"No."

"All right, give me the names of the two kids," he said. "And don't tell me it's confidential. You're not even a private investigator."

I gave him Greg and Winn's names. He wrote them down and said, "They visited Gerall in juvie," Viviase said putting the notebook away. "I knew who they were."

"Just trapping the coyote," said Ames.

"Very colorful," Viviase said.

"Anything new on the Horvecki daughter?" I asked.

"Nothing I plan to share."

Which, I concluded, meant that he had nothing more than what Dixie had given me and probably a lot less.

Viviase left.

Seconds after he was gone, the door to my bedroom opened and Victor Woo came out with a girl. She was no more than fifteen, dark, cute, still holding on to a little baby fat. She wore faded jeans and a white tucked-in short-sleeved blouse with a flower stitched over her left breast.

"Is my father gone?" she asked, standing back in case Viviase decided to return. His footsteps had clacked down the stairs and, unless he had taken off his shoes and tiptoed back up, he was gone, at least for now.

"He's gone," I said. "How did you find me?"

"Your name is in my father's address book. I went to where you were supposed to be, but there was no building."

Victor moved to the floor in the corner. Elisabeth Viviase glanced at him.

"I asked a sad fat man in the car rental place. He told me where you live. Why is that man sitting on the floor in the corner?"

She sat in one of the two chairs on the other side of my desk.

"Penance," I said, sitting.

"For what?"

"Ask him."

She turned to Victor and said, "Why are you doing penance?"

"Murder," he said softly.

With a veteran policeman as a father, the possibility of murder in close proximity was not confined to CSI on television.

"Why here?" she asked. "Why do penance here?"

"I killed his wife," Victor said flatly.

Elisabeth turned back to me, tried to figure out if this was some comic routine with her as the butt of the joke. Whatever she saw in my face, she decided to change the subject.

"Ronnie didn't kill Horvecki."

"How do you know?"

"Because he was with me," she said.

"When?"

"A week ago on Saturday," she said.

"What time?"

"From seven till midnight."

She sat with back straight and false sincerity masking her face.

"The murder took place after midnight," I said.

"Well, I may have left Ronnie's at one or later."

"I was just testing you," I said. "Horvecki was actually killed no later than noon."

"Well," she said, sliding back as far as she could go. "Now that I think of it, I was with Ronnie from seven to midnight on the day before the murder. On the day of the murder, I was with him as early as eleven in the morning, maybe earl . . . You're testing me again."

She looked away.

She returned to the self-certain statement of "Ronnie didn't do it."

"You didn't go to the police with your alibi for Gerall," I said.

"You kidding? My father would find out in five minutes. I wanted to tell you so you could find the real killer without telling my father about, you know, my coming here."

Victor suddenly stood, and asked, "Would you like a Coke?" The move reminded me of James Coburn when he tilted his hat back and suddenly stood erect, ready for a showdown with his knife against a gun.

"Diet Coke," she said.

Victor looked at me.

"Nothing for me," I said.

Victor left. Elisabeth and I listened to his footsteps on the stairs.

"Gerall's your boyfriend?"

"I wish," she said eyes looking upward.

"You told Greg Legerman and Winn Graeme about me."

"Yeah."

"Tell me about them."

"Greg is kind of electric-cute, super-smart, dancing around, adjusting his glasses, a walking public service ad for hyperactives anonymous."

"He get in a lot of fights?"

"No. He just talks, makes people nervous. Winn is his only friend. He takes a lot from Greg."

"But they stay friends?" I asked.

"Go figure," she said.

"Greg talks. What does he talk about?"

"You think I pay that much attention to Long-winded Legerman?"

"I think you pay attention to a lot of things."

She gave me a questioning look.

"That's a compliment," I said.

The quizzical look was replaced by a minimally appreciative smile.

The door opened. Victor and Ames entered together. Victor moved to my desk with an offering of Diet Coke for Elisabeth who said, "Thank you."

"It's warm," he said.

I knew a twelve-pack of Diet Coke was in the back of his car.

"That's okay," she said.

She popped the tab and drank from the can.

Victor went back to his bedroll and Ames leaned against the wall.

"Anything else you can tell me?" I asked.

"About what?" she said, looking over her shoulder at Ames and Victor.

"Greg, Winn, Ronnie, Horvecki. A man named Blue Berrigan."

"Blue Berrigan? I can tell you about him. I have his three CDs. Haven't listened to them in a long time. I was a big fan. I've still got my Blue Bunny night slippers, but if you tell anyone, I'll come back here and claim you raped me."

"I won't tell anyone," I said.

She took a big gulp from her Diet Coke.

"Hot Coke is gross. Am I through?" she asked, placing the can on the desk.

"How'd you get here?"

"Walked from school. I can catch a bus home."

"Victor can drive you home."

She looked at Victor who had returned to his place in the corner.

"No, thanks," she said, looking at the man who had called himself a murderer.

"Ames can give you a lift on the back of his scooter."

I looked at Ames. He had a strong avuncular feeling for children.

"Has he murdered anyone?" she asked.

"Not recently," I said.

"I'll take the scooter."

"Do you know the first line of a book, any book?"

" 'The event on which this fiction is founded has been supposed, by Dr. Darwin, and some of the physiological writers of German, as not of impossible occurrence.' "

I asked her to repeat it slowly. She did, while I wrote on a pad from my desk drawer.

"The book?" I asked.

"*Frankenstein,*" said Victor.

"That's right," said Elisabeth. "We had to memorize a paragraph from a novel on our reading list. I picked *Frankenstein.*"

"Because it's scary?" I tried.

"Because it was written by a woman," she said.

"You want to be a writer?"

"I want to be an FBI agent," she answered. "But don't—"

"Tell your father."

"He's not ready for it," she said. "And I might change my mind."

I got up to show I had nothing more to ask or say. She stood and headed for Ames and the door. She paused at the door and said, "You won't tell my—"

"I won't tell," I said.

Ames and the girl left. I was making some assumptions. I assumed the timing was such that my investigation of the Horvecki killing, the bullet through the window of Augustine's car, the shooting of Darrell Caton, and the murder of Blue Berrigan were all tied together. What if I were wrong? I had two suspects I hadn't yet spoken to, Esau Williams, the cop in Venice, and Jack Pepper in Cortez Village—two people whose names were in files in a cabinet in the mobile home of an ex-Cincinnati cop named Pertwee. Both had sworn to make Philip Horvecki pay for what he had been accused of, the rape of Esau's mother and aunt when they were young girls and the attempted rape and beating of Pepper, whom Horvecki had tried to sodomize. Pepper lived north, just outside of Cortez Village, and Williams south, in Venice.

When night came, I lay in bed silently for I don't know how many minutes listening to traffic on 301, thinking of something I could say or do to induce Sally to stay.

I had nothing to offer. Armed with addresses that I had gotten from Pertwee's files, I got up just before six in the morning and asked Victor, who was cross-legged on his bedroll reading a book, to tell Ames I was going to Cortez Village and that I'd be back in a few hours.

There are no hills in Florida south of Ocala unless we're talking about man-made ones. Construction is constantly going on in Sarasota—streets torn up and widened, new streetlights, hotels, mansions, developments, high-rise apartments, new malls. From time to time a pile of dirt resembling a fifteen-foot hill will rise and occasionally a dazzled teen or preteen will climb up and be knocked down or even buried in a small dust-raising avalanche. The flat landscape of Sarasota County is paled over with nonnative palm trees and trees that thrive on enough water to drown most other fauna and with tall, sometimes fat condominium buildings that present a view of heavily trafficked roads and other condos.

I passed a mess of construction heading north on Tamiami Trail.

Wooden yellow-and-black traffic horses and dingy red cones created a minor maze that slowed vehicles and made ancient drivers, pregnant mothers, and slightly drunken men mad with the challenge.

It took me almost an hour to make the trip to Cortez Village. Ames had installed a thirdhand junkyard radio in the car. It worked just fine, so I was accompanied by the soothing voice of a man with a Southern accent. The voice wasn't strident; he was confident and sounded as if he were smiling as he spoke. I had been told when I called Jack Pepper's phone number that he was at the studio doing his show. The woman told me the address of the station's studio and number on the dial where WTLW could be found. I found it and listened as I drove.

"You know, friends," the man said, "the Jewish people are holy. They are the people chosen by God to redeem the land of Israel, the sacred land of our Lord Jesus Christ. We must support the Jewish people in their quest to survive against heathen hordes. Palestine does not belong to the Arab. Palestine comes from the biblical word 'Philistine.' The Philistines were neither Arab nor Semite. The Emperor Hadrian designated the land as Palestine. The Arabs can't even say the word. They call it 'Palethtine.' "

He almost sounded as if he were crying.

"We can't let the Jewish people be pushed into the sea. We cannot let the land of Israel once again go into the hands of those who would make of it an unholy land. If there need be another Crusade, we must march in it armed with truth."

And a lot of heavy firepower, I thought. Pepper was just getting warmed up.

"There will come a time," he said, "when our Savior returns and those who have believed in him will be saved and shall sit in the house of the Lord and bask in the warmth of Christ."

And what about the Jews? I thought, but Jack Pepper let it hang in the air.

Cortez Village, on the Gulf of Mexico, still has a few small fishing companies and some independent fishermen making a living pretty much as fishermen have been doing there for more than a century. The air was salty with the smell of fish.

The radio station was a little hard to find. It was about thirty yards down a narrow dirt street, at the rear of a small frame church on a white pebble-and-stone parking lot. Four cars were parked in the lot. A four-foot sign indicated that I was indeed not only in the parking lot of the Every Faith Evangelical Church but that if I followed the arrow pointing toward the rear of the church, I'd find radio station WTLW, *THE LORD'S WORD.*

There was a seven-foot-high mesh steel fence with three strands of barbed wire surrounding the lot. Inside the fence there was a patch of crushed white stone and shell about the size of my office. About twenty yards beyond the enclosure was a three-story steel radio tower.

On the patch of grass on my side of the fence was the door with a freshly painted white cross about the size of an ATM machine. Next to the cross was a gate with a button and a speaker just above it. I pushed the button. The clear but speaker resonant voice of a woman said, "Who is it?"

"Lew Fonesca. I'm here to see Jack Pepper."

"Reverend Pepper," she reprimanded.

"Reverend Pepper," I said.

"Why?"

"Philip Horvecki," I said.

Long pause. Long, long pause.

"Why?"

This time it was a man's voice, the same voice I had just been listening to on the radio.

"Detective Viviase of the Sarasota Police suggested I talk to you," I lied.

Another long pause.

"I do not wish to testify," he said.

"Ronnie Gerall may not have done it," I said.

I could hear the man and woman talking, but I couldn't make out what they were saying. One of them must have put a hand over the microphone. I could tell that the woman sounded insistent and Pepper sounded resigned.

"Come in," said Pepper. "Close the gate behind you."

Something clicked and I pushed the gate open.

The door at the end of the path was painted a bright red. It looked as if a new coat of paint had been applied minutes earlier. The station's call letters were painted in black in the middle of the door with a foot-high brown cross under them.

"Come in," came the man's voice.

I opened the door.

"Take off the hat please," the man said. "This station is part of the House of the Lord."

I took off my Cubs cap, stuffed it in my back pocket, stepped in, and closed the door behind me.

The room was about the size of a handball court. There were three desks with chairs lined up side by side on the left, and on the right stood a narrow table with spindly black metal legs. The table was covered in plastic that was meant to look like wood, but it looked like plastic. On the table there sat a computer and printer and boxes of eight-by-ten flyers I couldn't read from where I stood. There were eight folding chairs leaning against the wall. Beyond all this, through a large rectangular window, I could see a studio barely big enough for two people. In fact, two people were in there. One had a guitar. One was a man. One was a woman. They were obviously singing. They were smiling. I couldn't hear them.

I looked over at an ample woman of no more than fifty whose dark hair was a study for one of those "before" pictures on early-morning television.

"Speak," she said.

I looked at the man behind the second desk. He was gaunt and had red hair and an almost baby-like face. He could have been any age.

"You're Reverend Pepper?"

"I am," he said. "And you are?"

"An investigator hired to see if Ronnie Gerall killed Philip Horvecki. Want to go someplace more private?"

"Whatever you have to say to me can be said in front of Lilly."

"Philip Horvecki," I said. "He was not a good man."

Lilly closed her eyes and nodded her head.

"He wasn't punished for what he did to you," I said.

"It was my word against his. The police said that wasn't enough," Pepper replied.

"He wasn't punished," I said.

"Yes he was, but not by the law. His punishment was delayed, but the Lord was not in a hurry."

Lilly was slowly nodding her head to the rhythm of Pepper's voice and the eyes of Jack Pepper vibrated back and forth.

"Where were you Saturday night?"

"What time?"

"Evening, at about ten."

"In my home, my aunt's home where I live. She looks after me. Lilly was there too."

"I was," Lilly said.

"Lilly came to dinner and to talk about a tour I have been planning. I'm sorry. I have to get back in the studio. Gilbert and Jenny are almost finished with their song."

"And today, about eleven in the morning?" I asked.

"Another crime?"

I said nothing.

"I was here, doing the morning call-in show," he said.

Before I could question Lilly, the theory I had been putting together about recorded shows and lying alibis seemed to come apart. Maybe I had just seen *Laura* too many times.

Jack Pepper rose with the help of two aluminum forearm crutches. He leaned forward as he slowly came out from behind the desk.

He looked up at me with what may have been a touch of pain and said, "MS. Multiple Sclerosis. The Lord has chosen to touch me with this affliction. Would you like the name and number of my doctor to see if I'm telling the truth?"

"No," I said.

"Fonesca? Italian. You are a Catholic?" he asked.

Lilly was shaking her head yes. She was either answering for me or at the brilliance of Jack Pepper's observation.

"No," I said.

"Lapsed?"

"No. I'm a lapsed Episcopalian."

"We are all one in Christ," he said.

"Except for the Jews and a long list of others."

"They are welcome to join the faith and be embraced as brothers and sisters and be saved," he said.

"Amen," said Lilly softly.

"You believe that in spite of what God has let happen to you?"

"Because of what God has let happen to me."

"Philip Horvecki sodomized you," I said gently.

"No," he said with a smile. "He tried and failed. The Lord did not choose to let it happen."

I shut up and watched him make his painful way toward the door to the studio in which I could see that the two singers had wrapped up. Then he stopped and looked back at me.

"The Lord has allowed something bad to happen to you, too," he said. "You are filled with grief and sorrow."

That could have been said of just about everyone I knew or had ever known. But, it hit me. He opened the door to the studio a few seconds after the red light over the door had gone off.

"You have a favorite first line of a book?" I asked.

"Genesis one," he said.

"Something else."

He paused and said, " 'Ours is essentially a tragic age, so we refuse to take it tragically.' "

"What's that from?" I asked taking out my index cards and pen.

"*Lady Chatterley's Lover*," he said.

He entered, and the studio door closed behind him.

Never underestimate the ability of a human being to surprise.

"There are many roads to enlightenment and belief," Lilly said.

If there were that many roads, why wasn't I on one of them? I looked at her. She was beaming, her eyes fixed on the studio door.

"All are welcome to this church," she said.

"Then why the barbed-wire fence?" I asked.

"There are people on this earth who have been put here to challenge, vex, and destroy to keep us from spreading the faith."

"Vandals," I said.

"Minions of the devil," she said.

I thought I might save a little time, so I simply asked, "You didn't happen to kill Philip Horvecki and Blue Berrigan?"

"I don't know any Blue Berrigan and I don't believe in killing."

"You happen to have a favorite first line from a book?"

" 'It was a pleasure to burn. It was a special pleasure to see things eaten, to see things blackened and changed,' " she said. "*Fahrenheit 451.*"

With that, I went to the door.

"Feel free to come back," Lilly said.

I had no intention of doing so. When I got back into the car and turned on the radio, I was greeted by the voice of the Reverend Jack Pepper:

". . . a special prayer for the soul of Lewis Fonseca, one of our Lord's lost children."

"Fonesca," I said softly. "Not Fonseca."

I turned off the radio and drove amid the sound of silence.

10

Essau Williams was in the Venice telephone directory. I sat in the Saturn and punched in the number I had written on one of my index cards.

The phone rang three times before a man answered with a sleepy, "Williams."

"Fonesca," I said. "I'm from Sarasota. I'd like to talk to you about Philip Horvecki."

"He's dead."

"I know."

"I'm not sorry."

"I'm not surprised. Can I talk to you?"

"Who are you?" he asked sounding a little more awake. "A reporter?"

"No, a friend of the family."

"Whose family?"

"Ronnie Gerall."

"You want me to contribute to his defense fund? Put me down for an anonymous fifty dollars. No, make that a hundred dollars. Any killer of Horvecki is a friend of mine. And since you're calling me, I think you know why I'm being generous."

"Can we meet?" I asked. "I'd like to gather information about Horvecki that might help justify what Gerall did."

"Where are you?"

"I'm in Venice," I said.

"Come over."

He gave me directions and we hung up without good-byes.

Essau Williams's house was not near the beach. It was in Trugate West, a development about three miles south of the hospital. What it was west of, I have no idea. His was a small ranch-style house, one of hundreds built in the 1950s to house the middle-class migrants who didn't have enough money to buy near the beach. They did have a little more money than the retirees who moved just outside of what was then the city limits into the mobile homes lying on tiny patches of grass that most of them tried to make homey with flowers and bright paint.

The green grass, really the weeds that passed for grass in Florida, was mowed short. The two trees, one a small palm, the other a tangelo, grew on opposite sides of the narrow concrete path that led to the front door.

I knocked. Essau Williams opened. He wasn't big, he was huge. He wore a pair of blue shorts and a gray T-shirt with the name ESSAU in red block letters across his chest and the number 8 under it. He had a yellow towel draped around his neck, and sweat was thick on his forehead, cheeks, and arms. He was all muscle and probably could have made a career with his body if he had a face to match. Essau Williams, light brown with a brooding brow, looked a little like my cousin Carmine, who was not the beauty of our family. Williams had the additional drawback of a raised horizontal white scar across his forehead.

"Go around back," he said and closed the door.

I walked through the grass to the back of the house where Williams was placing two tall glasses of what looked like lemonade on a wooden picnic table.

"Have a seat," he said.

I sat. It was hard to tell how big the yard was. It was dense with fruit trees, succulent bushes, flowers, and vines. The picnic table was on a round redbrick island that left no room for anything but the table.

"Nice," I said, looking around.

On a mat a few yards from the table was a plastic-covered bench. A series of bars and weights were lined up evenly next to the bench.

"Thanks. If you go that way, down the path . . . See it?"

"Yes."

The lemonade was cold with thin slices of lemon and clinking cubes.

"There's a fountain over there with a small waterfall. You should be able to hear it."

"I hear it," I said.

"Okay, maybe I can save us some time." He took a deep drink of lemonade and looked in the general direction of the running water. "Philip Horvecki raped my mother and aunt when they were kids and got away with it. Eight years ago Philip Horvecki came to my mother and my aunt's home, threatened them, and left them crying. He warned them not to tell anyone or he would come back and kill them."

I nodded. There was nothing else to do. He went on.

"My mother was sixty-four, my aunt sixty-six. I was on the force in Westin, Massachusetts. They didn't tell me what had happened till I came down for Thanksgiving. That was three months after the attack. I went to the sheriff's office and demanded that Horvecki be arrested. My mom and aunt filed criminal complaints. Only the word of my mom and aunt against Horvecki, who had the best lawyers money could buy. They tore at the reports, said they were filed by two sexually frustrated, old black women who changed their minds about selling the house for what he called 'a fair price.' He also said they were angry because he wouldn't accept their advances. His lawyers brought up medical histories, family history. We didn't have a chance."

"So . . ."

"Didn't even go to trial," he said, shaking his head. "He walked. Then I moved here, took a job with the Venice police and began watching everything Horvecki did or said. My mother and aunt moved back north. They've both been in therapy. They're recluses.

They seldom go out, and they've got guns and know how to use them. They think Horvecki's going to make good on his promise to kill them."

"Didn't you feel like doing more than watching him?"

He was nodding now, considering. Then he leaned forward toward me.

"I wanted to kill him. I told him I would. I told him I'd pick my own time. I wanted to turn him into a pile of frightened jelly."

"Did it work?"

"No," he said. "After a while, he didn't believe me. The fact, which I'll deny, is that I had a date set, the anniversary of what he did to my mom and aunt, to beat the bastard to death. Three weeks from today. I'm glad someone beat me to it."

"Horvecki was rich," I said.

"Very. Worth about sixty or seventy million. Real estate. He made at least two million of that from my aunt and mother's house and property."

"You know who gets his money?"

"His daughter I guess. Who cares? My mother and my aunt are lost. You know what it's like to lose someone you love? You know what it's like to become obsessed with punishing him?"

"Yes," I said.

He looked at me long and hard over the rim of his lemonade and then said, "Maybe you do. When you see him dead in a funeral home, the feeling of vindication doesn't come. You just feel flat, empty."

"I know," I said. "Did you kill Horvecki?"

"What?"

"Did you kill Philip Horvecki?"

"No. I told you. I thought you were trying to find information that would justify what Gerall did, not come up with another suspect. Who do you work for?"

"Ronnie Gerall. I told you. He says he didn't do it."

"Surprise. A killer denies his crime. If you find out someone else did it, I'll give that hundred dollars to his defense. Now I think you better leave."

He stood up, but I didn't.

"I think there's something you're not telling me," I said.

His fists were clenched now. The scar across his forehead distended and turned a clean snow white.

"Get out," he said, kicking the bench.

"You've got a temper," I said. "How angry are you?"

"You want to find out?"

He was around the table now standing over me. I didn't want to find out.

"You lose your temper easily," I said.

"Maybe."

He had me by the front of my shirt, now, and pulled me to my feet.

"You are about to have an accident," he said. "A bad one."

"Don't think so," came a familiar voice from the corner of the house.

Ames stood there with a pistol in his hand.

"Best put him down and back away," Ames said.

"You have a license for that weapon?" asked Williams.

"No, but if I shoot you dead, legality of the weapon won't mean much, will it?"

He still had my collar and was squeezing more tightly. I gagged.

"You won't shoot," Williams said.

"He will," I gagged. "He's done it before."

Williams lifted me farther. I felt myself passing out. Ames fired. He was a good shot, a very good shot. The bullet skidded between Williams's feet leaving a scratch in the bricks. Williams let me drop. I tumbled backward, fell over the bench, and landed on my back.

"You all right, Lewis?" he asked.

I had trouble answering. My back was a flash of pain, and my throat wouldn't allow words to come out. I made a sound like "Mmmm," which in the universal language of the beating victims of the world could mean no or yes.

Williams stood still, looking at Ames.

"One question," I rasped, getting to my knees.

"I didn't kill Horvecki," said Williams.

"Not my question," I said, making it to my feet. "Have you got a favorite first line from a book?"

Williams turned to look at me. "No," he said.

I staggered to Ames's side, and he said, "Let's get my scooter in your trunk and get out of here."

I didn't argue. Ames kept his weapon trained on Williams, who was now ignoring us and sitting on the bench again. He had poured himself another large lemonade.

On the way home, Ames explained how he had found me. He knew the names of the two suspects I was out looking for. The files Pertwee had given me were on my desk. He used the same telephone directory I had and made his way to the house in Venice.

"He kill Horvecki?" Ames asked as I drove.

"I don't think so," I said.

"The other fella, Pepper?"

"I don't think so."

"Where do we go now?"

"You have a favorite first line from a book?"

"Yes."

Ames is the best read person I have ever known. His room across from the kitchen and near the rear door of the Texas Bar and Grill was jammed with books neatly arranged on floor-to-ceiling shelves Ames had built. He always carried a book in his pocket or in the compartment of his scooter. The last book I saw him reading was *Dead Souls.*

"What is it?"

Ames was silent for a moment. He looked down at the barrel of the shotgun between his legs and said, "People don't read much anymore."

Then Ames said, " 'In a village of La Mancha, the name of which I have no desire to recall, there lived not so long ago one of those gentlemen who always have a cane in the rack, an ancient buckler, a skinny nag, and a greyhound for the chase.' "

"Which one of us is Quixote and which one is Sancho Panza?" I asked.

He looked straight ahead and said, "Let's find us more windmills."

We were making good time going north on Tamiami. We were both quiet while I thought about what to do next. Then I spoke. I didn't think about what I was saying. There were consequences, but there was the promise of windmills.

"How are things at the Texas?"

"Fine," he said.

"Think you might want to become my partner?"

"Already am."

"Officially, I mean."

"The pay would be bad, the hours all over the place, the job dangerous sometimes, no benefits?" said Ames.

"And those are the incentives," I said.

"Sounds good to me," said Ames.

"And there's always a chance I'd get in this car one morning and just drive away for good."

"Understood."

"And your job at the Texas?"

"Could still do the cleaning up in exchange for my room. Big Ed'd be amenable."

"Then it's done?"

"Seems," Ames said.

And it was done. I wasn't sure what it meant, but I knew something had happened, something I would have to talk to Ann Hurwitz about.

"Dunkin' Donuts to celebrate?" I asked.

Ames had said enough. He nodded in agreement and we pulled into the parking lot of the Dunkin' Donuts across from Sarasota Memorial Hospital.

Our partnership was confirmed over coffee and chocolate iced doughnuts.

"Someone's been following us," Ames said after wiping his mouth.

"Blue Porsche."

"Yes."

"She parked in the lot?" I said.

"Yes."

"Maybe we should bring her coffee and a muffin?"

"No need," Ames said, looking past me. "She's coming."

There were three chairs at our small table, the only table at which anyone was sitting. The sound on the television set mounted on the wall was off. On the screen, a very pretty blonde with full red lips and perfect teeth was looking out at the world and talking seriously about something.

The woman from the blue Porsche sat between me and Ames.

"Can we get you a coffee and doughnuts or a muffin?" I asked.

"Coffee, black, that's all," she said.

She was Corkle's daughter and the mother of my teenage babbling client, Greg Legerman. She was dark and beautiful, her makeup perfect, not a hair out of place. Her skirt was blue and her long-sleeved cashmere sweater white. A necklace of large Chinese green jade and small jet black beads was all the jewelry she needed.

For an instant, just an instant, I remembered Catherine on the night we went to a concert at Orchestra Hall in Chicago. The symphony played Grieg and Brahms, and I watched my wife smiling and held her hand.

"You all right?" Alana Legerman asked.

"Perfect," I said.

I introduced her to Ames. He nodded in acknowledgment. She didn't offer her hand. Ames rose and headed for the counter to get her coffee. She sat up straight, probably a payoff from yoga classes.

"You didn't give my son back the money he paid you to find out who really killed Horvecki."

"If he wants his money back—"

"He won't take it," she said.

"No, he won't."

"You'll get my son killed."

Ames was back. He placed the coffee in front of Alana Legerman.

"Who would want to hurt him?" I asked.

"Whoever killed Horvecki," she said, looking at the steaming coffee but not picking it up.

"You don't think Ronnie Gerall did it?"

She considered the question. She took a breath, picked up the coffee, and said, "Ronnie has a temper and caustic verbal bite, but he hasn't the fire inside for the kind of brutal thing that was done to Horvecki."

"You know Gerall well?" I asked.

"Well enough."

I pictured the two of them together. She was twenty years older than he was, but she was a beauty, and he was a good-looking kid. Stranger things had happened.

"How did you meet him?"

"That's not relevant," she said, drinking some coffee.

A fat man sat two tables away with a small bag of doughnuts and a large coffee. He was wearing a suit and a very serious look on his face. I watched him attack the bag and come out with an orange-iced special.

I looked at Ames, who sat with his large hands folded on the table. He understood what I wanted. Neither of us spoke. It was her move.

"I'd like you to continue to look for whoever killed Philip Horvecki. You return whatever money my son and my father gave you, and I'll give you double the amount in cash. In addition, you make it clear to everyone you come in contact with that you are working for me. I'll do the same."

She touched the corner of her mouth with a little finger to remove a fleck that wasn't there.

"So, whoever killed Horvecki won't have any reason to harm your father and your son?" I asked. "If the killer wants my investigation to stop, he'll go after you."

"Yes," she said, "if that's what it comes to. Whoever it is is already trying to kill you."

I didn't see how changing clients would make a difference to someone who might want to kill me because I was looking into Philip Horvecki's murder, and I wasn't sure how accepting her offer might make her father and son a lot safer than they were already.

"How about this?" I said. "I keep the money you, your father, and your son give me, and the killer has to do a lot of thinking before going after your family. What's Greg's father like?"

"As some of Greg's friends might say, Greg's father is, like, dead. Heart attack. The world did not grieve at his passing."

"Nine hundred and thirty dollars," I said.

"A nice round number," she said, reaching into her oversized Louis Vuitton purse. "Will a check do?"

"Nicely," I said. "Make it out to cash."

She had a checkbook in front of her and a lean silver pen in her hand. When she finished writing the check, she tore it out of the book and handed it to me.

"Then there's nothing more to say," she said, getting up.

"You could thank my partner for the coffee."

"I'm sorry," she said. "Thank you."

This time she held out her hand, and Ames took it.

"Report to me when you have anything and try not to upset my father and Greg. Oh, and one last thing. When I said 'everyone you come in contact with'—don't tell them you are working for me."

She gathered up her purse and moved quickly toward the door. The fat man in the suit paused in his chewing to admire Alana Legerman as she went into the sunlit morning.

"Pretty lady," Ames said.

"Very pretty," I agreed.

"What's next?"

"We do just what she doesn't want us to do. We talk to Greg and Corkle."

Greg was still in school. I left a voice message asking him to call as soon as he could.

D. Elliot Corkle answered the phone. I asked if I could come over.

"Something happen to Gregory?"

"No."

"Come on over."

"Be there in half an hour."

He hung up. On the way to his house we stopped at a Bank of America and cashed the check. I gave half the cash to Ames. Alana Legerman hadn't followed us—we would have known. It's hard to hide a neon blue Porsche being driven by a beautiful woman.

The Saturn still made some voodoo sounds. Ames said he would engage his magical skills and take care of the Saturn's remaining problems the next day.

My cell phone rang.

"You weren't going to call me, were you?" Sally asked.

What was it I heard? Disappointment? Simple weariness? A headache in progress?

"I don't know."

"Dinner Saturday. Just you and me. No kids. Walt's. Six-thirty."

"You want me to pick you up at home?"

"You have a car?"

"Bought it today."

"Acquiring property."

"It can be abandoned or given away," I said. "It's not worth much."

"Or you can drive it into the sunset," she said.

"Yes."

Ames had put on his glasses and was reading a small blue book to let me know he was in no hurry for me to end the call.

"Pick me up at six-thirty," she said.

"Six-thirty," I repeated.

She hung up.

Ames took off his glasses and put the book back in his pocket. I drove. We were on our way to talk to an odd and possibly demented man with many millions of dollars.

Corkle answered the door. He was wearing a green polo shirt and navy pants with a welcoming smile.

"Can we come in?" I asked.

Corkle stepped back and wrung his hands just the way he did in his infomercials when he was about to offer "a sweet deal." He may not have needed the money, but he couldn't resist two customers.

"This is my partner, Ames McKinney."

It was the first time I had said that. I felt a little like Oliver Hardy introducing himself in one of their movies—"I'm Mr. Hardy and this is my friend Mr. Laurel. Say hello Stanley." —but Ames was no Stan Laurel.

Corkle stopped wringing his hands and reached out to shake. He looked delighted as Ames took his extended hand.

"Come in," said Corkle. "The library. You remember the way Mr. Fon . . . Fonesca."

"Yes," I said.

"Beer? Lemonade?"

"Lemonade?" Ames asked as I started toward the area with the yellow leather furniture.

"Yes, thanks," I said.

"Three glasses," said Corkle.

Ames and I sat on the uncomfortable leather sofa and waited. Corkle appeared in a few seconds with a tray on which rested a pitcher of iced lemonade and three glasses.

"Best lemonade in the world. Made with whole lemons from the tree right outside, seed and rind turned to a smooth pulp. More nutritious than the juice alone and it can be made in my D. Elliot Corkle Pulp-O-Matic in five seconds. Of course, you have to add sugar. I'll give you a Pulp-O-Matic when you leave."

All three of us drank. He was right. The lemonade was the best I had ever tasted.

"Blue Berrigan. Name mean anything to you?"

"No," he said. "D. Elliot Corkle has never heard of him."

"He was an entertainer," Ames said. "Sang kids' songs, had his own television show."

"Didn't know the man," Corkle said, holding up his glass of lemonade to the sun to watch the tiny pieces of pulp swirl like the snowy flecks in a Christmas bubble.

"You knew Philip Horvecki," I said. "You said . . ."

I paused to pull my index cards out of the day planner I kept in my pocket. I flipped through the cards and found the one I wanted.

"You said, 'Horvecki is not a nice human being.' "

He sat back, folded his hands in his lap and looked up at the ceiling for about ten seconds before saying, "D. Elliot Corkle is considering lying to you. I could do it. I can sell almost anything, especially a lie."

"But you won't," I said.

"I won't. I knew Philip Horvecki. He had a three-acre lot at the fringe of downtown. He wanted me to buy it from him. I wanted to buy it, but not from him. D. Elliot Corkle did a background check. He was a weasel. I told him so. He didn't like it."

"You didn't happen to kill him?" I asked.

"No."

We all had more lemonade.

"Did you ever threaten to kill him?" I asked.

"No. Am I a suspect in Horvecki's murder?"

"Ask the police that one," I said.

"Then why are you still looking for someone else besides Gerall for the murder? Gerall is a smart-ass and a . . . a . . ."

"Weasel?" asked Ames.

"Weasel," Corkle confirmed. "He bamboozled my grandson and my daughter. Neither has the good judgment of a John Deere tractor, which, by the way, is one of the finest pieces of machinery ever invented.

"You know what happened to Augustine?" he asked. He was looking directly at me, lips tight.

"I think he went back to acting," I said.

"He's a terrible actor. I used him on some of my infomercials because he looked tough and had muscles and D. Elliot Corkle wanted someone who could try to open The Mighty Miniature Prisoner of Zenda Safe, which can go with you wherever you go and is housed inside a candy or cigar box you could leave in plain sight."

"I remember that," said Ames.

"I'll give you one when you leave," said Corkle. "The Mighty Miniature Prisoner of Zenda Safe could not be opened unless you had a blow torch, but it had two defects. Want to guess what they were?"

"You advertised the safe on television," I said. "People know what the safe looked like."

"Several million people," Corkle said, proudly pouring us all more lemonade. "Yes, it was hard for D. Elliot Corkle to come up with someplace the little safe could be hidden in the average house. And then, how was I to let them know where the safe should now be hidden? What's the other problem with it?"

"The safe might be hard to open, but it can be carried away and opened somewhere else later," said Ames.

"On the button," said Corkle, closing one eye and pointing a finger at Ames. "Still sold enough to make a small profit on them."

"I've got some questions," I said.

"Shoot," said Corkle.

"Do you know who killed Horvecki?"

"I believe in our justice system, in our police," he said emphatically. "It's the sacred duty of any citizen to help the police in any way that citizen can. People should not commit murder. Evidence should never be withheld."

"Are you withholding evidence?" I asked.

"There are secrets inside the office of D. Elliot Corkle. Next question."

"Secrets? Evidence?" I asked.

"Next question," he said.

"No, that'll do it," I said. "Sorry about the intrusion. Thanks for your hospitality."

At the front door, Corkle said, "Wait."

We stood there until he returned with two boxes for me and two for Ames.

"You each get a Pulp-O-Matic and a Mighty Miniature Prisoner of Zenda Safe."

"Heavy," said Ames, holding a gift box in each arm. "You could beat a man's head in with either one of these."

"Wait," Corkle said hurrying off, ducking into the closet and popping right back out with two more packages, both small. "The Perfect Pocket Pager."

He stuck one in one of my pockets and did the same for Ames. We left the house and started down the path. It wasn't until we hit the street that we heard the door close.

"Secrets," Ames said. "Believe him?"

"Strongly suggests that he knows who did it or has a pretty good idea," I said.

"Think he has something?"

"Maybe we can find out," I said.

I had some trouble getting the trunk of the Saturn open, but when I did we placed our gifts inside, got in the car, and drove away from the Bay and from Corkle.

"Where to now?" asked Ames.

"Ronnie Gerall."

11

Ronnie Gerall agreed to see us when I sent him a message saying that I had something important to tell him. Ames stayed in the waiting area of juvenile detention with his book, and I took off my Cubs cap and followed the guard down a brightly lit corridor that smelled of Lysol and bleach.

Ronnie Gerall was waiting for me when the door to the visitors' room was opened. Ronnie was getting special treatment because he was accused of murder—and murder of a prominent, if not much loved, citizen.

Ronnie, his hair freshly combed, looked good in orange and a sullen pout. He did not offer to shake my hand, and I wasn't about to be rejected.

"I have a new client," I said as I sat.

I got an impatient look at this news.

"A client who's willing to pay for a new lawyer," I said.

"Why would I want to replace the guy from the public defender's office? He's inexperienced, stupid, and has no confidence. I was thinking of representing myself. Who's my benefactor?"

"A woman who thinks you're innocent."

He stiffened and I knew he would come up with the right name if I pushed him.

"I thought you were going to find out who killed Horvecki and set me free to enjoy the sunlight, baseball, and pizzas."

"It's always good to have well-paid backup," I said.

"What do you want to tell me?" he asked.

"Do you know Blue Berrigan?"

"Blue Berrigan? The dolt who used to have the stupid kid show on television?"

"Yes."

"I don't know him," Gerall said.

"Someone murdered him yesterday."

"I'm sorry, but I have problems of my own."

"I'm pretty sure he was killed because he knew who killed Philip Horvecki."

This got Gerall's interest.

"Then nail him," Gerall said. "You know what it's like in here? You have any idea of what kind of people are in here, people I have to be nice to when I want to punch their few remaining teeth out?"

"I'm still trying to find Horvecki's killer. But I need you to answer one question."

"What?"

"Does Corkle or Greg know about you and Corkle's daughter?"

"Know what?"

His fists were clenched and he started to rise from his chair. I sat still and looked at him. I was getting to know his moves. I met his eyes. The menace slipped away.

"No, they don't know," he said sitting. "But when this is over, they'll be told."

"Why?"

"Because Alana and I are going to get married," he said.

It didn't have to be said, and I didn't say it, but the observation hung in the dusty room. Either Corkle or Greg might prefer to have Ronnie in prison than living as Corkle's son-in-law and Greg's stepfather.

"I know what you're thinking. She's old enough to be my mother, but you've seen her," Ronnie went on as if he were announcing the new issue of a Salmon P. Chase postage stamp. "She loves me."

"I'm happy for you both," I said.

There was nothing else to say. Ronnie folded his arms and watched me head for the door.

Ames and I split a medium moussaka pizza—eggplant, cheese, sausage, and extra onion—at Honey Crust on Seventeenth Street. We were celebrating our partnership.

"Too many suspects," he said, wiping his mouth with a napkin.

He was right.

"Who's your pick?" I asked.

"Don't know, but Corkle's looking ripe for it."

"His grandson, daughter, Pepper the Preacher, Williams the Cop, and Ronnie Gerall. Just because he's in jail it doesn't mean he's innocent."

"And maybe Gregory's friend Winston," said Ames.

"And half the students at Pine View."

The next line should have been one reflecting incredulity that someone might murder over retaining a high school educational program. But both Ames and I knew that people had been murdered over a lot less. A few days earlier a Bradenton police officer had interrupted a ninety-dollar drug sale, and the buyer killed him. Two homeless men in Sarasota had fought, and one had died from a jagged Starbucks Frappuccino bottle to the throat. The fight had been over who had more teeth. Homeless Man Number One had more teeth, but Number Two said his were in better shape. Number Two pushed Number One into the concrete arch of a medical office building on Bahia Vista. Number One lost most of his remaining teeth and his life, blood and Frappuccino dribbling down his chest.

"What do we do now?" Ames asked.

"I'm going home to bed."

"It's three in the afternoon."

"A good time to close my door, pull down the shade, take off my shoes and pants, and go to sleep."

But such was not to be.

My cell phone sang "Help!"

The number of people who had my cell phone number, at least the ones I wanted to have it, was four: Ames, Flo, Adele, and Sally.

"Yes," I said.

"Lew," said Sally. "Darrell walked out of the hospital less than an hour ago."

"Is that good or bad?"

"Bad," she said. "He put on his clothes and walked out before he was discharged. He's supposed to be at home resting."

"You try his mother? Their apartment?"

"I called her. He isn't at the apartment and he didn't call her."

"We'll find him," I said.

"Call me when you do, all right?"

"I'll call you," I said.

Sally hung up. So did I.

"Darrell?" asked Ames as he stood up with a box holding the last three slices of the pizza.

I nodded and put a twenty-dollar bill on the table. I was on my feet now and heading for the door. Nothing had to be said. Both Ames and I would have given twenty-to-one odds that we knew where Darrell was.

And we were right.

When I opened the door to my new home, Darrell Caton was sitting in the chair behind my desk. Victor Woo sat across from him. They had been talking. I tried to imagine what the two of them would have to say to each other. Then I saw the small photograph in front of Darrell. I knew what it was. I had seen it before, on a table in the booth of a bar in Urbana, Illinois. Victor had shown me the photograph of his smiling wife and two small, smiling children.

"Mind reader, Lewis Fonesca," said Darrell. "Knew where to find me and knew I was hungry. What kind of pizza you bring me?"

"Moussaka with extra onion," I said.

Ames placed the box on the desk. Darrell opened it and examined the pizza.

"What the f . . . hell is musical pizza? Beans?"

"Let's get you back to the hospital," said Ames.

"Hell no," said Darrell, handing a slice of lukewarm pizza to Victor. "They've got diseases and all kinds of shit in there. Worst place to be when you're sick. I read about it."

"Let's get you back," Ames said again.

"Your mother's worrying about you. Sally is worried about you," I said.

"Think about it, Lewis Fonesca," said Darrell. "Four people may be worrying about me. Four. You. Big Mac here. My mother and Ms. Porovsky. Him?" he added looking at Victor. "I don't know what he's thinking."

"What about Flo and Adele?" I said.

"They know I escaped from Alcatraz?"

"No."

"Then they can't be worried, can they? Pizza's good. What's that yellow thing?"

"Eggplant," I said.

"Woo," Darrell said. "I'll wrestle you for the last piece."

Victor shook his head no. Darrell picked up the last slice of pizza. He tried to hide a wince as he brought it to his mouth. Darrell was fifteen. No father. His mother had kicked a crack habit two years earlier and was holding down a steady job at a dollar store.

"You're going back to the hospital," Ames said.

"Don't make me run," said Darrell chewing as he spoke. "You won't catch me and running could kill me. Besides, if you do get me back in the hospital, I'll just get up and leave again."

"Why?" Victor asked.

We all looked at him.

"Why?" asked Darrell. "Because I'd rather die than be hooked up to machines waiting for Dr. Frankenstein and a bunch of little Frankensteins to come in and look at me."

"Fifteen," said Victor.

"Fifteen little Frankensteins?" asked Darrell.

"You are fifteen. You wouldn't rather die."

Victor looked at me. There were times after Catherine died that I wouldn't have minded dying, but I never considered suicide as an option. There were times, I knew, that after he had killed Catherine, Victor had considered death as an option.

"Mr. Gloom and Mr. Doom," said Darrell. "You didn't answer your damn phone. I broke out because I have to tell you something, Lew Fonesca."

"Tell it," I said.

"You should have brought more pizza."

"That's what you have to tell me?"

"Hell no. I had a visitor during the night in the hospital. I was asleep and drugged up. Room was dark. Machine was beep-beep-beeping, you know. Then I heard him."

"Who?"

"A man, I think, or maybe a woman. He was across the room in the dark. He thought I was asleep. At least I think he thought I was asleep. He said something like, 'I'm sorry. My fault. Silky sad uncertain curtains.' Shit like that. Creepy. Then he said he had to go but he'd be back. I could do without his coming back. So, I got up and . . ."

"Anything you could tell from his voice?" I asked. "Young? Old?"

"Like I said, couldn't tell," said Darrell. "No, wait. He had one of those English accents, like that actor."

"Edgar Allen Poe," said Ames.

"Edgar Allen Poe, the guy who wrote those scary movies?" asked Darrell.

" 'The silken sad uncertain rustling of each purple curtain wrought its ghost upon the floor,' " said Ames.

"Yeah, creepy shit like that."

"It's from a poem by Poe, 'The Raven,' " said Ames.

"I guess. You know him? This Poe guy?"

"He's been dead for a hundred and fifty years," I said.

I knew one person involved in all this that had what might pass for an English accent.

"I don't believe in ghosts," said Darrell. "You should have bought more pizza. Next time just make it sausage."

"Let's get you back to the hospital."

"Let's order a pizza to go," said Darrell. "Do that and I go back to the hospital."

"Ames and Victor will get you the pizza and take you back to the hospital."

Darrell looked decidedly unwell when they went through the door. I called Information and let them connect me with the number I wanted. The woman who answered had a pleasant voice and a British accent. She told me that Winston Churchill Graeme wasn't home from school yet, but soon would be. She asked if I wanted to leave a message. I said no.

When I hung up I walked over to the wall where the Stig Dalstrom paintings were and looked for truth in black jungles and mountains and the twisted limbs of trees. I focused on the lone spot of yellow in one of the paintings. It was a butterfly.

I folded the empty pizza box and carried it out with me. At the bottom of the steps I dropped the box into one of the three garbage cans and called Sally. With no preamble, I said, "We found Darrell."

"Where?"

"My place. Ames and Victor are taking him back to the hospital."

"I'll call his mother."

"Are you at work?"

"Yes."

"What can you tell me about Winston Churchill Graeme?"

Twenty minutes later I was parked about half a block down and across the street from the Graeme home on Siesta Key. The house was in an ungated community called Willow Way. The house was a lot smaller than others in the community, but it wasn't a mining shack.

Winn Graeme hadn't called back to set up a time to talk. I wondered why.

I didn't think Winn Graeme was home yet but, just to be sure, I called the house. I was wrong again. He answered the phone.

"This is Lew Fonesca," I said.

"Yes?"

"I'm parked on your street, half a block West."

"Why?"

"I'd like you to come out and talk."

"You can come in."

"I don't think you want your mother to hear what we have to talk about."

"I don't . . ."

"Your visit to the hospital last night."

It was one of those silences, and then, "I'll be right out."

There was no one on the street. A white compact car was parked in the driveway of the house from which Winn Graeme emerged. The house was at the top of a short incline with stone steps leading down to the narrow sidewalk. Trees and bushes swayed in the cool wind from off the Gulf.

Winn saw my car, adjusted his glasses, and headed toward me. He walked along the sidewalk, back straight, carrying a blue gym bag. He walked like a jock and looked like a jock.

He opened the passenger-side door and leaned over to look at me before he decided to get in. The door squeaked. He placed the gym bag on the floor in front of him.

"I have soccer practice in half an hour," he said, turning his head toward me. "Someone is picking me up."

"We shouldn't be long," I said. "You have a car?"

"Yes," he said. "It's in the garage. Why?"

"Early this morning," I said. "Say about two o'clock. Where were you?"

"Why?"

"Darrell Caton," I said. "The hospital."

Winn Graeme took off his glasses, cleaned them with his shirt and looked through the front window into a distance that offered no answers. Then he nodded, but I wasn't sure whether he was answering my question or one he had asked himself.

"Is he going to be all right?"

"I don't know."

"We're fragile creatures," he said.

"You told him you were sorry. Sorry for what?"

"For not stopping what happened."

"Greg shot Darrell, right?"

No answer from Winn, so I went on.

"He was aiming at me, but Darrell got in the way."

Still no response.

"Okay, not Greg. You shot Darrell."

Now he looked at me, and I at him. I saw a boy. I wondered what kind of man he was looking at.

"To scare you into stopping your investigation," Winn said.

"First he hires me and then he tries to stop me," I said.

He said nothing, just nodded, and then, after heaving a breath as if he were about to run a hundred-yard dash, he spoke.

"He found out something after he hired you, something that made him want you to stop. Firing you didn't work. You found someone else to pay you. So he tried to frighten you into stopping. He hoped you would weigh your safety and possibly your life against the few dollars you were getting. He only made it worse."

"He shot at me in the car with Augustine, and then he shot Darrell."

"Who's Augustine?"

"Cyclops."

Winn looked out his window. A woman was walking a small white dog. She was wearing a business suit and carrying an empty poop bag. Winn seemed to find the woman and dog fascinating.

"Both times he shot at me he sent someone else to the hospital," I said.

"Your life is charmed."

"No, Greg's a terrible shot."

The god of irony was at it again.

"Blue Berrigan," I said. No response, so I repeated, "Blue Berrigan."

"The clown," he said softly.

"He wasn't a clown."

"Greg didn't do that."

"Horvecki?"

"Greg didn't do that. We weren't unhappy about it, but he didn't do that."

"Did you?"

"No," he said.

A yellow and black Mini Cooper turned the corner and came to a stop in front of the Graeme house.

"I've got to go," he said. "I told you all this because I'm sorry that I didn't do anything to stop Greg. He's my friend. Whatever I've said here I'll deny ever saying."

"Why?" I said though I knew the answer.

"Why what?"

He had the door open now.

"Why is he your friend?"

"We need each other," he said as he got out of the car. "Greg didn't kill anybody."

He closed the door, crossed the street, and raised his hand in greeting to the boy who leaned out of the window of the Mini Cooper.

The boy in the car was Greg Legerman.

Greg looked back at me and ducked back through the window. Winn Graeme crawled in on the passenger side, and they drove off.

I could have confronted Greg Legerman, but sometimes it's better to let the person you're after worry for a while. I had learned that as an investigator with the state attorney's office in Chicago. Patience was usually better than confrontation, especially with a nervous suspect, and they didn't come any more nervous or suspicious than Greg Legerman. I wasn't afraid of Greg's not talking. I was afraid that he wouldn't stop.

I did follow the little car down Midnight Pass and off the Key, but I kept going straight when they turned left on Tamiami Trail.

My cell phone rang. I considered throwing it out the window, but I answered it.

"Lewis, I have a death in the family," said Ann Hurwitz.

"I'm sorry."

"My cousin Leona was ninety-seven years old," she said. "She's been in a nursing home for a decade."

"I'm sorry," I said.

"Lewis, you are one of the few people I know whose expression of sorrow over the death of a very old woman you don't know I would believe. I must cancel our appointment tomorrow so I can attend the funeral in Memphis."

"All right."

"But I have an opening today," Ann Hurwitz said.

"When?"

"Now."

"I'm on the way."

"You did your homework?"

My index cards were in the notebook in my back pocket.

"Yes."

"Good. Decaf with cream and Equal. Today I feel like a chocolate biscotti."

"With almonds?"

"Always with almonds," she said and clicked off.

Fifteen minutes later I picked up a pair of coffees and three chocolate biscotti from Sarasota News and Books and crossed Main street. I was about to go through the door to Ann's office on Gulfstream when he appeared, mumbling to himself.

He was black, about forty, wearing a shirt and pants too large and baggy for his lean frame. His bare feet flopped in his untied shoes. He looked down as he walked, pausing every few feet to scratch his head and engage himself in conversation.

I knew him. Everyone in this section of town near the Bay knew him, but few knew his story. I'd sat down with him once on the park bench he lived under. The bench was across the street from Ann's office. It had a good view of the small boats moored on the bay and the ever-changing and almost always controversial works of art erected along the bay. He had been evicted from his bench in one of the recurrent efforts to clean up the city for tourists. I didn't know where he lived now, but it wasn't far. Even the homeless have someplace they think of as home.

"Big tooth," he said to himself as he came toward me.

"Big tooth," I repeated.

The bag in my hand was hot and the biscotti must have been getting moist.

He pointed across the street toward the bay. There was a giant white tooth which was slowing the passing traffic.

He scratched his inner left thigh and said, "Dentist should buy it. Definitely."

One of the charms of the man was that he never asked for money or anything else. He minded his own business and relied on luck, the discards of the upscale restaurants in the neighborhood and the kindness and guilt of others.

I reached into the bag and came up with a coffee and a biscotti. He took them with a nod of thanks.

"You, too?" he asked, tilting his head toward the nearby bench—not his former residence, but the one right outside Ann's office.

"Can't," I said. "Appointment."

"Old lady who talks to ghosts and crazy people?"

"Not ghosts," I said.

"I'm not a crazy person," he said.

"No," I agreed.

"You a crazy person?"

"I don't know."

"You should maybe find out," he said, moving toward the bench, his back to me now.

"I'm working on it," I said and stepped through the door.

Ann's very small reception area was empty except for three chairs, a neat pile of copies of psychology magazines, and a small Bose non–boom box playing generic classical music. The music was there to cover the voices of any clients who might be moved to occasional rage or panic, usually directed at a spouse, child, sibling, boss, or themselves. The music wasn't necessary for me. My parents never raised their voices. I have never raised mine in anger, remorse, or despair. All the passion in our family came from my sister, and she more than compensated for it with Italian neighborhood showmanship.

Ann was, as always, seated in her armchair under the high narrow horizontal windows. I handed her the bag. She smelled it and carefully removed coffee and biscotti and placed them on the desk near her right hand.

"No coffee for you?" she asked, handing me a biscotti.

"No," I said. "Caffeine turns me into a raging maniac."

I took off my Cubs cap and placed it on my lap.

"Levity," she said, removing the lid of her coffee and engaging in the biscotti-dipping ritual.

"I guess."

"Small steps. Always small steps. Progress," she said. "Biscotti are one of the tiny treasures of life. When one of my clients tells me he or she is contemplating suicide I remind them that, once dead, they will never again enjoy coffee and biscotti."

"Does it work?"

"Only one has ever committed suicide, but I can't claim that the biscotti approach has ever been the reason for this high level of success. Did your mother make biscotti?"

"No, she ate it. My father made *pignoli*. My uncle made biscotti."

"*Pignoli*?"

"A kind of cookie with pine nuts."

"My mother made mandel bread," Ann said. "That's like Jewish biscotti, made with cement, at least the way my mother made it."

I looked at the clock on the wall over her head. Five minutes had passed.

"You want to know when we are going to start," she said. "Well, we already started."

"I asked Ames to be my partner."

"Putting down roots," she said, finishing her biscotti. She had eaten it in record time.

I handed her mine.

"You sure?" she asked. "I didn't have time for lunch."

"I'm sure about you having my biscotti. I'm not sure about asking Ames to be my partner."

"Why?"

"He'll expect me to stay around."

"Yes."

"Besides, I make just enough to live on."

"Yes, but you asked him and he said yes.

"He said yes."

"Sally's leaving, moving North. Better job."

Ann said nothing, just worked on her biscotti, brushing away stray crumbs from her white dress with dancing green leaves.

"Did you ask her to stay?" she said finally.

"No."

"Do you want her to stay?"

"Yes."

"Is there anything you could say or do that would make her stay?"

"I think so. Maybe."

"But you won't say it."

"I can't. You want to hear the first lines I've collected?"

"Not this session," she said.

The phone rang. She never turned off the phone during our sessions and I guess she didn't turn it off during anyone else's sessions either. She had too much curiosity to turn off her connection to anyone who wanted to confess or try to sell her something.

"Yes, I'll take it," she told the caller after listening for a few seconds. She hung up.

"I'm going to give you a conundrum, an ethical dilemma, a moral puzzle," she said. "With that call, I just paid to become beneficiary of a life insurance policy for a ninety-one-year-old man. He gets paid with my cash offer immediately. I double or triple my investment when he dies, providing he dies before I do and, given my age, while the odds are in my favor, I stand some chance of losing. I have six such policies. What do you think?"

"Do you meet these people?" I asked.

"Absolutely not," she said, sitting back and folding her hands.

"Life insurance is gambling on beating or forestalling death," I said.

"Precisely, Lewis. Still?"

"I don't know. It doesn't feel right."

"No, it doesn't, but why not? Does it challenge God or the gods who might decide to strike you down instead of the person from whose death you would profit?"

Her eyes were dancing. We were getting somewhere or going somewhere. She leaned forward.

"I lied, Lewis," she said. "I didn't buy life insurance for a dying man. I told my stockbroker to go ahead and buy pork belly futures. I'm betting on people who might profit from the slaughter of pigs."

"That's comforting."

"Your opinion of me faltered for a moment," she said.

"Yes."

"But it's all right if I profit from the death of pigs."

"Yes," I said.

"We bet against death every day," she said. "But it is taboo to bet for death. We don't want to make those gods angry even if they exist only in our minds."

"Someone may be trying to kill me," I said.

"This has happened before."

"Yes."

"You invite it?"

"I don't know."

"You gamble with your life."

"I suppose," I said.

"And the irony is that you keep winning."

"I don't want to die anymore," I said.

"I know. But you haven't decided what to do about staying alive."

"I don't want anyone else I know to die."

"But they all will," she said, looking over her shoulder at the clock on the wall.

"Some of them have."

"Catherine," she said.

"Yes."

"The world is not perpetually sad in spite of the fact that the ones we love will all die," Ann said.

"Yes it is," I said.

"Time to stop. Next time, I hear your first lines."

She clapped her hands and rose. Her fingers were thin and the backs of her hands freckled with age. The wedding ring she wore looked too large, as if it would fall off.

I got up and put my Cubs cap back on my head. We faced each other for a moment. She seemed to be trying to convey some question with the tilt of her head and a few seconds of silence. I felt the answer but had no words for it. I nodded to show that I had at least a glint of understanding. I got twenty dollars out of my wallet and handed it to her.

When I stepped out into the sun, the homeless man was still on the bench squinting out at the setting sun. He had finished his coffee and biscotti, and his arms were spread out, draped over the bench. He was at home. He scratched his belly. I sat beside him and looked at the boats bobbing in the water. He didn't acknowledge my presence.

"You have a favorite first line from a book?"

"Uh-huh."

"What is it?"

"'Kelsey Yarborough hated grits with salt but he ate them anyway because his mother told him it was good for him.'"

"What's the book?" I said, writing the line on one of my cards. I had a neat little packet of them now.

"*Kelsey Plays the Blues.*"

"Who wrote it?"

"Kelsey Yarborough."

I looked at him, but he was too busy looking toward the sun. I thought I knew the answer to the unstated question, but I said nothing.

He helped me out by saying, "Me. I'm Kelsey Yarborough." He pointed a thumb at his chest.

"You wrote a book?"

"Hell no," he said. "I wrote the first line of a book. The rest of the book's in my head and it's never gonna come out. I wrote the music for the first notes of a song. That ain't never gonna come out either. You know why?"

"No."

"Because," he said, tilting his head up so he could catch the dwindling warmth of the setting sun. "Got no creative juice. Got no interest. Now I got a question for you, but I don't want no answer. My time's too precious to spend getting involved."

"The question?"

"Who is in that car comin' this way down the block. Been circling ever since you went into the doctor's office."

I looked down the street. There was a dark Buick of unknown age moving slowly in our direction. When it got close enough, I could see that its windows were tinted and dark.

The passenger side window facing us came down slightly and the car stopped about fifteen feet in front of us.

"Get down," I said, going to the pavement prone and scurrying under the bench.

Kelsey didn't move other than to look down at me. The two shots came in rapid succession. Both seemed to whiz precariously close to Kelsey.

Then the car sped away with a screech. I turned my head to catch the license plate number. I think it was one of the save-the-manatee plates, or tags, as they call them in Florida. It began with the letters C and X. The rest was obscured by dirt.

I slid out from under the bench, picked up my hat, dusted it, and then wiped away the worst of the garbage that covered the front of my shirt and jeans.

"That was for you," he said. "Only reason anyone wanting to be shooting me is because I'm a black man and a homeless eyesore. More likely the message was for you."

"It was," I said, putting on my cap.

I left him sitting on the bench and moved down the street to my Saturn. There was a folded sheet of notebook paper, the kind with ragged edges and punched holes. I retrieved the note. It read:

What Part of Stop Don't You Understand?
Would you understand a death march band?
Listen to the distant Orleans clarinet.
Turn away. There's still time yet.

It was written in a cursive script you don't often see anymore.

I had learned something in my session with Ann. I tried to figure it out as I drove, but I was distracted by the background voice on a talk radio station. The host, who had a New York accent, wanted callers to tell him what they thought about bombing Iran and sending troops if Iran continued to defy the United States and continued their race to build a nuclear weapon.

The car from which someone had shot at me was not the one Greg Legerman had driven to pick up Winn Graeme. The shots that had been fired at me a few minutes earlier had not come from a pellet gun, but from something with real bullets. Either Greg had another car and a more impressive gun, or this was a new shooter.

About seven or eight minutes later I was parked outside the Texas Bar and Grill on Second Street. I was calm with a this-isn't-real calm. My hands didn't tremble. I didn't weep.

When I stepped through the door of the Texas, Big Ed was behind the bar. He nodded at me and adjusted his handlebar mustache. Guns of the old West hung on the walls, and the smell of beer and grilled half-pound burgers and onions perfumed the air. Around eight round wooden tables people, almost all men, were having a heavy snack before heading home for healthy dinners.

"Ames here?" I asked Big Ed.

"Back in his room," Big Ed said, nodding over his left shoulder.

Ed was a New Englander who loved old Westerns and would have worshiped Lilly Langtree were she to return in ghostly form.

"You know Wild Bill Hickok wasn't holding aces and eights when he died? Bartender made it up. No one knows what he had. Grown men still feel a little panic when they look down at the dead man's hand in a game of poker."

"I didn't know that," I said.

"You want a beer, a Big Ed Burger?"

"Beer and a Big Ed with cheese."

Behind the bar there was a horizontal mirror with an elaborately carved wooden frame, painted gold.

"The same for Ames," I said.

I looked at myself in the mirror and saw a short, balding Italian with a sad face wearing a Cubs baseball cap.

"He told me," Big Ed said, adjusting the curl in his waxed handlebar mustache with both hands. "About partnering up with you."

"You all right with that?" I asked.

"Ames has partnered up with you since he met you. I'd like him to put in some hours here, too, in exchange for his room, providing you don't have too much work for him to do."

"I don't expect to overwhelm him with work."

"Good," said Big Ed after calling back to the tiny kitchen for two half-pound burgers.

He poured two mugs of beer from the tap and clunked them down in front of him.

"Work on your beer. I'll go back and tell Ames that you're here."

When Ames came out, tall, hair shampooed and white, he was dressed in his usual freshly washed jeans and a loose-fitting long-sleeved white flannel shirt with the sleeves rolled up.

We moved to a table next to two guys speaking in Spanish and sounding like they were having an argument half the time and telling each other jokes the other half.

"You play poker?" I asked Ames.

"I do."

"How good are you at it?"

"Middling good," he said. "But then most I've played think they're middling good."

"I'm less than middling bad," I said. "Remember Corkle saying he had something on Ronnie Gerall?"

"I do."

"We're going to try to find it."

We listened to the guys speaking Spanish and drank our beers until Big Ed motioned and Ames moved around the tables to pick up our burgers.

"You good enough in a seven-card stud game to help someone else win?" I asked.

"Depends on who's watching and playing."

We ate as we talked. More people, including the two Spanish speakers at the next table, left and a few others came in. Big Ed handled them all, nodding just right at each new customer as if he had known them all his life.

"Players are multimillionaires . . ."

"Corkle," said Ames.

"Yes, and four others. They have a game every other week at Corkle's house. Stakes are fifty and a hundred. You need four thousand to sit down."

"I've got two thousand," he said.

"I've got another two," I said. "We'll borrow a few thousand more from Flo in case we run out."

"Not like you to be beholding."

"Little by little, day by day, I'm trying to change," I said.

"How's it going?"

"Not too good," I said, taking a bite of burger.

The grilled burger was handmade by Big Ed from extra-lean meat and cooked to greasy perfection by the kitchen cook. I was hungry. The slightly burnt beef reminded me of a taste from the past that I couldn't quite place.

"How you gonna get in this game?"

"Kidnap one of the players," I said.

Ames gave me a slight nod and worked at chewing the large bite of burger in his mouth.

"Only way?" he said.

"Only one I can think of," I said. "You in?"

"We're partners," he said. "When we doing this?"

"Tonight," I said. "It's game night. Wednesday."

"What'll I be doing while you're playing poker?"

"Searching through Corkle's office."

"Corkle carries a handgun," Ames said.

"I know. I'll be careful," I said, pushing the now-empty plate away.

"I trust you," he said.

"I know."

"What time?"

"Midnight," I said.

"You planning to win?"

"No," I said. "Just to fold a lot, hang in as long as possible and not lose everything."

"If they catch us?" Ames asked. "They'd have to own up to gambling for big stakes."

"Yes, and it'll be in the newspapers and on television," I went on.

"The fines won't mean anything to them, but the fact that they'll have to close down their game for good will mean something. And Corkle might have to leave the house and go downtown."

The bar in the Texas was a small one. Not much space behind it and only six high, wooden swivel stools. At that moment a man and a woman were arguing at the bar and getting louder—loud enough for us to hear the drunken slur.

The couple were probably in their fifties and looked like they had spent their days behind desks taking and giving orders.

She slapped the man hard, a slap that stopped conversation and echoed around the room. The man was exhausting his vituperative vocabulary now, and quickly worked his way up toward a punch. Before he could throw it Big Ed reached over his arm and grabbed his wrist. That gave the woman an opening to attack again. This time she punched. The man slipped from the stool and fell flat on his back, his head thumping on the hardwood floor.

"You want to help Big Ed?" I asked.

"No," said Ames. "He's happy. Genteel barroom brawl."

"See what the boys in the back room will have," I said, watching the woman dropping to her knees on the floor and touching the fallen man's cheek.

"Warren," she whimpered, "I'm so, so, *so*, so sorry."

The bar noise level in the room went back to prebrawl level. It was then that I noticed Ed Viviase, alone at a table near the window. He must have come in while the man and woman were doing battle.

When he saw that he had our attention, he got up and sat between me and Ames.

"See the fight?" I asked.

"Yeah. Over in one minute of the first round. You're easy to find, Fonesca. You only go to five places regularly. I found you at the third one on my list."

"A beer?" asked Big Ed.

"On the clock," said Viviase.

We sat at a table, Viviase, Ames, and me. The detective watched as the woman helped the fallen man to his feet and then out the door, an arm draped over her shoulder.

"Love," Viviase said with enough sarcasm so we wouldn't think he was genuinely moved. "Always a bad call for a cop, couple fighting. They don't want a man or woman of the law stepping between them. Sometimes a cop will get hurt more than the battlers. I once got a steak pounding mallet on the side of the head—you know the kind with the nubs?"

"Yes," I said.

Viviase shook his head, remembering.

"She was a chef," he said. "I was lucky she didn't have something even more lethal in her hand, like whatever it was that killed Blue Berrigan. The chef and her husband were divorced a few months after I met and arrested them. Neither of them did time. I had headaches for more than a year."

"Tough," I said.

"There are tougher things," Viviase said. "Like finding out your daughter went behind your back to involve a process server in a murder case."

"I'm sorry," I said.

"Of course you are. People who commit crimes are always sorry when they get caught."

"She didn't hire me," I said.

"I know. The hell with it. I'll have a beer. A beer ain't drinking."

It was Edmond O'Brien's line from *The Man Who Shot Liberty Valance*, forever to be honored by alcoholics.

Ames rose to get the beer.

"I'll get the tape back to you," Viviase said.

"No hurry," I said. "You ground her?"

"For what? Disappointing me?"

"Guess not."

"You really think Gerall didn't kill Horvecki?"

"Yes. And he couldn't have killed Blue Berrigan. He was in jail."

"Who says he killed Berrigan?" asked Viviase as Ames came back with three beers.

"The angel of common sense," I said.

"Only thing holds the two murders together is you," Viviase said, drinking the beer directly from the bottle. "And I'm reasonably confident that you didn't kill either one of them, unless you've gone Jekyll and Hyde on me."

"The Gerall boy's a bad apple, but he didn't kill anybody," said Ames.

"Ames and I are partners now," I explained.

"Partners in what?" asked Viviase, shaking his head. "Operating an illegal office of private investigation."

"We find people," I said.

"You find people who commit murder," Viviase said.

"Sometimes," I admitted.

"Ames have a process server's license?"

"Not yet," he said.

"Not never," answered Viviase, after nearly finishing his bottle of beer. "He's a convicted felon."

"We'll work on that," I said. "He's my partner either way."

"You and Ames here bothered a Venice policeman, a detective."

"We talked to Detective Williams," I said.

"Mr. McKinney here fired a weapon at him after you practically accused him of murder."

A bustle of businessmen and -women came through the door, laughing and making in-jokes that weren't funny, but when you want to laugh any flotsam of intended wit will do.

"What does he want?"

"Nothing now, but for you to stay away from him."

I knew why. If Ames and I were arrested, the story of his aunt and mother being raped would hit the media again.

Viviase finished his beer while Ames and I kept working on ours. He rolled the empty bottle between his hands. No genie emerged. Viviase got up.

"You find anything, let me know," he said. "Don't do anything stupid."

He left.

Then Ames and I decided to do something stupid.

II

PLAYING FOR KEEPS

12

I was holding two pair, jacks and fours, in a five-card stud game. That was the only game being played in the card room of Corkle's house. The old doctor with the slight tremor was the only one left in the hand with me. The pot stood at four hundred dollars and change. The doctor had a pair of sevens showing. He could have had three of them or, since one of his cards showing was a king, he could have had a higher two pair.

On my left was Corkle, clad in a green Detroit Lions sweatshirt. Next to him was a bulky man who had been introduced as Kaufmann. "You know who he is," Corkle had said in his initial introduction when I had sat at the table three hours earlier. I didn't know who Kaufmann was, but about an hour into the game Corkle asked him something about a union meeting. On his left, across from me, was a kid, college age. Corkle introduced him as Keith Thirlane. Keith Thirlane looked like an athlete, a very nervous athlete trying to look calm. He was tall, blond, and wearing black slacks and a black polo. The last player at the table was "Period Waysock from out of town." Period was about sixty, bald, and slowdown fat. He did everything from betting to going to the snack table with the deliberation of a large dinosaur.

I pushed in another hundred dollars and looked at the steel clock on the wall. It was almost one in the morning.

Ames and I had pooled our money. I had cashed the check from

Alana Legerman. We came up with the requisite four thousand, with another thousand borrowed from Flo Zink. We had a slight cushion. Then I had called Laurence Arthur Wainwright, who was one of the poker players Corkle had mentioned and the only one whose name I recognized. Wainwright was a state representative, a lawyer who owned pieces of banks, mortgage houses, property, and businesses worth who knows how much. Wainwright made the local news a lot, partly because he did a lot of donations to charities and looked good in a tuxedo at society dinners. Wainwright, also known as LAW or Law by the *Herald-Tribune*, was in constant trouble for his business practices, which were often barely legal.

On the phone, I told Wainwright that I had some documents he had been looking for. There are almost always documents a person like Wainwright is looking for.

"What documents?" he had asked.

Ames had gone through past newspaper articles mentioning Wainwright and come up with a list of four prime names. The best bet seemed to be Adam Bulagarest, a former Wainwright business associate who had moved out of Florida before the law could catch up with him.

"Does the name Bulagarest ring a bell?" I asked.

"Is this extortion?"

"I hope so," I said.

"How did you get these documents?"

"They're originals taken from papers in possession of Mr. Bulagarest. You can have them for a nominal fee. We will provide you with a signed and notarized guarantee that there are no copies."

There was no chance Wainwright could check on my tale with Bulagarest. In researching the poker players, Dixie had discovered Bulagarest was serving time in a Thai jail for child molestation.

"How do I get these documents?" Wainwright asked with a tone of clear skepticism.

"Come tonight to the Ramada Inn at Disney World. Register as F. W. Murnau. We'll meet you at the bar at midnight."

"To Orlando tonight? What's the hurry?"

"My associates and I are not comfortable in Florida. Bring one hundred thousand dollars in cash. If you don't come, we have another buyer."

"I don't . . ." Wainwright said, but I hung up.

People like Wainwright always had piles of cash handy in case the real law was about to knock at their door.

I waited an hour and then called Corkle to ask when there might be an opening at his poker table.

"You have four thousand dollars?"

"Yes."

"You're in luck. One of our regulars can't make it."

Two hours into the game, I was ahead about three hundred dollars. After three hours I was ahead by almost eleven hundred dollars. It wasn't that I was a particularly good player. They, including Corkle, were all incredibly bad, but I was learning that in a five-handed game, the odds of one of the bad players getting lucky was fairly high. Besides, I had to remember that I wasn't there to win, just to keep the players busy.

From time to time, when they were out of a hand, the others at the table either ambled to the snack table in the corner for a plate of nuts and a beer or to the toilet just off the room toward the front door.

I didn't meet the first raise on the next hand and moved toward the small restroom. It was a minute or two after one. Law Wainwright was sitting in a hotel room at Disney World with one hundred thousand dollars or a pistol with a silencer in his lap. I didn't care which.

I looked back. The players were bantering, betting, acting like their favorite television poker pros. I moved past the restroom, turned a corner and went to the hall beyond to the front. I opened it quietly. Ames, flashlight in hand, stepped in. I closed the door and pointed to a door across the hallway. He nodded to show that he understood and showed me the Perfect Pocket Pager, one of the gifts Corkle had given us. I had an identical one in my pocket. Both Ames's and my pager were set on vibrate. Each pager had originally been offered not for $29.95 or even $19.95, but for $9.95 with free shipping if you ordered now, but the "now" had been a dozen years ago and, until we had tested them, we didn't know that they would work.

On the way back to the poker table, I reached in and flushed the toilet. The same hand was still being played, but only Corkle, who never sat out a hand, was still in it against Waysock from out of town. The pot, a small mountain of crisp green, looked big.

Corkle won the hand with a pair of fours. Both men had been bluffing.

I was worried about Ames. He wasn't carrying a gun. I didn't want a shoot-out and Ames was not the kind of man to give up without a fight. Ames and I were partners now. I was, I guess, senior partner. I know he felt responsible for me and to me. I felt the same.

Ames was going through Corkle's office in search of the evidence Corkle had mentioned—evidence that might tell us who had killed Blue Berrigan and Philip Horvecki. Or maybe it wouldn't. Maybe it was just another invention proceeding from Corkle's heat-oppressed brain.

I was having trouble concentrating on the game.

"Two hundred more," Keith the Kid said.

He hadn't been doing badly. At least not in the game. He was a little over even. He winced in periodic pain or regret and gulped down diet ginger ale.

We were down to three players in the hand. I saw the bet and, for one of the few times during the game, Corkle folded. When the next cards were dealt to Keith and me by Kaufmann, Corkle got up and headed for the restroom. I watched him walk past it. I pressed the durable and easy-to-clean replaceable white glow-in-the-dark button on the pager in my pocket.

"Your bet, Lewie," said Kaufmann.

"What's the bet?" I asked.

"Three hundred," said Kaufmann. "Keep your eyes on the prize."

Period Waysock from Out of Town had waddled to the snack table.

I was holding two fours down and a third four showing on the table with one card to go, a set of three in a five-card-nothing wild game. The Kid could have had three sevens, eights, or jacks or just a pair of each. He wasn't betting like a player with a set. I reluctantly folded, got up from the table and hurried after Corkle.

I caught up with Corkle in the foyer where he was pacing and talking on a cordless phone in front of the front door.

"No, D. Elliot Corkle is not sorry that he woke you. There are more important things than sleep. I did not make my money by sleeping. I made it by staying awake. You can sleep later."

He looked around at the three closed doors and the elevator and kept pacing as he listened.

"Not everyone who goes to jail gets raped," he said. "D. Elliot Corkle will put up the bail in the morning. Watch him all the time. Do not let him run away . . . All right. Let me know."

Corkle pushed a button on his phone and I ducked into the bathroom and closed the door. I heard him walk past, come out, pushed the button on the pager twice and watched while Ames stepped out of Corkle's office. He headed for the front door holding up an eight-by-eleven brown envelope for me to see. Then he went through the front door and closed it as I turned to return to the game.

Keith the Kid was standing across the foyer looking at me. He didn't say anything, but he did give me a look of slight perplexity.

"Stretching my legs," I said. "Bad knee."

"What'd you have?" he asked. "That last hand."

"Queen high," I said.

"No," he said. "Not the way you bet."

"I figured from the way you were betting that you had a set. The odds were against me."

"You gave me the hand," he said. "I don't want anyone feeling sorry for me."

"I don't," I said. "I didn't."

He touched his cheek nervously.

"I thought I could make back some of the money I lost here last time," he said. "My father was a regular in this stupid game. He's not well enough to play again. Heart. I took his place. I don't want to lose, but I don't want any gifts either. Besides the ones Corkle gives out in boxes as we leave."

"Kaufmann won't play a hand unless he's holding an initial pair,"

I said. "Period bluffs half the time, no pattern. Corkle never folds unless he's beaten on the table."

"And me?"

"You shouldn't be playing poker."

"You?"

"I don't like to gamble," I said.

"Then . . ."

"Hey, you two," Corkle called. "Clock is moving and a quorum and your money are needed."

I moved past Keith and took my place at the table. Keith came behind me and sat.

"Question," Period Waysock from Out of Town said. "You wearing that Cubs cap for luck or because you're going bald."

"Yes, in that order," I said.

"Let's play some poker," Corkle said, and we did.

At two in the morning, the last hand was played, the cash was pocketed, and the lies about winning and losing were told. I estimated that Ames and I had come out about five hundred dollars ahead.

On the way out, Corkle handed each of us a small box about the length of a pen.

"See Forever Pocket Telescope with built-in sky map," he said. "Specially designed lenses. You can clearly see the mountains of the moon or the party your neighbors are having a mile away, providing trees or buildings aren't in the way."

We thanked him. I was the last one at the door. Corkle stopped me with a hand on my arm and said in a low voice, "D. Elliot Corkle knows what you did here."

I didn't answer.

"You did some losing on purpose," he said. "You're a good player. You're setting us up for next time."

I didn't tell him that I was sure I had come out ahead and not behind.

"Well," he went on. "I don't think that opportunity will be afforded to you. You're a decent enough guy, but not a good fit here."

I agreed with him.

"One more thing," he said. "My daughter has bailed out Ronnie Gerall."

He looked for a reaction from me. I gave him none.

"She stands to lose a quarter of a million if he skips," said Corkle. "I'll be grateful with a cash bonus of four thousand dollars if he doesn't skip."

He didn't tell me why Alana Legerman would bail Ronnie out, but I could see from his face that we were both thinking the same thing.

I took my See Forever Pocket Telescope with sky map and went out the door.

Ames, leaning over so he couldn't be seen from the door, was in the backseat of the Saturn. He didn't sit up until we hit Tamiami Trail.

"What'd you find?" I asked, looking at him in the rearview mirror.

"Our chief suspect has a lot of explaining to do," he said.

Victor wasn't around when we got to my place.

Ames waited for me to sit behind my desk, and then produced the envelope he had taken from Corkle's office. He opened it and placed the first two sheets next to each other in front of me.

They were birth certificates. The one on my left was Ronald Gerall's. It said that he was born in Palo Alto, California, on December 18, 1990. The birth certificate on the right gave his date of birth as December 18, 1978. If the certificate on the right was correct, Ronnie Gerall was twenty-nine years old.

"I'm betting that one," Ames said pointing at the certificate on my right, "is the right one and the other one's the fake."

"We'll find out," I said. "You know what this means?"

"Gerall started high school here when he was twenty-five or twenty-six years old," said Ames.

He reached back into the envelope and came out with two more pieces of paper. He handed them to me and I discovered that our

Ronnie had graduated from Templeton High School in Redwood City, California, and California State University in Hayward, California.

"Best for last," Ames said, pulling one more sheet of paper out of the envelope.

It was a marriage certificate, issued a year ago in the State of California to Ronald Owen Gerall and Rachel Beck Horvecki. Ronnie was married to Horvecki's missing daughter.

We had more questions now. Why had Ronnie Gerall posed as a high school student? Where was his wife? What was Corkle planning to do with the documents that were now on my desk?

It was three in the morning. We said good night and Ames said he would be back "an hour or two past daybreak." I told him nine in the morning would be fine.

I handed the papers back to Ames and said, "You keep them. If Corkle finds that they're gone, he might think I'm a logical suspect."

Ames nodded and put the documents back in the envelope.

When Ames left I went to my room and closed the door. The night-light, a small lamp with an iron base and a glass bowl over the bulb, was on. I had been leaving it on more and more when night came. I put on my black Venice Beach workout shorts and went back through my office to the cramped bathroom. I showered, shaved, shampooed my minor outcropping of hair; I did not sing. Catherine used to say I had a good voice. Singing in the shower had been almost mandatory—old standards from the 1940s had been my favorites and Catherine's. "Don't Sit Under the Apple Tree," "To Each His Own," "Johnny Got a Zero," "Wing and a Prayer." I had not sung or considered it after Catherine died. When I turned off the shower, I heard someone moving around in the office.

I got out, dried my body quickly, put on my Venice shorts and stepped into the office while drying my hair.

Victor Woo was sitting on his sleeping bag on the floor in the corner. He had placed the blanket so that he could look up at the Stig Dalstrom paintings on the wall. He glanced over at me. He looked exhausted.

"I called my wife," he said.

I draped the towel over my shoulder.

"What did you say?"

"I didn't. I couldn't. But she knew it was me. She said I should come home, that she's been getting my checks, that the children miss me. She didn't say that she missed me."

"Go home Victor," I said.

"Can't."

"I forgive you. Catherine forgives you. I don't think Cook County forgives you, but that's between you and the Cook County state attorney's office, and I don't plan to give them any information."

It was pretty much what I had been saying to him for more than two months. I didn't expect it to work this time.

"Forgive yourself," I tried. "Hungry?"

"No."

"You can do me a favor," I said. "In the morning, go to Starbucks or Borders, plug your computer into the Internet, and find some information for me."

"Yes."

"You might have to do some illegal things to get what I want. I want whatever you can find about a Ronald Gerall, probably born somewhere in California."

It was busywork. Dixie would get me whatever I needed in the morning.

"Yes," he said.

"You want me to turn the light out?"

"Yes."

"Good night."

I went into my room, placed the towel on the back of my chair, put on my extra-large gray T-shirt with the faded full-color image of Ernie Banks on the front.

I turned the night-light to its lowest setting and got on the bed. I stayed on top of the covers, lay on my back, and clutched the extra pillow.

The room was bigger than my last one in the office building behind the Dairy Queen. I looked up at the angled ceiling.

I like small spaces when I sleep. This room wasn't large, but it was bigger than I liked. I would have slept in a closet were there one large enough to sleep in. I cannot sleep outdoors. I can't look up at the vastness of the sky without beginning to feel lost, like I'm about to be swept into the universe. This room was tolerable, but it would take some getting used to.

I lay without moving, looking upward, growing too tired to move, going over whether Ronnie Gerall had killed his father-in-law and why, and wondering if he had killed his wife and Blue Berrigan.

Thoughts of Sally Porovsky came and went like insistent faces of forgotten movie actors whose names just managed to stay out of reach.

Sometimes when I fall asleep, an idea comes, and I feel energized.

Usually, if I don't write down the idea, I'll lose it with the dawn. I did get an idea, then, or rather, a question. Why were all the Corkles paying me to save Ronnie?

His family would be better protected by having Ronnie locked away until he was too old to appreciate a handy dandy Corkle Electrostatic CD, LP, and DVD cleaner. I didn't write down my idea, but this time I remembered it. When I sat up in the morning, I heard my dark curtains open, saw bright morning light, and looked up at Greg Legerman and Winston Churchill Graeme.

"He's out," said Greg, handing me a steaming Starbucks coffee.

"Who?"

"Ronnie. Who did you think I was talking about, Charlie Manson?"

"What time is it?"

"Almost nine," said Greg.

"I know Ronnie's out," I said. "Who let you in?"

"The Chinese guy," said Greg.

"He's Japanese," Winn Graeme said.

"He's Chinese," I said.

Greg took the only chair in the room and pulled it over to my bedside.

"You want your money back?" I said. "Fine."

"No, you need it. You live in near squalor."

"Greg," Winn warned.

Greg Legerman's response to the warning was to reach up and punch the other boy in the arm. Winn took it and looked at me.

"How long have you known old Ronnie?" I asked.

Greg thought about it, but Winn answered.

"He transferred to Pine View after his sophomore year. Came from Texas, San Antonio."

"He have a girlfriend?"

"Lots. He had a fake ID," said Greg. "Went out to bars, picked up women. Said he wasn't into high school girls. Why?"

"He ever mention Rachel Horvecki?"

"Horvecki's daughter? No," said Greg. "I don't remember. Why?"

"Have any idea where he might be now?"

I got up and went to the closet for a clean pair of jeans and a blue short-sleeved Polo pullover.

"No," said Winn.

"Any idea where your mother is?"

"My mother?"

"Your mother."

"No. Home. Shopping. Buying. I don't know. I don't keep track of her. Why do you want to know where my mother is?"

"Just a few questions I need to ask her."

"My mother?"

"Your mother."

"I said no. Have you found out who killed Horvecki yet?"

"No, but I will."

Greg had clasped his hands together and was tapping his clenched fist against his chin.

"You need more money?"

"More time," I said. "Now, it would be nice if you left."

"Sorry," said Winn.

He adjusted his glasses and reached over to urge his friend out of the chair.

"I've got more questions," said Greg.

"I can't give you answers now," I said. "Ronnie's out on bail."

Greg reluctantly rose from the chair, nodded a few times as he looked at me, then turned and, after a light punch to Winn's arm, went through the door. Winn Graeme hesitated, looked at me and whispered, "Nickel Plate Club."

Then he was gone. I stood listening while they opened the outer door and moved into the day.

I put on my Cubs cap and stepped into my outer room. Victor was sitting on the floor on his sleeping bag, a cardboard cup of coffee in his hand, looking up at one of the Stig Dalstroms on the wall.

A cup of coffee sat on my desk alongside a paper bag which contained a Chick-Fil-A breakfast chicken sandwich. I sat and began working on my breakfast. I put the coffee in my hand next to the one on my desk.

"I looked," he said.

"At . . ."

"Internet. Ronald Owen Gerall."

The door opened, and Ames came in bearing a Styrofoam cup of coffee. He nodded at Victor and handed the coffee to me. I put it alongside the others.

"I just had a visit from Winn and Greg," I said working on one of the coffees. "They think we haven't made any progress. Progress is overrated. Victor has some information for us about Ronnie."

"He is married," said Victor. "To Rachel Horvecki."

"That a fact?" Ames said, looking at me for an explanation for why we were listening to something we already knew.

"Ronald Owen Gerall spent a year in a California Youth Facility when he was sixteen. Assault."

That was new information.

"There's a little more," said Victor, showing more signs of life than I had ever seen in him before. "Because he was underage when he came to Sarasota and he claimed to have no living relatives, he needed someone to vouch for him, help him find a place to live, and accept responsibility."

"Who?"

"Sally Porovsky."

While Ames, riding shotgun, went off with Victor to try to find Ronnie Gerall, I went to Sally's office at Children and Family Services to do the same thing. I could have called to find out if she was in or off to see a client, but I didn't want to hear her say that she was too busy to see me. Besides, I don't like telephones. I don't like the silences when someone expects me to speak and I have nothing to say or nothing I want to say. I use them when I must, which seemed to be a lot more of the time.

I parked the Saturn in the lot off of Fruitville and Tuttle where Children and Families had its office. Then I picked up my ringing phone and opened it. It was Dixie.

"Your Ronnie Gerall problem just got a little more complicated."

"How?" I asked.

"Ronnie Gerall is dead."

"When?"

"Six years ago in San Antonio," Dixie said. "Which means . . ."

"Ronnie Gerall is not Ronnie Gerall. He stole a dead boy's identity."

"Looks that way," she said. "But there's more. I tried a search of the back issues of the San Antonio newspaper for a period a year before your Ronnie got here. I tried a match of the photograph of him in the Pine View yearbook."

"And?"

"Bingo, Bango, Bongo. Newspaper told me his name is Dwight Ronald Torcelli. He fled an indictment for felony assault. Then I did a search for Dwight Ronald Torcelli. He's twenty-six years old. His birthday's tomorrow. He'll be twenty-seven. Maybe you should buy him a cake or give him some Harry & David chocolate cherries."

"Is that a hint?"

"Hell yes. I love those things. Want me to keep looking?"

"Try Rachel Horvecki or Rachel Gerall," I said.

"They may have a license and a minister's approval, but they are definitely not married."

"I wonder if she knows that."

"Good luck investigating, Columbo."

We hung up, and I looked at the entrance to Building C of a complex of bored three-story office buildings that couldn't decide whether to go with the dirt-stained brick on the bottom half or the streaked once-white wooden slats on top. Building C was on the parking lot between A and D. There was a neatly printed sign plunged into the dirt and grass in front of the space where I parked. The sign said there was an office suite available and that it was ideal for a professional business.

The offices were almost all occupied by dentists, urologists, and investment counselors who promised free lunches at Longhorn for those who wanted to attend an equally free workshop on what to do with their money. A four-man cardiology practice had recently moved out and into a building they had financed on Tuttle, about a mile away.

Cardiologists, cataract surgeons, specialists in all diseases that plagued the old and perplexed the young are abundant in Sarasota, almost as abundant as banks.

John Gutcheon was seated at the downstairs reception desk making a clicking sound with his tongue as he wrote on a yellow pad.

John was in his mid-thirties, blond, thin, and very openly gay. His sharp tongue protected him from those who might dare to attack his life choice, although he had told me once, quite clearly, that it was not a choice and it was not an echo. His homosexuality was a reality he had recognized when he was a child. There were those who accepted him and those who did not. And he had come to terms with that after many a disappointment.

"Still wearing that thing," he said, looking up at me and shaking his head. "Lewis, when will you learn the difference between an outrageous fashion statement and bad taste."

"I like the Cubs," I said.

"And I like sea bass but I don't wear it on my head. There are other ways of expressing your bad taste," he said.

"My wife gave me this cap," I said.

"And my cousin Robert wanted to give me an introduction to a predatory friend at a gay bar," he said. "I made the mistake of accepting that introduction. You could at least clean that abomination on your head."

"I'll do that," I said.

"Lewis, 'tis better to be cleanly bald than tastelessly chapeaued."

"I'll remember that."

"No, you won't, but I feel as compelled as a priestly exorcist to remind you."

"Sally in?" I asked.

"All in," he said folding his hands on the desk.

"How is your writing coming?"

"You remembered," he said with mock joy. "Well, thank you for asking. My writing career is at a halt while several online and one honest-to-God publisher decide whether it's worth continuing."

"Ronnie Gerall," I said.

He looked up. I had struck home.

"He . . . I can't discuss clients," he said, measuring his words careful. "Lawsuits. Things like that. You know."

"You've talked to me about lots of clients."

"Have I? Shouldn't have. She's in. I assume you didn't come to see me."

"You have a favorite first line of a novel?" I asked.

He pulled open a drawer of his desk and came up with a thin paperback with ragged pages. He opened the book and read: " 'Where's Papa going with that ax? said Fern to her mother as they were setting the table for breakfast.' "

"Stephen King?" I guessed.

He held up the book to show me its cover. *Charlotte's Web*, by E. B. White. Then he said, "Where's Lewis going with that ax?"

"No ax," I said.

"Liar," said Gutcheon.

"No," I said.

"Always a pleasure to talk to you," he said as I headed for the elevator.

The elevator rocked to the hum of a weary motor. I wasn't fully certain what I was doing here or what I expected when I talked to

Sally. I had a lead. I was following it. At least that's what I told myself.

The elevator door opened slowly to a Wall Street stage, only the people in front of me in two lines of cubicles were dealing in human misery, not stocks and bonds and millions of dollars. It was a busy day for the caseworkers at Children and Families. There was no shortage of abuse, anger, and neglect.

A few of the dozen cubicles were empty, but most were occupied by a caseworker and at least one client. Almost all the clients were black. Sometimes the client was a tired parent or two. Some were sullen or indifferent, others were frightened. Some were children. The mornings were generally for taking in clients at the office. The afternoons and evenings were for home visits throughout the county. Sometimes the day was interrupted by a court appearance. Sometimes it was interrupted by something personal—personal to the life of the harried caseworker, something like Lew Fonesca.

Sally's back was to me. In the chair next to her desk sat an erect black man in a dark suit and red tie. In the man's lap was a neatly folded lightweight coat. He was about fifty and lean, with graying temples. He looked at me through rimless glasses. He reminded me of a sociology professor I had at the University of Illinois, a professor who, when he looked at me, seemed to be in wonder that such a mirthless silent specimen should have made it to his small classroom.

I stood silently while Sally went over a form in front of her. When she spoke, she had to raise her voice above the hubbub of voices around her.

"He's in school now?" she asked.

I stood back, knowing that she would eventually turn and see me, or her client would gaze at me again and catch her eye.

"Yes, he is. At least he is supposed to be."

His voice was deep, even.

"Thurgood is a good student?" Sally said, looking up from the form.

"When he goes to school, and if you should meet him, he will not answer to the name 'Thurgood.' His middle name is Marshall. Thurgood Marshall Montieth."

"He is," said Sally, "twelve years old."

"Soon to be thirteen," said Montieth. "And, if I may, I will encapsulate the data you have in front of you in the hope of speeding the process so I can get back to work. My name is Marcus Montieth. I'm forty-seven years of age. I am a salesman and floor manager at Joseph Bank clothing store in the Sarasota Mall. My wife is dead. Thurgood is my only child. He is a truant, a problem. He has run away four times. I do not beat him. I do not slap him. I do not deprive him of food. I do not try to instill in him a fear of God because I do not believe in a god or gods. My health is good, though there is a history of heart attack in my family."

"Thurgood is an only child?" asked Sally.

"And for that I would thank God were I to believe in one. May I ask you two questions?"

"Yes," said Sally.

"What can be done for my son, and why is that man hovering over our conversation?"

Sally turned enough in her desk chair to look over her right shoulder at me.

"Lewis, could you . . ." she began.

Something in the way I looked told her this was not one of my usual visits. Usually, I called before I came. Usually, I waited downstairs and listened to John Gutcheon while I waited for her to be free. Usually, there was no sense of urgency in my appearance. Usually, I did not hover near her cubicle.

"I'll be with you in a few minutes," she said.

I thought it unlikely she would ever be with me. I had let Sally Porovsky move into my life—no, to be fair, I had moved into hers—and let the ghost of Catherine begin to fade a little, but just a little.

"Mr. Montieth, when would it be possible for you to come back with Thurgood?"

"Please remember to call him Marshall. During the day he is supposedly in school. In the evenings I work. He comes home to my sister Mae's apartment after school. I do get Wednesdays off."

"Wednesday after school?"

"Yes," he said. "Time?"

"Four-thirty," said Sally, reaching over to write in her desktop calendar.

"We will be here," he said rising.

He was tall, six-four or six-five, and when he passed me I expected a look of disapproval at my intrusion. He smiled in understanding, assuming *What? A fellow parent with a troubled child? A homeless creature in a baseball cap, some scratches on his face?*

"I've got a client coming in ten minutes, Lewis," she said.

I stepped forward but I didn't sit. She looked up at me.

"What is it?"

"Ronnie Gerall," I said. "When he supposedly transferred from San Antonio to Pine View, you vouched for him, signed papers of guardianship, found him a family to live with."

"Yes," she said. "Lewis, please sit."

Her full, round face was smooth, just a little pink, and definitely pretty. She was tired. Sally was tired much of the time.

I sat.

"What's your question?" she asked with a smile that made it clear that she did not expect me to ask if she would run away with me to Genoa.

"Two questions to start," I said. "How did Ronnie Gerall get in touch with you? How old was he when he entered Pine View School for the Gifted?"

Sally blew out a puff of air as she leaned back in her chair and looked up at the white drop ceiling.

"A letter and records came from Ronnie's caseworker in San Antonio addressed to me. The caseworker said Ronnie's parents had recently been killed in a small plane crash and that Ronnie had no other relatives, though his father had once had a brother in Sarasota. There was a possibility that other relatives might be found. The records showed that Ronnie was sixteen when he arrived here.

"I called the number I'd been given," she said. "A woman answered, gave her name, said she was Ronnie's caseworker and had heard of me through an attorney who had moved to San Antonio a few weeks earlier. She didn't have his name, but could get it if I needed it."

"You were conned," I said.

"I know."

"Ronnie Gerall was twenty-five when he came here," I said.

"Almost twenty-six," she said.

"His real name is Dwight Torcelli. When did you find out?"

"Two years later," she said. "Just before I met you. How did you find out?"

"Dixie."

Sally shook her head. She looked more tired than I had ever seen her.

"I was suspicious," she said. "Dwight Torcelli is a very good-looking, charming, smart, fast-talking young man. With my experience, you might think I wouldn't fall for things like this, but he took me in and made it clear that he was interested in me as someone other than a caseworker."

"And?" I said, knowing, almost welcoming yet another blow.

"I let him get close, not so close that we . . . but close. By that time I knew he wasn't a teenager. I should have turned him in, but he was persuasive, claimed he had never finished high school, that he wanted to go to college and . . ."

"Yes?" I said.

"By that time he was in his senior year. We saw each other once in a while, but we never . . ."

"I believe you."

"Don't," she said closing her eyes. "There were two times, both in the last year. I . . . I'm forty-three years old, two young children, a job that never stops, sad stories around me all day and here was a young man who reminded me of a very white-toothed young James Dean."

"That's why you're moving?" I said. "Because Torcelli is here?"

"That and the other things we talked about."

We were silent for a while, looking at each other.

"You think he killed Horvecki?"

"I don't know," she said. "Why would he?"

"He's married to Rachel Horvecki. She inherits her father's money."

Sally looked over the top of her cubicle at the ceiling.

"If Ronnie left Sarasota, would you stay?" I asked.

"Probably not. I broke the rules, Lew," she said, turning in her chair and putting a hand on my arm. "I'm sorry."

The phone rang. Sally picked it up and said, "All right."

When she hung up, she said, "My next appointment's here."

I stood.

"You know where I might find him?"

She pulled over the notepad on her desk, paused to look at the framed photograph of her two kids, and jotted something down. Then she tore it from the pad and handed it to me.

"I'm really very good at what I do here," she said.

"I know."

"I'm sorry. Lew . . ."

"Yes."

"Get the son of a bitch."

I nodded, said nothing and left the cubicle. It was the first time I had heard her utter any epithet more harsh than "damn." I didn't want to run into Sally's next client or clients getting off the elevator. I didn't want to imagine what it would be like for Sally after our conversation. I took the stairs.

John Gutcheon looked up at me with sympathy. He knew.

"I'm sorry," he said.

Everybody seemed to be sorry, including me. I wondered how Gutcheon had found out about Dwight Torcelli and Sally, but I guessed that he had seen it in Dwight's triumph and Sally's guilt. He saw a lot going by as he sat behind that reception desk. Sometimes one learns more by sitting and watching than running and listening.

13

I called Ames.

"We've been parked outside Gerall's apartment," said Ames. "Nothing yet."

"That's not where he is," I said.

I told him where I was going and asked him to get there soon, and armed.

"You sound like someone hit you with an andiron."

"Yes," I said. "I know. I've got some things you should know. I'll tell you when I see you."

"Saturn needs more work," Ames said. "Best do it in the morning."

"Right," I said, and hung up.

Saturn, Mars, Jupiter, and the Earth all needed more work. The Universe needed more work. I tried to concentrate on a new metallic banging under the dashboard. It sounded like an angry elf had had enough of this rust of metal and motion. Up Tamiami Trail into Bradenton and a turn at Forty-seventh. I parked at the address Sally had written for me. Gerall's car was there. So was a perfectly polished, sporty-looking new Mazda with all the bells and whistles one could buy, enjoy, and show off. I probably wasn't too late. He could have run away on foot. Unlikely. He could have taken a cab. Possible. Someone could have picked him up and taken him to another refuge. I sat and waited for Ames to arrive.

The apartment building was small, two stories, brick, in need of a serious blasting to reveal whatever color was under the dirty earth and etched-in dripping patterns from the building's old drains. The weight of leaves, brush, twigs, and tree branches gave the illusion of a sagging middle to the roof. A sign, as abused as the building, said that choice studio apartments were available in the Ponce De Leon Arms. The dried-up tiny fountain near the take-it-or-leave-it sign let tenants know they had not come to the right place if they were planning to live forever. What the building and the sign did say, without words, was, "If you're low on the pole and looking for what you can get by on, this is as good a place as any."

Victor pulled his car in behind mine and remained behind the wheel, while Ames got out wearing his weathered yellow duster.

"I'll go in first. You stand outside his door," I said.

Ames nodded in understanding. We crunched over a layer of dead and dying yellow, orange, and black leaves dropped by two massive native oak trees. The entryway door of the building was open. The small foyer, tiled in cracked, ancient squares, had nothing to offer but a bank of twelve mailboxes, one of which hung open, and a collection of flyers and giveaway newspapers promising two slices of flavorless pizza for the price of one. The apartment marked GERALL was number seven.

We went through the inner door, also open, and down the narrow, carpeted corridor to apartment seven. Someone inside was talking. I could have strained to pick up some of the conversation. The voices belonged to a man and a woman.

I knocked.

The people inside the apartment stopped talking and went silent.

"Who is it?" came Ronnie's voice.

"Police," Ames said.

The room went silent. The pause was long.

"Police," Ames repeated. "Open it or step out of the way."

The lock was unbolted as Ames stepped back against the corridor wall where he couldn't be seen unless Dwight Torcelli or whoever was inside stepped out to look. The door opened slightly more than a crack.

"Fonesca?"

"Who is it?" a woman's voice from inside the room asked.

"Not the police," Torcelli said.

"May I come in, Dwight?" I asked.

"How did you find . . . ?"

He stopped after quickly and silently going through the very short list of those who would know about this second apartment and his real name.

"Sally," he said.

"May I come in?" I asked again.

He stepped back to let me enter and closed the door behind me. Alana Legerman stood in the center of the room next to the bed on which a large brown cloth suitcase stood open. It looked full and ready to be closed.

"Sally who?" asked Alana.

"My caseworker," he said.

His denim pants were tan, pressed, creased, and tight fitting. His shirt was a Polo pullover, green and white stripes, and not tight fitting.

"We're in a hurry here, Mr. Fonesca," Alana said.

"I'll bet you are. Bail jumping, especially on a murder charge, can make someone move in a hurry. You're going to lose a lot of money."

"I can afford it," she said. "You plan to tell anyone?"

"Yes, the police."

She motioned to Torcelli to close the suitcase. He did and pulled the cracked leather straps tight.

"You still work for me, Mr. Fonesca," she said.

"I resign. Job-related stress."

"I have a secret you may wish to know before you make a decision," she said.

"You're really his mother," I said, nodding at Torcelli.

"No," she said, pausing to show that she didn't appreciate my attempt at humor at her expense. "You stole something from my father."

"What?" asked Torcelli.

"I don't know," she said. "He just told me Fonesca and the old man he hangs around with broke into the house and stole something."

"The old man is my partner," I said. "His name is Ames McKinney. And a copy of what we stole is here."

I took the folded pieces of paper from my pocket and handed them to her.

"We have to go," Torcelli said while she looked at what I had handed her.

"I find people for a living," I said. "I'm good at it. It may be the only thing I'm good at. I could find you no matter where you go, and so could the police."

"Not true," he said, folding his arms and standing erect with his arms folded. "Alana, those things in your hand are fakes. He's . . ."

She held up a hand to indicate that she wanted him quiet while she looked over the papers. After no more than two minutes she handed me the documents and spoke.

"Two questions, and I expect the truth: First, are you really twenty-seven years old? Second, are you married?"

The answer was a long time coming, and he looked at me with something less than friendship before answering.

"Yes, and no," he said. "I am twenty-seven years old. At least I will be tomorrow."

"Happy Birthday," she said, folding her arms across her chest.

"I can explain why I . . ."

"Are you married?"

"No," he said. "I was. She died."

"You married Philip Horvecki's daughter," I said. "Is she dead?"

"No."

Alana Legerman was freeze-framed in a look of disappointment which turned to anger and then to acceptance with a shake of the head.

"Alana," he said. "You know I love you."

"You love me? Who are you?"

"His name is Dwight Torcelli," I said.

"Mr. Fonesca, do you have any objection to my leaving?" she asked.

"No."

"I won't be missing anything else I should know?"

"No."

"Good. Don't let him get away. Good-bye."

"If you let me . . . ," he began, but he didn't finish because she was out the door and gone.

I wondered what she would make of Ames in the hallway with a shotgun. There was no scream. I heard no voices through the thin door.

"I didn't kill Horvecki or anyone," he said. "I swear. Believe me."

"What I believe doesn't matter."

"You're taking me back to jail."

"But not to juvenile. You're an adult. We'll let the district attorney's office figure it all out."

"No," he said. "When you give them those documents about me, I probably won't even be able to get a public defender who believes I didn't kill Horvecki."

I wanted to ask him about Sally, but I didn't. He would either lie or tell the truth, and both would hurt.

"Let's go," I said.

"No," he repeated.

"Suit yourself. Run, hide. Maybe Alana Legerman won't turn you in. Maybe she really won't care about losing the bond money. Maybe."

I stepped away from the door. He picked up his suitcase and moved toward me.

"Step away," he said.

I stepped away, but something I couldn't control came over me. I moved in and punched him in the nose as hard as I could. I felt bone break and electric frozen pain in my knuckle.

There was no satisfaction in throwing the punch. It just felt like something I had to do.

He let out a groan and dropped the suitcase. Blood gushed from his nose. Rage was in his eyes and his fists were clenched. He was almost twenty years younger than I. I was in good shape from my almost daily workouts at the downtown YMCA, but I was probably not a match for him. The one thing I was sure of was that I could take whatever he threw and keep on coming. I didn't know how much he was willing to take.

"You lunatic," he screamed, doing nothing to stop the blood.

He looked like a much different person from the one who had opened the door. This was not a young James Dean sans mustache. This was Mr. Hyde played without his hair draped haphazardly down his forehead. His now inflamed nose suggested drunkenness. His eyes were wide and wild.

"You broke in here and tried to kill me," he said.

I knew where this was going. I took a step toward him. A gun, a small gun, appeared in his right hand. He wiped blood from his nose with the back of his left hand.

"You told me that someone hired you to kill me," he said. "Maybe Corkle."

"Might work," I said. "But probably not."

He was flexing his grip on the gun, which was now aimed at my stomach.

"Why aren't you scared?" he almost screamed.

"Nothing you'd understand," I said. "Lift the gun a little if your plan is to hit my heart."

"You are a lunatic," he said.

His gun hand moved down so that it was now aimed at the floor. That was when Ames came in, shotgun at the ready and aimed at Torcelli who took a step back.

"You okay?" Ames asked me. "You've got blood on you."

"His," I said.

"I'm the one hurt," Torcelli said, pointing to himself to be sure we knew who and where the injured party was.

"Put your little gun down," said Ames, "and we'll get that bleeding stopped."

Torcelli placed the gun on the bed.

Ames asked, "What happened?"

"He punched me. No warning. Just punched me in the nose," said Torcelli.

Ames looked at me before saying, "That a fact?"

"Yes," said Torcelli. "It's a fact. I'm running out of blood."

"Let's go save your life," said Ames. "Where's the bathroom?"

"There," said Torcelli, bloody shirt pulled up to his nose.

Ames touched my shoulder as he followed Torcelli through a door. Then I heard running water. Then my legs began to shake. There was a chair against the wall next to the door. I managed to sit. My hands were trembling now. Was it because Torcelli had almost shot me? No, that didn't feel right. It was because I had felt something uncontrollable and powerful when I hit him. The operative word being "felt." *Feeling*, strong emotion had come back, if only for a few seconds. I almost didn't recognize it. I know I didn't like it. I didn't like it at all.

When they came back in the room, Torcelli was holding a towel to his nose. His voice was muffled, but I could understand him.

"You could have driven bone into my brain," he said.

"You'll be fine," said Ames, standing behind him.

"Yeah," said Torcelli, sitting on the bed.

"Why did you do it?" I asked.

He took the towel from his face and looked at it to see if his nose had stopped bleeding. It hadn't.

"I didn't kill anyone," he said.

"No, everything else."

"It's a long story."

"Make it short," said Ames.

"What am I going to look like?" Torcelli asked. "I have to look good. It's what I've got."

"Story," Ames said.

Towel to nose, he turned to look at Ames over his shoulder then back at me.

"I met Horvecki's daughter in San Antonio. I was working in a Sharper Image store in a mall. She came in. She was visiting a fellow high school friend from Pine View. We started to talk. I said we should talk more. So we made a date for that night. And the next.

And the next. I learned that her father was rich. Her father was a jerk. No way he would just accept me."

"You had already discussed marriage?" I asked.

"We applied for the license the second week I knew her."

"Love?"

"On her part. I've done some acting. I was convincing. I got the idea of using information she had given me to persuade Horvecki to give me a job and pay me at a level that would suit his son-in-law."

"That didn't work, did it?" I asked.

"He said that he had another idea. I'd have to register as a high school student at Pine View. He would handle the paperwork. All I had to do was gather examples of how the school was screwing up. He said he wanted to bring down Pine View and the Bright Futures program. I'm sure he also wanted to see how low I would sink to be sure Rachel and I would inherit his money. He had hired a detective to look into my past. He insisted that I change my name, even told me how to do it and how to get a convincing set of documents that established me as Ronald Gerall, a transfer student in very good standing. He said he'd provide us with enough money to keep us comfortable while I accomplished what he demanded."

"You brought these documents to Sally," I said.

"I did."

"What about running from a grand jury in Texas?" I asked.

"A mistake."

"A mistake Horvecki used to keep you in line."

"One of them. Maybe I should see a doctor about this nose. The blood is still coming."

Ames produced a dry towel from behind his back and handed it to Torcelli, who dropped the bloody one on the floor and pressed the fresh one to his nose.

"Thanks."

"Welcome."

"Sally authenticated these documents," I said.

"With a little friendly persuasion," Ronnie said.

I should have been able to muster enough anger to at least consider another punch to Ronnie's expanded red-and-purple nose, but I found nothing to call on. Hitting him again would not take care of what I was now feeling.

"Last question," I said. "If you get it right, you win the prize."

"Okay," he said.

"What really happened the night Horvecki died?"

"I called him, told him I wanted to see him, that he was screwing me around, that he was just trying to stall until he could get rid of me, poison Rachel against me. I told him I was coming over. He said, 'Not now. I've got a friend visiting.' "

"Did he sound like he meant it?"

"He smirked," Ronnie said.

"Over the phone?" I asked.

"Yes. Philip Horvecki was good at that."

"Go on."

"When I got there, the front door was open. I went in. Someone was going out the window. Horvecki was on the floor. I could see he was dead. Rachel was in the bedroom doorway. I told Rachel to get out of the house, get down to Main Street."

"Why?" Ames asked.

"I panicked," he said. "I had to almost push her out. She went, and I ran after her, looking for whoever had gone through the window."

"You didn't see anyone?" I asked.

"I did," he said. "There was someone in a pickup truck across the street. I had seen him when I went into the house. I thought he was waiting for someone in one of the other houses. I told you all this."

"We like hearing it," said Ames.

"I went back in the house. I was sure Horvecki was dead, but I went over to him to be sure. I've seen people beaten, but nothing like this. His face was a mess. A bone in his left arm was pushed through the skin. I started to get up to call 911. The door opened. Two cops were pointing guns in my face. Find Rachel. Find the guy in the pickup truck. Rachel and the guy in the truck both saw the killer go through the window. That's the story. It's true."

"You believe him?" I asked Ames.

"Some."

"It's the truth. Oh, shit. Is this a piece of bone?"

He pinched a small piece of something between his thumb and nearby finger and held it up.

"Can't tell," said Ames. "Maybe."

"I'm going to need a plastic surgeon," Ronnie said.

"Probably, but you can afford one now," I said. "If Horvecki really left his money to his daughter."

"That do it for here?" asked Ames.

I nodded. Ames helped Torcelli to his feet.

"I'm still out on bail."

"I don't think the police are going to want you out on the streets of Sarasota, or Rio, or Brussels," I said. "We've got a place you can stay for a while."

"You're taking me in," he said.

"No, not yet," I said. "We're taking you somewhere safe."

"You'll be safe," Ames said.

"Safe from what?"

"From whoever it is who's going to try to kill you. My guess is that if he or she catches you, you'll decide to commit suicide," I said.

"Why would I kill myself?"

"Guilt over killing your father-in-law," I said.

"Remorse," said Ames.

"Case closed," I added.

"The killer will try to make it look like I killed myself?"

"That's what I would do," I said. "Tell us about Blue Berrigan."

"The clown?" he asked, examining the second blood-drenched towel. "I told you before. I don't know anything about who killed him. I didn't. Why would I?" He paused to look at us. "You're going to find the killer and keep me out of jail?"

"At least for a day or two, if we can," I said. "Ames, I forgot the introduction. This is Dwight Torcelli."

"Can't say I'm pleased to meet you," Ames said.

"Okay. I'm sure Alana will get me a real lawyer. I can talk her into it. She'll calm down. Now, will you please take care of my nose."

I wasn't as sure as he was about Alana Legerman coming up with money for a lawyer.

14

He wasn't wearing his uniform when he came through my door that night. The door had been locked, but Essau Williams was a cop. There are many ways to get through a locked door, short of breaking it down. Besides, most people carefully lock their doors at night but leave their windows open with only a thin screen to protect them.

I was lying in bed, my eyes closed, my reading lamp still burning on the chair next to my bed. I had fallen asleep with a book on my chest. The book was a list of boys' names and their meaning. Lewis means "fame and war." I hadn't looked up Essau.

He grabbed me by my blue Chicago cubs sweatshirt with the sleeves cut off and lifted me from the bed. We were face-to-face. There was no anger in his face. There was nothing but frigid appraisal. Before he had come in, and before I fell asleep, I was considering a last stop in the restroom. Now I had to pee. I had to pee very badly. I did not tell him.

"I did not kill Horvecki," he said.

"Okay," I said.

"The Gerall kid did it. Don't come to my house again."

I didn't answer. I had nothing to say.

"You understand?"

"Yes," I said.

"Say what you've got to say," Essau said.

He hadn't addressed that to me but to someone I now made out in the darkness near the door. Jack Pepper, Reverend of the Self-Proclaimed Ministers of God, stepped forward.

"Do you know who killed Philip Horvecki?" asked Pepper, every bit as calm as Essau Williams, who stepped back from me but continued wearing a look of menace. He had it down. He was playing bad cop to Pepper's good Reverend. Or maybe he wasn't playing.

"Was it Ronald Gerall?"

"I don't think it was Gerall."

"If you discover who the person was who killed the bastard of hell, you will call one of us," said Pepper stepping forward. "But it might be best if no one finds out who did it. You understand?"

"Yes."

"But if you find the avenging angel—" Pepper began.

"I call you so you can do what?" I asked.

"Protect him," said Pepper. "The killing was not murder. Whoever did it, it was an execution. You find him. You tell us. You go about your business. You understand?"

I nodded, but the nod was too small and went unseen in the darkness.

"Understood?" asked Essau Williams.

"Yes," I said.

"Good," said Pepper.

"No," I said. "I understand, but I won't do it."

Essau Williams got a one-handed grip on my already crumpled shirt.

"You could have lied to us," said Pepper. "You're an honest man. But honesty is not always its own reward."

"I have a question," I said.

"Yes?" asked Pepper.

"How did you two team up?"

"In search of retribution from the system of men," said Pepper, "we've encountered each other through the years in our several attempts at trying to seek justice for our families and punishment for Philip Horvecki."

"Find him, tell us," said Essau.

"We decided that neither of us would exact physical retribution," Pepper continued ignoring Essau Williams. "But if someone were to do so, we would put the full extent of our gratitude toward him and pray for the mercy of Jesus upon him."

"*You* would pray for the mercy of Jesus," Essau Williams amended.

"What will you do?" asked Pepper, now only a few feet from me.

"Get a lock for my door," I said.

Silence. I prepared to be hit, as well as anyone can prepare. The instant the blow came I would go with it, fall back. Then again, Essau Williams might simply decide to strangle me.

"You're not afraid," Pepper said.

"No."

"You know you are in the hands of Jesus," said Pepper.

"No."

"Then . . . ?" Pepper asked.

"I have another question," I said.

"What?" asked Pepper.

"Do you have a favorite first line from a book?"

" 'Behold, I send my messenger before thy face, which shall prepare thy way before thee. Prepare ye the way of the Lord, make his paths straight.' The Gospel according to St. Mark."

"You left out a little," I said.

"What the fuck is this?" Williams said. "Are you both crazy?"

"I was going to ask the same thing," I said.

"We have a damn good reason if we are, Philip Horvecki. What's your damn good reason?"

"There's someone in the dark," I said.

"What is that supposed to mean?" Williams said.

"Me," came the voice from the door.

Victor Woo had entered while they were doing their best to intimidate me.

Williams and Pepper turned toward the door. Victor flipped on the light switch. He was barefoot, wearing clean jeans and an orange University of Illinois sweatshirt with the sleeves rolled up. In his right hand was the old aluminum softball bat I'd found in the closet when I moved in here.

I could see now that Williams was also wearing jeans. His long-sleeve T-shirt was solid blue. Pepper, pale, his straw hair slightly tousled, wore brown slacks and a white shirt and tie. I wore my underpants with the penguins and my Cubs sweatshirt with the cut-off sleeves. No one wore a smile.

"Victor batted leadoff for two Tigers farm teams," I said.

I might analyze that instant lie sometime later with Ann Hurwitz. Anyway, it didn't seem to have any effect on my visitors.

"We've said what we have to say," Pepper said calmly.

"You can put the bat down, Jet Li," said Essau Williams.

Victor moved away from the door so they could pass. Pepper went out first. Williams paused at the door and said, "'Once upon a time, there were three bears, a papa bear, a momma bear, and a baby bear.' A favorite first line. My mother used to tell me that one when I was a baby. That was long after Philip Horvecki raped her and my aunt, and long before he came back eight years ago and turned her and my aunt into cowering old women and ended my family's history."

He closed the door behind him. Victor followed them out to be sure they left and then returned, bat still in hand.

"Tea?" he asked.

"Sure," I said. "You?"

"I don't like tea," he said. "But I have Oreo cookies and milk."

"That'll work for me."

We woke Dwight Torcelli, who was sleeping on a blanket in the room next to mine. Victor had been in that room, too, lying on his bedroll in front of the door to keep Torcelli from deciding to wander. There was a strip of white tape across his swollen nose. The skin under both of his eyes had turned purple. I almost apologized, but I wouldn't have meant it.

"What?" he asked sitting up, blinking, not sure of where he was, and then slowly understanding.

"You had visitors," I said. "You missed them. Victor and I are going to have Oreo cookies and milk. Want to join us?"

"I guess," he said, looking at me and then at Victor, who still bore his softball bat.

I was reasonably sure now who was responsible for the death of both Philip Horvecki and Blue Berrigan. When I got up in the morning, I'd share my thoughts with Ames.

I checked the clock when we went back into the room where my desk sat. It was almost three in the morning.

We had cookies and milk.

I was up by six. I showered, shaved, shampooed what little hair I have remaining with a giant container of no-name shampoo-conditioner purchased at a dollar store, and examined the scratches on my face. It didn't look as bad as I thought it would. I certainly looked better than Jeff Augustine.

I was dressed in my jeans and a fresh green short-sleeve knit shirt with a collar. It didn't go well with my blue and red Cubs cap, but I had no plans for meeting royalty. If I did run into any, I could tuck my cap away. Lewis Fonesca was prepared for anything except intruders, unbidden emotions, disarming surprises, life's horrors, and the pain and death of others.

When Ames and Darrell Caton walked in together just before eight, I was eating an Oreo cookie with the full understanding that I would have to brush my teeth again.

"Met him downstairs," Ames explained.

"Takes me a while to get up the stairs since I got shot with an Uzi," said Darrell.

"It was a pellet gun," Ames said.

"Shot is shot," said Darrell. "I can't go around telling people I was in the hospital for three days because I was shot in the back with a BB."

"Guess not," said Ames.

It was obvious Ames and Darrell liked each other, though I couldn't quite figure out what the essence of that friendship might be.

"Cookies?" I asked.

Both Darrell and Ames took one.

"He safe?" asked Ames, pointing at the door of the second bedroom.

"Victor's in there with him," I said.

"With who?" asked Darrell.

"Visitor," I said.

"You're my big brother, big sister, uncle, Santa, whatever," said Darrell. "You're supposed to tell me things. Share confidences, you know?"

"You're getting a bit old to have a big brother," said Ames. "And what are you doing roaming the streets when you're supposed to be in bed."

"Okay," said Darrell, "we'll call it even. Then we're . . ."

"Friends," said Ames.

"Friends," I agreed.

"Sometimes I think my mother would rather have me hang with safer friends, like drug dealers and gangbangers."

I offered him another cookie. He took it. Ames decided one was enough.

"Let's get some breakfast," Ames said. "We can bring something back for Victor and our guest."

"You two are playing with me," Darrell said. "That's it, right?"

"No," I said. "Let's go downstairs slowly and walk over to the Waffle Shop and I'll tell you the story about two night visitors."

"No," said Darrell, "I know that one. Amal and camels. I know that shit."

"This one," I said, "is about different night visitors. I think you'll both like it."

"Okay," said Darrell. "Let's get waffles."

It was Saturday morning, bright, sunny, cloudless, Floridian-winter cool. No one shot at us as we walked down the stairs, Ames in front, Darrell second, me in the rear. Darrell moved slowly, wincing, trying to cover it. We were only two blocks from the Waffle Shop but I suggested we drive. Darrell said no.

When we entered the Waffle Shop it was crowded, but a family of four was just getting up from a table at the front window. We waited, then sat, and I pretended to look at the menu, which both Ames and I had long ago memorized.

Greg Legerman and Winn Graeme came in about two minutes later, looked around, saw us, and headed for our table.

Greg and Winn stood next to our table. Greg's arms were folded over his chest, his look a demand before he spoke.

"Where is he?" he asked.

"Greg, Winn, this is Darrell Caton," I said by way of introduction. "He was shot and almost killed on the steps of my office a few days ago."

For a beat they both looked at Darrell who held out his hand. First Greg, and then Winn, took the extended hand.

"They look kind of shook," said Darrell first to me and then to Ames. "One of them shoot me?"

"Possible," said Ames.

"This won't work," said Greg. "You are working for everyone in my family and you owe me the information first. We're worried about Ronnie."

"We?" I asked.

Greg and Winn had to pull in close to the table as one of Gwen's daughters came by with an armful of platters, calling, "Out of the way."

"We," Greg repeated. "Me, Winn, my mother, my grandfather. We."

"Find a seat," the now-platterless waitress said just above the patter of the other customers.

She said it with a smile, a warm voice, and a hand on Winn's shoulder, but it was a command.

"Sit," Ames said.

They sat, losing the supposed advantage of our looking up at them.

"I'll be right back for your order," the daughter said. "Coffee?"

"Yes," said Greg.

"Orange juice," said Winn.

"How'd you know Ames and I were here?" I asked.

"Went to your place," Greg said. "Your car, the Chinese guy's car, and the old cowboy's scooter were there. The Chinese guy wouldn't let us in, said you were out for breakfast, so we . . ."

"His name is Victor," said Ames. "Victor Woo. Mr. Woo till he tells you to call him otherwise."

Ames was calm, but I knew by the number of words he had used that he was not pleased by our new breakfast companions. The only one who had spoken less was Winn Graeme, who sat reasonably erect and adjusted his glasses.

"We didn't mean any disrespect," said Greg. "I'm a flaming all-inclusive open-the-borders liberal. Right, Winn?"

He gave Winn a shoulder pop with his fist. Winn nodded to confirm Greg's political assessment.

"My mother bailed Ronnie out," Greg said. "We all hired you. We want to know what's going on."

"His name isn't Ronnie," I said.

"What?" asked Greg.

"His name is Dwight Torcelli," I said. "He's twenty-six years old and he's married to Philip Horvecki's daughter."

Greg looked stunned. Winn sat silently. It was time again to adjust his glasses.

"Your mother wants to know where he is?" asked Ames.

Greg looked at Ames as if Ames had not been paying attention.

"My mother . . ."

He was interrupted by Gwen's daughter bringing breakfast for Darrell, Ames, and me, orange juice for Winn, and coffee for whoever wanted it. Darrell, Ames, and I were all having the waffle special with eggs and three slices of bacon.

"Go ahead," said Greg. "We don't mind if you eat."

He said the last part of this after the three of us had already begun to eat.

"Okay," came a shout above the voices and clattering plates and cups. "Listen up."

Two tables from us, a trucker in a blue baseball cap and a denim vest over his T-shirt was standing and waiting for attention. His beard was just beyond stubble and he looked more than serious.

"My friend here says Elvis never ate here, that Gwen's mother just put up that poster and the sign."

"That's right," said the friend, now standing.

He was shorter than the other guy but in better shape, biceps like cement.

"February 21, 1956, Elvis played the Florida Theater in Sarasota," said Winn aloud. "He had breakfast here on the morning of February 22 and headed immediately for an appearance that night in Waycross, Georgia."

The breakfast crowd applauded.

"The kid don't know *shit*," the muscled trucker said, with a special emphasis on the word "shit."

The restaurant went silent.

Gwen's other daughter, the one with two babies and another on the way, was behind the counter where I usually had breakfast.

"You calling my family liars?" she said.

"My grandfather was here when Elvis came in," said Winn.

"Bullshit," said the trucker.

"His grandfather's still alive and almost ninety-five," added Greg. "Reverend Graeme of the First Episcopalian Church of Christ the Redeemer would, I'm sure, be happy to come by and settle this."

People began to applaud and laugh. The defeated trucker mumbled a few obscenities and sat down as the first trucker raised a hand in historic triumph.

"Your grandfather really in here when Elvis came in?" asked Darrell.

"Don't see how he could have been," said Greg. "He was in Korea."

"Yes," said Winn.

"And," added Greg, favoring his friend with another punch in the arm, "he's dead and he wasn't Reverend Graeme. He was Russell Graeme, co-owner of Graeme-Sydney Chrysler Motors in Sydney, Australia."

Greg was grinning.

Darrell mumbled something to himself and went on eating. I was sitting next to him and heard, though no one else did.

"Rich white kids," Darrell had said.

"That the truth about Ronnie?" asked Winn.

"Truth," I said.

"Why do you want to find him?" asked Ames.

"To talk to him about getting a new lawyer," Greg said leaning forward. "My grandfather said he'll pay to get the best available defense team in the nation. The plan was for us to set it up with Ronnie and you keep looking for whoever killed Horvecki. But he's not Ronnie. I don't understand."

"What about Berrigan?" asked Ames.

"Berrigan?" asked Greg.

Gwen's daughter, the one who had waited on us, touched Winn's shoulder and quietly said, "Your breakfasts are all on the house."

Then she moved away to the waving hand of a customer who wanted more coffee or his check.

"Blue Berrigan," I said.

"What kind of name is that?" asked Greg.

"Dead man's," said Ames.

Winn Graeme's eyes were closed for an instant. Then he removed his glasses, opened his eyes, and put the glasses back on.

"The singer?" he asked.

I nodded.

"Where? When did he . . . ?" asked Greg.

"Day ago," said Ames. "Beaten in his car."

Darrell was giving his full attention to the conversation now.

"Who is Blue Bennignan?" Darrell asked.

"Berrigan," Winn corrected. "I used to watch his show when I was a kid. My mother took me to see him when he was at the Opera House in Sydney when I was six."

"You going to cry?" Greg asked his friend in disbelief before looking around the table to see if anyone else found this particularly bizarre. No one seemed to.

"I know a guy in a gang in Palmetto called Black Brainbanger," said Darrell. "And there's a whore up on the Trail goes by Red Alice because . . ."

"Her hair's red?" said Ames.

"You know her?" asked Darrell.

Ames took it and Darrell laughed.

"Got you, old cowboy," Darrell said.

Ames gave a small shake of his head. No one joined the laughter.

Darrell looked at me and said, "I'm just breaking it down and bringing it down Fonesca. Lightening it up, you know what I'm saying?"

Unordered breakfasts for both Greg and Winn arrived, the same thing all of us had.

"Anything Ronnie needs?" asked Greg.

"His name is Dwight Torcelli," Winn said.

"The best criminal defense attorney in the United States would help," I said.

We ate for a while, and I thought in silence.

Then Darrell whispered to me, "You don't need more money? I do. Rich white boys probably have their pockets full of twenties. You take it, give it to me. I keep a little and give the rest to my mother."

I shook my head, but it didn't stop him. He whispered to me as he finished his breakfast.

"I took a bullet in the back for you, Fonesca," he said.

"Pellet," I said. "Maybe you were the one being shot at."

"People from my part of town don't use pellets and BBs after they're five years old. They don't shoot people with toys. Someone after me'd have a serious weapon."

"Because you're so bad?" I asked.

"No," he said. "I'm just saying."

"You didn't tell people you got shot with a pellet gun."

"Hell no."

After we were finished with breakfast, Greg and Winn stood, and Greg said, "You'll let me know?"

"I'll let you know," I said, though at this point I wasn't sure about what it was I would be letting him know about.

"Sorry," said Winn, though at this point I wasn't completely sure what it was he was sorry about.

When they left, Ames finished a second cup of coffee and said, "Smart boys."

I wasn't sure how he meant it, and I wasn't going to ask him to explain.

We picked up carryout breakfasts for Victor and Torcelli. The same truckers we had seen earlier were in line behind us at the cash register.

The one with muscles and, I could now see, fading tattoos on his arms, said to Ames, "Your grandkids cost me forty bucks."

I touched Ames's arm in the hope that he wouldn't respond, but he said, "Cost yourself forty dollars."

"Not the way I see it," said the trucker.

"Let it go, Ben," said the trucker who had won the bet.

"You let it go, Teek. Easy for you. You won. Way I see it, old bones here owes me."

It was our turn to pay now. I handed over cash for the carryout to Gwen's daughter at the register. She pushed it back to me.

"Ames owes you shit," said Darrell. "Right, Fonesca?"

"Right," I said.

"Mess with Ames, he'll shoot your ass," Darrell said. "Mess with Fonesca he'll break your nose. Ames shot and killed a man and Fonesca just broke a fool's nose."

"That a fact?" said Ben the trucker with the biceps.

"Fact," Darrell said.

The trucker reached for Darrell. Ames put his arm in the way.

"You want to take this outside," said Ames. "I'll accommodate."

I led our happy band out the door.

"Parking lot," said Ben.

"I'm having no part," said Teek.

When we got to the parking lot next to the restaurant, Ames opened his jacket so Ben could see an old, but very large, well-cleaned, and shining pistol tucked into his belt.

"Bullshit," said Ben, now glaring. He took a step toward Ames, who calmly removed the weapon from his belt and fired into the ground at the trucker's feet.

"Another step and you'll be on your way to the emergency room," said Ames.

"He means it," I said.

Ben backed away three steps and raised a fist, but didn't say anything.

Teek took Ben's arm and started to pull him away.

"Crazy old fucker," said Ben, looking over his shoulder as he wisely allowed himself to be escorted from the lot.

I didn't ask either trucker if they had a favorite first line from a book.

"You did him, Ames," said Darrell holding up his right hand for a high five, which Ames didn't deliver.

"Best we go now," Ames said.

"Best," I agreed.

15

"I'm not an unreasonable man," Horvecki said, professionally looking at the camera and away from the SNN interviewer.

He was looking directly at me as I sat in my room with Ames, Darrell, Victor, and Ronnie watching the DVD Greg Legerman had given me.

Horvecki had the raspy voice of a smoker and a haunted look. He was slightly frail and definitely on the verge of being old. He had a well-trimmed, close-cropped head of dyed black hair and the slightly blotched skin of a man who had spent too many hours outside without benefit of sunblock.

"I pay taxes—a hell of a lot of taxes to this country, this state, and this county," he said, looking back at the interviewer, a pretty young brunette who couldn't have been more than twenty-two and who was definitely uncomfortable as she tried to control the interview. "So do thousands of other people who don't have children in school, don't have grandchildren in school. We pay to give a third-rate education to kids who aren't even ours, and no one gives us a choice. Well, I'm fighting for that choice."

"But this is a matter of funding a much-needed program for gifted students," the young woman tried.

"So all students aren't created equal?" he said. "Some get a better education. No one asked me what I thought about that. Did they ask you? Your parents? Did you go to Pine View?"

"No," the girl said protectively, "I went to Riverview."

"Education should be paid for by parents and anyone who wants to give money," Horvecki said. "I don't want to give money for the children of the people who should be paying."

"And Bright Futures?" she asked.

"Same thing," he said. "A big, phony boondoggle. Take lottery money and tax money and give it to smart kids instead of distributing it evenly among all the kids who want to go to college."

"That's what you believe, that the money that—?"

"I don't think there should be any Bright Futures program or any Pine View School funded by my BLEEP money."

"So?" she asked.

He turned again to face the camera and said, "Vote no on the funding referendum."

Cut to a silver-haired man behind a desk with sheets of paper in his hand.

"Philip Horvecki," he said. "Man on a mission with a gift for making political enemies and a record of convincing voters in the past fifteen years to vote for his self-named Self Interest Initiative Voters Alliance."

The television screen went gray with thin white fizzling lines.

Darrell reached over, ejected the disk and turned off the television.

"See," said Torcelli. "That man was a monster."

"Your father-in-law," said Ames. "Your wife's father."

"Yes," Torcelli said, touching the bandage on his nose to be sure it was still there.

"So you went to see him because of your commitment to Bright Futures," I said.

"Yes," he said.

"Nothing to do with your wanting to be his true son and heir?" said Ames.

"A little, maybe, but does that negate what I was trying to do?"

"A little, maybe," Ames said.

"I'm a con man, a fraud, an opportunist, a—"

"Asshole," said Darrell.

"All right," Torcelli conceded, "but if you came from the background I had—"

"Wrong road to go down with me," said Darrell. "I'll take you home for the night, and we'll tour my neighborhood. We'll play Mr. Rogers. And check out Fonesca's tale. His—"

"Where is your wife?" I interrupted.

Torcelli shook his head to show that none of us understood the weight of his life or the toll it had taken.

"She's not well," he said.

"Sorry to hear that. Where is she?" I asked again.

He looked past us out the window at the slightly fluttering leaves of the tree outside.

"Want to have Viviase ask the same question?" I said. "He might add a few questions about your friendship with his daughter."

"She's a kid," he said.

"Your wife or Viviase's daughter?"

"My wife is staying at the Ocean Terrace Resort Hotel on Siesta Key," he said. "Waiting for her father's lawyer to tell us what she's inherited."

"You told us you didn't know where she was," I said.

"You said you wanted us to find her to give you an alibi," Ames said.

"I did. I did, but I wanted to protect her. I was confused and you were . . ." He put his head in his hands.

"She's registered under the name Olin. I'll call her and tell her to talk to you."

"Don't call," said Ames.

"You got anything to eat in the refrigerator?" asked Darrell.

"You just had breakfast," said Ames.

"I'm still growing and I need food to keep me going. I was shot and almost dead. Remember that?"

"You plan on letting us forget it some time?" asked Ames.

"Hell no," said Darrell.

"Go look in the refrigerator," I said. And he went off to do just that.

"You believe me about what happened?" said Torcelli. "You believe I'm innocent?"

"Greg Legerman thinks you're innocent," I said, "but then, he doesn't know about you and his mother."

"Don't tell him," Torcelli pleaded.

"You were using Alana Legerman as backup in case your wife didn't get Horvecki's money?" I said.

"I wouldn't put it like that," he said, touching his bandaged nose again.

"Course not," said Ames.

Darrell came back into the room with a bowl of Publix sugar-frosted wheat and milk.

"What'd I miss?" he asked.

"Nothing," said Torcelli sullenly.

Victor got up and left the room, brushing past Darrell who crunched away at the cereal.

"The State of Florida is going to try to kill me when they find out I'm an adult, but my wife will get me a great lawyer and you'll keep looking for whoever killed Horvecki, right?"

"Your wife know you're not really married?" Ames asked.

"We'll get married again," he said.

I thought of him with Sally, overworked Sally, caring Sally, Sally with a deep laugh and a soft smile when she looked at her children. I tried to conjure up the other side of Sally I'd glimpsed a few times, the Sally who had no compassion for the parents who took drugs or were religious lunatics or just plain lunatics. She was calm and determined with such people. She was relentless and willing to fight the courts and the law to see to it that they couldn't destroy their children. She lost more often than she won, but she kept fighting. I thought about these two Sallys, and I tried not to imagine her with the man who sat across from me, the man whose nose I had broken, the man who wanted Ames and me to save his life.

Victor came back into the room. He had another bowl of cereal and milk. Less than an hour after breakfast Darrell and Victor were hungry. So was I.

Someone was knocking outside the door in the other room.

"I'll get it," said Ames, moving out and closing the door behind him.

Then we heard a voice, a familiar voice. I got up and went out to meet our visitor.

"He's here, isn't he?" said Ettiene Viviase.

"He's here," I said.

It wasn't rage in his eyes exactly, but personal determination. The source, I was sure, was his daughter's involvement with the man he still thought of as Ronnie Gerall.

"Haul him out," he said.

"What's happened?" I asked.

"Just came from my third visit to his apartment," he said. "This time I found something new, found it under a bookcase. I turned it over to the lab about ten minutes ago."

"What?" I asked.

"The weapon that was used to kill Blue Berrigan."

Ames went in to get Torcelli who came out black-eyed and slightly bewildered. The confident and angry young man of a few days ago had been replaced by this pained creature with a swollen and bandaged nose and black and blue eyes.

"What happened?" Viviase asked.

"I hit him," I said.

"You?"

"Yes."

"There's hope for you, Fonesca," he said. Then he looked at Torcelli and said, "Back to a cell. We've got lots to talk about."

"Fonesca, tell . . ." Torcelli began, but he was no longer sure about who he might call for help.

"I didn't kill anyone," Torcelli insisted as Viviase put handcuffs on him behind his back. "Fonesca, we're both Italians, Catholics. I swear to Jesus. I swear on the life of the Pope. I didn't kill Philip Horvecki."

"He's Italian?" said Viviase.

I didn't bother to tell Torcelli that I wasn't a Catholic and that some of my best enemies were Italian.

Victor and Darrell came out of my room, bowls in hand, still eating their cereal.

"You make an interesting quartet," Viviase said. "One more thing. What did your two middle-of-the-night visitors want?"

I didn't answer, so he added, "We had a man watching last night. Thinks he recognized Essau Williams, a Venice police officer. Who was the other man?"

"It was personal," I said.

"The other man," Viviase insisted.

"Jack Pepper, a radio evangelist from Cortez," I said.

"Mind telling me what they wanted, or did they just drop by to give you legal and spiritual counseling and a cup of tea?"

"They wanted me to find a way to get Dwight Torcelli free of the murder charge."

"Dwight Torcelli?"

"Ronnie's real name, but we can still call him Ronald. It's his middle name. He's twenty-seven years old today."

"You can prove that?"

"Listen . . ." Torcelli started to say, but Viviase was in no mood to listen to him.

"You can prove it," I said, and told him how to do it.

"No point in my telling you not to do anything dumb," he said. "You're going to do it anyway."

When Viviase and his prisoner were gone and Darrell and Victor had finished their second breakfast, we all got into Victor's car, Ames in front, Darrell and I in the rear.

"How come you're not telling me to go home?" Darrell asked.

"Because," I said, "you'd remind me that I'm responsible for you all day. You'd tell me that being with me when I'm working is the most important thing in your life."

"I'm into girls now," he said. "Don't overestimate your charisma." He hit each syllable in the word.

"I'm impressed."

"You're learning," Darrell said as Victor drove to Siesta Key.

"I'm entering a new phase," I said.

And I was pretty sure I was.

The Ocean Terrace Resort Hotel was on Siesta Key. It had a swimming pool, but it was no resort. It was a one-story dirty green stucco line of thirty-five rooms and a slightly moldy-smelling carpet in the hallway. The Ocean Terrace lived on the spillover from the bigger, fancier, more up-to-date and upscale motels that called themselves resorts and sold postcards proclaiming that they were the place for Northerners, Canadians, Frenchmen, Germans, Norwegians, and Japanese to spend a week, or the whole winter. The Ocean Terrace offered nothing but its own existence.

The desk clerk, a woman with an unruly pile of papers in front of her and a head of equally unruly dyed red hair looked up at us as we entered the lobby. She was maybe in her fifties, clear-skinned, buxom, and looking as if she had suffered a few setbacks in the last ten minutes.

"What have we here, the road company of the Village People? A baseball player, a cowboy, a Chinese guy, and a black kid," she said.

We didn't answer her.

"Sorry. That was uncalled for," she said. "We have no vacancies and you appear to have no luggage. Would you like a bottle of water?"

"Sure," said Darrell.

"Rachel Olin," I said.

The woman bent down out of sight and then came up with a bottle of water which she handed to Darrell, who said, "Thanks."

"A guest," I said. "Rachel Olin."

"Checked out about an hour ago," the woman said.

"She pay with a credit card?" I asked.

"Cash. Who are you?"

"Her husband is looking for her," Ames said.

"He's pining for her," said Darrell.

She looked at Victor but he had nothing to add.

"Left with a man," she said.

"She call him anything?" Ames asked.

"No, I don't think so."

"What did he look like?" I asked.

"Who are you?" she asked.

I produced my process server license card and handed it to her.

"You look different in that baseball cap," she said, handing the card back. "These gentlemen are your backup?"

"Ames is my partner," I said. "I look after Darrell on Saturdays."

"And I killed his wife," Victor said.

She turned her attention to Victor, who was definitely not smiling.

"The guy she went with was a little older than you maybe," she said. "Good shape. Nice-looking."

"Anything else?"

"Yes," she said. "He had a patch over his left eye."

"Thought he left town," Ames said from the front seat as Victor drove through Siesta Key Village, avoiding collision with shopping bag–laden tourists.

"So did I," I said.

"Who?" asked Darrell.

"His name is Jeff Augustine," I said.

"He kidnapped her?" asked Darrell.

"I don't know. Maybe. Doesn't look that way," I said.

"He's not the upchuck who shot me, is he?"

"Someone shot him, too," Ames said.

"Fonesca, what is going on?" Darrell asked, turning in his seat to face me as fully as he could.

"I'm not sure," I said.

"Can't do no better than that?" he asked.

"Can't do *any* better than that," I said. "I'm not sure, but I'm getting some ideas."

"Good ones?"

"I don't know."

"Where are we going?"

"To the home of D. Elliot Corkle," said Ames.

"Why?"

"So he can give you a handy dandy super automatic CD sorter which normally sells for nineteen ninety-five," I said.

"I don't need a CD sorter," Darrell said.

We were crossing the bridge off the Key.

"Don't worry," said Ames, "he's got lots of things he likes to give away."

Ames told Victor how to get to Corkle's. When we hit the mainland, Victor turned north on Tamiami Trail.

"Victor," I said. "Would you do me a favor?"

"Yes."

"Stop telling people you killed my wife."

"But I did."

"You may want to hear it, but other people don't."

"You don't want me to say it, I won't."

"I don't want you to say it to anyone but me when you feel you have to."

"I'll remember," he said.

There were no cars parked in front of Corkle's or in his driveway, but that didn't mean no one was home. If he had told me the truth, Corkle didn't leave his house. Doctors, barbers, dentists, I'm sure, came to him. I wouldn't have been surprised if he had an operating room somewhere behind the walls.

The last time I was in Corkle's home, Ames stole the Ronnie documents, and I won a few dollars playing poker. This was not a place I wanted to be.

"Ames, find a way in the back," I said. "See if you can find her."

Ames looked straight ahead. Victor looked at the steering wheel and Darrell said, "No way. You said he'll give us something?"

"We'll come up with something," said Ames.

Ames stayed seated while I went up the path to the front door. A tiny lizard skittered in front of me. I pulled my foot back to keep from stepping on it. A flock of screaming gulls spun over the Gulf of Mexico about forty yards down the street to my right.

I took off my cap, put it in my back pocket, and rang the bell. It didn't take long, maybe forty seconds. Corkle opened the door.

"Ah, the thief in the baseball cap. Come in."

He stepped back and looked over my shoulder at Victor's parked car. Corkle was wearing blue slacks and an orange shirt with the words CORKLE'S RADIO TO OUTER SPACE. Under the lightning black letters was a picture of a plastic radio the size of a cigar box.

"You like the shirt?" he asked, leading me toward the office Ames had broken into. "On the way out, remind me and I'll give you and your friends in the car one each."

"Could you really hear outer space?" I asked as he opened the door to his office and let me pass.

"I'll give you one. You try it. Let me know. Truth is, you can tune in outer space on any radio. You just won't hear much of anything. But the CROS is perfect for AM and FM and has an alarm clock that plays 'So in Love with You Am I.' Have a seat."

I sat, not across from him at his desk but at a table in the corner near a window.

Corkle picked up a glass sphere about the size of a softball. He shook it gently and held it up so I could see the snow under the glass gently falling on . . .

"Rosebud," he said. "This is an exact replica of the one in *Citizen Kane*."

He handed it to me.

"See the sled?"

"Yes," I said handing it back. "You sold them for nine ninety-five?"

"No, I didn't sell them. I had this one made to remind me not to go looking for other people's Rosebuds. Are you looking for someone's Rosebud, Lewis Fonesca?"

"My own maybe," I said.

He made a sound I took as a sign of sympathy or understanding. Then he put the glass ball gently atop a dark wood holder on the table and began rummaging through the drawers of his desk.

"I don't stay in this house because of any phobia," he said. "I just don't find things out there very interesting anymore. You know what I mean."

"Yes."

"I wasn't asking a question," he said, bouncing from the chair and looking at his shelves for something else to play with. "I know the answer."

"What's the answer?" I asked.

"Catherine," he said. "Am I right or am I right?"

"You're right," I said. "Now I've got a question."

"Want a drink? You drink Diet Coke, right? Or how about lemonade?"

"Not now, thanks. The Kitchen Master Block Set."

"A good seller, not great, but good. Sold seventy-four thousand in 1981."

"There was a meat pounder in the set," I said.

"Meat tenderizer," he corrected.

"A big wooden mallet with ridges on the head."

"Yes. You want one?"

"My sister has one."

"Nice to know it's still in service," he said. "Sturdy. Made in the Philippines."

"I think one of them was used to murder Blue Berrigan," I said. "I saw the postmortem photographs. They left a dent in his skull like a fingerprint."

"Could be a different manufacturer's," he said.

Corkle found what he was looking for in the deep file drawer in the desk. It was a jar full of what looked like pennies. He rolled the jar in his hands. The coins made the sound of falling rain as it turned.

"You give away a lot of Kitchen Master Block Sets here in Sarasota?"

"I give my Corkle Enterprises helpful house, car, and kitchen aids to anyone who comes in this house. I give them for Christmas, Hanukkah, Kwanzaa, and birthdays."

The rolling coins in the jar grew louder as he moved toward me.

"You're a generous man," I said.

"I like to think so."

"You haven't asked me about Ronnie Gerall."

"I assume that you'll tell me if you have anything to say that will help him."

"His name isn't Ronnie Gerall, but you already know that."

"Do I?"

He was behind me now. I didn't turn my head, just listened to the coins.

If I were ever to really believe in God, a primary reason would be the existence of irony in my life. There had to be some irony in the possibility of my getting killed with a jar full of pennies.

There is a mischief in me, even with the coins of death over my head. Death wish? Maybe. Ann Hurwitz thought so. Now she thinks I may be getting over it. If so, why did I then say, "Jeff Augustine."

The coin rattling turned to the sound of a thunderstorm in the Amazon and then suddenly stopped.

"He didn't leave town," I said.

Corkle moved back to the wall, deposited the jar, and sat behind his desk.

"He convinced you he was going, didn't he?"

"Yes," I said.

"Good actor. C-plus real-life tough guy."

"Where is he?"

"I don't know," Corkle said, "but I do know where your cowboy friend is."

"Where?"

"Searching the rooms upstairs for Rachel Horvecki."

He pushed a button under the desk and a section of the bookcase popped open to reveal a bank of eight full-color television screens. They were all numbered. On number three Ames was talking to a young woman sitting on a bed.

"Why did you take her?"

"Protect her," he said. "My daughter and grandson believe in Ronnie's . . . What's his real name?"

"Dwight Ronald Torcelli. He's still Ronnie."

"I don't want her threatened to the point where he feels he can't proclaim his innocence."

"You think he'd do the noble thing?"

"No," said Corkle, swiveling his leather chair so that it faced the window and presented me with the back of his head. He had a little monk's bald pate you couldn't see unless he was seated like this and leaning back.

"Don't ask me why my daughter and grandson believe in him."

"Their belief may be eroding."

"I wouldn't try to talk them out of it," he said. "On the other hand, I wouldn't say a word against . . ."

"Dwight Torcelli," I said. "You let us steal those documents about Ronnie Gerall while we played poker the other night," I said. "You dropped a hint about them and left them on your desk. You had a pretty good idea we would come the night I bought into your poker game."

"Why would I do that?"

"To give us reasons to believe that he was guilty without handing us evidence."

"You think I'm that devious?"

"You're that devious," I said.

He swiveled back to face me and looked up at the television monitors.

"Persuasive," he said.

I looked at the monitors. Ames and the young woman were coming out of the bedroom. He led the way to some narrow steep stairs just off the kitchen. The young woman followed him.

"Augustine?" I asked.

"You think he killed Horvecki and Berrigan?"

"The thought had entered my mind."

"Anything else?"

"Are you paying me to clear Torcelli or to find something against him?"

"Given his relationship with your friend Sally Pierogi . . ."

"Porovsky."

"Porovsky," he amended. "Given that, I think you might have an interest in proving Torcelli is not a nice person. There, they've left the house."

I looked up at a screen in the lower left-hand monitor to see Ames and the young woman hurrying across the back lawn.

"You're good at all this," I said.

"Couldn't have sold forty-eight thousand copies of the Guitar Master Twelve-Lesson Plan and almost twenty thousand guitars to go with it if I weren't good at sizing up the potential customers."

"What are you trying to sell me?" I asked.

"I'm buying," he said.

"What?"

"The truth," he said. "Not the big truth. Just a small one about who killed Horvecki. If it clears the dago weasel, so be it. You don't believe me?"

"No. Police will be coming to talk to you about what they found in Torcelli's apartment."

"The meat tenderizer?"

"The meat tenderizer."

"They're waiting for you in your car," he said.

He got up and so did I.

"You get your choice of items in the closet," he said.

"Some other time," I said, going to the office door.

"D. Elliot Corkle has irritated you," he said following me. "The dago remark? I was just pulling your chain." He reached up and pulled once on an invisible chain.

"I know," I said.

He grinned and pointed a finger at me to show I had hit the mark.

"Answer four questions and we're friends again," I said.

"Ask."

We crossed the foyer to the front door.

"You know a policeman named Essau Williams and an evangelist named Jack Pepper?"

"D. Elliot Corkle knows who they are," he said. "Wait a moment."

He hurried to the closet off the front hall, opened it and disappeared for no more than a few seconds before coming out with a white cardboard box and handing it to me. "Second question?"

"Have you given money to either one of them?" I asked as we went out onto the redbrick path.

"Nothing to Williams but I did volunteer to put up a suitable headstone of his choice for his mother when they die. Five thousand dollars to Pepper to help support his ministry."

"In exchange for?"

"Nothing, but I did indicate to both of them that I appreciated their efforts to bring Philip Horvecki to justice."

"Blue Berrigan?" I asked.

"Unfortunate. No, tragic. No, shocking. A terrible coincidence. If you see my daughter . . ."

"Yes?"

"Nothing," he said. "She'll come back here. She always does when her funds get down to the level of the gross national product of Poland. Another question."

"Does Jeff Augustine play golf?"

"Why? Do you want him to join you on the links at the Ben Hogan Gulf Club? I don't know if he plays golf. I do know that if he does it will be a bit difficult for him now with but one eye."

He closed the door and I carried my prize to the car, where Rachel was sitting in the front passenger seat. I got in beside Ames and Darrell.

"Where are you taking me?" Rachel Gerall said.

"Wherever you want to go," I said.

"To see Ronnie," she said, her voice in twang from the center of the State of Florida.

She was frail and pale, red of hair and green of eyes. She should have been Irish. She had a pinched face and thin lips. She could have been cast as a tubercular resident of an Irish mining town a century ago. Either that or a hardcore drug user.

"Who are you people?" she said, half turning to look at me.

"People trying to help the police find whoever killed your father," I said.

"I don't trust you," she said, giving me the evil eye.

"Trust him," Darrell said. "He ain't lying."

"Ronnie's in jail," I said.

"Big boy jail," said Ames.

"And his name ain't Ronnie," Darrell added.

"That's no never mind to me," she said. "I want to see him."

"Do you know what happened to the one-eyed man who took you from the motel?" I asked.

"No."

"Would you like a drink?"

"Of what?"

"Whatever you want to drink," I said.

"I'd like an iced tea with lemon," she said.

"We'll stop," said Ames.

Victor drove to the Hob Nob on the corner of Seventeenth and Washington. The Hob Nob isn't trying to look like a fifties diner. It is a fifties diner. It hasn't changed in half a century. It's open air with a low roof, picnic tables, a counter with high stools and bustling waitresses who call you "honey." Smoking is permitted. You could be sitting next to two local landscape truckers, a couple who've just escaped from a drug bust, or a retired stockbroker from Chicago and his wife. There's not much privacy at the Hob Nob, but the food is good and the service is fast.

Darrell lived within walking distance of the Hob Nob, passed it almost every day, ate at it almost never. He ordered a burger and a Coke.

"I know what you want," Rachel said after I ordered her an iced tea with lemon.

Ames, Victor, Darrell, and I all wanted different things, none of which we could imagine Rachel providing.

"You want me to tell you that Ronnie killed my father."

"Did he?" Ames asked.

"No, he did not," she said, raising her head in indignation. "It was that other man."

"What other man?" asked Ames.

"The one who went out the window. I heard the noise, my father shouting. I was in my room. I opened the door and saw this man climbing out the window and Ronnie, all bloody, kneeling next to my father."

"What can you tell us about the man who went through the window?" I asked. "White, black, tall, short, young, old?"

"He was white and he had an orange aura," she said with confidence.

"Orange aura?" asked Darrell.

She turned to Darrell and said, "Orange is anger. Yours is green, nervous."

Connecting thoughts did not seem to be a strong element of Rachel's being.

"You watchin' too much TV," said Darrell. "A wife can't be forced to testify against her husband, but if she wants to nail his ass, it's party time. If you want to help him, you'd be best off sticking with the guy through the window and forgetting auras. Tell her, Fonesca."

"He's right," I said.

Her iced tea had arrived. She slowly removed the straw from its wrapper, dropped the wrapper in the black plastic ashtray on the table, and inserted the straw into her drink.

Rachel was a little slow in everything she did—thinking, talking, moving. My first thought was drugs, but my second thought was that heredity had not been kind. Or maybe it had. There was an almost somnambulatory calmness to the young woman. Daddy had bullied his way through life. His daughter was sleepwalking through it.

She sipped her drink loudly with sunken cheeks.

"Could your husband have killed your father, maybe with the other man's help?" I asked.

"You're trying to trick me, like the one-eyed man," she said coming up for air.

"The one-eyed man tried to trick you into saying Ronnie killed your father?"

"He did," she said emphatically. "But I told him no such thing. He was on television."

"The one-eyed man?"

"Yes. I watch television," she said. "Good, clean entertainment if you are discerning. *Rockford Files* on the old TV channel."

"He was on the *Rockford Files*?" Ames asked.

"What's the *Rockford Files*?" asked Darrell.

The marriage of Torcelli and Rachel had been made in heaven or in hell. He exhaled a slick veneer of deception and she floated on a vapor of ethereal innocence.

"Did he kill your father?" Ames asked.

"The one-eyed man?" she asked, bubbling the last of her iced tea through the straw.

"Your husband," I said.

She thought, looked down at her drink, and said, "May I have another one?"

I ordered her another iced tea. Rachel wasn't brilliant, but she wasn't a fool. If she was playing with us, we were losing.

"Ronnie," I repeated. "Did he kill your father?"

She sucked on her lower lip for a few seconds as she considered her answer and said, "I wouldn't have blamed him if he did. My father was not a good man. He never hurt me, but he wasn't a good man. No, he was definitely a bad man. Ronnie saved me from him. When I finish my second iced tea, I'd like to see him."

"You're very rich now," I tried.

"Lawyer said. Policeman said. Man with one eye said," she said. "Ronnie married me for the money."

"He did?" I asked.

"He did," she said as she worked on her drink. "He never denied it. He said when my father died we would be rich and he would be a good husband. Ronnie's a looker and though I am somewhat plain and wistful, he treats me nicely and I tell him he is smart and beautiful which he delights in hearing provided I don't overdo it, and he pleases me in bed or on the floor. He likes sex."

"More than I need to know," said Darrell with a mouthful of hamburger.

"Did Ronnie kill your father?" I tried once more.

"No. I saw the other man do it."

"You actually saw him do it?" asked Ames.

"Yes. He was all bloody. He was there earlier. Had words with my father, who called him a 'shit-bastard-cocksucker.'"

"And you didn't recognize the killer?" I asked.

"I had a little dog and his name was . . . ?" she said with a smile.

"Blue," said Ames.

"Yes," she said.

"Old song," said Ames.

"New suspect," I said.

"Please take me to Ronnie now, after I pee," Rachel said.

Victor got the washroom key and walked with her to the rear of the Hob Nob, where he waited outside the door.

"Lady's on a cloud," said Darrell finishing off his burger. "What time's the next cloud? I might want to hitch a ride."

"Believe her?" Ames asked.

"You?" I answered.

"She didn't see Berrigan kill her father, just heard it," said Ames.

"Or maybe didn't hear it. Or maybe just wants to get her husband off the hook and the murder of her father blamed on a dead man."

"She's just acting?" asked Ames.

"If she is, she's really good."

"Ain't nobody that good," said Darrell.

"Yes," I said. "There is."

16

"He's too smart for that, the little bastard," Detective Ettiene Viviase said.

He was seated behind his desk at police headquarters on Main Street. Ames and I were across from him, in wooden chairs that needed a complete overhaul and serious superglue to forestall their inevitable collapse.

Victor and Darrell were at Cold Stone ice cream store, across the street and half a block away.

Viviase was talking about Dwight Torcelli.

His door was open. Voices carried and echoed from the hallway beyond, where the arrested and abused sat after they got past the first line of questioning and into the presence of a detective.

"The weapon we found in Torcelli's apartment is a now-bloody wooden meat pounder."

"Tenderizer," I said.

Viviase was working on a plastic cup of coffee of unknown vintage.

"The girl makes little in the way of sense."

"Some things she said make sense," I said.

"What?"

"Berrigan."

"Says her father knew Berrigan, used him as a greeter at a weekend sale at his Toyota dealership in Bradenton."

"He owned a Toyota dealership?" I said.

"Now she owns it and if luck or you turn up something to keep Torcelli from going to jail, the Horvecki estate will be his too. And the weirdest goddamn thing is that they both really seem to like each other. She said she'd remarry him."

I said nothing. I didn't want to open the door to Alana Legerman and possibly to Sally and possibly to who knows how many others.

"Treats her like a nine-year-old," said Viviase, finishing his coffee and looking into the cup to see if he had missed something.

"She says Berrigan killed her father," I said.

"Convenient," Viviase said, looking into his empty cup for some answers.

He dropped the cup into the garbage can behind his desk.

"Williams and Pepper," I said.

"You make them sound like a law firm, a men's clothing store, or a mail-order Christmas catalog."

Someone screamed down the hall, not close, but loud enough. I couldn't tell if it was a cackle, a laugh, or an expression of pain.

"Williams and Pepper both have solid alibis for the times of death of both the Horvecki and Berrigan murders."

"They weren't each other's alibis, were they?"

"I'm in a good mood, Fonesca. Truly. I don't look it, but I'm in a good mood. My daughter, I've discovered, has not been fooling around with our heartthrob prisoner."

"That's good."

"No," he said. "She's been fooling around with a high school senior. She assures me and her mother that 'fooling around' is all that she's been doing, whereas if she were fooling around with Ronnie the words would take on a whole new meaning. So, I'm in a good mood. I'm waiting for a DNA report on Horvecki and the blood on the meat pounder."

"You checking Berrigan's DNA too?"

"We are."

"I think the blood on the tenderizer is Berrigan's, not Horvecki's."

"Why would our boy want to kill Berrigan?"

"Maybe he wouldn't, but somebody else might and then hide the murder weapon where it was sure to be found in Torcelli's apartment.

"Life is complicated," I said.

"Life is uncooperative."

"Yes."

"Can I talk to him?"

"He doesn't want to see you. He's only talking to his wife and his lawyer—the lawyer courtesy of your very own D. Elliot Corkle and his daughter, the same daughter who put up the charming Ronnie's bail."

The first words Ames uttered since we entered Viviase's office were, "We'd best go."

"Fine," said Viviase, turning to me. "Let me know if you and your sidekick find more of Ronnie's or Torcelli's wives or girlfriends kicking around."

His eyes didn't meet mine but I sensed something and that something was the name of Sally Porovsky.

Rachel didn't want a ride. She asked the receptionist at the jail to call her a cab so she could be taken to the nearest hotel, which happened to be the Ritz-Carlton on Tamiami Trail just outside of downtown. The Ritz-Carlton was about a three-minute ride from the jail. She told Ames, who was waiting for her, that her husband had reminded her she was rich and could now stay anywhere she liked and didn't even need to pick up the clothes she had left at her father's house.

"How did she seem to you?" I asked.

"Something on her mind wherever her mind was," Ames said as he, Victor, Darrell, and I walked over to the pizza shop next to the Hollywood 20 Movie Theaters on Main Street.

"So," said Darrell, "who killed those two guys and who shot at me and you, Fonesca?"

"I'm not sure," I said.

"But you think?" said Darrell.

"Yeah," I said.

Victor said nothing. Victor was extending his silence. He was waiting for something, something for me to say or do, or something he had to decide to do, or something that came down from heaven or up from hell.

"Movie?" asked Darrell as we all shared a large sausage pizza.

"Next week," I said.

"When's the last time you went to a movie, Fonesca?" Darrell asked.

It had been June 6, 2003. Catherine and I went to see *Seabiscuit* at the Hillside Theater. We both liked it. We usually liked the same movies. Since then the only movies I had seen were on videotape or television, almost all made before 1955, almost all in black and white.

"I don't remember," I said.

"We're right next door to the fucking place," Darrell said. "They've got *Saw 8* or *9* or something. And you, Ames McKinney, what was the last time you went to a movie in a real, honest-to-god theater?"

"Can't say I remember," Ames said. "Maybe forty, fifty years ago."

"I need some help here," said Darrell. "Victor, you, when? Or don't they have movies in China?"

"I've never been to China," said Victor. "I went to this movie the night before last."

"That settles the issue," said Darrell. "The Chinese guy who's not from China and me are going to see *Saw*."

"No," said Victor. "I won't see movies in which women or children are killed."

"Fonesca, I'm pleading with you," said Darrell.

"All right," I said. "I'll go."

"I guess I will, too," said Ames.

"Depends," Victor said.

We spent two hours in darkness watching beautiful women with too much makeup saying they were witches and trying to kill bearded guys who looked like Vikings by sending monkey-faced creatures riding on short but fast rhinos with short fire-spitting spears in their hands. Darrell drank a seemingly gallon-sized Coke and a giant popcorn.

When we got out, it was dark.

"Help that near-crazy lady," Darrell said as we let him off outside the apartment building on Martin Luther King in which he lived with his mother.

I didn't answer. Neither did Ames. We drove off with Victor.

"Someone beat Horvecki to death," Ames said. "Someone killed Blue Berrigan almost in front of our eyes. Why? Who?"

"And someone shot Darrell in the back and put a pellet through the window of Jeffrey Augustine's car," I said. "Who? Why?"

Victor parked in the narrow driveway next to the house. We all got out.

"You've got some ideas," said Ames.

"An idea," I said.

"Partners, right?"

"Right," I said.

"Ideas?"

I told him. He rolled his scooter out from under the stairs and drove back to his room at the back of the Texas Bar and Grill.

Victor took a shower and then settled into his sleeping bag in the corner of the office. I got into my black Venice beach shorts and my *X Files* black T-shirt and spent about an hour in bed, just looking up at the ceiling. I considered calling Sally. I didn't. Sleep snuck up on me, as it usually does just when I'm convinced insomnia will have me waiting for the sun to rise.

No wandering preachers or wayward policemen woke me. No new great ideas came to me in dreams. I remembered no dreams. I woke up three minutes after six in the morning. My *X Files* shirt was soaked with sweat, though the room felt cold. I got up, dressed in clean jeans and a plain blue T-shirt, and picked up the Memphis Reds gym bag I had purchased for two dollars at The Women's Exchange.

In the outer office, Victor was tossing on his sleeping bag. Half of him was on the bag. The other half was on the floor. I made it out the door without waking him and went down the stairs to retrieve my bicycle from the shed under the stairs.

The morning was cool, maybe in the seventies. The sky was clear and traffic on 301 was lighter than usual. The YMCA was on Main Street in the Mall next to the Hollywood 20 Movie Theaters.

I saw a few people I knew as I did my curls with fifteen-pound weights. It felt better after I got them done and began my second set. Then I did crunches, bends, and heartbreakers until my shoulders began to ache.

After I finished my workout, I showered, put on my clothes, and stepped out onto Main Street where someone took a shot at me.

I stood on the sidewalk for a few seconds, not quite registering what had happened. A trio of teens passed me laughing, noticing nothing. An elderly woman with a walker slowly crossed the street, looking forward and moving slowly. Nothing seemed unusual until the second shot fell short, pinging off the hood of a shiny new red Honda Accord a few feet away from where I was standing. I could see the small dent in the car showing silver metal under the red paint. With the second shot I held up my gym bag and bent at the knees. Something thudded into the bag I held in front of my face. I ducked for cover alongside the Honda, hoping the shots were coming from the other side of the street and not from either side of me.

I sat on the sidewalk, my back to the car, my Cubs cap about to fall in my lap. A couple in their fifties came down the sidewalk. They tried not to look at me.

"Down," I said. "Get down."

I motioned with my hand. They ignored me, probably considering me an early-morning drunk. They walked on. No more shots.

After a few minutes I hadn't been killed, so I stood up carefully and looked around. There were places to hide, doorways to consider, rooftops, corners to duck around. I looked at the front of my gym bag. A pellet was lodged in the fabric. I pulled it out, pocketed it, and went to get my bicycle from where it was chained around a lamppost. There was a Dillard's bag dangling from the handlebars. I looked inside and found a folded handwritten note.

Should you survive, think no ill of me.
Folly is as folly always does.
Folly is and never was completely free.

Stop or hear again the bullet's buzz
and it will be as if Fonesca never was.

"High school kid," said Ames, looking down at the poem that lay flat on my desk. "Maybe a girl."

"Real men don't write poetry?" I asked.

"They might write it, but they don't show it to anybody."

"Why write a poem?" I said. "Why not just a note saying, 'Stop trying to help Ronnie Gerall or I'll shoot at you again and next time I won't miss.' "

"Guns are easy to get," Ames said. "Why shoot at you with a pellet gun, especially after having been less than gentle, beating two men to death?"

"Maybe," said Victor who stood looking out the window at nothing.

Ames and I both looked at him.

"Maybe," Victor continued, "the person shooting at you is not the killer of Horvecki and Berrigan."

With my Bank of America pen, we made a list of everyone we could think of who would know I was trying to find a suspect other than the former Ronnie Gerall. The list was long.

"Where do we start?" Ames asked.

I told him and he said, "Dangerous out there for you."

"Whoever is shooting at me," I said, "is a rotten shot. Plus, he won't shoot at me again till he knows I haven't dropped the case."

"She," said Ames.

"Right," I said. "He or she."

"Let's do it," said Ames and we went out the door and down to my car.

Victor sat in the back, Ames next to me. I turned the key and the Saturn powered on with something approaching a purr.

"Worked on it early this morning, before church," Ames said.

"Sounds great," I said.

"It'll do," he said.

I didn't ask Ames what church he belonged to, though I knew he would tell me. I didn't ask Ames if he had a weapon under his well-worn tan suede jacket, though I knew there was one there.

We got to the church in Cortez just before noon. Services were over, but the Reverend Jack Pepper was delivering a pensive message on station WTLW.

"Vengeance is mine, sayeth the Lord," came Pepper's voice over the radio as we sat listening to the man in the small studio in the building just beyond the tall metal mesh gate. "But we are the vessels of the Lord, the instruments of the Lord. What if the Lord calls upon us to seek his vengeance?"

He paused for a few seconds to let his listeners consider what he had just said. I imagined a 1930s farm couple, Dad in his overalls, Mom wiping her hands on her apron, son on the floor looking up at an old Atwater Kent radio as if it might suddenly turn into a television set. I wondered how many people actually listened to Jack Pepper.

"Ponder this further," Pepper said. "How will we know when it is the Lord commanding us? We have free will for the Lord has given it to us along with many of the blessings of life including the bounty of the seas right in our own waters—fish, shrimp, crab, scallops, lobster. When are we really hearing the Lord? I'll answer this after these messages from the good Christian business in our own neighborhood."

I got out of the car after telling Victor to get behind the wheel and Ames to stand by the gate and be ready. I wanted to talk to Jack Pepper alone.

As Ames and I walked to the gate, I could hear Victor behind us, listening to Jack Pepper urging his good listeners to buy their bait and tackle at Smitty's Bait and Tackle.

I pushed the button next to the gate. Pepper, complete in suit and tie, came out, told the dog to go sit "over there," and let me in.

"You find something that will help Gerall?" he asked opening the gate to let me in.

"Maybe," I said. "I've got a few questions."

"I've got to get back on the air," he said, motioning for me to follow him. I did.

There was no one but Pepper and me in the reception room, and through the glass window I saw no one in the studio. Pepper opened the studio door, hurried in and sat just as the commercial ended. The speaker connected to the studio crackled with age, but it worked. Pepper put on his earphones, hit a switch and said, "You are waiting for an answer to the question I posed before the break, and I'll give it to you. You'll know that it is the voice of the Lord because your heart is cleansed and you follow the Ten Commandments and the teachings of Jesus. The wayward will hear the voice of the Devil; the good will hear the voice of the Lord."

He said he would take calls if anyone wished to ask questions or give testimony. He gave the number and repeated it.

The phone rang.

"A call," Pepper said hopefully. He picked up the phone in the studio and said, "Jesus and I are listening to you."

At 1 p.m. Jack Pepper signed off, saying, "WTLW will return to the air tomorrow morning at ten. Join us if you can and trust in the Lord."

Back in the reception area, Jack Pepper said, "We've got Dr Pepper, Mr. Pibb, canned iced tea, and all kinds of Coke in the refrigerator."

I declined. He moved behind the receptionist and manager's desk and came up with a can of Coke, which he opened, drank from, and said, "Parched."

"Which of you was at Horvecki's house the night he was murdered?"

He swished some Coke around in his mouth wondering if he should lie.

"Rachel Horvecki and Ronnie Gerall both say they saw a pickup truck in front of Horvecki's house that night," I went on. "There was a man in it. You or Williams?"

"And if I say neither?"

"Then you'd be lying and Ronnie would be one step closer to death row."

"I think the Lord sent you," he said softly. "It was me. We'd been watching Horvecki's house whenever we could, waiting for him to commit a new abomination. A man cannot help being the creature the Lord created, but he can do battle with his nature."

"You saw and did what?"

He took another drink, let out an "aah," and said, "A few minutes after midnight I hear voices inside the house, voices filled with hate. And then a thudding sound. Ronnie comes down the street just about then and goes in the house. Man in a watch cap climbs out the window at the side of the house and goes running down the street. Ronnie comes outside like a flash, looks around, and goes back inside."

"How loud were the noises and voices inside the house before Ronnie showed up?" I asked.

"Loud enough," he said. "Police came just about then, went in, and you know the rest."

"How long between the time Ronnie came out to look around and the time the police arrived?"

"Less than a minute," he said. "No noise. Police there almost instantly, which could mean—"

"Whoever called 911 did it before Ronnie got there," I said.

"The murderer called 911?" asked Pepper.

"Where was Williams that night?" I asked.

"I'm not my brother's keeper," he said.

"Did either Ronnie or Rachel see you in front of the house?"

"Probably," he said. "I wasn't hiding. I wanted Horvecki to know I was there watching. The police will want a statement from me, won't they?"

"They will," I said.

"There is a restraining order against Essau and me. I prayed it wouldn't be necessary for me to come forward," he said. "I prayed that the real killer would step forth or be exposed before I had to speak out, but it looks as if the Lord has chosen me to speak the truth. It will be in the newspapers won't it?"

"Yes. I'm sorry."

He clasped his hands, closed his eyes, and dropped his head in prayer.

I left the building.

The dog got up, looked at me, and growled deeply. I wouldn't make it to the gate if she didn't want me to, and she didn't look as if she wanted me to. I looked at the door. Pepper did not come out.

"Steady on, girl," Ames called.

The big dog took slow, stalking steps in my direction. Pepper still did not appear. The dog rocked back, ready to pounce, when Ames's voice boomed with authority.

"I said steady on."

The dog looked at him as he took another step toward me. Ames came out with a small gun, which slipped out of his sleeve and into his hand.

I hadn't moved, but the dog had. She was a few steps from me, now, and growling again. Ames fired into the air and the dog scampered off to a far corner. Then Pepper appeared in the doorway of the building. He looked at me and Ames and then at the dog.

"You shot her," he said.

"No," I said. "She's just frightened."

"So are we all," said Pepper. "So are we all."

17

A lean white heron stood on one leg atop the rusting pickup truck on Zo Hirsch's lawn. The bird looked at me, and I looked back. He considered putting his foot back down but changed his mind as I walked up the cracked concrete path to the front door.

"You," Hirsch said opening the door and looking up at me.

"Me," I admitted.

"You've got the papers, right? More courts and lawyers after me? Okay, bring it on."

I handed him the envelope with the summons enclosed.

"They can't get blood out of a banana and I'm a banana."

"Your wife?" I asked.

"And the third-rate shortstop," he said. "I made an offer they couldn't refuse, and they refused it. I'm down to selling off some of my collection. Interested in buying a genuine Cleveland Indians sweatshirt once worn by Larry Doby?"

"How much?"

"Two thousand."

"What do you have under a hundred?"

"Baseball autographed by George Altman, a Cub. Led the National League with twelve triples in 1962."

"How much?"

"My pride is gone. I'll take what you offer over fifty dollars."

I took out my wallet, found two twenties and a ten and handed it to him.

"Can we talk?" I asked.

"We are talking."

"Can I come in?"

"What the hell."

He pocketed the money and stood back to let me in. I moved into the living room and sat down. Black baseball players in poses and smiles looked down at me. Zo Hirsch, summons and the cash I had given him in hand, hurried off to the back of the house and returned almost immediately with the baseball. He tossed it to me. Then he sat in the chair across from mine.

"You want something to drink? I'm down to store-brand ersatz cola and root beer from a dollar store. It tastes vaguely like something besides tap water."

"Tempting," I said, "but no, thanks."

"Simply put," he said, "what do you want from me? There isn't much left, but what there is, with the exception of a few treasures, is for sale."

"Horvecki," I said. "You were his only friend."

"Friend," he repeated the word, more to himself than to me. "We talked baseball, had drinks."

"He talk about anything else? What did he care about?"

"Guns," said Zo Hirsch, "and his daughter, Rachel. I only saw her a few times a couple of years ago. Cute kid, too skinny, didn't talk. My ex-wife was not too skinny and she could talk, mostly in Spanish. She called me 'Pequeño.' You now what that means?"

"Little," I said.

"At first she said it with a smile and a touch. Later she said it with a hiss and folded arms. A piece of work."

"Horvecki," I reminded him. "What else?"

"He liked the ladies. They didn't like him. He paid for companionship. Come to think of it, so did I."

Zo Hirsch sat back in the chair and drummed his fingers on the arms.

"Pine View and Bright Futures," I said.

"Oh yeah, almost forgot. He hated them both. His kid got turned down by Pine View. He was determined to bring the school and that Bright Futures program down. He didn't talk about it much, but when he did, that was what he said. He supplemented his daughter's education by teaching her how to ride, shoot, learn his truth about history, which was wacky. Next question."

"Wacky?"

"Phil had a long list of groups he hated. The School Board, the ACLU, the Democratic Party, lawyers, psychiatrists, teamsters, television writers, professional tennis players—"

"Enough," I said. "I get it."

"You gotta give him credit," said Zo Hirsch. "The man knew how to hate."

"Your friend?"

"No," he said. "But the man knew baseball."

"He was ruthless in business," I said.

"He was a giant five-story steamroller in business. He crushed and was proud of it."

"What was in it for you?"

Zo Hirsch squirmed a little in his seat, shook his head and looked toward the recently repaired front window.

"He bought baseball memorabilia from me, paid more than top dollar, never even questioned authenticity. Philip Horvecki was a substantial part of my income."

"He was a—"

"Sucker," said Zo Hirsch, "but he knew it. I think he was buying a friend. I was happy to sell. The guy really did know baseball and he served good lunches."

"Why you? There are plenty of people for sale."

"He liked showing me off," said Zo Hirsch. "It made people uncomfortable. A little black man. He liked making people uncomfortable. One more question. Then I've got to go see my lawyer to find out if there's anything to salvage. I hope he suggests that I hire a hit man and get rid of my ex-wife and the shortstop. You on that bicycle again?"

"No. I've got a car."

"Good. You can give me a ride. On the way, I'll give you my all-time favorite Cubs lineup and you can do the same."

I put the slightly tarnished George Altman autographed ball in the glove compartment and drove Zo Hirsch to an office building on Orange, just north of Ringling.

When Hirsch got out of the car, he hesitated and said, "Phil Horvecki was a shit, but he was my friend, sort of, the poor bastard."

I watched him walk to the big double-thick glass doors and reach up for the handle. He pulled the door open with dignity and strength and disappeared inside.

I wondered how he planned to get back home.

After I called her, Alana Legerman met me at the FourGees Coffee Shop on Beneva and Webber. She was reluctant. I was persuasive. I didn't try to tell her that I was still trying to save Ronnie. I told her I wanted to talk to her about her son.

The lunch crowd had cleared out. I had a choice of the bright, sunny room where there were small tables, but I chose the back room, dark and minimally plush, with music piped in at a level where one could still have a conversation.

She came in after I did, just as the last customers, three women, moved out of the side room and left. She saw me, walked over, and sat, hands in her lap. She wore a light blue dress with short sleeves and a black belt with a big silver buckle. She was doing Grace Kelly ice princess, and she was good at it.

"I'm waiting," she said.

A lean girl, barely out of her teens, came in to take our order.

"Coffee and a scone," I said.

"Prune?"

"Plain."

The waitress turned to Alana, who said, "Tea, mint."

"That's it?" asked the girl.

I said it was, and Alana went back to her patient waiting pose.

"Does Greg own a pellet rifle?"

"My son owns whatever he wants. His grandfather doesn't deny him anything."

"So, he owns a pellet rifle?"

She shrugged.

"Who knows? I've never seen him with one."

"Why does Greg want to save Ronnie Gerall?"

"They're friends. That's how I had the bad fortune to meet Ronnie."

"What kind of friends?" I asked.

This time she cocked her head back in a becoming look of surprise.

"You're suggesting my son and Ronnie had a homosexual relationship?"

"No. That didn't occur to me, but I'll think about it. Did Ronnie rule in their relationship?"

"Probably," she said.

"Have you ever seen Ronnie act violent?"

"No."

"Does Greg have any other friends besides Winston Graeme?"

"No. I don't think so."

"When did they become friends?"

"About a year ago. No, two years ago. Winn Graeme is very protective of my son. My father and I are both very grateful for it, though I must confess that I don't understand why the boy puts up with Greg."

"Greg keeps punching him in the arm," I said.

"A token of my son's inability to come up with a painless way of expressing his friendship. His therapist assures me that when he gets to Duke he will mature. What is this all about?"

Our coffee and tea came. I picked up the check. We drank in silence for a few seconds, and then I said, "Does Greg write poetry?"

"Poetry? You ask the damnedest questions. Greg writes poetry, short stories, does sketches and paintings that could earn him a scholarship, and he reads at a rate that is not a treat to watch. He doesn't just read. He devours books."

"Do you and your father want Ronnie to go to prison for murder?"

"We'll be satisfied to have him sent away for pretending to be a high school student or, better yet, whatever he did in Texas that he and his wife ran away from."

"Your whole family hired me to find evidence that he didn't kill Horvecki."

"My father and I have changed our minds," she said, finishing her coffee. "The job has changed. If you find evidence that he killed Horvecki or that other man . . ."

"Blue Berrigan."

"Blue Berrigan," she repeated with a shake of her head. "What kind of people have we gotten ourselves involved with? No answer is required."

I gave none.

"Are we finished?" she asked.

"Yes."

"Good. I have another appointment."

She got up, picked up her purse, and said, "Nail the bastard."

"Someone else said the same thing."

"A woman?" she asked.

"Yes."

"Of course," she said and strode away.

When she was gone, I made a call and got through after two rings.

"This is Lew Fonesca."

"I know," said Winn Graeme.

"I'd like to see you."

"When?"

"Now."

"Where?"

"FourGees. It's—"

"I know where it is. You have something?"

"Maybe," I said.

"I'll be right there."

I had a refill of coffee and waited, listening to Rufus Wainwright sing "Not Ready to Love."

It took him twenty-five minutes before he came into the backroom. He adjusted his glasses to be sure I was the person he was looking for.

"I'm missing golf practice," he said, sitting down in the same seat Alana Legerman had been in. "I had to tell the coach and tell him my mother called and said she wasn't feeling well."

"He believed you?"

"I don't know. He didn't call me a liar. I don't like lying. What's going on? Why isn't Greg here?"

"You go everywhere together?"

"Pretty much," he said. "We're friends."

The waitress came back to take our order and get a good look at Winn Graeme.

"Are you Winston Graeme?" she asked.

"Yes," he said.

"I saw you play Riverview," she said. "You had twenty-four points. My boyfriend was Terry Beacham, but we're not together anymore."

It was a clear invitation, but not to Winn, who said, "You have a caffeine-free diet cola?"

"Just Diet Coke."

"I'll have that," he said, looking at me and not at the girl, who got the message and moved away.

She had forgotten to ask if I wanted a refill or something else.

"Why?" I asked.

"Why what?"

"Why are you and Greg friends?"

"He's smart and we get along. Sometimes you can't explain things like friendship."

"I think I can explain it," I said. "How much does Greg's grandfather pay you to take care of his grandson and pretend to be his friend."

Winn put his head down and then brought it up, adjusting his glasses again.

"Mr. Corkle pays me fifteen hundred dollars a month in cash."

"How long has he been doing this?"

"Since Greg's sixteenth birthday party. My father lost his job when I was fifteen. He had a drinking problem. He was sixty-one when he lost the job. Since then he's made some money at home on his eBay trades. Some money, but not a lot, and my mother stands on her feet eight hours a day selling clothes at Beals. I need a scholarship. I need Bright Futures. I need fifteen hundred dollars a month. Wherever Greg goes to college, I'll go to college so the money won't stop."

"What else would you like?"

"I'd like it if Greg didn't find out about his mother and Ronnie and about me taking money from his grandfather."

"You think I'll tell him?"

"I don't know," he said.

"I won't tell him. You own a pellet gun?"

"No, why?"

"Someone's been trying to shoot me with one."

"If I were trying to shoot you would I tell you I had a gun?" he asked.

"Good point. People sometimes admit things they shouldn't."

A man in his late forties or early fifties and a woman who might have been his daughter came in the back room. He was wearing a business suit and tie. She was wearing less than she should have been. The man looked at Winn Graeme and me. Then the two of them sat on a sofa in the shadows under the speaker.

"You know that girl?" I asked.

"Why?"

"She nodded at you."

Winn shook his head before saying, "I know her. She graduated from Riverview last year. She was a cheerleader. Her name is Hope something."

"Small town," I said, looking at the pair, who were whispering now, the girl shaking her head.

"That's not her father," Winn said.

"How do you know?"

"That's Mr. Milikin, lawyer downtown. Wife, four kids. He's on the board of everything in the county."

I looked at the couple. Mr. Milikin looked as if he were perspiring.

His eyes darted toward the archway leading into the other room. He didn't want to see any familiar faces.

"Ronnie's going to be like that if he lives long enough," Winn said.

"Like Milikin?"

"No."

"Horvecki," I said.

"We didn't kill him."

"We?"

"Greg and I. We tried to talk to him a few times. So did others. Didn't do any good."

"You went to his house?"

"Once. He wouldn't let us in, threatened to call the police if we didn't go away. He said he had the right to bear arms and protect himself, his family, and his property. He said, 'Under my roof, we know how to use a gun!'"

"And?"

"We went away. Is that all?"

I looked at him and he forced himself to look back for an instant before giving his glasses another adjustment.

"That's all," I said.

Winn Graeme stood up, started to turn, and then turned back to me to say, "Don't hurt Greg."

"That a warning?"

"A plea."

He didn't look toward Mr. Milikin and the former cheerleader as he left. The girl glanced at him, but Milikin was so busy pleading his case that he didn't notice. He just kept perspiring.

I had almost enough information now. There was only one more person I had to see. I paid the waitress, who said, "He's a fantastic basketball player. Jumps like a black guy. You know where he's going to college?"

"Yes," I said and went around the tables and through the door.

I was careful. I could have been more careful. Ann Hurwitz would know why I didn't exercise more caution. Pellets might fly. I might catch one in the eye like Augustine. I was reasonably sure of who the shooter would be, but Augustine was the person who could make it a certainty.

The shot didn't come until I opened the door to get into the Saturn, which was wedged between two SUVs at the far end of the lot, a few spaces from the exit on Webber.

The shot didn't come from a pellet gun.

The first bullet shattered the driver's side window showering shards on the seat. I turned to look in the direction from which I thought the bullet had been fired.

Something came at me from around one of the SUVs. It hit me, knocked me backward to the ground, and landed on me. I panted for breath. A second shot came but I didn't hear it hit the ground or my car or the pavement.

I lay there for a beat, the weight on my chest and stomach, an arm covering my chest, and looked up to see, inches from my nose, Victor Woo.

"You all right?" he asked.

I tried to answer but couldn't speak. He understood and rolled off to the side. I started to get up but he held a hand out to keep me down. He listened, watched for about half a minute, and then helped me up.

"He's gone," he said.

The shooter wasn't trying to frighten me off anymore. We had gone beyond that, to murder.

"I followed you," Victor said at my side.

"Thanks," I said trying to catch my breath.

"That last shot might have killed you," he said.

"Might have, yes," I acknowledged.

"It would have hit you."

He was trying to make a point, but I wasn't sure what it was. He turned around so I could see where the bullet had entered his right arm through the red Florida State University sweatshirt he was wearing, the arm he had draped over my chest. There was remarkably little blood.

"It ricocheted off the ground before it hit me," he said.

"I'll drive you to the ER."

"No," he said. "I'll stop somewhere, clean it, put on a bandage and some tape. The bullet just scratched my arm. It's not inside me."

Clichés abound from old movies. "It's just a flesh wound." "I've had worse bites from a Louisiana mosquito."

"Suit yourself," I said.

"I want to go home," he said. "I saved your life. It is all I can do. It doesn't make up for killing your wife, but it's all I can do."

"I forgave you for killing Catherine."

"But when you said it before, you didn't mean it," he said. "This time you do. I've been away from home too long."

I reached out to shake his hand. He winced as he briefly held my grip.

"My bedroll is in my car," he added. "I'm leaving from here. If I can ever be of any service . . ."

"I know where to find you," I said, but we both knew I would never call.

"You know who's trying to kill you?"

"Yes," I said.

"Stop them," he said.

And he was gone. I held up my hands. I felt calm, but my hands were both shaking. Can the body be afraid when the mind isn't? I knew the mind could be afraid when the body of a policeman went through the door of an apartment where a crazed father held a gun to his ten-year-old daughter's head, or when a fireman made a dash into a burning building where he heard the cry of a cat. It was a question for Ann.

When I opened the car door, I saw the folded sheet of paper with the words:

I whisper your name in the book of one more tomorrow
knowing your yesterdays were filled with sorrow.
Migrating birds soar South then North again.
North into night flying over your solitary den.
Luck will not last.
Move fast.
Move past.

Thou hast
No more tomorrows.

I cleaned up as much of the glass on the seat and the floor as I could and got in my car. Once I was seated I saw more shining shards on the passenger seat. I swept them on the floor with my hand and called Ames.

"Real bullets this time," I said.

"You all right?"

"Yes."

"Same shooter?"

"Yes."

"Sure?"

"I'm sure. Where are you?"

"The office."

"I'll pick you up in ten minutes. A weapon would be in order."

"Got one," he said.

When I got to the house, Ames was coming down the steps. The day was cool enough that his lightweight leather jacket wouldn't draw attention and whatever weapon he was carrying would remain hidden.

"Watch out for the glass," I said as he started to get in the car.

"I'll fix that window when we're done," he said swiping away at some of the glass bits I had missed.

He sat, looked at me and said, "Let's do it."

18

"Took you a while," Corkle said, opening the door. "Come in."

He was wearing tan slacks, a dark lightweight sweater and a blue blazer. Well dressed for a man who never left his house.

Ames and I followed him as he led the way to the rear of the house and onto a tiled, screen-covered lanai. The kidney-shaped pool was filled with clear blue-green water.

A glass pitcher of something with ice and slices of lemon in it sat on a dark wooden table. There were five glasses.

Behind the table stood Jeffrey Augustine, black eye patch and all.

"It's just lemonade," said Corkle. "Mr. Augustine will pour you both a glass, and we can sit and talk."

Both Ames and I took a glass of lemonade from Augustine. I took off my Cubs cap and put it in my back pocket.

"I feel like one of those rich bad guys in a fifties movie," said Corkle, glass in hand, sitting on a wooden lawn chair that matched the table. "Like what's his name, Fred . . ."

"Clark?" I said, sitting next to him.

Ames stood where he could watch Augustine, who was also standing. Augustine wasn't drinking.

"Yeah, that's the guy," said Corkle. "Bald, heavyset sometimes, a little mustache. That's the guy. Fonesca, D. Elliot Corkle is not the bad guy here."

"You kidnapped Rachel Horvecki," I said.

"Mr. Augustine brought her here to protect her," said Corkle, looking at the lemonade after taking a long drink. "She came willingly, and you two executed a flawless rescue."

"Protect her from what?"

"She's rich now," he said. "Someone might be inclined to take a shot at her or drop a safe on her in the hope and expectation of getting her money."

"Ronnie."

"Ronnie Gerall, otherwise known as Dwight Torcelli," he said. "I've known Rachel since she was a baby. Always been a little bit in outer space. Her father put her there. Good kid. She deserves better than Torcelli. So does my daughter."

"Someone tried to kill me about an hour ago in the parking lot at Beneva and Webber."

"With a pellet gun?" he asked looking at Augustine whose fingers automatically reached for his eye patch.

"With a rifle."

"You know why?" he asked, drinking more lemonade.

"Because I've been talking to people."

"People?"

"People who told me who killed Philip Horvecki and Blue Berrigan."

Corkle held up his lemonade and said, "Pure lemonade with small pieces of lemon evenly distributed throughout. Good, huh?"

"Very good," I said.

"Made with the Corkle Mini-Multi Mixer Dispenser. Put in the water, the ice, lemons, push a button. It works almost silently; you just place the individual glass under the spout, and it fills automatically. Same perfect taste every time. Works with lemons, oranges, berries, any fruit or vegetable. Cleans with one easy rinse. I like orange-banana."

"You know who killed them," I said.

"I'll give you both a Corkle Mini-Multi Mixer Dispenser when you leave," he said. "Parting gift. Much as D. Elliot Corkle enjoys your company, he doesn't think we can be friends. Are you owed more money for your troubles?"

"No," I said.

"If there's nothing else . . ."

"Nothing else."

Ames had placed his empty glass on the table and folded his arms in front of him.

At the front door, we waited while Corkle got us each a boxed Corkle Mini-Multi Mixer Dispenser. Ames handed his to me. They were lighter than they looked.

When we cleared the door, Ames said, "I'll take that now." He took his Corkle Mini-Multi Mixer Dispenser and added, "He was armed. Augustine."

"I know," I said.

"I think it best if I keep my hands free till we're away. Where to now?" Ames asked.

"To see a baby and get something to eat."

"I'll watch for snipers," he said.

About a block from Corkle's I said, "Victor's gone."

"Where?"

"Home."

"Good."

"He saved my life when the shooting started."

"He was waiting for something like that."

"You knew?"

"I figured," said Ames.

"I should have," I said.

Flo was home alone with Catherine who toddled toward us, arms out for Ames to pick her up, which he did.

"Gifts for you," I said, handing her both Pulp-O-Matics.

"Those are the things I saw on television years ago," she said. "Almost bought one then. My friend Molly Sternheiser had one. Said it was a piece of shit. Tried to get her money back. Never did. Now, for some reason, I've got one and a backup."

Flo had given up her flow of curse words when Adele and Catherine came into her life. Every once in a while, however, a small colorful noun bursts out unbidden.

"Don't try to understand," I said. "Just mix."

She reached up, took my cap from my head and handed it to me. I pocketed it.

The music throughout the house wasn't blaring, but it was as present as always.

"That's Hank Snow," she said. "'Moving On.'"

Flo was wearing one of her leather skirts and a white blouse. She only had six or seven rings on her fingers. She was dressing down.

"Hungry?" she asked.

"Yes," I said, watching Catherine and Ames, who were almost face to face and both very serious.

The baby reached up and touched his nose with pudgy fingers.

"I'll find something to eat," said Flo.

"Adele?"

"School," she said. "How about chili? Got a lot left over from dinner yesterday."

"Fine," I said.

She went to the kitchen while I sat and listened to Hank Snow and watched Catherine and Ames. After a minute or so he handed the baby to me and went toward the kitchen to help Flo.

Catherine was pink and pretty, like her mother. She sat on my lap and started gently bumping her head against my chest until Flo called, "Come and get it!"

The chili was good, not too spicy. We drank Diet Cokes and talked.

Catherine in her high chair worked on crackers. I watched her. I was here for a few minutes of sanity.

I told Flo that Ames and I were now officially partners.

"That a fact?" she said.

"Fact," Ames confirmed.

"How's the new place working out?"

"Fine," I said.

Ames ate his chili straight. I filled mine with crumbled crackers.

I had been aware for some time that if Ames indicated something beyond friendship in his relationship with Flo, she would be receptive. Flo was somewhere around sixty-five years old. Ames was over seventy. Flo had a built-in family to offer—herself, Adele, and the baby, plus the money her husband, Gus, had left her.

I didn't think Ames was in the market, but the door was open.

Adele called. She was going to be late. Flo told her we were there. Adele said she was sorry.

Catherine was in Flo's arms and George Jones was singing "He Stopped Loving Her Today" when we left. Ames went out first and looked around to be sure no one was about to shoot at me. There was no real cover around the houses in the area, which was almost without trees and bushes. The trees that did exist were, like the houses, only five or six years old.

"Next stop?" asked Ames, riding shotgun again as I drove.

"I've got dinner with Sally," I said.

"Best be looking for whoever's shooting at you."

"I think I know."

I told him. He nodded.

"So," he said. "I keep an eye on the shooter."

"Yes."

We met at Miss Saigon just across 301 from the Greyhound bus station. The restaurant was in a small, downscale mall with mostly Hispanic businesses: a tienda, a travel agency, a beauty shop, a check-cashing service. One of the shops in the mall was, according to Ettiene Viviase, a legitimate business and a front for a neighborhood mom-and-pop numbers racket.

I arrived first, putting my Cubs cap in my pocket. I didn't want it stolen through the broken window of my car. I wore a clean pair of tan wash-and-wear pants and a white shirt with a button-down collar. The cap didn't really go with the dressed-up version of Lewis Fonesca.

I ordered Vietnamese iced tea. Sally arrived ten minutes later, touched my shoulder as she passed, and sat across from me. Coming separately had been Sally's idea.

"I don't want any front-door good-byes," she had said.

"I understand," I had said.

"Sorry I'm late," she said.

"Not very."

"Not very sorry or not very late?" she asked with a smile that could have used more enthusiasm.

She ordered an unsweetened iced tea.

When the waiter returned, I ordered noodles with short ribs. Sally ordered duck soup.

We ate in silence. The restaurant was small and busy, with mostly Vietnamese customers. Vaguely Asian music was playing in the background. Voices were low.

"Did you . . . ?" she began, pausing with chopsticks raised. She stopped, question unanswered but understood.

"He'll go away soon," I said.

"Soon?"

"Maybe the next few days."

"Far?"

"Far," I said.

"How do you plan to persuade him?"

"You'll know in a few days."

I didn't use chopsticks, though I could have. My wife had taught me how to use them. At first I had been a poor student, but I caught on. Now, I couldn't bring myself to use them. It was something I did only with Catherine, a small thing but a fine silkscreen for memories.

"Lewis," she said.

"Yes."

"You drifted off somewhere."

"Sorry," I said. "With Ronnie gone, you won't have to leave."

"It was hard for me to come here tonight," she said, looking down at the bowl in front of her. "Hard for me to face you. I can't imagine seeing you day after day."

"You won't get any accusations from me," I said.

"I know, but you don't need any more pain from man or woman."

"Don't leave," I said.

"That's probably the nicest thing you've ever said to me, but where do we go if I stay?"

"Where do you want to go?"

"You answered a question with a question," she said. "I do that all the time with clients."

"So?"

"You don't even know how I look nude and we've never been to bed together," she said. "Almost four years, Lewis."

I tried to stop it, but the image of Sally and Dwight Torcelli in bed came to me. It would come back to me, too. I was sure.

"We can work on it," I said.

"You, me, Ronnie, and Catherine in bed together," she said. "You don't forget anything, Lew. I'll bet you even know the name of your grade school gym teacher and exactly how he looked."

"She," I said, remembering. "Shirley Ann Stoffey. Her husband was Jerry Stoffey, a staff writer for the *Chicago Tribune*. Mrs. Stoffey had a small purple birthmark above her left wrist. She had a Baltimore accent and a tarnished tin whistle she always wore around her neck."

"You see? You can't forget and you can't bring yourself to lie about your memories. You never forget," Sally said.

I didn't say anything. I should have, but I couldn't. This was the moment for sincere, simple eloquence, but it wasn't in me. Sally was right.

She sighed deeply and said, "I'll tell you what. The job in Vermont is open-ended and I could always come back here. I might even get a raise. The kids would be happy if we stayed. I'll tell you what. In Vermont, a year from today, we meet and see . . . Lewis, I'm leaving, not just you but my own memories."

"You can't run away from memories," I said. "I tried. They follow you."

"I've made my decision," she said.

"I understand."

And I did. Sally usually had coffee after dinner. Not this time. I said I would pay. She let me. She gave me a quick kiss and left me sitting there.

I paid in cash and left a big tip. I don't know how much fifteen or even twenty percent is. I don't know how much nine times seven is.

I had counted on Catherine to do that. I had counted on Sally to do it, too.

Sally was right, right about everything.

I got in my Saturn, put on my cap, and drove to the place where I was reasonably sure of finding the evidence I needed to convince the police.

I parked a block away and walked back. At the window, I checked, double-checked, and checked again to be sure no one was inside. The next shot from the person who lived here would likely be up close and with a shotgun. The window wasn't locked. I climbed in.

Less than ten minutes later, pocket flashlight in hand, I had found everything I needed. I left it all in place and left.

Tomorrow, it would be over.

It was about eleven at night when I climbed the long flight of stairs to my rooms. With Victor gone, I would be spending my first night alone here. I was looking forward to it. But first I had to deal with the visitor standing on the landing at the top of the stairs.

"Where have you been?" asked Greg Legerman. "No, wait. I take that back. It's none of my business. What I should say is, How is the effort to save Ronnie going? That is my business."

"It'll be over tomorrow," I said.

I opened the door, reached in to turn on the lights. He followed me inside. I closed the door and he moved to the chair behind my desk. I could have told him I didn't want to talk. It would have been true, but I sat.

"Where's Winn?" I asked.

"Home, I think. We don't spend all our time together. Well, most, but not all. I've decided I'm going to Duke. So is Winn."

I shifted my weight, took out my wallet and counted out cash, which I placed on the desk in front of Greg.

"What's this?" he asked.

"What you paid me minus the time I spent working on your case."

"Why?"

"Let's say your mother and grandfather have paid me more than enough."

"I don't understand," he said, looking at the money.

"You will tomorrow."

"'Tomorrow and tomorrow and tomorrow creeps at a petty pace,'" he said. "That's Shakespeare, sort of."

"I know. Very poetic."

He looked around the room wondering what to say or do next.

"Do you know the history of your semiprofession in the United States?"

"No."

He got up, leaving the cash on the desk, and started to pace as he spoke.

"The first U.S. marshals were appointed by George Washington to serve subpoenas, summonses, writs, warrants, and other processes issued by the courts. They also arrested and handled all Federal prisoners."

"I'm not a U.S. marshal. I'm a private contractor."

"I know, I know. But you see the history, the connection. Our lives, our history, and the history of the entire country—the entire world—are connected by slender threads of seemingly random events."

"Interesting," I said. "Would you like a can of Coke?"

If he said yes I would have given him the caffeine-free variety. Greg Legerman needed no more stimulation.

"I'm sorry," he said. "I get carried away."

"You have any idea who killed Blue Berrigan?"

"No, but I have to tell you something about him. Berrigan."

"Tell."

"I hired Blue Berrigan to lie to you, to tell you he had evidence that would clear Ronnie."

"He tried."

"He wanted more money from me. Said he'd tell the police I had killed Horvecki."

"And you wouldn't give it?"

"No," he said. "I didn't kill him. I don't know who did, probably whoever killed Horvecki."

"Maybe," I said. "How did you know Berrigan?"

"He used to work for my grandfather on his infomercials and at his mall appearances. I've known him all my life. He always needed money. It was a bad idea."

"Very bad."

"I got him killed," said Greg.

I didn't say anything.

"What happened to the Chinese guy?" Greg asked. "His bedroll's gone."

"Went home. A place far away and exotic."

"China?"

"Oswego, Illinois."

"Cheng Ho, fifteenth-century admiral, diplomat, explorer, son of a Muslim, descendant of Mongol kings, was the first real Chinese explorer extending his country's influence throughout the regions bordering the Indian Ocean."

"Greg," I said, trying to slow him down as he paced, speaking so quickly that I missed some of the words.

"Fifteenth century," he said. "Do you know how the Romans numbered the centuries before the Christian era?"

"Greg," I said again as he paused in his pacing to glance at the dark Dalstrom paintings on my wall.

I thought he was going to shift from the Roman calendar to something about art, but he stayed with his history.

"Eleven months, a three-hundred-and-four-day year. But my question was a trick. Your answers to me have been tricks. The Romans didn't number their years. When a new year came, they called it something like 'The Year of the Counsels of Rome.' They didn't think of decades or centuries. Time meant something different to the Romans."

"Greg, how did you get here?"

"I drove, of course."

"How about staying here tonight?"

"Why?"

"Do I have to tell you?"

He went back to the chair, sat, played with the money, scratched his forehead and said, "No."

"I'll call your mother."

"No," he said. "Not necessary. She isn't sitting up waiting for me."

"Your grandfather?"

"No. I won't be missed. I'm never missed. I am a trial and a tribulation to my family," he said, finishing with a broad grin. "Don't worry. I've brought some of my quiet-down tranquilizers. I'll be fine."

"Bathroom is over there. I'll get my sleeping bag out of the closet."

"I need a pillow."

"I'll get you one."

"Thanks. I'll take that Coke now."

"Caffeine free," I said.

"I'll take it."

I got it for him. He used it to wash down three pills he fished from a small plastic bottle.

"I'll resist telling you about the developmental history of tranquilizers," he said.

"Thank you."

"You remind me of your grandfather," I said.

"Is that an insult or a compliment?"

"Observation."

"Others have said the same. I long to be away at the Duke campus, built and endowed by . . ."

I sat listening as he slowly talked himself down, drank two Cokes, used the bathroom twice, and finally, at a few minutes past midnight, took off his shoes. I got him a pillow. He took it and moved to what had been Victor's corner.

I turned off the lights and got into bed. It would not be the first night I slept without a pillow. I'd have to put the purchase of a guest pillow on my mental list of things I needed.

There was no problem. I lay in darkness in my T-shirt and shorts and let the thoughts of both Catherines, of Sally, and of what I had to do in the morning come. They came and went, and I slept well. I slept dreamlessly.

Greg was gone when I got up a few minutes before eight the next morning. The sleeping bag was rolled up with the pillow plumped on top of it. The cash I had laid out was still on the desk and there was a scribbled note I could barely read:

I have the feeling that what you will do today will be something other than what I would like. Consider the cash payment for your putting up with me last night. Greg Legerman is not an easy town.

I called Ames and told him I would pick him up in half an hour.

"Did you get any sleep?" I asked.

"Some."

"Our shooter?"

"Didn't move."

"You have breakfast?"

"Not yet," he said. "Okay if we eat here?"

"Sure."

Half an hour later I was seated at a table in the Texas Bar and Grill and being served by Big Ed. We ate chili and eggs and didn't say much.

"Thanks," I said.

"For?"

"You fixed my car window last night," I said. "Or was it the car window fairy?"

"Me. Took a few hours off when our shooter was tucked in."

"You armed?"

Ames pulled his jacket open to reveal a small holstered gun.

"Leave it here," I said. "We won't need it where we're going."

I called Ettiene Viviase and he agreed to meet us at the jail just down the street when I told him what I wanted to do.

We could have walked to the jail from the Texas, but I drove and we found a space with a two-hour meter. I dropped enough quarters into it and we met Viviase in the reception area in front of the bulletproof window, behind which sat a uniformed woman.

"She's here," Viviase said. "Make it good."

He took us through a door and into a small room where lawyers and clients, relatives and inmates, cops and criminals met to talk and lie and threaten and plead.

Torcelli, wearing an orange uniform, sat at the table.

He looked at me and said, "You've come to get me out."

"No," Viviase said. "He came to be sure you stay in here. You killed Philip Horvecki."

Torcelli's nose was covered by a wide bandage that didn't hide the spreading purple. The cavities of his eyes looked as if they had been painted black.

"I didn't . . . What? I didn't kill Horvecki. Tell him, Fonesca."

"Go ahead," said Viviase. "Tell us."

I told my tale slowly and carefully so Torcelli wouldn't make any mistake about what he was hearing.

The first words from him when I finished talking were, "I want my lawyer."

"He withdrew from your case," said Viviase. "He has a bad cold."

"His feet are cold," said Torcelli. "Alana stopped paying him, didn't she? Find Rachel. Rachel will pay him."

"We're looking for her," Viviase said.

"This is a mistake," Torcelli said again, this time looking at Ames, who said, "Take it like a man."

"I didn't touch your daughter," Torcelli tried, turning to Viviase. "A kiss, maybe. What's the harm in that?"

"She's fifteen," Viviase answered.

"Fonesca, you were supposed to help me," Torcelli said, his voice dropping, his head in his hands.

"I guess I failed," I said.

19

"You sure?" Viviase asked.

"Sure," said Ames. "Followed the taxi right here."

The sky was almost black. Thunder from the north. Lightning flashes. The rain was light. It would, I was sure, turn heavy. It was a typical Florida rainstorm.

We had backup, two patrol cars running without sirens or lights, two armed police officers in each.

"Let's get it done," said Viviase, walking up the path to the door with one of the police officers, ringing the bell and stepping to the side.

Ames and I stood off to the side on the sidewalk, watching the other cops, two left, one right, circling around the building. Viviase rang again and then used a key to open the door and step in, his back against the doorjamb.

"You need a warrant," a voice came from the darkness inside. "You have a warrant?"

"We don't need a warrant," Viviase said as a single small light came on, and Rachel Horvecki stepped forward inside the room. "This is a crime scene."

"I want him," I heard her say.

"Fonesca," called Viviase. "You want to step in here a minute? The lady wants to talk to you."

Ames and I stepped forward and through the door. The shades and curtains were all down and closed. The room was a funereal black.

Thunder rolled toward us. Then lightning, and in the flash we saw Rachel standing completely nude and carrying a shotgun that looked big and powerful enough to down a large, charging rhino.

We stood in darkness.

"Your husband confessed," Viviase said.

"To what?"

"To killing your father," Viviase said. "He says you helped him and it was all your idea so you could get your father's money."

"He didn't say that," she said.

"You're under arrest," Viviase said firmly. "Tell her, Fonesca."

Imperative. An order. Tell the naked woman in the dark with the shotgun how you figured out she and her husband murdered her father.

"I came here last night," I said. "You were out, looking for me. You were followed by Mr. McKinney. I found your father's collection of shotguns and rifles in the back room and some photographs on the wall of you and him. You were about thirteen and cradling a weapon almost as big as you were. Your father has his hand around your shoulder in all the photographs."

I could hear her move a little. I glanced at a shadow moving past the window to her right as she said, "If they shoot, I shoot."

"No one's shooting," said Viviase.

"I found some of your poetry in a drawer in your room," I said.

"You had no right," she shouted.

"Crime scene, remember?" said Viviase. "Your father died just about where I think you're standing."

I knew there were still bloodstains on the floor.

"You tried to kill me," I said.

"Why would I want to kill you? You were helping Ronnie."

"You were afraid I'd find out that your husband really did kill your father."

"Not true," she said.

"True," said Ames.

A slight *tink* of metal as I sensed the shotgun moving toward Ames.

"Ronnie, or both of you, killed your father early that night," I went on. "You chose that night because you knew you had a nearly perfect witness. Essau Williams, a policeman, or Jack Pepper, a minister, would be parked across the street watching your father's house, wanting to be watched as they returned to that spot across the street, like men punching into work. It was Pepper. And what did he see? Hours after your father was already dead, the Reverend Jack Pepper saw Ronnie enter the house just as a man in a coat and watch cap came through a side window and run down the street. Almost immediately, Ronnie came back out the door and looked both ways for the man in the watch cap. He looked around and he went back inside. You had already called 911 and said there'd been a murder. There was a car there almost immediately. A bloody Ronnie was kneeling by the body. The police didn't find you, because you were the man in the watch cap. There was only one problem."

"What?" she asked.

I was sure the shotgun was getting heavier. It was probably pointing down at the floor.

"Jack Pepper didn't immediately come forward about the man who came through the window and about seeing Ronnie in the house for only a few seconds. He didn't want to explain why he was sitting in his car in front of your house. There was a restraining order against him. You waited a while before coming forward with your story about seeing a man in a watch cap kill your father and go through the window. Your father was already dead. You were the one in the watch cap. When Pepper showed up, you talked loud enough for Pepper to hear a muffled voice and something thudding, probably you hitting the wall."

"Pepper should have come forward sooner," she said.

"He's come forward now," said Viviase.

"Want to give me that shotgun, miss, and go put on some clothes?" said Ames gently.

There was a sound of movement and she turned on a shaded table lamp.

She looked dazed.

"Ronnie said I killed my father?"

"He did," Ames said. "We heard him."

"It's on tape," said Viviase.

"Ronnie's not a bad man," she said. "He likes my poetry. He's so gentle in bed. I know he can't stay away from other women, from girls, but he always comes back to me."

And your father's millions, I thought.

"This is unfair," she said. "My father was a monster. He did things to me I . . . it's unfair. The police could never stop him—him and his lawyers. He deserved to die."

The shotgun rose and pointed directly at Viviase's chest.

"Could I have a glass of water?" Ames said.

She looked at him.

"And could I maybe sit down?"

"Water?"

"Juice would be fine, too, but not grapefruit. Doesn't sit well in me."

"I like your poetry," I said.

"You're just saying that because you don't want me to shoot you."

"That, too, but I like your poetry. None of it is happy, is it?"

"No," she said. "Never was. Looks like it never will be. I've got fresh orange juice. Will that do?"

She handed the shotgun to Ames, who said, "It'll do just fine."

"So," said Viviase while a policewoman walked with Rachel to her room to dress. "One down. Which one killed Berrigan and why?"

Ames had removed the shells from the shotgun and handed it to one of the police officers who had come into the house from all entryways.

"That's a mystery," I said.

"You didn't answer the question," he said.

"I don't have an answer."

"You have a pretty good idea," said Viviase.

I shrugged.

I drove to my place and let Ames out.

"Certain you want to do this yourself?" he asked.

"Certain."

"I'll be here," he said.

I knew the odds of reaching the person I had called were slight, and I was right. I left a message saying we had to meet at four at Selby Gardens.

"Walk along the path till you see me. I'll be sitting on a bench," I had said.

It was almost one when I got to the Dairy Queen on Clark Street. There was a huge photograph on the wall of the original DQ with old cars and long-gone people around it. I didn't order the Chocolate Covered Cherry Blizzard. I wasn't sure why. Instead I had a medium Banana Chocolate Oreo Blizzard. I also ordered a burger and a large fries. When my order came, I put the fries in a bag and worked on the blizzard and burger. It wasn't the DQ I had lived behind for almost four years. The owner was nice, but he wasn't Dave.

By three I was at Selby Gardens sitting on a bench facing the water. A white heron landed next to me, its wings flapping to a close, searching for something from the human on the bench. I did not disappoint. I placed three fries on the bench. He gobbled them up and was joined by two other small, brown, iridescent birds. After the fries were gone, the birds lingered, looking at me. They left only when they were certain I would give no more. The heron was the last to go. He flapped his wings and flew off over the bay.

At ten minutes to four, Winston Churchill Graeme sat next to me, right where the heron had been. He cleaned his glasses on his shirt and turned his eyes in the same direction mine were pointed.

"When I was sixteen, I thought about quitting school and joining the Navy."

"What stopped you?"

"The fact that my parents didn't object. They thought it was a pretty good idea. They thought going to college and becoming a lawyer was an even better idea."

"What happened?"

"I didn't become a sailor. If I had, I might be out to sea instead of sitting here with you.

"Why are we here?" Winn asked.

"So you could tell me why you killed Blue Berrigan."

20

There was a single fry left. I had missed it, but I spotted it now as I was about to crumple up the bag and drop it in the nearby trash basket. I handed him the bag.

"For the birds," I said. "One left."

He nodded, adjusted his glasses, and threw the fry in the general direction of a pair of nearby pigeons.

"Why do you think I killed him?" he asked.

I reached into my pocket and pulled out the white and red golf tees.

"I found these in the backseat of Berrigan's jeep."

"So, he played golf."

"No, he didn't. I looked in his room and his closet and asked his landlady. He didn't play golf. You do."

"Maybe they didn't belong to whoever killed him. Maybe they had been there a long time," he tried.

"No," I said. "Both tees were on top of a splatter of blood. The killer lost them during the attack."

"I'm not the only one who plays golf," he said.

"No, you're not, but you're the only one who would kill Berrigan for blackmailing Greg. Greg told me that Berrigan tried to get more money out of him."

"Yes."

"And you told me you would do anything to protect your friend."

His hands were shaking now.

"What happened, Winn?" I said.

He paused, looked into the DQ bag as if there might be a miracle fry in it, and then spoke. "I was with Berrigan when he went to see you at that bar. I wanted to be sure he would go through with saying he had evidence to clear Ronnie. I stayed in the jeep."

"But?"

"He got frightened, panicked. You said something to him in the bar. He told me he wanted more money, a lot more money. He was hysterical. He said he'd tell you, tell the police that Greg had murdered Horvecki. He drove to his place and parked in front. He kept saying things like 'What am I doing? What am I the fuck doing?' He didn't get out of the jeep, just sat there looking over his shoulder down the street, hitting the steering wheel hard with the palms of both hands. I told him to get out. He wouldn't move. He kept saying he would tell the police that Greg killed Horvecki. I couldn't let that happen."

Winn closed his eyes.

"So you hit him with something in the backseat."

"Yes, one of Greg's grandfather's mallets."

"Then you got out of the jeep and ran before I got there."

"Yes."

"You went to Ronnie's apartment and put the mallet under his bookcase. He was in jail for one murder. Two wouldn't make a big difference, right?"

"You know, I could hit you with something and throw you in the bay," he said.

"No, you couldn't," I said.

"No, you're right. I couldn't. What are you going to do?"

"Nothing," I said. "You're going to go to Elisabeth Viviase's father and tell him what happened."

"I can't. My mother . . ."

"The odds are good that eventually, probably soon, a strand of hair, a string of cloth, a DNA trace is going to lead to you. You already left the two tees. What else did you leave?"

"I don't know."

"Turn yourself in, get a good lawyer. I'm sure Greg's grandfather will pay for one. You're still a minor. Think about it."

"Yeah," he said. "I'll think about it. Thanks. Will you turn me in if I don't do it?"

"You'll do it," I said. "Do you know who George Altman is?"

"Cardinals outfielder in the sixties?"

"And a Cub before that. Here."

I took the autographed baseball I had purchased out of my pocket and handed it to him. He took it and looked at me, puzzled.

"It's yours," I said.

"Why?"

"I don't know."

I got up.

Winn Graeme looked down at the ball cupped in his hands as if it were a small crystal ball.

"Mr. Fonesca," he said. "What will Greg do without me?"

At ten the next morning, I carried my tribute of coffee and biscotti into the office of Ann Hurwitz who motioned me into my usual seat. She was on the phone.

"I'm not investing in alchemy," she said patiently. "I want secure stocks and bonds. I do not want real estate, neither malls nor parking lots nor the foreclosed property of others."

There was a pause while she listened, accepted a bagged biscotti and coffee, nodded her thanks, and then spoke into the telephone as she jangled the heavy jeweled chain around her thin wrist:

"We've been through this many times, Jerome. You are forty-four years old. I am eighty-three years old. Depending on what chance and heredity bring your way, you will live about forty more years according to current actuarial projections. I, on the other hand, should have, at most, another seven to ten years. I am not interested in risking what my husband and I have saved. It is not because we intend to retire to Borneo on our savings. We wish to give to a set of charities, charities that support the continuation of human life. Get back to me when you've thought about this."

She hung up and looked at me.

"Lewis, you are the only one of my current clients who does not believe in God and does not want to live forever."

"If there is a God, I don't like him," I said.

"So you have indicated in the past. Almond or macadamia?" she asked, hoisting a biscotti.

"Almond."

"Tell me about your week," she said, "while I enjoy your gift."

I told her, talked for almost twenty minutes, and then stopped. She had finished her biscotti and coffee and my almond biscotti.

"Progress again," she said.

"Progress?"

"You made a commitment to Ames. You offered something resembling a commitment to Sally. After four years you are putting down tentative tendrils in Sarasota."

"Maybe."

"Have you done your homework?"

I reached into my pocket and came out with the stack of lined index cards on which people's favorite, or just remembered, first lines were. She took them.

"Why did I have you collect favorite first lines rather than jokes?"

"I don't know."

"I think it is time for you to have a new beginning," she said, quickly going through the cards, glasses perched on the end of her nose. "And now yours, Lewis, your book."

"*Moby-Dick*," I said.

"What do you think the book is about?" Ann asked.

"A lone survivor," I said. "I bought a copy of the book at Brant's and copied the line."

I took out my notebook.

"Is it that hard for you to remember? Almost everyone knows it. 'Call me Ishmael.' "

"Yes," I said. "Can I read what I have on the card?"

"All right," she said, lifting a hand in acceptance, "read."

" 'It was the devious-cruising *Rachel,* that in her retracing search after her missing children, only found another orphan.' "

"That's not the beginning of *Moby-Dick*, Lewis," she said.

"No," I said. "It's the end."